His Sec

MARIE FERRARELLA
CARLA CASSIDY
CINDY DEES

MILLS & BOON

Published in Great Britain 2015
by Mills & Boon, an imprint of Harlequin (UK) Limited,
Eton House, 18-24 Paradise Road, Richmond, Surrey, TW9 1SR

HIS SECRET BABY © 2015 Harlequin Books S.A.

The Agent's Secret Baby, *The Cowboy's Secret Twins* and *The Soldier's Secret Daughter* were first published in Great Britain by Harlequin (UK) Limited.

The Agent's Secret Baby © 2009 Marie Rydzynski-Ferrarella
The Cowboy's Secret Twins © 2009 Carla Bracale
The Soldier's Secret Daughter © 2009 Cynthia Dees

ISBN: 978-0-263-25211-8
eBook ISBN: 978-1-474-00390-2

05-0415

Harlequin (UK) Limited's policy is to use papers that are natural, renewable and recyclable products and made from wood grown in sustainable forests. The logging and manufacturing processes conform to the legal environmental regulations of the country of origin.

Printed and bound in Spain
by CPI, Barcelona

THE AGENT'S
SECRET BABY

BY
MARIE FERRARELLA

To
David McCallum
who, as Illya Kuryakin
in *The Man From U.N.C.L.E.*,
is responsible
for my falling in love with
secret agents and black turtleneck sweaters

Chapter 1

It took her a second to realize that the sigh she heard echoing in the small, converted bedroom that served as her office was her own.

Lost in thoughts of the past and preoccupied, Dr. Eve Walters had thought that the deep sigh had come from Tessa, the German shepherd she'd rescued from a sadistic owner a little more than two years ago. On occasion Tessa, currently curled up under her desk, was given to sighing just like a human being. Considering the life she'd led both B.R.—before rescue—and A.R.—after rescue—the sighs were more than merited. Before, Eve was certain, the dog's sighs had been of the fearful, hopeless variety while now, with Tessa's weight a third more than what it had been when she'd first been rescued, the German shepherd's sighs sounded as if she was exceedingly content with her new life and just couldn't believe her good fortune.

Lately, Eve had become aware of sighing a great deal herself, as if she couldn't catch her breath. And couldn't believe the twists and turns that had brought her to this point.

She supposed she could just shrug her shoulders and attribute her deeps sighs to the fact that she wasn't accustomed to carrying around this much weight, but if she were being honest, the cause for her sighs went a great deal deeper. Never in her wildest dreams did Eve think she would find herself in this position: approaching thirty in a few months, single, alone and very, very pregnant.

Tears suddenly gathered in her eyes and she held them back by sheer will. God, but she was emotional lately. Well, she *was not* going to cry. She wasn't.

Another sigh escaped.

How in heaven's name had she come to this state?

Okay, she was gregarious and fun-loving, but never, ever would anyone have called her reckless. She was always known as the stable one, the one everyone else turned to in times of crisis.

When her mother, Evelyn, had died suddenly on Eve's second day of middle school, Eve was the one who was there for her veterinarian father, Warren, and her older sister, Angela—not the other way around. This while she secretly yearned for someone to comfort *her.* But she couldn't indulge herself, couldn't sink into self-pity no matter how much she wanted to. Others depended on her. And she always came through.

Beneath her genial, warm smile she was the living

embodiment of the old adage, "Look before you leap." Not only did she look, she would take out a surveyor's level and plot every single step from there to here each and every time. It wasn't that she didn't like surprises; she just didn't like being caught unaware. And it certainly wasn't like her to give in to impulse and allow herself to be so completely swept away, especially by a man she'd hardly known.

A man she didn't know at all, Eve thought bitterly.

Eve blew out a breath and dragged a hand through the flowing mane of wayward dark blond hair. She stared at the computer screen on her laptop, silently seeking answers she knew weren't about to materialize. Barring that, she needed a distraction.

My kingdom for a distraction, she thought whimsically.

After shutting down the animal hospital for the night, the animal hospital that had once borne only her father's nameplate across the front door and where she had grown up, surrounded by animals in need of care and a kind, gentle father, Eve had gone home and retreated to her inner office. She'd turned on her computer to do a little research into the condition of the near-blinded dachshund that had been brought in today, searching for a possible way to reverse, or at least halt the condition. Searching, she supposed, for a miracle.

How she'd gotten to a chat room for expectant single moms was almost as mysterious to her as how she'd gotten in this condition in the first place.

Actually more so, she mused.

Of course she knew all about the mechanics of becoming pregnant, but it was how and why she'd gotten to that point that utterly mystified her. In hindsight, it just didn't seem possible.

She knew exactly what she wanted to do with her life, had known ever since she could remember. At least she'd known professionally. She was exactly what she wanted to be: a veterinarian, caring for a host of dogs and cats just the way her father had.

What she wanted for her private life was another matter. Oh, she knew that she wanted to go the traditional route. Wanted a husband and a family. Eventually.

She would have sworn that she hadn't wanted to reverse that order, but apparently she had no choice in the matter now.

Unless, as her sister in Sacramento had urged, she give up the baby.

There was no way Eve wanted to do that. Not because she viewed the little passenger she was carrying around as a love child, the living testimony of the passion that had existed between her and Adam. No, that didn't enter into it at all. The baby, whose due date Eve's ob-gyn had calculated was still a long two weeks away, was an extension of her, a little person whom for reasons that were beyond her, God had seen fit to entrust to her.

She was even looking forward to holding the baby in her arms. But she wasn't looking forward to dealing with being alone at a time when the baby's father's emotional support would have meant so much.

The latter was her own fault, she supposed.

No one had told her to pick up in the middle of the night and flee from Santa Barbara, secretly running back home to Laguna Beach.

"But how couldn't I?" she said aloud.

Tessa, dead to the world only a heartbeat ago, raised her head and looked at Eve with deep brown eyes. The next second, seeing that there was no emergency, Tessa went back to sleep.

Leaning over, Eve ran her hand over the dog's head, struggled to bank down her agitation. Petting her dog usually helped calm her.

But not tonight.

Tonight, the agitation refused to leave, refused to budge.

Maybe it was because tonight was Halloween, she thought. Maybe that was why she couldn't seem to shake the feeling that someone was watching her.

She sighed again.

Adam Smythe had been almost stereotypically handsome, not to mention the last word in "sexy." Added to that he was charming and he had taken her breath away from the very first moment she'd walked into his rare, first-editions bookstore. The moment he had looked her way, she'd felt as if an arrow had been shot straight into her heart.

At the time she'd been looking for a special birthday present for her father. Warren Walters loved everything that had ever come from Mark Twain's pen. What she'd wound up getting, along with a fairly well-preserved first edition of *A Connecticut Yankee in King Arthur's Court,* was a prepackaged heartache.

Oh, Adam hadn't looked like a heartache at first or even at tenth glance. He looked like a drop-dead gorgeous specimen of manhood who, given that this was California, she wouldn't have been surprised if the tall, dark-haired, green-eyed man had said he was just running the bookstore until that big acting break came that would propel him into being the country's next great heartthrob.

To add to this image, Adam was soft-spoken, slightly reserved, and he exuded such a powerful aura of authority that he'd instantly made her feel safe.

Eve laughed now, shaking her head at her incredible naiveté.

Talk about getting the wrong signal.

There had been nothing safe about Adam. He made her lose control in a heartbeat. Some of the boys in high school, and then college, she recalled, had referred to her as the Ice Princess.

"I certainly melted fast enough with him," she told her faithful, sleeping companion. Tessa didn't even stir this time.

One dinner.

One dinner had been all it had taken and she was ready to completely surrender her self-imposed code of ethics and abandon the way she'd behaved for her entire adult life without so much as a backward glance. When Adam had leaned over to brush back a loose strand of hair from her cheek, she turned into a furnace. Raging heat flashed through her limbs. Through her entire body.

And then he'd kissed her.

God, when Adam kissed her, she'd felt as if she were literally having an out-of-body experience.

And suddenly, without warning, Adam had drawn away and she came crashing down to earth like a speeding meteorite. A very confused meteorite.

She was accustomed to men being the aggressors, to having to somehow diplomatically hold them at bay without hurting their feelings or their egos. But this had been the other way around. Adam had been the one who had pulled back. And she had been the one who ultimately pushed.

Very simply, there'd been something about Adam that had turned her inside out. Their night together was the stuff of fantasies.

And then, just like that, all her thoughts centered around him. She couldn't wait until the next time they were together, couldn't wait to hear the sound of his voice, to catch a whiff of the scent that was the combination of his shaving cream mixing with his aftershave.

Adam had become her sun and anytime she wasn't around him, she felt as if she'd been plunged into soul-consuming darkness.

What a crock.

How could she, a heretofore intelligent woman, have been so blind, so dumb?

Smitten teenage girls—very young smitten teenage girls—felt this way, not a woman who practiced veterinarian medicine, who was a responsible, levelheaded and dedicated person.

Except that she had.

Into every paradise, a snake must slither and her paradise was no different. It occurred shortly after the first time—the only time—that they made love.

Made love.

The phrase lingered now in her brain like a haunting refrain.

Even today, knowing what she knew, it was still hard

not to feel the excitement pulsing through her body at the mere memory of those precious, exquisite moments she'd spent lost in Adam's arms, in his embrace. Even though it seemed impossible, he was simultaneously the most gentle, caring, yet passionate lover ever created. And he had been hers.

Looking back, she could honestly say, if only to herself, that they hadn't made love. They had made poetry.

Remembering the moment, Eve felt her body aching for him.

"Stop it," she upbraided herself.

Tessa raised her head, this time quickly, as if she was ready to dart away, afraid that she'd caused her mistress some displeasure. Displeasure that brought punishment with it.

Eve instantly felt guilty. "No, not you, girl," she said in a soothing voice, running her hand over the dog's head and stroking it. "I'm just talking to myself." She looked at the dog and smiled sadly. "Too bad you can't talk, then maybe my thoughts wouldn't keep getting carried away like this."

Calmed, Tessa lowered her head again, resting it on her paws. She was asleep in less than a minute, this time snoring gently.

Eve smiled at her, shaking her head. "I love you the way you are, but I wish you were human."

She craved companionship, someone to communicate with. But her father was gone. He had died less than a month after she'd come back home. Heartbroken, she'd handled all the funeral arrangements. Angela and her family had come down on the day of the funeral and had left by its end. Angela had left a trail of excuses in her wake. Eve didn't blame her. Angela and her family had a life to get back to.

It was several days after her father's funeral, as she wandered around the empty house, looking for a place for herself, that she finally had to admit what she had been trying desperately to ignore. She was pregnant.

At least her father had been spared that, Eve thought, forever trying to look on the bright side of things.

Eve knew he would have been there for her, supporting her—unlike her sister—no matter what her decision regarding the baby's future. But somewhere deep down inside, Eve was fairly certain her father would have felt disappointed. He'd always thought of her as perfect.

Again, she shook her head, her sad smile barely moving the corners of her mouth. "'Fraid not, Dad. So far from perfect, it would boggle your mind."

Just then, she felt a sharp pain. The baby was kicking. Again. It had been restless all day.

Probably tired of its closed quarters, Eve thought. Maybe he or she was claustrophobic, the way she was.

Without thinking, Eve lifted one hand from the keyboard and placed it over the swell of her abdomen, massaging the area that was the origin of the pain this time, even though it did no good.

Was it her imagination, or was she growing bigger and bigger by the hour?

"Won't be long now, baby," she murmured to her stomach.

She had a little more than two weeks to go. Part of her couldn't wait to finally have this all over with, to give birth and meet this little person who had turned her world completely upside down. The other part of her was content to let this state continue. She was terrified of the delivery. Not of what she imagined would be the pain, she'd helped birth enough animals to know exactly what to expect in that respect. No, she was afraid of what lay ahead after the birthing pains had subsided. When the real challenge kicked in.

"You know it's selfish of you to keep it," Angela had told her for the umpteenth time when she'd called last week. There was a knowing air of superiority in her sister's voice. Angela was convinced she *always* knew what was best. "It needs a mother *and* a father. Since you decided to have it, you really should give it up for adoption."

"'It' is a baby," Eve had shot back, one of the few times she'd lost her temper. But she was thoroughly annoyed at the flippant, cavalier way her sister was talking to her. Angela was acting as if she had the inside track on how to live life the right way just because she was married and had the idyllic number of children: two, a boy and a girl. "And what the baby needs is a mother who loves unconditionally."

"Obviously," had been Angela's snide retort. Eve knew that her older sister referred not to her loving the baby, but to the situation that had resulted in the creation of this baby. "Look, why won't you tell the father that he has a responsibility—"

Eve cut her short. "Because I won't, that's all. Subject closed," she'd said firmly.

She wasn't about to tell Angela the reason she wouldn't notify Adam of his paternity. Even under perfect conditions, she wouldn't have wanted the father of her child to feel obligated to "step up and do the right thing," as Angela had declared. When she did get married, it would be because the man who had her heart wanted to marry her, not because he felt he *had* to marry her.

And conditions were far from perfect. She hadn't even told Angela Adam's name, much less what it was that had sent her running back home to get away from the potential heartache that Adam Smythe—if that was even his name—represented.

Eve closed her eyes, remembering that night. She might have even still been in Santa Barbara, running the animal clinic there, if she hadn't overheard Adam on the phone. Closing early for the night, she'd decided to surprise Adam and arrive early for their date. He was on the telephone, his back to her, talking to a potential customer. As she listened, waiting for him to finish, she realized that he wasn't talking to a customer about one of the books in his shop, but someone calling him about obtaining drugs.

Horror filled her as she realized that the man who had lit up her world, who was her baby's father, was one of the lowest life-forms on this earth: a drug dealer.

The bookstore was just a cover.

Her soul twisted in disappointment. She couldn't even bring herself to confront him, to demand to know why he hadn't told her he was immersed in this dark world before they'd gotten involved with one another.

Before she'd fallen in love with him.

She'd felt so sick, so betrayed and so lost. She'd slipped out of the store quickly and silently. Hurrying to her apartment, she'd called him, struggling to hide her anger and hurt, and told Adam that she wasn't feeling well. Sympathetic, he'd offered to come over to keep her company, but she'd turned him down, saying she was afraid she might be contagious. Promising to call him the next day with an update, she'd hung up.

It took her less than an hour to pack.

She'd left Adam a note, telling him she knew what he was involved in and begging him to get out before he became just another dead statistic. And then, after calling the clinic and telling her assistant that there was an emergency and she had to leave, Eve did just that.

All water under the bridge, she told herself now wearily. Can't unring a bell. Adam was what he was— and she was pregnant. She was just going to have to make the best of it.

Right now, that actually involved doing something else she'd never thought she would do: pouring out her heart to a perfect stranger.

But then, that was exactly what made it so safe and cathartic. She was never going to see the stranger she'd found online, never going to meet MysteryMom, the woman who ran the support Web site she'd discovered several weeks ago. At the time, she hadn't thought she would write more than once, but venting, getting it all out, proved to be almost euphoric. And it really did make her feel better to unburden herself like this, cloaked in anonymity. Though she wanted to be, she just couldn't remain tight-lipped right now.

Besides, confession was supposed to be good for the soul, right?

God knew, she hadn't intended on going back to the Web site when she'd sat down tonight, but it had been a long, trying day and after hunting for answers regarding her nearly blind patient, answers that had turned out not to be very optimistic. She'd found herself drawn back to MysteryMom and the woman's easygoing, low-keyed common sense. It was like having a friend, and right now, she could stand to have a friend. A female friend who seemed to know exactly what she was going through.

Once she logged on, all it had taken were a few well-intentioned questions from MysteryMom and suddenly the floodgates had been tapped and Eve found herself typing so fast, there was almost smoke coming from her fingers.

Maybe tomorrow, she'd regret all this, Eve thought philosophically. But then, how could she possibly be in any worse shape than she already was? Wildly in love nine months ago, then wildly disappointed—and now, wildly pregnant.

Hell of a journey, she thought, typing words to that effect to the sympathetic MysteryMom.

And then Eve stopped, leaning back in her chair. She glanced toward her sleeping shadow. "I just hope that 'MysteryMom' isn't some cigar chomping, hairy-knuckled oaf getting his jollies by pretending to be a sympathetic single mom," she said to Tessa.

Tessa merely yawned and went back to sleeping.

Eve was about to type another thought when she heard the doorbell ring.

More trick or treaters.

With a sigh, Eve gripped the arms on her chair and pushed herself up.

She missed being able to spring to her feet, but she supposed it could be worse. At least she could still see her feet. When Angela had been pregnant with her first child, Renee, she couldn't see her feet after entering her seventh month.

Tessa was on all four of hers, padding quietly behind her, a four-legged, furry shadow determined to remain close.

Eve passed a mirror on her way to the front door. "At least I don't look like a blimp," she consoled herself.

A goblin, a fairy princess and what looked like a robot, none of whom could have been over ten, shouted "Trick or treat!" at her the moment she opened the door. Delighted, Eve grabbed a handful of candy from the bowl she had placed by the front door and divided the candy between them.

The goblin paused, relishing his booty, and obviously staring at her. "What are you supposed to be?"

Eve didn't even hesitate. "A pumpkin." It sounded better to her than "beached whale."

"But you're not orange," the robot protested.

Eve snapped her fingers. "Knew I forgot something. Thanks for letting me know."

Only the fairy princess said nothing beyond, "Thank you," looking at her knowingly, as if, even at that age, there was an unconscious bond that existed within the female gender.

And then her little visitors ran off, laughing, all beneath the distant, watchful scrutiny of one of their parents.

As she slowly closed her front door, Eve realized that the feeling was back. The one that whispered there was someone out there, watching her. Hoping to either catch him or her, or render a death knell to the unnerving feeling, she swung open her door again and looked around.

Nothing.

Again.

She frowned, closing the door all the way this time. The excitement over, Tessa turned away from the door. "If there is someone out there, promise you'll rip them limb from limb if they try to break in, Tessa."

The dog gave no indication that she heard any of the request. Instead, she trotted back to the office and reclaimed her position beneath the desk.

"I feel so safe now," Eve murmured to the dog as she lowered herself into the office chair again and once more immersed herself in the comforting words of MysteryMom. It wasn't that she was a believer in the old saying that misery loved company. It was just that knowing someone else had gone through what she was going through and survived made her feel more heartened.

It was something to cling to.

Chapter 2

After more than two years undercover, disappearing into the shadows had become second nature to Adam Serrano.

Usually the object of his surveillance was an unsavory character involved in the ever-mushrooming, lethal drug trade, not a female veterinarian with killer legs, liquid blue eyes and a soul Snow White would have been in awe of.

The anonymous tip that had appeared without warning on his computer yesterday morning had been right. Eve Walters was right here in Laguna Beach, practically right under his nose.

Who would have thought it?

The irony of the situation was still very fresh in his mind. She had disappeared on him eight months ago, doing what he hadn't been able to bring himself to do: leaving. Reading her letter, a letter he still had in his possession, had cut small, jagged holes in his soul. His first instinct had been to go after her, to find her and bring her back.

But he'd forced himself to refrain.

It hadn't been easy. Eventually, his common sense had prevailed. This was for the best.

Though he missed Eve more than he would have ever thought possible, Adam had every intention of allowing her to stay out of his life. Being part of his life would have been far too dangerous for her.

The nature of his "business," searching for the source of the latest flood of heroin, had brought him here, down to southern California. These days, the hard reality of it was that, despite his agency's efforts, the drug culture was alive and thriving absolutely everywhere. The drugs on the street apparently knew no caste system, bringing down the rich, as well as the poor. The only difference was that the rich didn't need to knock over a liquor store, or rob an elderly couple or kill some unsuspecting innocent to feed their habit. That's what Mommy and Daddy were for, blindly throwing money at the problem instead of helping their spoiled, pampered offspring morph into respectable people.

Life didn't work that way. But it was obviously still full of surprises.

Not the least of which was that his work had brought him down here, almost at Eve's door, as it were.

But moving the base of his "operation" to Laguna still wouldn't have had him skulking around, camping out in unmarked cars and hiding in doorways to catch a glimpse of her or acting like some wayward guardian angel if that anonymous message on his computer hadn't knocked him for a loop.

"Eve is pregnant with your baby." The terse sentence was followed by an address. Nothing more.

He'd presumed the address belonged to Eve. Minimal effort via his computer had proven him right. He recalled her mentioning that she had grown up somewhere in this area and that her dad had had an animal hospital here.

When he looked up the animal hospitals in and around Laguna, he found an "E. Walters" listed. He remembered her telling him that her father's name was Warren. That meant that she was now running the Animal Hospital of Laguna Beach.

And she was pregnant, supposedly with his baby.

Even so, Adam had debated ignoring the message, telling himself it was some kind of trick to have him come forward. And even if it wasn't a trick, he could do nothing about the situation. It was her body, not his. Whether or not she kept this baby was up to her, not him.

That argument had lasted all of ten minutes, if that long. Even as he posed it, Adam knew he had to see for himself whether or not it was true.

He fervently hoped that it wasn't.

But it was. Or, at least, she was carrying someone's child.

In his gut, he knew it was his.

Juggling things so that he could put everything else temporarily on hold for the evening, Adam stationed himself in a nondescript vehicle on the through street that ran by Eve's house. He was careful to park on the opposite side, waiting to catch another glimpse of the only woman who had managed to break through his carefully constructed barriers.

It was Halloween and he knew the way Eve felt about kids. The same way she felt about helpless animals. No way was she going to be one of those people who either left their home for the evening every Halloween or pretended not to hear the doorbell or the noise generated by approaching bands of costumed children.

Personally, he never liked the holiday. Dealing with the scum of the earth for the last ten years, he knew what was out there. And what could happen to trusting children.

Hell, if he had a kid…

He *did* have a kid, Adam realized abruptly. Or would have one. Soon, if his math served him.

Damn, he hadn't gotten used to that idea yet.

A father.

Him.

Maybe the baby wasn't his, Adam thought. A woman as beautiful as Eve Walters had to have a lot of men after her. A lot of men trying to get her to sleep with them…

Even as he made the excuses, Adam knew they weren't true. Eve wasn't the type to sleep around. He'd known that even before they'd made love. And when they had, he'd discovered to his everlasting surprise that she was a virgin. He'd been her first.

How?

How the hell had this happened? he silently demanded. He'd made sure he used protection. Pausing in the middle of heated passion had been damn awkward, but he had done it, mindful of the consequences if he didn't. Even so, she had made him lose his head and it had been all he could do to hold on to his common sense.

Common sense, now there was a misnomer. Common sense just wasn't common. If he'd actually had any, he would've gotten a grip on himself then and there. Instead of reaching for a condom, he would have reached for his jeans and walked away.

Adam shook his head. Who the hell was he kidding? A saint couldn't have walked away from Eve, not when things had reached that level. Not with that delicious mouth of hers. Not with that body, slick with sweat and desire, his for the taking. And God knew he wasn't a saint—far from it. He was just a man. And she had made him vulnerable.

And now, apparently, he had returned the favor and done the same to her.

He had no family, not anymore. And when it was only him, the danger didn't matter.

But now it mattered.

If she was pregnant, he was going to need to protect her. If these rich lowlifes he dealt with found out she was pregnant with his baby, there was more than a slim chance, if things went awry, that they would do something to her. He put nothing past them, nothing past the middle man he was currently working with, a college senior majoring in heroin distribution. Danny Sederholm might kidnap Eve—or the baby— if it gave the kid the advantage and secured leverage against him. Nobody trusted anybody in this so-called "business."

Adam shifted in his seat, feeling restless and confined. Where were the hoards of kids, wandering around the neighborhood and ringing doorbells in their quest for cavities? Had they all suddenly come to their senses and abandoned the trick-or-treating ritual?

Get a grip, Serrano.

He wasn't usually this impatient. But this was different. This wasn't just about him.

Hell, he would have felt a lot better just knowing who the message had come from.

The fact that it could all be a trap was not lost on him. No computer novice, he'd spent a good part of yesterday trying to trace where the message had originated. A good part of yesterday was spent in frustration.

Striking out, he'd gotten in contact with his handler, Hugh Patterson, who in turn had turned Spenser onto the task. Spenser was a wunderkind when it came to the computer. When Spenser failed to find where the e-mail had come from, he knew that they were dealing with a five-star pro.

Good pro or bad pro?

Adam hadn't the slightest idea, but for now, his anonymous tipster didn't seem to have an agenda, other than passing on this tidbit of information. Why he or she had done that, Adam hadn't a clue. Was it to taunt him, to show him he was vulnerable, or to get him to stand up and do the right thing? Or was this tipster just out to entertain himself or play deus ex machina behind the scenes?

Adam wished he knew.

But he did know what his next step had to be. And he took it.

Laura Delaney sat down at her desk, getting back to her Web site. Jeremy was finally in bed, asleep, or at least, asleep for the time being. She had no doubt that at least some of the candy he'd collected tonight had found its way into his bottomless tummy despite her strict rules about his only eating two pieces tonight and evenly doling out the rest for the following week. She'd offered those terms, hoping that a compromise would be reached at five. Maybe six.

Bid low, go high, she thought, amused.

She loved this holiday, loved seeing the excitement in her young son's eyes. Taking after her, Jeremy had started planning his costume right after school began in September. Most of all, she loved seeing life through his deep brown eyes. Everything felt so fresh, so new again seeing it from Jeremy's perspective. After all the time she'd spent in the CIA, this new outlook was a godsend to her.

Getting pregnant with Jeremy was definitely the best thing that had ever happened to her.

Although it certainly hadn't felt so at the time.

At the time, making the discovery a week after her intense debriefing in Singapore, the pregnancy had knocked the pins right out from beneath her world. And there was never any question as to who the father was. Jeremy's father was a dynamic, larger-than-life handsome man who had quite literally saved her life.

The whole thing had been almost like a scene out of

the movies. The one where the hero put out his hand to the heroine and growled darkly, "Come with me if you want to live."

She'd wanted to live all right. Pinned down in a hopeless situation, knowing she'd be dead by dawn if she stayed, she'd had no recourse but to come with the man who had suddenly burst into her life.

In true knight-in-shining-armor style, he'd used his body to shield hers and had hustled her out of what would have been a terminal situation. A hairbreadth away from being captured by the people she, as a CIA operative, had been sent to spy on, Laura had had no illusions about her situation. Had he not suddenly materialized in that embassy room, seemingly out of nowhere, she knew she would not have lived to see another sunrise.

Instead, she'd lived to watch the sunrise in a small fishing hut, sequestered in his arms. Funny how almost dying makes you so anxious to live, to experience and savor everything. The escape, the pursuit and then hiding in a fishing village, posing as fishermen, had all contributed to her heightened desire to live. Her desire to seize all that life had to offer.

What life had offered was a man whose name she never learned.

She had learned that she hadn't been afraid to seize the moment, and neither had he. They were drawn to one another like the missing two halves of a whole. Their coming together was nothing short of earthshaking. It had been predestined.

Then came the dawn and the rest of life.

He smuggled her out of the village, put her on a

transport plane and then, much too quickly, faded out of her life. Faded even though she asked more than one operative who the masked man was. Time and again, she received conflicting answers. The upshot was that no one seemed to know who he was or where he came from. It was almost as if he was a phantom.

Laura went on asking more urgently when she discovered that she was pregnant. But the result remained the same. No one could tell her. The few leads she had all ended in a dead end, taking her to operatives who turned out not to be the man who had saved her life and planted another inside her.

Pregnant, she had another life to think about other than her own. Laura decided she had no choice but to leave her present life behind. Because of her love of animals and having been raised on a ranch, she took up horse training in an effort to create a stable—no pun intended—normal life for her son.

These days, the life she'd once led almost seemed like a dream, or an action novel she'd read a long, long time ago. The only thing left to remind her that she had once actually been a CIA operative was her ability to utilize information—and sources—to allow her to find people. Ironically, despite numerous tries, she couldn't find Jeremy's father, but once she'd read Eve Walters's e-mail and learned the woman's story, she had used all the information available to her to see if she could track down the so-called "drug dealer" who had impregnated the woman.

As she read Eve's story, her gut almost immediately told her that the man who had fathered Eve's baby wasn't the drug pusher the woman believed him to be.

Laura knew the life, knew the deceptions that were so necessary in order to maintain a cover. Something she couldn't put into words told her that Eve's "Adam" was part of some kind of government agency.

A little research and calling in several favors from old friends proved her right.

Adam Smythe was actually Adam Serrano, a DEA agent who had been working undercover for the last two years. There was more background on the man, but that was all she was interested in. Laura saw no reason to delve into the man's history any further than was absolutely necessary. The life she led now made her acutely aware of the need for, and seductive appeal of, privacy. She gave Adam Serrano his.

Armed with this information, it took little for her to find both Adam's Internet server and with that, his e-mail address. Her stark e-mail message to him went out the moment she secured it.

If Adam was anything like her, she reasoned, his sense of family would leap to the foreground, especially since he had none. She was fairly certain that he would lose no time trying to track down the mother of this unborn child he hadn't realized was in the offing.

Laura was more than a little tempted to e-mail Eve and let her know that Adam was coming, but that might have made the woman bolt. Bolting was the last thing she needed to do at this late stage in her pregnancy.

Eve needed exactly what she was most likely going to get.

What she, herself, would have loved to get, Laura thought wistfully.

But, except for an occasional daydream, she had

given up the fantasy that had her mystery man knocking on her door, the way she envisioned Adam doing now, or definitely in the very near future, on Eve's door.

Laura smiled as she replayed the thought. It wasn't every day a girl got the chance to bring Adam and Eve together, she mused, more than a little pleased with herself.

With renewed purpose, Laura went on to read the next e-mail that had been sent to her site from another single mom.

The doorbell was ringing.

Eve pressed her lips together. She had just shut down her computer for the night. Glancing at her watch, she saw that it was almost nine o'clock.

Nine o'clock and she was struggling to keep her eyes open.

Some party girl she was, Eve mocked herself. She could remember going two days without sleep when she was in college. Three days once, she recalled. There was no way she could do that now. But then, this pregnancy and the tension that had come with it served to drain her and make her overly tired more than she cared to acknowledge.

This was probably nothing compared to how tired she was going to be once the baby learned how to walk and get into things, she thought. She was looking forward to that, she realized. Looking forward to being a parent—

The doorbell rang again.

What kind of a responsible parent allowed their child to still be out, trick-or-treating at this hour? The little ones needed to be home, asleep in their beds, or at least in their beds.

Most likely it was another one of those high school kids, she thought, bracing her hands on the chair's armrests and pushing herself to her feet. She'd had several of those tonight, costumed kids who towered over her. One looked old enough to shave.

She hated the way they abused Halloween, horning in on a holiday that was intended for little children to enjoy. Oh, well, she still had some candy left over. She might as well give it to them. It was better for her that way.

Eve knew her weakness. If there was candy hanging around in a bowl, no matter what she promised herself about being good, the pieces would eventually find their way into her mouth. The problem was, Eve thought, she had never met a piece of candy, chocolate or otherwise she didn't like.

"Time to get rid of the temptation," she told Tessa. Gently snoring, the dog ignored her.

Picking up the bowl, Eve carried it with her as she made her way to the front door.

"Some guard dog you are," she quipped, tossing the remark over her shoulder. Tessa still didn't stir.

About to open the door, she had to stop for a second as yet another pain seized her, stealing her breath and causing her to all but double over. This was getting very old. Just as perspiration broke out all along her brow, the pain receded. She let out a long breath and then reached for the front door.

Since she was right-handed, Eve had to shift the bowl over to her left side and then open the door with her right.

But this time, no chorus of "Trick or treat!"—even a baritone chorus—greeted her.

Instead, the uncostumed, tall, dark and still pulse-racingly handsome man who was standing on her doorstep said, "Hello, Eve."

The lights in the living room behind her seemed to dim slightly, even as her head began to spin about. Eve struggled to catch hold of it. Reality and everything that went with it distanced itself from her.

The bowl she was holding slipped out of her hand and onto the light gray tiled floor, shattering the second it made contact.

It was only by sheer luck that she hadn't gone down with it.

Chapter 3

Adam. Here.

How?

Stunned, the first coherent thought that shot through Eve's mind was to somehow cover up the rounded expanse of her belly so that Adam wouldn't notice that she was pregnant.

But it was far too late for that.

Those emerald-green eyes of his that she'd once loved so much slid down, taking in the swell of his child.

Her mouth felt as dry as cotton as she struggled to access her brain. The organ became temporarily paralyzed by the sight of the man whose very touch had once been able to move the earth beneath her feet.

Then, as she watched, to her utter amazement Adam

dropped down to his knees right in front of her. For just the tiniest fraction of a second, she thought he was going apologize profusely, swearing by everything he held dear that he'd completely reformed and had been frantically searching for her these last eight months. She knew it was just a hopeless fantasy on her part. Adam would never beg for any reason. It would have been completely out of character for him.

As out of character as a supposed scholar dealing in drugs to provide himself with a lucrative sideline, she thought with no small touch of sarcasm.

As her mind came back into sync, it still took Eve more than a moment to draw in enough air to form any words.

"What—what are you doing here?" she finally managed to ask, addressing the question to the top of his thick, black hair.

"Right now, picking up a bunch of broken glass and several tiny bags of Halloween candy," Adam answered. The bowl had smashed into almost a dozen pieces, too many for him to hold in his hand at one time. Looking up, he asked her, "Do you have a bag or something that I can put this mess into?"

The question sounded so casual, so natural, as if they had never been apart. As if this was just another evening in their lives, following scores of other evenings exactly like it.

But it wasn't just another evening, and they *had* been apart. Moreover, if she'd been successful in her escape from Santa Barbara, they would have remained that way forever.

Despite everything, just looking at him intensified

the longing she'd struggled against almost daily. Eve vaguely remembered a lyric she'd once heard, part of a song whose title she'd long since forgotten. *Leaving him was a lot easier than staying away.*

Truer words were never uttered.

Seeing Adam now, Eve wanted to throw herself into his arms. To hide there, in the shelter of his embrace. In effect, she wanted to hide from the man she'd discovered Adam to be by seeking refuge in the arms of the man she'd thought Adam was.

How crazy was that?

Very.

Her head hurt and her heart ached.

"Or," Adam went on when she continued to stand there, making no reply, "I could just go get it myself if you tell me where you keep your bags."

She needed to regroup, to stop feeling as if she was on the verge of hyperventilating and tell him in no uncertain terms that he had to leave.

The words wouldn't come.

Buying herself some time, struggling against yet another wave of pain emanating from her belly, Eve turned on her heel and went to the kitchen. She braced her hand on the counter and opened the bottom drawer situated just to the right of the sink. It was stuffed with plastic grocery bags waiting to be pressed into service. After taking one out, she made her way back to the front door and prayed she was hallucinating.

She hadn't imagined it.

Adam was still there, crouching with his hands full of broken glass, watching her. Waiting for her to come back.

Adam's very presence mocked the notions that had filled her head such a short time ago. Notions that comprised the happily-ever-after scenario she'd once woven for herself, thinking that *finally* she'd found that one special someone she wanted to face forever with.

Until there was Adam, she'd never been in love before, never even experienced a serious crush. At twenty-nine, she'd begun to think that she was destined to face life alone. But then she'd walked into the secondhand bookstore and lost her heart. Just like that.

She'd even joked with her father when she saw him shortly thereafter, gifting him with the first edition Mark Twain book she'd bought in Adam's store, that she'd never believed love at first sight was anything but a myth—until she'd fallen victim to it.

Victim.

Now there was a good word. Because she really was the victim here. She and this baby. A victim of her own stupidity and her far-too-trusting nature. Otherwise, maybe she would have noticed some things that were awry, things that she should have scrutinized more closely. Warning signs. They had to have been there if she hadn't been so blind, so willing to love.

She bit back a sigh. She wasn't up to this. Wasn't up to dealing with seeing Adam, especially not now, when she felt as sluggish as an elephant that had been hit with a giant tranquilizer dart.

Eve held out the plastic grocery bag. Adam took it from her, murmuring "Thanks," and smiling that lopsided, sensual smile of his she discovered she still wasn't immune to.

She stood there, trying not to think, not to feel, as

Adam gathered up the last of the glass and disposed of it in the bag.

Just then, as if suddenly hearing the sound of his voice, Tessa came charging out of the office to investigate. Seeing him, she immediately dashed toward Adam, wagging her tail like a metronome that had been set at triple time.

"Hi, Tessa," Adam said with a laugh, petting the excited dog and trying not to let her knock him over. "How've you been, girl?"

In response, Tessa licked his face.

So much for allies, Eve thought.

Still petting the dog, Adam looked at her. "I think I got it all," he told Eve. "But to be on the safe side, I'd suggest you vacuum the area." Standing up, taking care not to let the excited dog overwhelm him, he decided to augment his statement. "Better yet, tell me where you keep your vacuum cleaner and I'll vacuum the area for you." Anticipating an argument, Adam added, "It's the least I can do—seeing as how the sight of me made you drop the bowl in the first place."

Eve squared her shoulders. *Don't let him get to you, damn it. Don't!*

"I can do my own vacuuming," she told him in a voice that had a slight tremor in it.

He eyed her dubiously, his smile fading and becoming a thing of the past. "You sure? Pushing something heavy around like that might cause you to go into labor prematurely."

She wanted him out of here—before she wound up caving. "Did you get a medical degree since I last saw you?"

His eyes remained on hers. It took everything she had not to let them get to her. Not to just give up and hold on to him the way she couldn't seem to hold on to her anger.

"A lot of things happened since I last saw you," he told her, his voice low, "but my getting a medical degree wasn't among them."

It was the same tone that used to ripple along her skin, exciting her. Well, it didn't excite her anymore. *It didn't,* she fiercely insisted.

"I'm just passing on some common sense," Adam concluded.

She did her best to make him leave. "Always a first time," she answered sarcastically.

Adam waited for her to continue venting. When she didn't, he raised an eyebrow.

"That's it?" he asked. "Nothing more? No more slings and arrows and hot words?" He knew it was baiting her, but the way he saw it, she deserved to be able to yell at him, to put her anger into words. God knew she had the right.

But she just looked at him, the light leaving her eyes. That hurt him more than anything she could have said, because he knew that he'd done that to her.

"What's the point?" she countered sadly, half lifting her shoulders in a careless shrug.

"The point is that it might make you feel better," Adam told her. "It might help restore some equilibrium in your world."

She was a long way from having that happen, she thought. A *long* way. "The only thing that would do either would be if I'd never met you."

He had that coming and he knew it. He regretted

their time together only because it had placed her in jeopardy and it ultimately had hurt her. That had never been his intention.

In an absolute, personal sense, he'd never, not even for a moment, regretted having her in his life, no matter how short the time they had together had been. But, even though she didn't know it, she'd had her revenge. Eve had upended his world, showing him everything he'd given up to do what he did, to be what he was. She'd showed him everything he could have had if his life had gone differently.

At least he had a life, he reminded himself.

Which was more than Mona had.

Mona, his kid sister, had been bright, beautiful and blessed with the ability to light up a room the moment she entered it. Her family and friends were all certain that she could have had the world at her feet just by wishing it.

Instead, she opted to keep it at bay, losing herself in the dark, forbidding haze of heroin and meth until no one who loved her could even recognize her. Despite his alternating between pleading with her and railing at her, his sister had continued using even as she made him promise after promise to stop.

When she finally did stop, it hadn't been voluntarily. He'd found her lying facedown on the floor of the apartment he'd been paying for, a victim of a drug overdose. No frantic attempts at CPR on his part could revive her. His sister was gone, another statistic in the increasingly unsuccessful war on drugs. His crusade against drugs began that morning.

And the way he viewed it, it hadn't cost him anything. Until he'd met Eve.

"Where do you keep the vacuum cleaner?" he repeated, his voice a little gruffer.

"I said I'd take care of it," Eve insisted, holding her ground.

He let her win. Maybe she needed that. With a shrug, Adam bent down to pick up the spilled candy. Cradling the small bags, bars and boxes against his chest, he rose to his feet again.

"Where do you want me to put these?"

The answer flashed through her head, but it wasn't her way to say things like that, no matter how tempted she was or how warranted her flippant remark might have actually been. Adam might not have any honor left, but she still did.

Was that why she was carrying the drug dealer's baby? a taunting voice in her head mocked.

"Over there will be fine," she told him, nodding toward the coffee table.

Adam crossed over to it and let the candy rain down from his arms onto the table.

His back was to her. An image flashed through her brain. The way his back had looked as he moved to leave his bed after they'd made love. She felt her stomach tightening.

She had to stop that, stop torturing herself. He wasn't the answer to a prayer, he was the personification of a nightmare.

A nightmare in pleasing form.

Eve passed her tongue along her lips, trying to moisten them. They were so dry, they were almost sticking together.

"Why did you come?" she forced herself to ask, making it sound like an accusation.

He turned from the table and looked at her. Had she always looked so delicate? he wondered. "I heard you were pregnant—"

Eve widened her eyes. They had no friends in common and their worlds certainly didn't overlap.

"How did you hear?" she demanded. He just looked at her. "Who told you?" she pressed.

He waved her question away. "Doesn't matter. But I came to see for myself."

She drew herself up to her full five-foot-four height, then spread her arms, giving him an unobstructed view. After a minute, she dropped her arms again. "All right, you saw. Now please leave."

Adam remained where he stood, making no move to do anything of the kind. Tessa was nuzzling his leg and he stroked her head as he took a breath, fortifying himself.

"Is it mine?" he asked.

"No." The denial automatically rose to her lips and shot like a bullet through the air, primed by a she-bear's instincts to protect her unborn cub.

He didn't believe her even though part of him would have really wanted to. It would have made everything so much simpler. It would have taken away not just his sense of guilt, but of responsibility, too. Not to mention that he wouldn't need to feel obligated to protect the baby or her if she wasn't bearing his child.

The hell you wouldn't.

The other part of him fiercely rejected even the suggestion that the seed growing in her belly had come from anyone but him. Even if he never saw Eve again—

and until that anonymous e-mail had turned up on his computer he never planned to—Eve was his soul mate in every sense of the word. He knew that no matter how many women he came across, how many he took to his bed, this one would stand out. This one would always mean more to him than all the others combined.

And he knew her well enough to know that the child was his no matter what she said to the contrary.

"I don't believe you," he told her quietly.

Panic began to form within her. Why had he shown up? Why couldn't he just let her go? And more importantly, why did the sight of him make her yearn like this? She weighed a ton, for God's sake. Women who weighed a ton weren't supposed to suddenly want to have their bones jumped, especially not by someone they knew dwelled with the dregs of society.

Eve did her best to sound distant. "I don't care what you believe," she told him coldly. Tossing her hair over her shoulder, she ordered, "Now go, get out of here. I never want to see you again."

This was where he should retreat. She'd given him the perfect out. He'd come, he'd seen for himself that Eve was pregnant, now it was time to go. He was still undercover and the stakes were now larger than ever. The person he was after was the main player, the head of the drug cartel. The center of the drug trafficking that was filling the local colleges with heroin.

He couldn't jeopardize that. Eve had made it perfectly clear that she didn't want him around. And she'd heatedly denied that he was the father. That meant that he could walk away with a clear conscience.

But he couldn't leave.

It didn't matter what he wished, the fact remained that Eve had been with him a little less than nine months ago. With him in every sense of the word. He knew in his gut the baby was his. If he could do the math, someone else in the organization would do the same. The time to back away, to pretend she'd never been part of his life, was over. Eve and her unborn child were at risk. They needed his protection. He was *not* about to have them on his conscience.

He frowned, then calmly told her, "The calendar doesn't back up what you just said."

"Then get a new calendar," she retorted. "This is *not* your baby." Her voice rose in anger. "Don't you understand? I don't want anything from you. You're free to walk away. So walk," she ordered.

Instead of leaving, he pushed the door closed. The *click* echoed in her head. Nerves rose to the surface even as she struggled to at least look calm.

"Is this why you left?" he asked, his eyes indicating her swollen abdomen. "Because you found out you were pregnant?"

She took offense, although she didn't even know why. Her hormones raged, playing tug-of-war with her emotions.

"No," she retorted hotly, "I left because I found out that you were a drug dealer."

He needed for her to be safe. Needed to watch over her. He knew that he couldn't just post himself on her block indefinitely. This was the kind of neighborhood where an unknown car would attract attention if it was seen lingering for more than a few minutes—and that would inevitably result in a call to the police.

The last thing he wanted was to get involved with the local law enforcement agency, at least not until he could bring down the leader of this little high-class operation. Otherwise, he and a lot of other people would find themselves throwing away two years on a failed mission. And another drug lord would find himself with a free pass.

He owed it to Mona not to let that happen.

In order to do what he needed to do, he knew he needed to lie.

To Eve.

Again.

"Then you'll be happy to know," he told her, "that I'm not part of that world any longer." His eyes held hers and he hated himself for what he was doing, but at the same time, he knew he had to. "I'm just a simple used book dealer."

For just a moment, Eve's heart leaped up in celebration. She was ready to seize the information and clutch it to her chest like an eternal promise. But he had lied to her before—who knows how many times—and once that sort of thing happened, trust was badly splintered if not shattered. Rebuilding the fragile emotion was not the easiest thing in the world.

"How do I know you're not just lying?" she challenged, praying he had an answer that would somehow satisfy her.

"You don't," he admitted simply, surprising her. "You're just going to have to trust me."

And that, Eve thought, was the problem in a nutshell. More than anything in the world, she wanted to believe him. But at the same time, she knew that she just couldn't. Not yet. Not until he proved himself to her and gave her a concrete reason to believe him.

Just then, she thought she felt the baby begin to kick her again. Kick her harder than it had ever kicked before.

Caught off guard, immersed in this new drama, Eve gasped as tears welled up in her eyes.

Sensing both her mistress's anxiety and her pain, Tessa began to pace nervously about before her as Eve clutched at her belly.

Adam reacted immediately. His arms closed around Eve as if he was afraid that she was about to sink down to the floor.

"What's wrong?" he demanded, concern weaving itself through his voice. His eyes searched her face. "What can I do to help?"

Just hold me, Adam, the little voice in her soul whispered to him. *Just hold me and make everything all better again.*

Chapter 4

He didn't like the way she'd suddenly stiffened against him or the fact that her breathing began to sound labored. Why wasn't she answering him?

As he held Eve at arm's length to get a look at her face, he found nothing to reassure him. She was in physical pain.

"Talk to me, Eve. What's wrong?"

"Nothing," she managed to get out, fervently hoping that if she said it with enough conviction, it would be true. But it wasn't. The pain just got more intense. Why wouldn't it stop? "The baby kicked. He's been doing a lot of that today."

"He?" Adam echoed. If he hadn't known better, he would have said that something akin to pride stirred within him. "It's a boy?"

Trying to get behind the pain, or beyond it, Eve hardly heard him. "Yes." Belatedly, she realized what he'd asked her. "Unless it's a girl."

The only reason he felt a tinge of disappointment was because he liked knowing about things ahead of time. It always helped to be prepared. As for the possibility that he might have a daughter instead of a son, he found himself rather liking the idea. If she took after her mother, she'd be a force to be reckoned with.

"Then you don't know?" he concluded.

"No." He was still holding on to her shoulders and she shrugged his hands away. She'd decided to have her baby the old-fashioned way—that included not knowing its sex. "But then, I don't know a lot of things." She eyed him pointedly. "And contrary to the popular belief, ignorance is *not* bliss. It's setting yourself up for a fall."

She hit her intended target with that one. "I never meant to hurt you, Eve," he told her sincerely. "I swear I didn't."

She could almost believe him. But then, Eve thought ruefully, struggling to hold the hot pain burning in her belly at bay, she'd believed him before and look how that had turned out for her.

"You know what they say about the path to hell," she said in a pseudocheerful voice. "It's paved with good intentions."

Adam knew he could just walk away, that it might be better all around if he did, but the look in her eyes—a look he was fairly sure she wasn't even aware of—just wouldn't let him do it. She needed him.

"Look, I know you probably hate me—"

She shook her head, stopping him before he went on.

"I don't hate you, Adam. Hate's a very powerful emotion. I don't feel anything at all for you."

Her eyes were steely as she tried to convince him nothing remained between them but this child waiting to be born. She sincerely doubted if she'd succeeded because she hadn't even been able to convince herself.

She was lying. He *knew* she was lying. One look into her eyes told him that.

Or was he seeing things he wanted to see?

He wasn't the kind of man she deserved, the kind of man she had a right to expect. A nine-to-five kind of guy who left his work behind once he walked out of the office. His "job" was with him 24/7, even when he wasn't undercover and so much more so when he was. Eve deserved infinitely more than just half a man.

But that didn't change the fact that right now, when she was at her most vulnerable, he needed to look out for her. Needed to be her hidden guardian angel.

Damn, he should have never gotten involved with her, never given in to that overwhelming yearning that had stirred so urgently inside of him every time she walked into his store, into his carefully crafted make-believe life.

Up until that time, it had been easy. He'd been so focused on his job, on the target that Hugh, his handler, had turned him on to that he'd been able to successfully resist the women who crossed his path. Even the ones who had been very determined to extend their acquaintance beyond customer and seller.

But then *she* had walked into his store and everything changed.

It'd been raining that morning, an unexpected, quick

shower that had ushered her into the store along with a sheet of rain. Even soaking wet, her hair plastered to her head, Eve had been possibly the most beautiful woman he had ever seen.

He'd found himself talking to her for the better part of an hour, showing her rare edition after rare edition. Giving her a little capsulated history behind each book. He made it a point never to enter a situation without studying it seven ways from sundown and, in this case, he was supposed to be the scholarly owner of a small shop that dealt only with rare books. Consequently, he had a lot of miscellaneous information crammed into his head.

She'd appeared to hang on every word.

It had been the best time of his life and he wished he could recapture it. But he couldn't.

"All right," Adam said evenly, "you don't feel anything at all for me. I'm not asking you to, but I want you to know that I'm going to be here for you if you need me."

"Won't that be a killer commute for you?" she asked cynically. "Driving from here to Santa Barbara and back every day?"

"I won't be commuting that far."

She didn't understand, but was in too much pain to get the whole story. She blinked hard, clenching her fists at her sides as if that could somehow chase it away. "What about your bookstore?"

"I relocated it," he told her simply, then added an expedient lie. "I lost my lease and Laguna Beach seemed like a nice setting for the shop."

Before she'd discovered his dual life, she would have been thrilled with the idea that Adam had relocated to be close to her, that he had gone searching for her when she'd disappeared and once he'd found where she had gone, he'd rearranged his life just to be nearby.

But those kind of thoughts belonged to a naive, innocent young woman. She was no longer that, no longer naive. Or innocent. And the fault for that partially lay with him.

She needed to discourage him, to make him leave her alone—before she became too weak to follow through. "I don't need you to be 'here' for me, Adam. I've moved on. I'm seeing someone," she informed him tersely.

A sharp pain flared in his gut. He'd lost her. Before he'd ever really had her.

Schooled in not showing emotion, his expression remained unchanged. "Is it serious?"

The lies didn't get easier, but she had no choice. She needed to protect her baby at all costs, and that meant protecting the child from its father.

"Yes. Very. Josiah wants to adopt the baby." Silently, she apologized to Josiah Turner, but the seventy-year-old man's name was the first one to pop into her head. The man was like an uncle to her. She'd known him all her life, from the time she would frequent her father's animal clinic. Whenever he wasn't away on business, Josiah would bring his dogs to her father for routine care. And when he was away, he would board them at the clinic.

When her father died shortly after her return, the retired widower had arbitrarily appointed himself her guardian angel, determined to protect her, especially when it became apparent that she was pregnant.

"Good for you," Adam said, doing his best to infuse an upbeat note into his voice. He still intended to watch over her, but at least she wasn't going to be alone. This meant that he could maintain vigil from a distance. And if knowing that someone else would be holding her, making love with her, stuck a hot knife into his gut, well, that was his problem, not hers. "Then I'll be going."

But even as he told her, his feet didn't seem to want to move. Stalling for time until he could get himself to go, Adam took out one of the business cards he'd had printed just last week and held it out to her.

"In case you ever want to find another first edition," he explained.

When she made no effort to take it from him, he took her hand in his and placed the card with the new bookstore's address and phone number into her palm, closing her fingers over it.

The next moment, as he began to withdraw his hand, she suddenly grabbed his wrist and squeezed it. Hard.

She looked as startled as he was. Adam searched her face. "Eve?"

This time, she made no answer. Instead, Adam watched the color completely drain out of her face and heard her catch her breath the way someone did when they didn't want to scream.

It didn't take much for him to put two and two together. "It's time, isn't it?"

Her eyes were wide as she slanted them toward his. "No, no, it's not. It's not time," she insisted heatedly. "I'm not supposed to be due for another three weeks. Maybe four." Even as she said it, another wave of pain engulfed her. "Oh, God."

Still clutching his wrist, she almost buckled right in

front of him. Adam quickly put his arm around her shoulders. Drawing her to him, he held her up.

"Looks like the baby doesn't have a calendar in there," he told her.

"I'll be all right," she said fiercely, more to reassure herself than him. She glanced toward the living room. "I just need to sit down."

But when she tried to cross to the sofa, he continued to hold her against him. "You might need to sit down, but you're not going to be all right," he told her. She was about to protest again when Adam nodded at the floor directly beneath her feet. She followed his line of vision. The small pool made his argument for him. "Your water just broke."

"No," she cried in vain denial.

There was no time to go back and forth about this. She was in labor. "I'll drive you to the hospital," he told her firmly.

She didn't want him with her. This was far too intimate an experience to share with a man who still might be living in the criminal world. A man who had looked her in the face and lied to her. She didn't want him near her baby.

"I can call a cab."

"I'm sure you can," he told her, keeping his voice even as he continued holding on to her, "but I'm still driving you. If you're worried about this Josiah guy, I'm sure he won't mind my getting you to the hospital. I'll call him for you once we get there if you like," he promised.

"I—" The rest of the words she'd intended to say faded as she sucked in her breath again, all but gagging with the effort. Practically panting, Eve shook her head in silent, adamant protest.

"I never realized you had this stubborn streak," he commented. "But you're going to the hospital and I'm taking you. End of story," he declared firmly. *Or maybe, just the beginning.*

"No, I'm not." She wasn't going anywhere, and not because she didn't want to. There was horror in her eyes as she said between her teeth, "The…baby's… coming."

They'd already established that. "I know that, that's why I'm—"

Adam stopped talking. He assessed her expression and the way Eve was squeezing his wrist, as if she was about to break it off at any second. He realized she was trying to unconsciously transfer the pain. Which meant her pain level had increased.

"You're having the baby right now, aren't you?" he concluded. Concern gripped him in its giant, callused hand.

It took Eve a couple of seconds to regain her voice. "You think?"

The moment she confirmed his suspicions, Adam picked Eve up into his arms. Beside them, Tessa began to leap about excitedly, jumping up and trying to become part of the game.

"Not now, dog," Adam ordered gruffly. Tessa stopped leaping. Instantly subdued, she glanced from him to her mistress. "Which way to your bedroom?"

Why was he asking her that? She couldn't focus her eyes or her brain. "It's upstairs. But I don't think…"

"It would help if you didn't talk, too," Adam told her,

annoyed that he wouldn't be able to get her to the hospital in time. "I've got to get you onto a bed."

She couldn't seem to get in enough air. As he began to climb the stairs, she laced her arms around his neck, afraid that he might drop her. "That's the way this whole thing started."

"Still got a sense of humor," he observed, a thread of optimism weaving through him. Even pregnant, she hardly felt as if she weighed anything, he thought. "That's a good sign."

She didn't want a sign, she wanted this to be over with.

The room temperature felt like it had gone up by at least ten degrees, if not more, and she felt as if she was caught between a pending implosion and an explosion. The pain now raced through her entire body, generating from her epicenter and radiating out like the unnerving aftershocks following an earthquake.

Was this what birthing was all about? Suddenly, she felt infinite empathy for the pets she treated. How could animals willingly mate after the first time, knowing that this kind of pain was what was in store for them?

"I'm…too…heavy," she protested.

"Actually, you're not," he told her just as he made it to the landing. There were several doors on either side. "Which way?"

Her breath was temporarily gone. Instead of telling him, she pointed to the first door on the left.

The door was already open. Moving as swiftly as he could, with the dog shadowing his every step, Adam crossed the threshold and placed Eve down on her bed.

The moment she felt the mattress beneath her, Eve

grabbed the comforter on either side of her, bunching it up beneath her frantically clutching fingers.

Adam saw her bite down on her lower lip.

"You *can* scream, you know," he told her, watching her struggle. "That doesn't make you any less of a mother—or a woman."

"I'm not screaming," she retorted with passion.

She absolutely refused to have her baby coming into the world with her screams ringing in his or her ears. But bottling up the pain wasn't easy.

It took her a second to realize that Adam was asking her something. Even her eyes felt as if they were sweating.

"What?" she demanded breathlessly.

"What's your doctor's name?" Adam repeated.

"Mudd," she gasped.

He almost laughed out loud. He sympathized with her feelings. He'd once had a doctor's assistant in one of the little border towns in Mexico digging a bullet out of his shoulder. He'd felt the same way about the man.

"No need for name calling," he told her, banking down his amusement. "What—?"

"Her name is Mudd," she repeated. Gritting her teeth, she gave him specifics. "Geraldine…Mudd."

He nodded, owning up to his mistake. "Okay. Sorry about that."

Adam took out his phone and pressed the key for Information. Instead of ringing, he heard the irritating sound that told him his call couldn't go through. One glance at the screen told him his signal was all but non-existent. He swallowed a curse. The next second, Eve was grabbing the edge of his shirt. Before she could speak, another huge contraction had her arching her entire body up off the bed like a human tunnel.

She all but collapsed when the pain receded. "No time."

She knew her own body better than he did, Adam reasoned, flipping his phone closed again. He shoved it back into his pocket.

"Whatever you say. Don't worry." He did his best to sound reassuring despite the fact that he was worried himself. "I've had training."

"In what?" Her eyes were wide again as she looked at him.

His answer was carefully guarded, but he did want to assuage her fears. "In first aid and what to do if a woman goes into labor."

Was he telling the truth? But how could he be? "Drug dealing has gotten more complicated."

"I went to the Y. I like being prepared for all contingencies." It was a lie. He couldn't very well tell her that he'd taken the mandatory classes as part of his DEA training.

The next moment, any other questions she might have asked flew out of her head, chased out by the massive waves of pain sweeping over her. Sweat poured out of her even though the room was relatively cool.

She could feel her child pushing, trying to fight his or her way out.

With all her heart, she wished she could be bringing her baby into a better world than what waited for it. Wished that at least the baby would have not just a mother, but a father there, as well.

But the time for philosophical debates had long since passed.

In a vague, hot haze, she could feel Adam's hands on her, stripping off her underwear and pushing up the loose dress she was wearing.

Words, there were words. He was saying something to her. An apology? What was he apologizing for?

Oh, for having to undress her.

She laughed shortly. The time for that, too, was long gone. If she hadn't let him undress her in the first place, there would have been no need for him to undress her now.

"You're crowning," he declared, trying to mask his surprise.

He could feel excitement coursing through his veins. Despite the way she was behaving, he hadn't thought it possible for this process to be happening this quickly. If she'd been a race car, Eve would have literally gone from zero to sixty in a quarter of a heartbeat.

Oh, God, he hoped he could remember everything he'd been taught. Those lessons all seemed like he'd sat through them an eternity ago. He'd never had an occasion to put any of it into practice before.

Until now.

Taking a breath, he braced himself. "Okay, Eve, push."

Eve squeezed her eyes shut. She clutched the comforter, feeling the lace rip beneath her fingers as she held on to the material tightly and pushed for all she was worth. Through it all, she was vaguely aware of Tessa running back and forth near the foot of the bed.

Poor Tessa, the tension in the room had gotten to her, Eve thought.

"Okay, stop!" Adam ordered. "Stop!"

Eve fell back against the bed, her hair plastered to

the back of her neck, her head spinning almost wildly. "Is it here yet?"

Couldn't she tell the difference? he wondered, amazed. "No." It was all coming back to him, thank God. "I need you to relax and take a few deep breaths, then push again."

She did as he told her, knowing he was right even though she resented his presence, resented that he knew what to do. Resented him for bringing her to this state. Her body felt a kinship to a Thanksgiving wishbone being pulled in two separate directions. In agony, she was angry at the world.

"Now push, Eve," he was shouting at her. "C'mon, push!"

Exhaustion wore away her second wave of energy. She felt as if she had nothing left. Even so, she managed to muster together more from somewhere. Grunting as she followed orders, she pushed for all she was worth.

Again with nothing to show for it except possibly the vein she was certain had burst in her head.

Panting like a twenty-six-mile marathon runner at the end of the race, she fell against the bed again.

All too soon, she heard Adam asking, "Ready?"

If she had any strength, she would have hit him. "No," she cried hoarsely.

He was positioned to catch the baby when it emerged. Raising his eyes, he looked up at Eve. "I know this is hard—"

"How?" she demanded in an angry whisper. "How do you know?" He wasn't a woman, he had no right to say that he knew. He *didn't* know.

"Okay, I'm making an educated guess here," Adam

conceded. "But you can do this. I know you can do this. Women have been doing this since the beginning of time."

More proof that God wasn't a woman, Eve thought. But there really was no other choice. She had to do this or die. Propping herself up on her elbows, screwing her eyes shut, Eve bore down and pushed until she thought her head would pop off. And then she pushed some more.

Dying was beginning to sound like a very tempting option.

Chapter 5

"You're doing it, Eve!" Adam exclaimed excitedly, cheering her on. "You're doing it!"

It felt as if her insides were being ripped apart by some powerful, unseen hand. She squeezed her eyes shut so tightly, she saw concentric orbs of bright red and gold.

"I...know..." Eve panted. She could barely scrape together enough energy to push the words out of her mouth.

And then she heard it. A small, lusty wail.

Her baby? Was that coming from her baby? Or was she just hallucinating?

Belatedly, she realized that she still had her eyes shut. Her lashes were wet with perspiration and all but glued together.

When she opened her eyes, she saw what was in her estimation the most beautiful sight that had ever been created. Her baby in Adam's arms.

"What is it?" she asked breathlessly.

Unable to maintain her position a second longer, Eve's elbows went out from under her and she collapsed back onto the bed.

"Beautiful," Adam answered reverently, looking down into the dewy face of his daughter. He was completely mesmerized and enchanted. And utterly head over heels in love.

Had anyone asked, he would have said that his heart was impenetrable, that the only one who had ever managed to crack the exterior had been Eve. But this little being, this nothing-short-of-a-miracle that he had helped bring into the world, had seized his heart in her tiny hands the moment she made her debut.

He was in love with her, in love with this miracle who had come from nothing, who was the result of a chance, passionate coupling and a product malfunction.

"But what is it?" Eve asked, frustrated.

"It's a girl," he told her, still staring at the infant. He forced himself to tear his eyes away and look at Eve. "You have a daughter." He'd almost said "we" instead, but the very idea that the baby was half his still hadn't taken root. Besides, Eve had been the one to do all the work. The credit was hers.

He moved closer to Eve and tucked the naked newborn into her arms. Pressing the infant against her chest, awe instantly slid over Eve. She felt the newborn's warmth penetrating her skin.

"She's so little," Eve murmured in surprise, then looked up at Adam. "Where's the rest of her?"

The baby did seem little, Adam thought. Little and perfect. "She's whole, Eve."

"But it felt like I was giving birth to an elephant. The world's largest elephant," she amended. This was a little bit of a thing she should have been able to push out on a sneeze.

Adam laughed softly. "This is all of her," he assured Eve. Taking a step back, he glanced toward the hall, as if to check if the rest of the world was still there after this miracle had taken place. "I need to get a knife to cut the umbilical cord." He looked at Eve uncertainly. "Will you be okay if I leave you for a couple of minutes?" he asked.

The bonding was instantaneous, as was the surge of motherly pride and love. Eve couldn't get herself to tear her eyes away from this brand-new human being in her arms even for a second.

"We'll be fine, won't we, Brooklyn?" she asked the infant.

About to leave, the name stopped Adam cold in his tracks. He looked at her over his shoulder. "Brooklyn?" he echoed.

Eve nodded. Very gingerly, she skimmed her fingertips along the baby's clenched fist. Five fingers, there were five fingers, she assured herself. On both hands. She'd never felt anything so soft, she thought. Like snowflakes. Precious, precious snowflakes.

"My father was born there," she explained. "I always liked the sound of the name."

"Brooklyn," he repeated, rolling it over on his

tongue. Looking back at her and the baby, he slowly nodded. "Not bad." But right now, the baby and Eve were still very much attached. He needed to sterilize a knife and separate them. "I'll be right back," he promised.

Still looking at her daughter's face, Eve smiled. "We're not going anywhere."

He had to admit he liked the sound of that.

The moment he left, Eve raised her eyes to the doorway to be sure that he was gone.

"That was your father," she whispered to the infant in her arms. "He's a little unusual and he needs some work, but maybe with you here, we can fix him and make him into a good dad." She took a deep, fortifying breath. Her lungs had finally stopped aching. "At least it's worth a try."

She knew it was the euphoria talking, but it gave her something to hang on to.

Adam was back faster than she thought possible. As he'd said, he had a knife in his hand. But the look on his face as he regarded her was slightly dubious, as if he wasn't happy with what he was about to do.

"What's wrong?" Eve asked.

He regarded the knife and then her. He had no problem digging out a bullet in his own arm, but the thought of using a knife on her for any reason suddenly didn't seem like such a good idea.

"I don't know if this is going to hurt. Either of you," he added.

Considering what she'd just gone through, she felt she was pretty much beyond hurt. "Just do it and get it over with."

But he made no move to comply. "Maybe I should wait for the paramedics."

"What paramedics?" The euphoric bubble around her burst. Her eyes widened. When had he had time to place the call? "You called the paramedics?"

"Yes." He'd made the call in the kitchen. "I can't just toss the two of you into the back of my car or have you ride to the hospital on the handlebars of my motorcycle." The last was just an exaggeration. He *had* no motorcycle, at least, not here.

As far as she was concerned, the discussion was all just moot. "Why do we have to ride *anything* to the hospital?" she argued. "It's over, the baby's here." As she referred to her daughter, she couldn't suppress the smile that came to her lips.

"You both need to be checked out," he told her in a no-nonsense voice that said this wasn't up for debate.

Exhausted though she was, Eve felt her back go up. Where did he get off, telling her what she was supposed to do? "Nobody put you in charge."

"I got the position by default because you're not being sensible," he informed her. Seeing her frown, he added diplomatically, "It's understandable. You've just been through an ordeal and condensed eighteen hours of labor into about ten minutes flat. Anyone would have been addled by that—"

She cut him off. "I'm not addled, I'm fine. We're both fine," she insisted, looking at her daughter who now dozed. "And we don't need to go to the hospital." She just wanted to be left alone to enjoy her daughter. And rest.

His eyes narrowed. Something was off. For an ordinarily sensible woman, she was protesting too much. "What are you afraid of?"

"I'm not afraid," Eve retorted, but he kept on watching her as if he didn't believe her, as if he was waiting for her to tell him the truth. She pressed her lips together and looked up toward the ceiling. It kept the tears from flowing. "The last time I was in a hospital, it was to see the E.R. doctor pronounce my father dead. I just don't think I can handle being there."

The sound of approaching sirens pushed their way into the stillness, swelling in volume.

"Too late," Adam told her. "Besides, this is a completely different situation. Don't you want to know if Brooklyn's all right?" he asked her. With his free hand, he stroked the baby's head ever so gently. Something warm moved through him. He felt fiercely protective of this little being, instinctively knowing that he would kill for her if it came down to that. "I mean, she looks perfect, but just to be sure, you need to have a pediatrician confirm that."

She didn't think it was possible, not after all Adam had put her through, not after all the disappointment she'd felt when she discovered that he'd been lying to her the whole time they'd spent together, but her heart softened to hear him call their daughter perfect.

And she knew he was right. Her baby needed to be checked out by a doctor.

Much as she didn't want to, she had to go to the hospital, not for herself, but for her baby's sake. For Brooklyn.

She nodded toward the knife he'd brought. "I want you to cut the cord before they get here."

"Okay."

With one quick, clean movement, he severed the physical connection between mother and child. The moment Adam placed the knife down, he heard the front doorbell ringing.

"Looks like the cavalry has arrived," he told her. Turning on his heel, he left the room to admit the paramedics.

"No," she said softly to her daughter, glancing toward Adam's retreating back, "the cavalry's already here."

Rather than riding with Eve and the baby in the ambulance, or opting to go back home now that he'd helped Eve give birth to their baby, Adam decided to follow the ambulance to the hospital in his car.

Arriving at the hospital a half beat behind the paramedics, he left his vehicle parked in the lot designated for emergency room patients and stood at the back of the ambulance before the doors even opened. When they did, the first thing he saw was Eve's face. She was looking for him. When their eyes met, her smile widened.

It still got to him, that thousand-watt smile that always seemed to light up the room, or, in this case, the inside of the ambulance.

And the inside of him.

He supposed there was only so much a heart could be hardened.

This wasn't good, he admonished in the next moment. He needed a clear head to do what he was doing. Any distraction could prove fatal, not just to his operation, but to him, as well. He shouldn't be here.

Eve didn't need him. She was in professional hands now. These people were trained for this. They could more than take care of her and anything that she needed. As long as Eve was here, in the middle of a bustling hospital, she'd be out of harm's way.

Besides, as far as he actually knew, no one in this region knew about their connection. His connection, the self-centered college student, Sederholm, didn't know about Eve. This was all a preemptive strike on his part.

But he lived the life too long to be at ease, to hope that everything went well and that there would be no mishaps, no reason to believe that either Eve or the baby would be in jeopardy. He'd learned that when one of the agents had grown lax during the last undercover operation, he had gotten blown away. Literally. From where he stood, it was far better to be safe than live with a lifetime of regret.

"I need you to call Vera for me," she said to him the moment the paramedics mobilized the gurney, snapping the wheels in place. They immediately began to guide the gurney in through the automatic sliding doors.

Adam hurried to keep pace with the gurney. The name she'd just tossed in his direction meant nothing to him. "Vera?"

"Dr. Vera Lee. She's the veterinarian who works with me at the Laguna Animal Hospital. She's going to have to take over the appointments and have Susannah reschedule the ones that aren't emergencies until I can get back to work."

Which wouldn't be for a while if he had anything to say about it, he thought. Childbirth might be natural, but it could knock the hell out of a woman and Eve needed to give herself some time to recover.

"Susannah?" he repeated. Another name that meant nothing to him.

"Susannah Reyes. She's my tech and she doubles as a receptionist." Wanda Peeples had been her father's technician and receptionist for thirty years, but when he died, the woman, already in her seventies, had retired. Grief-stricken, she'd debated selling the practice for all of five hours, then decided to take over, rebuilding it from the ground up.

Frustrated, Eve shook her head. "I really thought I was going to have more time."

Who was it that said life was what happens while you were busy making plans? "Life's full of surprises," Adam told her.

And he should know that better than anyone, he thought, looking down at the infant cradled in her arms.

"All right, I'll call Vera and Susannah. Anything else?"

"Yes." She took a breath, then raised her head. Her eyes met his. "Thank you."

Adam hadn't been expecting that. Hearing Eve voice her gratitude brought a smile to his lips. "You're welcome."

The moment was quickly dissipated by the authoritative, stocky nurse who came up to him and hooked her arm through his. "You the husband?" the woman demanded.

Eve spoke up before he had a chance to. "He's the father."

Picking up on the difference, the nurse declared, "Good enough," and thrust a clipboard with several sheets clipped to it at him. "I need you to fill out some information."

Adam quickly scanned the top sheet. There was no way that he knew even half the information that was being asked. "Look, I can't—"

"I'm preregistered," Eve called out as the paramedics, rattling off pertinent information regarding both mother and child, turned her over to an orderly and another nurse. The duo paused for a moment as the gurney changed hands.

"Saved you some trouble," the stocky nurse mumbled to Adam, taking back the clipboard. Then, as Adam turned to continue following Eve's gurney, the woman placed her hand against his chest, stopping him in his tracks. "You can't go with her just yet," she informed him. And then she softened just a little. "They need to settle her in first, then they'll call for you."

Adam was accustomed to making his own rules as he went along, to coming and going as he saw fit without waiting for someone else's okay.

But this wasn't the kind of situation he ordinarily found himself in. Not wanting to draw attention to himself, he had no recourse but to go along with procedure. "What floor is maternity on?"

"Fifth." She clamped her mouth shut, as if she'd just given away a state secret. "But you can wait here," she went on, her eyes daring him to contradict the edict.

"I'll wait on the fifth floor," he told the woman. There was no arguing with his tone.

"All right, suit yourself. Just give the nurse at the desk your name when you get there."

He inclined his head, as if she had been the one to win and not him. "Yes, ma'am."

As he walked to the bank of elevators located to the

side, he heard the nurse mutter under her breath, "If I was just twenty years younger…"

A small, amused smile curved his mouth.

"How do you feel?" he asked Eve, walking into her private room.

It was more than thirty minutes later and he had begun to think that something had gone wrong. But then an intern had found him and gave him the all clear sign, telling him the number of Eve's room. He lost no time in getting there.

She'd just begun to doze off. The sound of Adam's voice temporarily banished any thought of sleep. She'd started to think that he'd taken the opportunity to leave the hospital.

That he hadn't coaxed a smile from her.

"Like I've been run over by a truck. Twice." Eve took a deep breath and pushed herself up into a sitting position. "They said that Brooklyn's fine."

Adam nodded. He'd been to the nursery before coming to her room. "I know. I asked."

She should have known he would. The man didn't believe in leaving stones unturned. "You're thorough."

Crossing to her, he stood at her bedside and struggled against the temptation to brush the hair away from her cheek. Instead, Adam shoved his hands into his pockets.

"Keeps the mistakes at a minimum," he told her.

She raised her eyes to his. For a moment, she was silent. And then she said, "At least some of them."

Was she telling him that she thought of their having made love as a mistake? That would mean that she considered the baby a mistake, which wasn't the impression he'd gotten. He'd seen love in her eyes when she looked down at Brooklyn.

"Some of them," he echoed.

She ran her fingers along the top of her hospital gown. There was so much she wanted to say, so much she wanted to ask him and somehow resolve. But she was so very tired again. Far too tired to think clearly.

As she fought off the drugging demands of fatigue, Eve tried to remember what it was that she'd asked him to do. And then it came to her.

"Did you call Vera? I didn't give you her number," she realized out loud.

"I found it," he assured her. "And I called her. She wanted to know who I was."

She looked at him warily. "And what did you tell her?"

"The truth," he said simply. "That I was someone you used to know."

"That's not the truth." Although she fervently wished that it was. "I didn't know you." *And still don't,* she added silently. "I thought I did, but I didn't."

"We can talk about that some other time if you want to," he told her, cutting her off. He glanced at his watch. It was almost two in the morning—as Vera had pointed out none too happily when he'd called her—until he'd explained why he was calling. "Right now, you need your rest."

It just wasn't in her to argue with him. She knew he'd win. "I am tired," she agreed.

"I'll see you tomorrow, Eve."

It was a perfunctory remark. Right now, he really didn't know if he was coming back, at least not in such a way where she could see him. And he did have work to attend to, both his actual job and what he did in order to maintain a cover for the outside world. There were times when his double life really got to be confusing. The less she knew, the better for everyone. He couldn't jeopardize the mission, not even for her.

Besides, he was fairly sure the woman didn't completely trust him. She would be better off if he stayed away as much as he could.

Bending over, he pressed a kiss to Eve's forehead. "Get some sleep," he instructed just before he started to walk away.

He was almost at the door when he heard her call his name.

"Adam?"

Turning around, he waited for her to continue. Did she have a lingering craving and want him to bring her back a pound of pistachios or some licorice? "Yes?"

"Stay with me. Just for a few minutes," she added, anticipating being turned down. "I don't want to be alone just yet."

Was she having doubts about what she'd just let herself in for, becoming a mother? He heard that a lot of new mothers suddenly worried about that once the euphoria wore away.

He retraced his steps to her bedside. "Sure."

Pulling up a chair next to the bed, he swung it around and straddled it, then waited for Eve to drift off to sleep.

Chapter 6

An ache woke her up. It shot through her entire body, from the very roots of her hair down to the tips of her toes. All except for two of her fingernails—one on each hand—and those felt numb because she'd clutched so fiercely at her comforter while pushing out her daughter.

Her daughter. She had a daughter?

She had a daughter.

Her eyes flew open, the very act instantly divorcing her from the dream she'd been having.

She didn't need to remember, she knew the dream by heart. It was the same dream that had invaded a third of her nights in the last eight months. A dream that echoed what she'd felt that one glorious night that she and Adam had made love.

Eve blew out a breath. She hadn't had that dream for at least a couple of weeks now and had begun to nurse the hope that she was finally over it.

Finally over him.

Having Adam pop back into her life had brought the dream back in vivid living color—both the bad and the good.

Adam.

Last night's events came rushing back to her, assaulting her brain and sending her system into high alert. She couldn't let her guard down. Now that she knew what he was, she had to remain vigilant—at least, until she was sure that he'd changed.

If only…

As she remembered the last words that had passed between them, her eyes darted toward the chair where he'd sat down.

It was empty.

A sinking feeling set in and she railed against it. How lame could she have been, asking him to stay with her a little while longer? What in heaven's name had gotten into her? Nothing had changed—and probably he hadn't, either. She wanted Adam to go, not stay. So why had she suddenly felt so vulnerable? Why had she asked him to stay with her like a child who was afraid of the dark?

A noise came from the doorway and she glanced over, half hoping—

Idiot!

A blonde nurse walked in. She looked as if she was about twenty-two. A young two-twenty at that. The nurse pushed a see-through bassinette before her.

"Someone here wants to see her mommy," the nurse all but chirped cheerfully.

Eve squinted ever so slightly, reading the nurse's name tag: Kathy.

As Kathy parked the bassinette at the foot of the bed, she scanned the room. "Your husband stepped out?" she asked.

It took Eve a second to make the connection. "He's not my husband," she corrected.

"Oh." The response seemed to squelch the nurse's enthusiasm, but just for the barest moment. And then the insuppressible cheerfulness returned. "Well, anyway, he seemed very devoted to you." Picking the baby up, Kathy made a few soothing noises to the infant and then placed the tiny bundle into Eve's arms.

Eve hated the fact that she was distracted even the slightest bit, but the nurse's comment had aroused her curiosity. She patted the baby's bottom as she asked, "What makes you say that?"

Kathy moved around the room, drawing back the curtains at the window, tucking the blanket in on one side. She seemed as if she needed to be in perpetual motion.

"Well, for one thing, he stayed here most of the night. He was sitting by your bed when I came on my shift this morning," she added.

Eve saw only one reason for that. "He must've fallen asleep."

But Kathy shook her head, a wistful smile curving the corners of her mouth. "Looked pretty wide-awake to me. Gail said he'd been there all night, just watching you sleep."

"Gail?"

"The nurse who was on before me." She smiled down into Brooklyn's face. Wide-awake, the infant appeared to absorb her surroundings. "The baby looks like him," Kathy commented. And then she raised her eyes quickly to look at her patient, as if she realized that she'd just tripped over her tongue. "He is the father, right?"

"Yes," Eve said quietly, gazing at her daughter's face. A face that had more in common with Adam than with her. "He's the father."

A shade under six feet with an almost painfully thin body, Danny Sederholm leaned indolently against the side of the cement steps of the renovated campus library. The renovation had been conducted, in part, thanks to his father and his uncle's generous contributions. Both were former alumni of the prestigious college, as was his mother. It made coasting easier.

The student's small, deep-set brown eyes unabashedly looked him over and took renewed assessment as he approached. Adam struggled to keep his contempt and loathing to himself.

"You look like hell. Something wrong?" Sederholm asked, trying to sound high-handed.

The marbles-for-brains twenty-two-year-old was leagues away from the kind of kid he'd been at that age, Adam thought. Circumstances had forced him to be a man early. Sederholm, he judged, would never be one no matter how old he was.

"Don't worry, it's nothing I can't handle," he told the snide senior, his tone firmly closing the door on any further speculation regarding the situation.

"Do I look worried?" Sederholm challenged. "Hey, as long as it don't interfere with 'business,'" he emphasized the word haughtily, "I don't care if you're juggling flying monkeys."

"'As long as it "don't" interfere?'" Adam knew he should let the comment slide, but bad grammar always got under his skin, especially when uttered by someone who gave himself airs. "How much did you say your father was paying for your education? Because whatever it is, it's way too much."

Sederholm's face darkened. "Like I don't have better things to do than go sit in a lousy auditorium with a bunch of competitive geeks." He puffed up his chest. "I'm making more money now than my old man ever did at my age—or when he graduated."

Adam knew exactly what tuition was at the school. It was part of his background research. "Then why would you bother registering? The $40K this costs could be better spent."

Sederholm shrugged, his large, bony shoulders moving carelessly beneath a sweater that would have set him back two months' pay. "It's his money and that's what he wants to do with it."

Adam saw through the blasé remark. "Can't figure a way to siphon it off, can you?" he guessed, not bothering to hide his amusement.

"I don't want to," the student snapped at him, annoyed. "In case your tiny brain can't figure it out, an Ivy League college campus is the perfect place to run my enterprise. As an undergraduate student," he spread his hands out wide, "I fit right in."

Adam saw a few obstacles to the senior's "brilliant"

plan. "You have to pass a few tests to stay in the game, don't you?"

Sederholm snorted, more than a little pleased with himself. "I've got that covered. There's this guy who, for the right price, can write an A-plus paper on any subject you throw at him."

There were always plenty of those around, Adam thought. Even when he was going to school. "What about tests?"

The student's smile was condescendingly smug. "I've got that covered, too." He lifted his chin, a lofty look in his eyes. "Why all the questions?"

"Just curious." Because that didn't seem to satisfy his contact, Adam added, "When I grow up, I want to be just like you," allowing only a drop of sarcasm to leak through.

Initially, the senior seemed to take the words as a compliment, but the frown that soon unfurled told Adam that the arrogant drug dealer realized he was being ridiculed.

"I can have you wiped off the face of the earth with a snap of my fingers," Sederholm threatened him haughtily, snapping his fingers to illustrate.

Obviously, the little twerp had probably come close to OD'ing on classic gangster movies, most likely starting with Cagney and Bogart. For two cents, he would have loved to squash the snotty senior like a bug, but he knew bigger things were at stake here than just mollifying his temper—no matter how good it might feel at the time. Like it or not—and he didn't— he needed this jerk to get hooked up to the head importer whose identity was still unknown to him.

"Before you snap again," Adam told him, lightly

catching hold of Sederholm's wrist, "I'd like to place an order for my people."

"Business before pleasure," the cocky student declared with an obliging nod of his head. Adam released his hand, wishing he could be wringing Sederholm's neck instead. "You know," Sederholm said, the smile on his lips as genuine as the smile on a cobra, "one of these days, you're going to push my buttons too hard."

I'm counting on it, kid, Adam thought just before he gave the college senior a list of just how much he was looking to score.

Sederholm seemed properly impressed. "That's almost twice as much as you bought last time."

Adam made certain to appear unfazed. "Word gets around. You've got a good product."

Sederholm nodded, preening. "Yeah, it's damn good all right." And then he frowned slightly. "But if you want that much of it, you might have to wait a little," he warned.

"If this is too much for you to handle, I can always take my business—"

"I didn't say it was too much for me," Sederholm cut in angrily. "It's just going to take a little longer to get it all together, that's all." Pausing, he was apparently trying to think, but there were times, like now, when the process appeared difficult for him. Undoubtedly, he'd been sampling "the product" again. "When do you need the stuff by?"

Adam eyed the student. "I was thinking now."

Sederholm was taken aback. And then he laughed. It was a nasty sound. "Right, like I carry that kind of stash on me. What are you, crazy?"

Again, Adam shrugged nonchalantly. "Got a lot of antsy customers."

Sederholm shut his eyes and scrubbed his hand over his face. "How's tomorrow sound?"

"Not as good as today," Adam replied without hesitation, "but it'll do. Where and when?"

"I'll call you," he said cavalierly.

Adam resisted the urge to pat Sederholm on the head, the way he might have to a dim-witted toady who'd tried too hard. He didn't want to put the kid off until the sting went down, and right now, the timetable was still unclear.

So instead, he smiled complacently and said, "You do that."

Adam waited until he was back in his car, driving north on University Road and away from the forty-five-year-old college campus before he put in a call to his handler via his Bluetooth.

"Looks like the plan's working," he told the man. "Sederholm's going to his source sometime between today and tomorrow."

"The big fish?" he heard Hugh ask.

He only wished. "Right now, it sounds like the medium fish. But it's only a matter of time. We keep doing business with him and we place an order big enough, medium fish is going to have to get in contact with big fish," Adam theorized.

"And then we'll reel them in." He heard Hugh allow himself a sliver of optimism. "Meanwhile, you know what to do."

"Yeah." He knew what to do. Continue leading his double life—and deceiving Eve. The longer he stayed undercover like this, the greater the odds were that someone was going to get hurt. One way or another, it seemed inevitable.

"Something wrong?" He and Hugh had been together long enough for him to know that though it didn't sound it, Hugh was concerned.

"I'm going to need a little time away from the job today," Adam told his handler.

"All right," Hugh allowed cautiously. There was leeway within their framework. "How little and is it going to get in the way of anything?"

"An hour, maybe less. Around one," Adam added. "And no, it's not going to get in the way of anything." *Just my conscience,* he said silently. "I've got someone covering for me at the bookstore." He didn't bother adding that the woman, somewhere in her sixties, was a dynamo who had reorganized all his shelves the first week she was hired. "You're going to have to get someone to keep tabs on Sederholm. The kid drives a 2009 silver Lexus SC 430 convertible. It shouldn't be too much of a problem spotting him wherever he goes."

Adam heard Hugh whistle. "Wish my mommy and daddy gave me a sixty-five-thousand-dollar car."

"More like sixty-seven point six," Adam corrected. Handing over the keys to that kind of vehicle to an immature brat seemed unfathomable to him.

"I can get Chesterfield to follow him," Hugh told him. "Chesterfield likes surveillance work."

Surveillance work was something he really hated. Though he considered himself tenacious, sitting in a car for hours on end drove him up a wall. He could literally feel life slipping through his fingers on a stakeout. He was a man who valued action, not stagnation.

"Different strokes for different folks, I guess," Adam commented. "More power to him."

"That's what makes the world go around," Hugh agreed. The next moment, the line went dead. Adam closed his cell phone. He was accustomed to Hugh's calls. The handler wasn't one to stand on ceremony. When he was done, he was done.

One o'clock had Adam hurrying down the corridor of the maternity ward. He carried a bouquet of red roses in one hand and a teddy bear sporting a pink bow and a pink tutu in the other. Neither, he knew, was exactly very original, but the offerings were the best he could do on short notice. Undertaking yet another life, bringing him to a grand total of three, was running him ragged.

Eve didn't even know his real last name. He was still lying to her and calling it the truth. How was she going to handle that? he thought uneasily. How was she going to feel when she found out that all of this, the second-hand bookstore, the so-called life of a drug dealer, all of that was just a setup, a sham, a means to an end?

Why was he even wondering about that, he upbraided himself. He would be out of her life before that happened, not settling in for good.

If a part of him yearned for love and family, well, he would have to bank it down. He knew what he was signing on for when he volunteered for this kind of work. There wasn't going to be a happy ending for him after two hours, when the credits rolled. This was real life and it was gritty.

When he reached Eve's room, he heard voices coming from inside. Specifically, a male voice. Was that her doctor?

The moment he opened the door, Adam knew the small, trim, older man, dressed in tan slacks and a dark blue sports jacket, was not a doctor. Doctors were given to scrubs and lab coats, not expensive suits he was fairly certain came from a high-end shop. Despite the unseasonably warm weather, the man wore a tie. The tidy Van Dyke gray beard he sported made him look old enough to be her grandfather. But Adam knew she didn't have one.

Who was this man?

Adam cleared his throat, crossed the threshold and gave the door a little push with his elbow, closing it behind him. When Eve looked his way, he said, "Hi."

Everything inside of her lit up before she could tell it not to. Why didn't she know better?

"Hi," she answered. Her eyes strayed toward the bouquet. There were at least a dozen and a half roses swaddled in green and white tissue paper with sprigs of baby's breath tucked in between the blossoms. "Are those for me?" Eve prodded when Adam made no effort to give her the bouquet.

"Well, they're not for me," the man on the other side of her bed observed. "For one thing, this young man had no way of knowing that I would be here."

"They're for you," Adam murmured, feeling damn awkward as he almost thrust the bouquet at her. This was a bad idea, he thought. He should have realized that she'd have company. She was far too outgoing a woman not to.

"They're lovely," she said, inhaling deeply. They were the fragrant kind, her favorite type of roses.

Adam could feel steely gray eyes regarding him for a long moment, obviously assessing him.

"And you are?" Eve's dapper companion finally asked as he passed the man while crossing to the sink. Opening the cabinet below, Adam took out a pink pitcher and filled it with water, then brought it over to Eve. Only once he deposited the bouquet, stripped of its tissue paper, into the pitcher and placed it on her table did he answer the man's question. "Adam. Adam Smythe."

The look on the older man's gaunt face seemed to say that he knew better. "Of course you are," he said with the air of man humoring someone of far less mental acuity. "Well, Adam Smith—"

"Smythe," Adam corrected, giving it the standard British pronunciation.

"Sorry, *Smythe,*" the older man amended, "I'm Josiah Turner."

Adam's eyes widened and he looked at Eve. "That's Josiah Turner?"

Until that moment, she'd forgotten that she'd referred to Josiah as the man she was currently involved with. Eve pressed her lips together. "I was in labor. I didn't know what I was saying."

Josiah's voice warmed as he turned toward Eve. "I've known Eve since she was a little girl. I'd bring my dogs in to be treated by her father and Eve would be there, soaking up everything her father did like a sponge. I knew she'd be a good veterinarian even then." The steely eyes narrowed as Josiah shifted his focus back to him. "And how do you know her?"

Adam had no idea how much or how little Eve wanted

him to admit, so he kept the narrative vague. "I met her when she came into my bookstore in Santa Barbara. She was looking to buy a first edition Mark Twain for her father. I had an original copy of *A Connecticut Yankee in King Arthur's Court.* Just yesterday I ran into her again." Adam looked at Eve. "Small world."

Josiah obviously had another take on the events. "You were stalking her?"

The accusation, politely worded, stunned Adam. "No," he denied vehemently. Who was this man?

Josiah didn't seem particularly convinced or contrite. Instead, his shoulders shifted in what constituted a minor shrug.

"My mistake." However, he gave no indication that he was ready to move on to another topic. "So you both just *happen* to transplant yourselves to the same city— or are you here on a visit, Adam?"

Adam felt as if he was being subtly grilled. "I relocated my shop."

"Interesting," Josiah commented. "And what is your shop called?"

"New Again," Adam told him.

Josiah nodded. "I must look you up when I get the chance. As it happens, I like first editions myself. Of course," he slanted a glance toward Eve, and Adam noted that the older man's look softened considerably as he did so, "I'm old enough to have been around for a great many of these books when they *were* first editions."

"You're not that old, Josiah," Eve insisted with a warm smile.

The man leaned forward and patted her hand. "You have no idea how old I really am, my dear. It's a state secret—and I intend to keep it that way." He took her hand in his. "Since you have a visitor, I'll take my leave now. But I'll be back tonight. Call me if there's anything special I can bring you when I return." He kissed her hand, then released it as he straightened. The smile on his face vanished as he regarded Adam. "Adam," he acknowledged with a nod of his head, and with that, moving with considerable grace and agility, Josiah Turner made his way to the door.

Adam watched the door close behind the man. "That's quite a character. Is he a relative?"

"In name only." When Adam looked at her quizzically, she explained, "When I was a little girl, I thought he was my father's uncle so I called him my great-uncle. He's a very sweet man. He had a daughter, but she's married and living out of the country. England, I think. I'm the only 'family' he has, if you don't count Lucas."

"Lucas?"

"His driver. Actually, Lucas is more of an assistant slash companion, although I doubt Josiah would call him that."

"How did he know you were in the hospital?" Adam asked, rearranging the roses so that they were more even. He had a thing about symmetry.

"I forgot he had an appointment this morning," she said ruefully. "Annual shots for his Doberman, Edgar. When he found Vera there instead of me, he asked her where I was and she told him that Brooklyn arrived early. He brought the baby a present." She'd assumed that the old man would, but she hadn't been prepared for what the gift turned out to be. She glanced down at the card Josiah had brought. "I've got to find a way to make him take it back."

Eve didn't strike him as the type to refuse a gift. Doing so would most likely offend the man and that didn't seem like something she would be willing to do. "Why? What is it?"

Instead of telling him, Eve took the card out of its envelope and opened it. She held up what had been tucked inside the card.

Taking it from her, he turned it around. It was a check. A rather large check. Adam looked at her incredulously. "He gave you a check for twenty thousand dollars?"

What kind of man just hands over a check for that amount of money?

She nodded, taking the check and putting it back into its envelope. For now, she put it into the drawer of her side table. It made her uneasy just looking at it. "It's the tuition to an exclusive nursery school," she told him. "He told me he had a friend who could get her placed near the top of the waiting list."

Adam looked at her sharply.

Chapter 7

Because of the deceptions he was forced to employ in his daily life, Adam's suspicions were immediately aroused. "Is this Josiah guy usually so generous?"

It was the largest monetary gift Josiah had ever given her, but as she thought back, Eve realized that the man had been generous to her over the years. There'd been a sizable "contribution" to her college fund when she'd gone off to become a veterinarian. And every birthday and Christmas were observed with cards. The cards were never empty.

"Pretty much," she confirmed. "From what my father indicated, Josiah has a sizable amount of money, more than he needs."

"How much is 'sizable'?" he asked her. Was Josiah involved in this drug cartel he was looking to bring down? Stranger things had turned out to be true. Maybe this man with no visible means of support actually made a living importing drugs.

"Enough," she answered carefully. She didn't like his tone. An uneasiness began to weave itself through her. She could feel herself growing very protective of Josiah. "What is it you're thinking?"

Adam shrugged. He couldn't very well come out and tell her what he was thinking. "Just wondering how he made his money, that's all."

That wasn't all. She was willing to bet on it. "The old-fashioned way," she answered tersely.

He'd annoyed her. That wasn't his intention. Adam backtracked and guessed teasingly, "He stole it? Printed it?"

"He earned it. Josiah was some kind of a businessman before he retired."

"What kind of business?" he asked casually.

"I don't know. But he did a lot of traveling, I know that. And when he did, he'd board the dogs with my dad." She drew in a breath, then let it out again slowly as she regarded the table over her bed and the check that was inside the drawer. "But I still can't accept a check that large."

"Sure you can." He saw the look that came into her eyes. She probably thought he wanted to use it. "Still don't trust me, do you?"

"You have to admit, it's a little hard." Especially when one minute Adam was all but accusing Josiah of being a robber baron, the next he's pushing her to take the money the man had given her. Just which way was Adam leaning? And why?

Adam inclined his head. "I can see how you might feel that way," he allowed.

And if you ever find out the rest of it, you really won't trust me.

Knowing how she might react if she found out the truth weighed him down. He found himself wishing that he could just be himself, in a position to tell her he was a law enforcement officer. But it was the undercover work that got drugs off the streets and provided the information that sent the dealers and suppliers to prison. He had to remember the game plan—and it didn't include falling for a civilian.

"Josiah didn't seem like the kind of man who would take kindly to having his gifts refused," Adam continued out loud. "If you don't want to use it for the baby, you can always donate the money he gave you to a charity—anonymously or even in Turner's name."

"To a charity," Eve repeated, rolling the idea over in her mind. She had to admit that Adam had come up with a decent, win-win suggestion. She knew that Josiah meant well, but she was hardly in a bad way. Her father's practice was a very established one and she could more than afford to take good care of her new daughter with the income she generated.

Adam's smile was encouraging. If only it wasn't so damn sensual, she thought. "Yes," he said. "To a charity."

She raised her eyes to his. "And not to you."

That caught him up short. But then, what did he expect? She thought he was a drug dealer. Reformed or not, that didn't exactly put him in the same league with martyrs and saints. And philanthropists.

"Why would you think that?" he asked.

"Because I'm not exactly all that clear about who or what you are."

The situation pained him more than he would have ever expected, but he could do nothing about it—at least, not yet. After this sting went down, then maybe he could tell her some things. Not everything, but enough to make her understand that he wasn't the devil assuming a pleasant form.

"Since that seems to be a stumbling block for you, why don't we just set that aside for the time being?" he suggested. "Let's just leave it at my wanting to come by to give you those." He nodded at the roses in the pitcher. "And to see how you were doing."

He sounded as if he was about to go. "You're leaving?"

It was better that way, he thought. For both of them. "I've got to get back to the store," he told her. "The sales clerk I hired might feel a little overwhelmed being in the store alone for so long."

"Oh? Doesn't he or she like books?" She was stalling, but who knew if she'd see him again once he walked out that door. Suddenly she wasn't ready to say goodbye.

"She," Adam specified. "And she doesn't like books, she loves them. That's just the trouble. Jennifer's busy reading instead of assisting customers." He laughed shortly. Now that the woman had organized everything, she'd dived right into worshipful reading. "She's practically ignoring them because they're cutting into her reading time."

He'd already asked Hugh to send him someone from the department to act as an assistant, in case he had to quickly "take care of business" during normal work hours. Hugh had told him he'd look into it.

Eve nodded. Without realizing it, she wrapped her arms around the teddy bear he'd brought, holding it close to her. The softness against her chin penetrated, and she flushed.

"I'll see that Brooklyn gets this," she promised, moving the teddy bear to one side.

"Good." Adam began to walk away, but he got no farther than ten steps when he abruptly turned around and doubled back. Reaching her bed, he framed her face and kissed her. The kiss was quick—he couldn't allow himself to linger, didn't trust himself to linger—but it still left an impression. On both of them. "Give her that, too."

"Not until she turns eighteen," Eve answered breathlessly, then realized her error as her words replayed themselves in her head. Her eyes darted to his. Damn it, why couldn't she just keep her mouth shut around him? She'd given too much away.

So what? she silently demanded the next minute. It wasn't as if Adam wouldn't have guessed that a very large piece of her heart still belonged to him, despite everything. Her problem was that she had a face that couldn't keep a secret.

Adam knew he should be on his way. For more than one reason. And yet, he found himself lingering a moment longer. "The baby's okay, right?"

"She's perfect."

"And you, the doctor says you're all right, too?"

Her own doctor had stopped by this morning, right after she'd woken up. Dr. Mudd had expressed surprise that she had delivered so early—and so quickly to boot. It wasn't unheard of, she'd told Eve, but it wasn't the norm, especially with first babies.

Eve smiled. "She said I'm none the worse for wear—just a little sore."

"So when are you being discharged?"

The doctor had given her a choice of tomorrow or the day after. She'd chosen sooner rather than later. "Tomorrow."

Adam nodded, more to himself than to her as he began rescheduling things in his head. "When?"

"Before noon."

That was doable. Especially if Hugh came through with someone. "Eleven-thirty work for you?"

"I don't— Why?" she asked, confused. And then it dawned on her. "Are you planning on taking us home?"

He couldn't gauge her tone, and her expression just registered surprise. "I thought, unless you made other arrangements, that I would, yes."

With everything so new and in fast-forward mode, she hadn't been able to think that far ahead yet. Now that she did, she supposed she could have Vera or Susannah take her home. And if something prevented that, she was fairly certain that Josiah would be more than delighted to come to her rescue.

None of these options made her skin tinge the way it did when she thought about Adam taking her home. That wasn't a good sign.

Eve pressed her lips together, doing what she could to seem indifferent, hoping she carried it off. "I don't want to inconvenience you."

"No inconvenience," Adam assured her, unconsciously flashing the smile that sent her stomach into a spin-dry cycle. "Okay, it's settled. I'll be here tomorrow before noon to take you and Brooklyn home," he promised, then forced himself to leave.

Even though he really didn't want to.

He was fifteen minutes late.

The meeting with his handler had run long and then the near-noon traffic seemed to conspire against him, moving slower than an aged inch worm.

On top of that, he'd had to park outside the hospital grounds because, apparently, everyone and his brother had decided that today was a good day to pay someone a visit. Twenty minutes of circling around the lots hadn't yielded a single empty space. He parked down the street, then ran back to the hospital.

Because waiting for an elevator would eat up more time—and who knew if there would be space for him when the elevator car arrived—he elected to take the stairs instead and ran up the five flights to the maternity floor. When he came hurrying in, doing his best not to breathe heavy, he found Eve sitting on her bed, dressed, with her hands folded in her lap like a school girl attending an old-fashioned parochial school.

Glancing at the clock on the wall, he apologized. "Sorry." It wasn't easy not sounding breathless, but he pulled it off. "Traffic," he tacked on by way of an explanation.

"You really don't have to do this," she told him. "I could have easily asked Vera or Josiah to take us home. Not that I don't appreciate it, but there was no need for you to break up your day like this."

Was she annoyed, or trying to distance herself from him? Either way, he wasn't here to get into a discussion. He was here to make sure she was safe. That was the main reason he was here, he told himself.

Adam quickly scanned the room. Nothing seemed out of place. The flowers he'd brought her yesterday had been transferred into a simple glass vase. The teddy bear was seated not too far from it.

"You have everything?" he asked her.

"I will once the nurse brings Brooklyn."

Adam laughed. "I meant other than that." He looked around again and came to the same conclusion.

"I didn't exactly have time to bring anything, remember?" There hadn't even been the traditional suitcase to grab because, confident that she still had several weeks to go, she hadn't bothered to pack one. So much for living up to the Boy Scout motto.

"Traveling light has its advantages," Adam commented. Moving the teddy bear right next to the flowers on the table, he asked, "What's the protocol? Are we supposed to buzz for the nurse to tell her you're ready to go, or should I go out and see if I can find her instead?"

We. The single, deceptively small word echoed in her head. He made it sound as if they were a unit. A family. But they were nothing of the kind, Eve reminded herself. Adam's sense of responsibility was warmly comforting, but she wasn't fooling herself. Her gut told her that this wasn't going to last. Not unless he'd actually told her the truth. That he meant what he'd said when he claimed to be through with his old way of life. It could happen. It could be true. He could have given his old life up, opting for a clean slate. Maybe this was him, trying to live his life as best he could.

Don't get caught up in a fantasy. You know *better.*

"I'll try buzzing for her." Eve reached over for the call button.

Very gently, he took the device from her. "I might have more luck," he told her when she looked at him in surprise. Putting the call button aside, Adam stepped out into the hall.

"You probably will," she murmured. She doubted many women could ignore Adam or say no to him.

He was back in less than a minute. She was about to ask if he'd changed his mind, then stopped when she saw that he was not alone. Shadowing Adam was the slender young nurse, Kathy, who had attended to her earlier.

"All set?" Kathy asked cheerfully.

"That I am," Eve assured her. Preparing to get up, she slid to the edge of the bed.

"I'll go get your little princess." The promise, Eve noted, was made not to her, but to Adam.

"She thinks Brooklyn is yours," Eve commented.

Adam's eyes met hers for a long moment. "She is," he reminded her.

After being on her own and thinking of the next eighteen years in terms of just the baby and her, sharing Brooklyn was going to take her a great deal of getting used to—and she wasn't really convinced that it was worth the effort. She'd had enough pain in her life without consciously leaving herself open for more.

But he was *the father.*

She'd think about it all later, Eve promised herself. For now, she just needed to get home.

"Here she is," Kathy announced, walking in with the swaddled infant.

Hesitating before Adam, the young woman seemed undecided as to whom to give the baby to. A moment later, the nurse opted for the traditional choice. She passed the sleeping infant to Eve.

"Wait right here, I'll bring in the wheelchair," Kathy told her.

"I can walk," Eve protested, calling after the nurse's back.

The young woman returned in a heartbeat, pushing the wheelchair in front of her. She pulled down the brakes on either side of the chair, then took the baby back for a moment, waiting for Eve to get into the wheelchair.

"Hospital policy. I could lose my job if I let you walk out the front door," Kathy told her.

Taking her arm, Adam helped Eve into the wheelchair. "Wouldn't want that."

It wasn't clear to Eve if he was addressing his words to her or to the nurse. Making the best of it, she put her arms out for the baby.

The second the transfer was completed, Brooklyn woke up and began to fuss.

It was happening, Eve thought, banking down the panicky feeling as she gazed down into her daughter's face. Brooklyn and she were on the cusp of starting their new life together.

Nerves undulated throughout her system. All the things she could do wrong with this baby suddenly paraded through her mind.

Her panic intensified. She wasn't ready.

"Don't worry," Adam whispered, lowering his lips to her ear so that only she could hear. "You're going to be great."

How could he possibly have known what she was thinking? Eve twisted around to look at him, a quizzical expression of disbelief on her face. "How did you…?"

The smile he gave her magically restored at least some of her confidence.

"Not so hard to guess what's going through your mind right now," he assured her.

Eve blew out a breath. It was going to be all right, she told herself. It was going to be all right.

If she repeated the sentence a few hundred times, she thought philosophically, she might just wind up convincing herself.

Maybe.

Adam glanced up into the rearview mirror. Again. He'd been doing it with a fair amount of consistency since they'd left the hospital.

He wasn't watching for tailgaters.

The last ten miles to her house, he wasn't certain if his imagination played tricks on him or if his instincts were dead-on. Either way, he could have sworn that a car was tailing him. A late-model domestic beige sedan followed two cars behind his. So far, he'd only managed to get two of the numbers on the license plate.

When he pulled up into Eve's two-car driveway, the beige car passed her house and continued down the street. Was he paranoid or were his survival instincts so finely tuned that he could spot a tail a mile away? Right now, he couldn't answer that with any kind of authority.

After parking his car, Adam quickly got out and rounded the back of the vehicle. He opened the passenger door and extended his hand to Eve.

Rather than resort to bravado, she reluctantly wrapped her fingers around his hand. Trying to get up on her own, she realized that he actually pulled her to her feet. She was still wobbly. So much so that she had to steady herself by grabbing on to his arm.

Surprised, concerned, Adam held her for a moment. "Are you all right?"

"Just a little light-headed," she admitted. "But I'm fine now. You can let go."

He did so, but only slowly, watching her carefully as he withdrew his arms.

She hated feeling like this. How had women managed to give birth and then continue working in the fields decades ago?

Turning carefully, she looked into the backseat. Brooklyn was strapped securely in an infant seat. An infant seat Adam had bought because she hadn't gotten around to it. Again, because she'd felt she still had a few weeks left in which to prepare.

"By the way, how much do I owe you?"

About to open the rear passenger door, he stopped and looked at her. "For what?" he asked incredulously. "For the ride home?"

"No, for the infant seat." She felt remiss in being caught so unprepared. But then, this whole pregnancy had caught her unprepared. "I was going to pick one up this weekend."

"And now you have one," he told her. "You don't owe me anything, Eve. The baby's half-mine, remember?"

Her mouth curved in amusement. "Which half are you claiming?"

"It's too early to tell," he quipped. "I'll get back to you on that."

After removing the belts from around his daughter, he picked her up and then gently tucked the baby into the crook of his arm as if he'd been doing this all his life. There was no need for Eve to know that he had bought a life-size baby doll at the toy store and had been practicing this since yesterday.

Adam slipped his free hand around her waist, ready to help guide her up the front walk. "Okay, let's get you both into the house."

The short distance seemed to stretch out before her like a twenty-mile run. Pressing her lips together, Eve walked up the path on shaky legs. She surrendered her key to Adam and waited for him to unlock the door. Once inside, she headed toward the sofa, relieved to be able to rest.

As she sank down on the sofa, she could feel Adam watching her. She hated letting him see her like this. It wasn't part of her self-image.

"This is just temporary," she assured him.

He shifted Brooklyn to his other side. "No reason to believe it's not," he agreed.

Under the pretext of closing the door, he looked out and saw the car he'd thought was tailing them pass by in the opposite direction. It was quite possible that the driver was lost, looking for an address in an unfamiliar neighborhood. But he hadn't lived this long in a dangerous field by being lax. He remained on his guard. The stakes were higher now than they had ever been.

Crossing to the sofa, he laid the baby down in the bassinette that stood beside the sofa. He'd purchased the item yesterday when he'd gone to get the infant seat.

"Look, I have to get back to the shop for a little while." Sederholm was going to call him this afternoon and he didn't want to have to take the phone call around her. "But I'll be back later."

He had already done more than enough. She needed to process things, to find a way to get used to dealing with all this—without becoming used to having him around.

"You don't—"

"—have to," he completed the sentence for her, banking down a wave of impatience. "Yes, I know. But you're obviously not yourself yet, and taking care of a newborn isn't a walk in the park." He remembered how exhausted his mother had been when his baby sister was first born. "It's demanding. So, unless you have some kind of support system in place, I'll be hanging around for a week or so until you can get on your feet again."

"A week?" she echoed.

"Or so," he added again.

"Or so," she whispered in disbelief.

She knew her hormones were in flux and she could always blame this roller-coaster ride on them. But right at this moment, sitting in the shade of Adam's unexpected offer, Eve wasn't sure if she wanted to laugh—or cry.

Chapter 8

"What's this?"

The question Eve asked pertained to the eight-by-eleven manila envelope Adam had handed her on his way to the kitchen.

Having taken care of business both at New Again, the rare first-edition bookstore in Newport Beach he supposedly owned, and with Sederholm, the latter involving humoring the college student, Adam had made a quick stop to pick up dinner for Eve and himself. He'd gone to an actual Mexican restaurant that had takeout on the side, rather than going to one of the numerous fast-food places that touted familiar Mexican meals. Time might be at a premium, but taste didn't necessarily have to suffer because of it.

"Dinner," he answered, assuming that she was asking

about the two large white bags he carried into the kitchen. Adam turned to look at her over his shoulder as he deposited the bags on the counter. "Don't worry, I made sure your portion wasn't too spicy, in case you're—you know." His voice trailed off as he avoided her eyes.

Considering the incredibly intimate contact they'd already shared, not just when they'd made love months ago, but during the far more recent process of bringing their daughter into the world, Eve found it strangely amusing and perhaps more than a little touching and sweet that Adam had turned suddenly shy.

"Well, just for the record, I am 'you knowing,'" she told him, making no attempt to hide her smile at his polite reference to her breastfeeding, "so that was very thoughtful of you, but I was actually referring to this." She held up the manila envelope. "What is it?" she asked again.

His back to her, Adam began to take their dinners out of the bags and placed the various wrapped selections on the granite counter. "Insurance."

She glanced back at the envelope, not sure if she even wanted to open the clasp and peer inside. "Against what?" she asked slowly.

"No, insurance," he repeated, turning around. She was still holding the envelope in her hands. Most women would have already ripped it open. That made her incredibly devoid of curiosity, he thought. "*Life* insurance," he emphasized, adding, "on me," when her expression remained bewildered.

Eve turned the envelope over in her hands, regarding it the way someone might a brand-new alien lifeform—and finding it displeasing.

"Okay. Again, why?" This was completely out of the blue and it made her feel uncomfortable without really understanding why. "Is there something wrong with you?" Even as she asked, the dark suspicion behind the words hit her. "You're not going to...?"

"Die?" he supplied with a touch of amusement. "Well, I'm not planning on it, but you never know." Especially considering his real line of work and the kinds of people he found himself dealing with on almost a regular basis. "And *if* something should happen to me, I want to make sure that Brooklyn's taken care of." He'd almost included her in the statement, but his gut told him that she would balk at that. He had more of a chance of her going along with this if she thought only the baby was named as a beneficiary.

Not that she seemed exactly thrilled with this revised version, either.

The expression that came over her face was like a dark storm rolling over the prairie, swallowing the terrain whole.

"What's the matter?" he prodded. "I'm just doing the responsible thing," he added when Eve didn't answer his question.

It hit her then. She knew why he was doing this. If he had really become a responsible person, he would have abandoned the life that had initially caused their separation.

"You're still involved, aren't you?" The evenly worded accusation was the only conclusion she could draw. Men his age didn't ordinarily think about death—unless they dealt with people who could make that sort of thing a reality. "In the drug world," she emphasized when he raised his eyebrows quizzically. She wasn't taken in by his act. "You didn't quit dealing," she cried angrily. "You *lied* to me," she accused, lightning all but flashing from her eyes. How stupid could she have been, believing him when he'd told her dealing was all in his past and he was here for a fresh start without the old ties.

Lies had always come easily to him. He considered them a necessary defense mechanism that he had to use in order to remain alive. What was lying but another form of pretense? Actors "lied" all the time when they assumed a role, pretending to be someone else on the screen or on the stage.

He was merely being a good, convincing actor, that's all.

But lying to this woman who had borne his child, who had managed to turn his world upside down, that was something else again. For reasons he didn't have time to fully explore, he found it difficult to continue deceiving her.

However, he had no choice. Far more people were involved than just him. Consequently, it wasn't entirely his secret to share.

So he twisted around her words. "Are you going to stand there and tell me that everyone who has a life insurance policy is a drug dealer?"

"No, but—"

"But I am, is that it?" His voice was low, quietly echoing barely controlled anger. Adam borrowed a few facts from his life, augmenting them to suit the occasion. "I originally took out this policy so that if anything happened to me, Mona, my kid sister, would be able to take care of herself." Mentioning his sister, even in passing, brought a wave of irate sadness to him. "Mona was never much good at hanging on to a job. I just wanted to be sure she'd be okay."

Then why had he given this to her for Brooklyn? She didn't have to open the envelope to know that he had obviously changed the designated beneficiary. "Where is your sister now?" she asked. An uneasy feeling slipped over her the moment the words were out of her mouth.

She saw his jaw clench. "She died."

"Oh." Sympathy flooded her. She knew what it was like to lose someone. More than one someone. "I'm sorry." Eve bit her lower lip. "What did your sister die of?"

"It doesn't matter. She's dead," he said with such dark finality, Eve felt as if she'd literally been pushed away. He began opening the top drawers that ran along the underside of the counter, looking for utensils. "I changed the beneficiary. The policy's in trust for Brooklyn until she turns twenty-one." He spared her a glance. "Until then, if the occasion arises, you manage it for her." He nodded toward the envelope. "Put that in a safe place."

She stared at the envelope, then shook her head as she pushed it toward him on the counter. "I don't want it."

"It isn't for you," he pointed out. "It's for Brooklyn."

He watched as she squared her shoulders like a soldier being challenged. "I can take care of my daughter—"

His eyes held hers. "*Our* daughter," Adam corrected pointedly.

She just couldn't figure him out, not on any level.

Here was an intelligent man who could have been anything, yet he had sunk down to the level of a drug dealer. Was perhaps still at the level.

"Most men would fight this tooth and nail," she said quietly. "Or at least insist on a paternity test, yet you're willing to accept that you're Brooklyn's father without any tangible proof."

Adam saw nothing wrong with that. Finally finding the utensils, he took out two knives and two forks, placing them on the counter. He pushed the envelope back in her direction.

"So?"

"So why aren't you asking for proof? A DNA test? Why are you taking just my word for it?"

"Maybe because you *didn't* ask me for anything." And then he shrugged. "The timing just works out." His eyes dipped down to her stomach. Even now, she seemed to be well on her way to regaining her figure— which, as he recalled, had been drop-dead gorgeous. "Besides," he raised his eyes to her face, eyeing her knowingly, "you're not the kind to have casual sex."

"How do you know that?" she challenged. Granted she'd been a virgin when they'd made love, but they hadn't been together long enough for him to have drawn this kind of a hard and fast conclusion. "What makes you think you know so much about me?"

His smile went straight to her gut.

Adam shrugged carelessly. "I just know. Call it a gut feeling."

It was more than just his gut that was involved, although that had been the initial proponent. When he'd received that e-mail that had sent him looking for Eve, he'd gotten Spenser at the department to do a little research for him. The reformed computer hacker put together a file that contained a great deal of information on the woman standing beside him.

Adam handed her a plate. "Now stop being stubborn and have something to eat before—"

As if on cue, the baby monitor on the counter came to life. Something that sounded very close to mewling filled the room.

"The baby cries?" she guessed, ending his sentence for him.

He nodded, then murmured, "Too late." He glanced over his shoulder, although there was no way he could see Brooklyn's room. "Eat," he told Eve, indicating her plate and the selection of entrees. "If you tell me which way to her bedroom, I'll go see what Her Majesty wants."

The aroma of the still-hot food caused her stomach to contract and growl. The spread before her proved to be too much of a temptation.

"It's upstairs," she told him. "Second room on your right."

She watched as Adam walked out of the kitchen. With all her heart, she wished she could banish her lingering suspicions about him. If it weren't for her nagging doubts, she would admit he was damn near perfect in this new paternal role.

He was rising to the occasion far better than she was, Eve thought, helping herself to a corn-husk-wrapped tamale. Though she dearly loved this brand-new addition in her life, a part of her was still afraid she was going to wind up being a very poor mother.

* * *

When Adam didn't return within a few minutes, carrying a hungry baby in his arms, Eve began to wonder what was taking him so long. Only one way to find out. Bracing her hands on the counter, she slid off the stool and went to investigate.

Although she wanted to hurry up the stairs, she forced herself to take it slow. It annoyed her no end that she still felt pretty weak. The last nap the baby had taken, she'd taken one, too. Filled with admiration for mothers who continued to be powerhouses, Eve couldn't wait to be her old self again.

Walking into the baby's room, she saw that Adam was at the changing table—one of the gifts Josiah had given the baby that she *had* accepted—putting the finishing touches on the disposable diaper he'd just secured around Brooklyn's tiny bottom.

He sensed rather than heard or saw Eve in the doorway. "She needed changing."

She crossed to him. "You change diapers?" she asked incredulously.

He'd changed more than his share of Mona's diapers. The knack was something akin to riding a bicycle. You never really forgot how—especially when plastic tabs were involved.

"It's not exactly like changing water into wine," he pointed out, glancing at her awed expression. "Anyone can do it if they need to." Picking his daughter up off the changing table, he smoothed down her tiny dress and turned around to look at Eve. "There, I think we'll all be a little more comfortable having her dirty diaper a thing of the past."

Who would have thought he'd take to parenting better than she did? "You are full of surprises, Adam Smythe." She didn't bother to hide the admiration in her voice.

They were sharing a moment. It took a great deal of self-control not to tell her that his name wasn't Smythe, but Serrano. But Adam managed to hold his piece and only commented, "You'd be surprised," making certain that the proper smile was on his lips.

Not entirely. The stray thought popped up in her head, taunting her. She banked it down, refusing to let it bring her down. The man was trying, that was all that mattered.

Taking the baby from him, she pointed toward the hall and the stairs that were beyond. "I'd better feed her. You go ahead and have dinner. Brooklyn and I'll be along as soon as she's finished."

"You know, if you prepare a few bottles ahead of time, we could take turns feeding her," he suggested, turning from the doorway.

Eve was already sitting in the rocking chair holding Brooklyn to her breast. The infant eagerly suckled as if she hadn't been fed for days instead of a little less than four hours ago.

Adam's breath caught in his throat. He couldn't remember when he'd ever seen anything even remotely as beautiful.

Belatedly, he realized he was staring. Clearing his throat, he abruptly looked away, even though he would have been content just to stand there, watching the scene all evening.

"I'll wait for you in the kitchen," he murmured to the bedroom door just before he left the room.

Eve smiled to herself. Again, his actions surprised

her. Adam Smythe was a very complex individual, with a lot of different layers. And she was getting a lot of mixed signals here. How did she tell them apart? Just what was real and what was imagined?

More than anything, she wished she knew what to believe and just who and what Adam Smythe really was. But she didn't see that happening anytime soon. And who knew? He might be gone tomorrow.

She tried to prepare herself, secretly hoping that tomorrow wouldn't come for a very long time.

Within a week, they fell into a routine, one that Adam was loathe to give up or even change in the slightest manner. Every night he would come home to her, to them, and share both the responsibilities and the rewards of caring for Brooklyn. And for what it was worth, all three of them seemed to be thriving.

The weather had even cooperated, in a manner of speaking. An unexpected storm off the coast of Colombia had sent residents along the coast scrambling for their lives. More importantly, at least for Adam, was that the shipment of drugs loaded into the belly of an airplane bound for California had been lost when the plane suddenly went down.

With great bravado, Daniel Sederholm had insisted that another shipment could be on its way as quickly as within ten days. Though the setback had his handler's teeth on edge, Adam had ten more days to enjoy this secret life he'd miraculously stumbled into. Ten more days to pretend that the world wouldn't come knocking on his door, dragging him away at a moment's notice.

Ten more days to watch his daughter grow and have

both Brooklyn and her mother burrow their way even further into his heart.

As if they hadn't deeply entrenched themselves there already.

"So I take it that he's moved in?" Josiah asked Eve.

It was midafternoon and her self-appointed guardian angel had come by for a visit. Outside, his driver, Lucas, sat in his restored classic Mercedes, engrossed in the latest page-turner put out by the current darling of the bestseller list. Meanwhile, Josiah sat in Eve's living room, quietly studying the young woman he regarded as another daughter over the rim of his teacup. Fragrant vanilla-flavored coffee wafted up to penetrate his senses, soothing him. He was flattered that she kept his coffee of choice on hand for his visits.

For his part, he'd been as patient as he could, giving Eve almost two weeks to settle into a routine before finally inviting himself over to see how she was doing. It had taken him exactly five minutes to deduce that his favorite veterinarian wasn't tackling parenthood alone.

"Adam's here temporarily," Eve was quick to correct. Having poured herself a cup, as well, she sat down opposite Josiah.

"And you're all right with that?" Josiah cocked his head slightly, as if that could help him assess the situation more clearly.

"I am."

His eyes seemed to delve into hers, as if accessing her very thoughts. "You don't mind that he plans to leave after a finite point?"

"Oh." She'd thought Josiah was asking her how she

was dealing with having Adam around, not if she minded the fact that he intended to leave in the near future. "To be honest, this is all still a little overwhelming for me. I'm not really thinking more than a few hours ahead at a time."

He nodded. Whether she knew it or not, that was what she had him for. He had always been good at looking at the big picture. His former line of work called for it. Josiah moved forward on the sofa, creating a more intimate atmosphere. "How much do you know about this man, Eve?"

"I know he's a good man." The moment the words were out of her mouth, she realized that she sounded defensive. She didn't want to be defensive and hoped Josiah would come to the right conclusion about Adam on his own. "He gave me his life insurance policy to hang on to for safekeeping. He named Brooklyn as his beneficiary."

Josiah nodded slowly, absorbing the information. "Admirable."

The word was polite, detached. "You don't like him, do you?"

Because he knew he couldn't say what she wanted to hear, Josiah avoided giving her a direct answer. "I'm not the one who counts here, Eve. And I'm just worried about you," he admitted. "And, I suppose, I'm worried about myself, as well."

Her eyebrows drew together into a puzzled line. "I don't follow."

"Well, if this Adam hurts you again—the way he did the last time," Josiah emphasized, "I will be forced to have to kill him, and truthfully, the prospect of 'doing time' at my age is not exactly pleasant."

Setting down her cup on the coffee table, Eve laughed. She leaned forward and placed her hand on his shoulder. "You won't have to kill him, Josiah. He's really nicer than you think."

Thin, aristocratic shoulders rose and fell in a careless shrug. "What I think doesn't matter."

"What you think matters to me, Josiah," she assured him. "You've always been like an uncle to me. If Adam does become a permanent part of my life," she went on, constructing her sentences carefully, "I'd want the two of you to get along." She abruptly remembered the holiday that was coming up. She really was living in a fog these days, Eve thought ruefully. "Tell you what. Thanksgiving is almost here. Why don't you come over to my house for dinner and maybe, properly wined and dined, the two of you can do a little more than just try to stare each other down."

Josiah looked at her, aghast. "But you can't cook, Eve."

"Why can't I?" she asked, confused. She'd cooked for him before. Was he blurting out what he really thought of her efforts? She'd always thought of herself as a good cook. "I've been doing it since I was ten."

"No, no, I mean, you just gave birth. Cooking is taxing, especially a big meal like Thanksgiving. You shouldn't exert yourself."

"By Thanksgiving it'll be closer to four weeks than to 'just,'" she pointed out, smiling at his concern. "And as for not exerting myself, I solemnly promise I won't go hunting for the turkey anywhere but the grocery store this year."

Josiah sighed. He knew it was useless to argue. Eve

had been a stubborn little girl and she had grown up to be a stubborn young woman. When she made up her mind about something, no one could talk her out of it. It was both a source of pride and despair for her father, Josiah recalled.

"You are a hard young woman to keep down, Eve Walters."

She smiled warmly at him. "So I've been told. Then it's settled? You'll come?"

"Yes, I will come. As long as you allow me to bring dessert."

Pleased, Eve put out her hand. He took it in his bony one and shook it. "Done," she told him. Just then, a lusty wail was heard over the baby monitor positioned on the coffee table. "Ah, I believe that's Brooklyn asking to see her great-uncle."

He rose to his feet, remarkably agile for a man in the latter half of his life. "Then let's not disappoint her." With a flourish, he bowed at the waist and offered the crook of his arm to her.

Rising, Eve hooked her arm through his. "Let's not," she agreed with a warm smile.

Chapter 9

It looked as if a tornado had made a pit stop in her kitchen, leaving pots, measuring spoons and cups, and ingredients—both large and small—scattered every which way.

At the moment, Eve felt just a shade away from overwhelmed. She scanned the formerly neat kitchen and sighed. The clock on the wall to her immediate right kept insisting on swallowing up minutes. She was running out of time and falling drastically behind.

Though she hated to admit it, Eve realized she'd bitten off a little more than she could chew. Okay, a lot more. She was seriously regretting having turned down Adam's offer. He'd volunteered to bring a fully cooked turkey dinner, prepared by a local caterer, to the table for her. At the time, she'd turned him down, confident that she could pull it off the way she had before.

Thanks to Adam's help every evening, she'd been getting more sleep and grew stronger. So much so that she thought, since it was nearly a month since she'd given birth to Brooklyn, she finally was back to her old self.

But standing here, in the middle of her chaotic kitchen, with the stuffing only half-baked and demanding her attention, the potatoes refusing for some unknown reason to cook to the point where they were soft enough to mash, and the turkey needing basting every fifteen minutes, not to mention that she had to stop periodically to feed or change an overly fussy baby, her goal of having everything ready by five o'clock was becoming the impossible dream.

Sound suddenly emanated from the baby monitor on the counter. Brooklyn was awake and crying. Again.

Eve pressed her lips together, trying to ignore the sound.

Brooklyn's wail grew louder.

Her daughter had gotten accustomed to being scooped up within moments of voicing her displeasure. Eve knew schools of child-rearing sometimes frowned on that, claiming that to deny instant gratification was actually good for the baby. But the sound of her baby's cries just twisted her heart. Besides, she reasoned, how could too much love be a bad thing?

Still, today would have been a good day to put one of those "let the baby cry a little" theories to the test. Eve tried and remained where she was.

She lasted all of a minute and a half. Throwing up

her hands, she wiped them on her apron then hurried to the staircase.

"Mama's coming," she called out, taking the stairs as quickly as she could.

The pitiful cries continued until she entered Brooklyn's room.

"Maybe you'd like to come down and give me a few pointers," she said to her daughter as she picked the infant up.

Brooklyn sighed deeply, as if some horrible wrong had just been righted, then lay her head down on her mother's shoulder, tucking herself against her mother's neck.

The missing piece of my puzzle, Eve thought, patting the baby's bottom. She could almost feel the deep affection in her chest doubling the moment Brooklyn lay her head down.

Remaining where she was for a moment, Eve drew in a deep breath. No offensive odor registered. "Okay, you don't need changing and you just ate an hour ago, so you're not hungry. You're just lonely up here, aren't you?" she murmured, stroking her daughter's back. It was a toss up who was more soothed by the action, Eve mused, Brooklyn or her. "Okay, come with me," she said cheerfully, leaving the room and heading for the stairs. "I know just where to put you."

On his last visit—yesterday—Josiah had brought yet another gift for the baby. It was what amounted to a motorized port-a-crib, complete with music some expert declared that babies enjoyed. He'd had Lucas put it together for her. The finished product currently stood in the family room.

"Time to put this little contraption to the test," Eve announced. Very carefully, she deposited Brooklyn into the port-a-crib.

The moment her back made contact with the thin mattress on the bottom of the crib, Brooklyn began to fuss again. Eve quickly wound the motor. The port-a-crib slowly swayed to and fro, the gentle action keeping time with the soft strains of a lullaby.

Brooklyn's eyes widened. Entranced, she stopped crying. Her expression became alert, as if trying to pinpoint where the sound came from.

If she didn't know better, Eve thought, she would have said her daughter was smiling.

"Bless you, Josiah," Eve murmured. With slow, careful movements, she repositioned the port-a-crib so that she could easily keep an eye on it from the kitchen.

Eve had no sooner done that than a loud hissing noise demanded her attention. The water in the pot with the potatoes had finally begun to boil, and just like that, it was boiling over. The water splashed onto the surface of the electric burner and cascaded down along the front of the stove.

The last time that had happened, Eve suddenly remembered, the stove had short-circuited, throwing the oven portion out of commission for an entire day. She didn't have an entire day to spare. She didn't even have half an hour to spare, she thought, trying to bank down a wave of panic.

"No, no, no," Eve cried, as if the urgent entreaty could somehow perform a miracle and send the water retreating like the Red Sea scene in the classic *The Ten Commandments*.

Grabbing a towel, Eve frantically stemmed the descending tide. In the background, she heard the doorbell ring.

Now what?

It was too early for either Adam or Josiah and his driver to arrive. People didn't sell magazines door-to-door around here on Thanksgiving, did they?

She decided to ignore whoever was on the other side of the door. But the doorbell rang a second time. And Tessa, suddenly alert, began to run back and forth from the front door to the kitchen.

Now someone was knocking instead of ringing. She glanced at her dog as she made a second round-trip dash. "What is it, Lassie? Did Timmy fall into the well?"

Tessa barked, as if in response to the question.

Feeling harried, Eve looked over toward Brooklyn to make sure everything was all right, then hurried over to the front door.

She pulled it open without bothering to ask who it was. If it was a serial killer, the dog would protect her. Or so she hoped.

It wasn't a serial killer. It was Adam. Early.

"Didn't I give you a key?" she asked him, an irritated note threatening her voice. Her dog, apparently, was overjoyed at the early appearance and behaved as if she hadn't seen him for months instead of a handful of hours.

Turning on her heel, Eve quickly returned to the scene of her pending disaster.

The scent of scorched surfaces and burned water faintly teased his nose as Adam followed her to the kitchen. Things weren't going too well, he noticed, but wisely kept the observation to himself.

"Yes, but that's only for emergencies, like if I think you've passed out and hit your head on something. Otherwise, I didn't think you would want me just waltzing in."

Thinking back, she realized that she had let him in each time. "You practically live here these days." The only time he left was to go to work or get a change of clothes. That pretty much constituted him living with her. "Having you let yourself in wouldn't have upset some delicate balance of power," she assured him.

Pausing to pet the dog, Adam then went directly to the port-a-crib. Brooklyn began gurgling and kicking her feet. Her big blue eyes appeared focused on Adam.

Hardly a month old and she was already a flirt, Eve thought with a shake of her head.

"Hi, short stuff," Adam teased, tickling the baby's belly.

The sound of Brooklyn's delighted laughter filled the air, warming Eve's heart.

Walking away from the crib, Adam crossed back to the kitchen. His eyes swept around the room. Keeping a straight face, he asked Eve, "Need help?"

"No." The word came out like a warning shot fired at a potential intruder. "I've got everything under control here."

Rather than dispute her claim, Adam slid onto the closest stool. Propping his upturned palm beneath his chin, he just stared unabashedly at her.

"What are you doing?" she demanded.

"Waiting for your nose to grow," he replied simply.

"Happened in a fairy tale. Little wooden boy lied, his nose grew something awful."

She held up her hand to stop him from going on. "I am aware of the fairy tale," she informed him through gritted teeth, "and I am *not* lying."

He gave her a knowing look, pretending to humor her. "Lucky for you, fairy tales don't come true." He slid off the stool and looked around. Enough was enough. It was time to get down to business. "All right, where do you want me to get started?"

She gave up the protest with a heartfelt sigh. "Do you have a magic wand?"

He laughed. "I don't think you need that much help. Just a little," he added, trying to bolster her morale. "Why don't we divide up the work? Would that make things easier on you?"

"I used to be able to handle everything," she told him with an air of helplessness.

The water in the pot finally simmered down, sinking to its new level. A lot of water had gone over the side. Wanting to replenish what was lost, she grabbed the pot by its handles in order to refill it and immediately yelped, releasing the pot again. Why she'd suddenly forgotten that there was no coating on the pot handles was completely beyond her.

Grabbing her hands in his, Adam quickly moved her toward the sink. He turned the faucet on and ran cold water over her palms.

What was wrong with her? She knew to do that, to instantly apply cold to the affected area in order to minimize the damage. Had giving birth completely diminished her brain power?

"And you'll be able to handle everything again—soon," Adam promised her, still holding her hands beneath the running water. "But for now, there's nothing wrong with accepting a little help when you're not firing on all four cylinders," he added mildly. Releasing her hands, he reached for a towel and offered it to her. "Why don't I take over the mashed potatoes—I am assuming they're going to be mashed." He looked at her, waiting for confirmation.

She bit back a wince as she wiped the towel over her tender fingers. "Yes, they're going to be mashed."

He regarded the potatoes for a moment, then raised his eyes to meet hers. "You make them with garlic, parmesan and mozzarella cheeses and milk?"

"That was the plan, more or less." She wouldn't have thought of adding the cheeses, but that did sound good.

"Great." He reached for the whisk she kept housed in a colorful jar on the counter, along with several other utensils. "I can take out all my aggression on the potatoes."

Opening the refrigerator to take out the one dessert she'd prepared last night, Eve stopped to give him a puzzled look. "What aggression?"

"Just a little joke," Adam assured her as he moved over to the sink and, using pot holders, drained the potatoes. A cloud of steam rose, but he deftly avoided coming in contact with it, drawing back his head. "Apparently very little," he commented more to himself than to her.

"I'm sorry, but you've thrown me off by coming now. I didn't expect you until later," she told him, then turned her attention to the stuffing she'd placed in the oven earlier.

Opening the top oven, she raised the aluminum foil

away from the rectangular pan, wanting to reassure herself that nothing was burning. This represented three-quarters of the stuffing. The remaining quarter was inside the turkey, absorbing the bird's juices for added flavor. She would make sure that Adam sampled it. She wasn't quite sure why she was so set on showing him she was a good cook, but in the last few minutes, it had become very important to her.

"Sorry, I didn't mean to throw you off," he apologized. "But the store's closed today and I had nothing to do. I don't like having a lot of time on my hands."

That much was true. There'd been a quick touching of bases with not only his handler—who was on his way to spend the holiday with his sister and her family—but with Sederholm, as well. He'd gone to see Sederholm to find out firsthand how things were coming along with the replacement shipment. He'd had to listen to the cocky college senior delineate his getaway plan, the one he intended to use on his parents by skipping out on the evening meal. Sederholm had sounded more than a little paranoid as he assured him that everything was on schedule and that he'd have his supply "soon."

Once he'd gotten all that out of the way, Adam caught himself thinking about Eve. Constantly. That very fact should have thrown up all sorts of red flags for him. He should be trying to stay away from her. It just wasn't working out for him. Being away from Eve only made him want to see her more. The trite saying was right. Absence, even absence involving a mere matter of hours, made the heart grow fonder.

Adam sighed. He was becoming entrenched in this

"helpful lover" role he'd taken on. So much so that it was taking center stage with him. He knew the danger. It made him let his guard down, interfered with his focus. Which in turn endangered not just him and the people he worked with, but Eve and Brooklyn, as well.

He couldn't allow anything to happen to them.

Maybe they'd all be better off if he just walked away.

Damned if he did and damned if he didn't. What was the right call? He honestly wasn't sure.

Tomorrow. He'd think about that and make up his mind tomorrow. Today, there were different priorities to consider.

"So I thought I'd come over and see if I could lend you a hand or at least some support," he continued. "My mother used to say that I was pretty handy in the kitchen."

"Your mother?" she echoed. He didn't strike her as the type to talk about his mother. She didn't think of him as warm and fuzzy.

"You sound surprised." Adam grinned, amused. "Even I had parents."

"I didn't mean to imply that I thought you didn't, but you don't exactly talk about your family."

Adam forced his voice to sound light, as if the subject and what had happened hadn't been carved into his heart.

"There's a reason for that."

Was it her imagination, or was he working that whisk particularly hard? He really *was* taking out his feelings on the potatoes. "And that is?"

"I don't have a family," he told her simply. "Not anymore."

He'd told her that his sister was dead, but he hadn't mentioned anything about his parents. She felt instant empathy in her soul. "Your parents are dead?"

"Yes."

The single word was completely devoid of any feeling, any telltale indications of the boy who had once been cut to the quick at the sudden deprivation. He hadn't had time to grieve. He had a sister to take care of and a life to carve out for both of them.

Eve turned away from the oven and toward him. "I guess that gives us something in common. I'm an orphan, too."

It felt odd to phrase it that way, because, after all, she was an adult and had felt like one for a very long time now. But the realization that there was no one to fuss over her, to wonder trivial things such as was she eating right and keeping warm, that occasionally made her feel detached from the world at large.

Adam looked into her eyes. It felt as if he delved into her very soul. "I know exactly what you mean," he affirmed softly.

Eve shifted restlessly. She felt herself reacting, not just to the words, but to him. To his very male presence within this, her female-dominated home. It seemed incredible that he still had that effect on her. Knowing what she knew about him, feeling as if he'd betrayed her, at least that initial time, she was still incredibly and irresistibly drawn to him.

She wanted to be with him. And not just with a table between them, but biblically, in the full sense of the word.

Out of the blue she remembered that she'd gone to see her doctor yesterday for her postpartum checkup.

After it was over, Dr. Mudd had expressed surprise at how quickly she'd healed and how fast her body seemed to have bounced back to its prepregnancy form.

When Dr. Mudd had told her that she was "good to go" in all aspects of the concept and could even begin contemplating giving Brooklyn a little brother or sister, Eve had felt herself going pale. Very politely, she'd informed her doctor that she had no intentions of going that route for a very long time to come. Maybe never.

Dr. Mudd had merely given her a knowing look and said the choice, as always, was up to her, but that she'd felt she had to tell her that she could have "relations" if she wanted to.

As if she wanted to, Eve had silently scoffed at the time.

But the problem was that whenever Adam was around, she found herself wanting to.

A lot.

Why was she thinking about this? Heaven knew she had more than enough to deal with right now and Vera was dying to have her finally return to the practice. She made plans to that end, thinking that she would get started next Monday. Between the baby and her career, she had more than enough in her life to keep her occupied. She certainly didn't need to complicate things even further by inviting a man into her life.

Into their lives, she amended. Because what affected her affected Brooklyn. They were a set now. The fact that the man she was contemplating—fleetingly—to allow into her life was Brooklyn's father didn't change anything. Hell, he was the reason she was feeling this edginess in the first place.

At bottom, despite the fact that he did pitch in on all

levels to help her cope with the changes in her life, and more specifically, to help her take care of the baby, she still couldn't bring herself to fully trust him or be able to take him at his word.

No matter how much she wanted to.

Chapter 10

"This has to be, by far, the best Thanksgiving turkey I've ever eaten," Lucas told Eve as he consumed the last bite of his dinner. Josiah's tall, muscular driver had the uncanny ability to appear both enthusiastic and quiet at the same time.

At first, when Eve had extended the invitation to join them at the table, the man had demurred, assuring her that he was fine with waiting for Josiah in the car. He'd held up the mystery he was currently reading and said that he would have an instrumental CD playing on the Mercedes's sound system.

When she'd pressed him as to what he intended to eat while they were inside, consuming a turkey dinner with all the trimmings, he'd produced a couple of those breakfast energy bars that boasted of having chocolate and raspberries in its mix.

Shaking her head, Eve had confiscated the bars, telling him that there was no way he was going to sit in her driveway gnawing on hardened granola, especially not on Thanksgiving.

Observing the exchange, Josiah had chuckled drily. "I wouldn't argue with her if I were you, Lucas," he'd told his driver. "I know for a fact that Dr. Eve can be a very stubborn young woman when she wants to be."

Listening, Adam had laughed. "Now there's an understatement if I've ever heard one. But he's right, you know," he went on to tell Josiah's driver. "She's going to keep after you until you give up. Might as well not let the turkey get cold and just give in."

He didn't appear to be the type who liked stirring things up. Lucas capitulated. Coming inside, he'd sat down at the dining-room table, taking a seat next to Josiah. When presented with the meal, he had eaten with gusto, consuming a great deal more than the man he had been chauffeuring around, plus the other two people at the table, as well.

Retiring his utensils, Josiah delicately wiped his mouth and added his voice to the praise. "Yes." He smiled at Eve warmly. "My compliments to the chef."

"Thank you," she replied, more than a little pleased. "But I really can't take all the credit," she protested in the next breath. "Dinner wouldn't have been ready at all if Adam hadn't helped."

His words belied the intense look in his eyes as Josiah regarded Eve's "helper." "Well, then it was an excellent collaboration. I highly approve." He patted what was still a very flat stomach. "I'm afraid that I am too full to move."

"Then stay. Stay as long as you like," she encouraged. She looked at Lucas. Her invitation was to both men. "I give you my word, no one's going to chase you out."

As she spoke, she rose to her feet and reached for Josiah's plate, intent on clearing away the dishes. Lucas was on his feet immediately. For a large man, he moved with impressive agility. He took the dish away from her and began piling the other plates on top of it.

"The least I can do after that fantastic meal is to clear the table for you and do the dishes," Lucas told her.

"Dishes don't need doing, Lucas. That's why God created dishwashers," she answered.

"Well, I can at least get them from here to there," he told her, piling the utensils on the top dish.

Beneath that polite exterior, she had a feeling that Lucas was as quietly determined to do the right thing as she was. She gave up trying to dissuade him.

Inclining her head, she politely accepted his offer. "Thank you."

Josiah took advantage to the temporary break in the conversation. He leaned forward, his eyes on Adam's. "So tell me, Adam, if you don't mind my asking, how do you like doing business down here?"

The man wasn't mildly curious, he was digging, Adam thought. Why?

"I like it," he said casually, as if he wasn't aware that the older man was placing him under a microscope. "The weather's nicer down here, the people friendlier."

"I see."

Ordinarily, he would have attributed Josiah's fishing to his needing to act as Eve's surrogate father. But something about the way the other man looked at him made Adam rethink this simple conclusion. Maybe the job was really getting him paranoid.

"Is there much money in bookstores these days?" Josiah asked.

"There is in the kinds of books Adam deals in," Eve told the older man. Something unnamed and protective had risen up inside of her.

As if Adam needed protectors, she quietly jeered.

"Still dealing in rare first editions, then?" Josiah asked, his eyebrows raised in query.

"Yes."

"And how is that done, exactly? Where do you find these treasures?" Josiah wanted to know.

Definitely grilling him, Adam thought. "I go to estate sales. You'd be surprised what you can find if you look hard enough," Adam replied.

"I'm sure I would be," Josiah agreed thoughtfully. He glanced toward the kitchen where Lucas was rinsing off plates and stacking them into the dishwasher. "My driver has an affinity for murder-mystery books. Would you by any chance have a first edition of an Agatha Christie book?" he asked, then became more specific in his choice. *"The Mousetrap."*

Adam chuckled. He had just had a mousetrap set for him. Lucky thing he had minored in English in college while working on his degree in criminology.

"The Mousetrap," he informed Josiah needlessly, "was a play, not a book."

The older man seemed properly embarrassed. "Ah, my error." His expression slowly turned hopeful. "Perhaps one of her other efforts?"

As it turned out, he actually had something to sell to Josiah—if the man wanted to continue with the charade. "I have *The Man in the Brown Suit*."

"Excellent," Josiah declared with just the right amount of enthusiasm. "If you give me the address to your shop, I'll make a point of stopping by next Wednesday. Christmas is coming, you know."

"It usually does after Thanksgiving," Adam commented drily. He reached into his pocket and took out his wallet. In the interest of maintaining his cover, he carried several business cards with him at all times and offered one to the other man.

Taking the card, Josiah studied it for a moment before tucking it into his own pocket. "Next Wednesday," he repeated.

"I'll be looking forward to it," Adam told him.

The old man was up to something. He would bet his last dollar on it. But what? That was the part that didn't make sense. Could it just be that the man was looking out for Eve? Or was there something else involved?

He'd been at this too long, Adam thought darkly. Being undercover for two years had a way of getting to a man. Now a rose was no longer a rose, but could very well be an elaborate listening device.

He missed the days of roses.

"Anyone for dessert?" Eve offered. But just as she rose to her feet, Brooklyn made a low announcement, letting it be known that she had woken up from her nap and now wanted someone—or everyone—to pay attention to her. Eve sighed, then flashed an apologetic smile at her guests. Dessert was going to have to wait. "Looks like I'm being paged."

"Why don't you do what you need to do?" Josiah suggested gently. "I can entertain your little bundle of joy for a few minutes. If I'm not mistaken, I haven't had the pleasing experience of holding the young lady yet," he added.

Bless Josiah, she thought. "All right, then, she's all yours." She turned to look at Adam. "Adam, could you please—"

She didn't have to finish her request. He knew what she needed him to do. Pushing himself away from the table, Adam rose to his feet. "No problem. I'll go get her for you."

Brooklyn had napped in the family room where the baby could easily be seen by her parents during dinner. Walking into the family room now, Adam bent over the port-a-crib and picked his daughter up.

A quick check of her diaper told him she was still miraculously dry, although he had to admit that the thought of depositing a slightly soggy infant onto Josiah's lap did have its appeal. Something about the older man didn't sit quite right. It was only a matter of time before he figured out why.

Holding his daughter, aware of her every movement and how incredibly soft she felt against him, Adam crossed back to the dining room. He made his way over to Josiah.

"Ah, there's the lovely lady. The spitting image of her mother," Josiah declared, his thin lips curving in a faint smile. He put out his arms, looking forward to holding the little girl.

Adam hesitated for a beat. "You know how to hold a baby?" he heard himself asking.

Damn, when had that happened? When had he begun making noises like some overprotective, clucking mother hen?

Josiah raised his gray eyes to look at him. The steely eyes reminded him of laser beams. "I've held a few babies in my time, Mr. Smythe," Josiah answered.

Banking down a reluctance that had no rhyme or reason to it, Adam handed his daughter over to the other man. Josiah accepted the small, wriggling bundle, a look akin to awe gracing the gaunt face.

It was Adam's turn to study the old man. There was no hesitation, no awkwardness. Josiah held the little girl as if he'd had infinite practice doing so. And then he remembered.

"Eve told me that you have a daughter."

"I do. And a granddaughter," Josiah added, never taking his eyes away from the baby in his arms.

"So I guess that makes you an old hand at this." Adam found that if he engaged someone in conversation enough times, eventually, he found what he was after.

Josiah spared him the most fleeting of glances, his attention completely focused on the tiny human being in his arms. "I wasn't around very much when my daughter was this age and by the time her daughter was, they were in England, so no, I'm not an old hand at this. Some things just require the right instincts," he pronounced.

The man became more and more of an enigma. "And what is it that *you* did for a living when you worked?" Adam asked, turning the tables on the older man.

"Whatever I had to," Josiah replied quietly, his attention still exclusively focused on the bright, animated small face before him. The barest hint of a smile graced his lips as he added, "You might say I was a jack-of-all-trades. Good at all," he added, changing the old saying to suit him. "The fact that I survived attests to my ability to remain alive even in the most adverse conditions."

He knew even less than he knew before, Adam thought. But now wasn't the time to continue digging. He had a strong suspicion that Josiah enjoyed weaving answers that went around in circles.

Adam nodded toward the kitchen. "If you're okay, I'll go lend Eve a hand."

"Of course I'm okay." Josiah addressed his answer to Brooklyn. He looked—and felt—younger just by holding this radiant life form. Powerful medicine, he mused, these newborns. "Why shouldn't I be?" he challenged mildly, finally looking up at Adam. "Go, help Eve. She isn't as strong as she'd like to believe she is. It usually takes more than a month to recover from bringing a child into the world."

Josiah said it with authority, as if familiar with the process. Just who was this old man who saw himself as Eve's benefactor and secret guardian? He hadn't a clue. Yet. But he would, he promised himself. He would.

Adam went to the kitchen, crossing paths with Lucas. The driver, finished loading the dishwasher, was on his way back to the dining room. The man nodded at him the way one tenant passing another in an apartment complex might, anonymous but friendly.

What was *his* story? Adam couldn't help wondering. Lucas looked a little too robust, too buff under his uniform to be just a driver. Did he double as the old man's bodyguard? And why would Josiah need a bodyguard?

"How much do you know about Josiah?" Adam asked Eve, lowering his voice so he wouldn't be overheard by the men in the other room.

The question surprised her. She regarded Josiah with nothing but deep affection. Being around the older man made her feel as if a piece of her father was still alive. "I've known Josiah all my life."

That didn't answer his question. He was certain that there'd been people who'd known Ted Bundy all their lives—or thought they had.

"But what do you *know* about him?" Adam pressed.

She stopped decorating the pumpkin dessert and turned to face Adam. "That he's a lonely old man who's very sweet and occasionally takes in rescued dogs when his own pass on." Her eyes narrowed as she looked at him, trying to guess what this was actually all about. "Why?"

Adam shrugged dismissively. "No reason. He's just trying to stare me down."

"He's curious about you," she corrected, going back to putting the finishing touches on one of the desserts. Shaking the can of whipped cream, she added a swirl right on the top, then drizzled the finished product with a handful of crushed pecans. "He thinks my judgment might be influenced by the fact that you are, after all, very good-looking and you're Brooklyn's father."

His mouth curved in amusement. "You really think I'm handsome?"

She pretended to be engrossed in what she was doing. "I believe the exact description I used was 'good-looking.'"

He was grinning now, not just smiling. "You want to quibble?"

What she wanted to do, Eve realized with a sudden jolt to her entire system, was make love with him. She found it unnerving that nothing had really changed. That incredible attraction that had drawn her to him in the first place was still there, alive and well. Perhaps even stronger than it had been originally.

The question was, what to do about it? Would she ignore what she was feeling, or give in to it?

Could she trust him, or was she just being an idiot? She really wished she knew, but the jury was still out on that.

Eve took a breath, trying to clear her head and focus. Finished with the whipped cream, she placed the last dessert onto the tray on the counter and then turned to Adam. "Would you carry that in for me, please?"

He paused to take in her handiwork, seeing it for the first time. He'd been too lost in thought to pay attention to what she was actually doing.

"This is like in a restaurant where they bring out a cart with a whole bunch of desserts for the customer to choose from," he observed. Josiah had brought a traditional apple pie with him. Obviously Eve had forgotten that she'd asked him to and had put in a great deal of work on this array. "When did you get a chance to do all this?"

"Yesterday afternoon while Brooklyn was napping. Cooking and creating different desserts relaxes me," she explained, though she figured he probably thought that was strange.

Making love relaxes me.

Adam stopped abruptly, slanting a look at Eve. Had he just said that out loud?

No, thank God. Judging by the expression on her face, he'd managed to keep his unexpected remark safe in the recesses of his mind. It was a lot better for both of them if it remained there.

Picking up the tray, Adam followed her back into the dining room.

Josiah's face lit up. The older man had, she knew, a sweet tooth that was never satisfied. "I'll have one of everything," he told her before Adam had a chance to set the tray down.

"I've got a feeling he's not kidding," Adam commented to Eve in a stage whisper.

Sitting beside his employer, shaking his keys above Brooklyn to entertain her, Lucas glanced in Adam's direction. "He's not," he confirmed.

"Why would I joke about something like that?" Josiah asked. "I have a weakness for pumpkin pie— pumpkin in any form," he added. His eyes swept over the offerings. He was unable to make up his mind. "It's times like this that I lament the fact that we have but one stomach instead of four, like cows."

"You can take some of them with you," Eve told him. She reached for her daughter, who was still in the crook of Josiah's arm. "Here, let me take her so that you can eat."

But Josiah shook his head, maintaining his arm around the baby. "She's fine where she is, Eve. She won't interfere," he assured her.

To prove it, he drew over the pumpkin parfait she'd made and sank his spoon into the center of the whipped cream. Bringing the spoon to his mouth, he closed his eyes for a moment and made a deep, satisfied sound as he savored the taste.

"You know, Eve," he said, his eyes still closed, "if you ever decide to stop being a veterinarian, you might consider becoming a pastry chef." He opened his eyes to see her reaction. "I'd stake you to opening up your own restaurant."

He noticed that Adam was studying him the exact same way he had studied the other man earlier. Josiah guessed at the reason. Adam was trying to figure out just where he had gotten all his money. The answer was a great deal simpler than the man would have dreamed. "The trick is to invest wisely and to know when to pull out."

"I didn't ask anything," Adam pointed out, somewhat surprised at the unsolicited advice that had just come his way.

"Not verbally," Josiah acknowledged, an enigmatic smile barely registering at the corners of his mouth. "But your eyes did."

Brooklyn shifted, waving her tiny arms. The scent of the tantalizing spices that had gone into making the dessert seemed to register. She began to fuss.

This couldn't be comfortable for Josiah, Eve thought. Again she reached to take her baby from him.

"Let me—" Eve started, but she never got the chance to complete the offer.

"You sit and take it easy," Adam told her. "I can take her."

He saw Josiah about to protest, but then decided to keep his peace. He didn't bother wondering what was up. He just took his daughter into his arms.

Chapter 11

Sitting on the sofa, Eve stretched her legs out so that they went far beneath the coffee table. She allowed her eyes to close for a moment. A long sigh escaped her lips. Josiah and Lucas had departed more than half an hour ago, leaving a host of compliments in their wake. Adam had insisted on putting Brooklyn to bed. With the table cleared and the dishes done, there was nothing left for her to do except enjoy the stillness.

Which she did, finding it almost seductive. She stretched out her legs a little farther.

"Tired?"

Her eyes flew open and she shifted in her seat, turning to look at Adam. But he had already rounded the sofa, dropping down on the cushion next to hers.

She smiled at him, infinitely grateful that he was

here, taking care of her. Who would have ever thought things would arrange themselves this way? Eight months ago, all she wanted to do was get away from him and the life she thought he represented.

"Yes," she admitted, quickly adding, "but very satisfied." She wanted this moment, this contented feeling to go on for a little longer. "It felt good doing that, hosting a dinner," she told him. "I didn't realize how much I missed cooking. Not that I don't appreciate all the take-out meals that found their way into my kitchen," she interjected quickly. Her eyes searched his face, afraid that Adam would take her initial words the wrong way.

He could almost read her mind. The idea made him laugh. "I wasn't about to take offense," he assured her. "And between you and me, your cooking tonight outstripped anything that I brought home this last month."

He realized his slip a second after it had come out of his mouth. He's referred to Eve's house as home. Not *her* home, but just "home."

Had she picked up on that? Looking at her, he couldn't tell.

He supposed in the last few weeks, he had come to think of Eve's place as home. Her house was where he spent most of his downtime.

Moreover, this was where his daughter was.

Careful, Serrano. You're just here to look after her, to make sure the scum you're associating with doesn't harm her or the baby. Nothing more. Don't let yourself get caught up in something you can't handle.

The father of her child. Eve realized she was smiling at him. Maybe it was the afterglow of a successful dinner party, small though it was. Or maybe she was just too tired to keep her guard up, but she was having some very kind, not to mention sensual, thoughts about Adam right now.

Maybe she'd been too hard on him.

After all, he didn't have to come around all these weeks and help her until she finally got her "mother" legs firmly planted beneath her. But Adam had come through for her with flying colors.

All this after she had, in essence, run out on him.

Don't forget why you ran out on him.

But he'd changed, Eve silently argued with herself.

She'd tried to cling to the belief that people were basically good and that, if they went down the wrong path, with enough effort, they could redeem themselves. They could get back to the right path again. There was nothing to indicate Adam had brought his old way of life with him or that he was still associating with addicts.

When would he have the time? His days were divided between the bookstore and the baby and her.

"You're awfully quiet," Adam observed after several minutes of silence had gone by. Despite her arguing to the contrary, *had* all this been too much for her? She usually wasn't this quiet. "What are you thinking?"

Not wanting to admit that she'd been thinking about him, that lately, most of her thoughts were centered on or around him, Eve said, "I was just thinking about going back to work at the animal hospital on Monday. Vera has been pretty swamped and she's had to close the place on Sundays. I don't like not being available to my patients one day a week."

He knew her. If she went back, she'd throw herself into her work wholeheartedly. It was easier to watch over her in her house. A lot of people came into the hospital. An assailant could easily slip in.

"You think you're up to going back full-time?" he asked. "Maybe you should try going back just part-time for now, work your way back up to frantic over the course of a month or two."

She'd already made up her mind. There was a place for the baby in the back office. She, Vera and Susannah could all take turns keeping an eye on Brooklyn.

"I don't like just dipping my toe in the water," she told him. "I like diving in."

The smile that came to his lips was automatic. "Yes, I remember."

Her cheeks suddenly turned a fascinating shade of scarlet. Adam did his best to bite back a laugh. As he did, he felt that same strong, breath-stealing stir whirl around his insides, the one he experienced whenever he would look at her, *really* look at her and realize just how beautiful she was.

Allowing his instincts to govern him, the way he would during a mission, Adam brushed his knuckles against her cheek. He saw a glimmer of desire flash in her eyes. Considering what was at stake, that should have been his red flag, his signal to back away. Now.

But he ignored it.

Ignored everything but this unmanageable yearning that was holding him a veritable prisoner. With one hand gently touching her face, Adam leaned in and lightly brushed his lips against hers.

Though his lips barely touched hers, it still had the

same effect as the first time he'd kissed her all those months ago. He felt as if a fist had been slammed into his midsection, knocking all the air right out of him.

Okay, this was where he *had to* pull back. He'd had his sample, had tasted how sweet her lips still were and had rediscovered just how overwhelmingly susceptible he still was to her. All his questions were concisely answered.

This was where he needed to cut and run, or at the very least, to retreat. There was no way this could lead to anything except for frustration. And the more he allowed this longing, this need, to build up within him, the more frustrated he'd be. There was no recourse but to leave. The woman had just given birth, for God's sake. She was literally in no shape to give him what he so badly craved—and that was a good thing because, deep in his soul, he knew she was a habit he needed to kick.

For her sake.

He had nothing to offer her except for bits and pieces of himself and a life that was forever being lived on the edge. If she were part of his world, *really* a part of his world, she'd be in danger all the time. And he would be worried about her all the time, her *and* the baby. The first thing he'd been taught was that an operative with a split focus was a dead operative.

He couldn't let himself go, for her sake more than for his.

So, with supreme effort, Adam drew away, his adrenaline racing through his veins as if he had his back to the wall and was facing down an entire squadron of drug dealers, every last one of them intent on slowly vivisecting him.

Stunned, Eve blinked. Oh, no, he wasn't going to do this to her. He wasn't going to stir her up, making her, in the space of hardly a few seconds, mentally forsake each and every one of the promises she'd made to herself just to pull back.

Was he trying to prove something to himself? That he could walk away from her at any time? Or was there more to it? Was he showing her that he still had power over her? That he could still press her buttons, make her need him more than she needed the very air to breathe?

Well, she would be doing the showing, not him.

Very deliberately, Eve wove her arms around his neck, her eyes more than her arms holding him in place. The next moment, she brought her mouth to his. Brought her soul to his, kissing him as if the very world would be doomed if she didn't.

Damn it, Eve, why are you making this so hard?

Pulling his head back, Adam gently but firmly removed her arms from around his neck. "We can't," was all he said.

She put her own interpretation to his words, praying she wasn't being the biggest fool the world had ever seen. That he wasn't just toying with her because he could.

"I'm all right," she whispered, her eyes on his. "The doctor told me that I could…be with you if I wanted to."

Be with you. What a tenderly innocent way to say it, he couldn't help thinking. Maybe, just maybe, if he could just have this one last time to make love with her, that would somehow sustain him. He knew all too well that making love with her wouldn't quench the fire, but at least it could dowse it for a small space of time, allowing him to reapply himself to what he really needed to concentrate on. With any luck, the worthless piece of trash he was dealing with would slip, giving him the name of the head supplier and the department could move in for the kill.

He wasn't naive enough to think that once this present head of the cartel was captured that would be the end of it. Like a hydra monster, if one head was cut off, one if not two more would suddenly pop up in its place. But with luck, there would be some downtime and maybe, the department could further clean up the streets.

With effort, they might make it more difficult for a new foothold to form in the high schools currently being supplied with narcotics. Any respite was better than none and who knew, maybe in that small time frame the users would see the upside of even partially regaining control over their lives. Maybe they would think twice before abdicating it again, allowing powders, pills and drug dealers to govern them.

But right at this moment, Adam had to admit that he had a great deal of sympathy for addicts. For the first time in his life, he could see things from their perspective because he was addicted to Eve. Addicted to the rush she created in his veins. Addicted to the memory of what was and to the incredible draw of the promise of what could be.

He *needed* her and could think of absolutely nothing else.

Was she losing the battle? Or was Adam trying to be strong for reasons she couldn't grasp? Eve didn't know.

All she knew was that she needed him. Badly. It was as if their lovemaking had taken place in another life, a life she needed to get back to.

She raised her eyes to his, silently entreating him. And then, when he made no move to take her back into his arms, she finally put it into words, quietly saying, "Adam, don't make me beg."

Her voice was low, but the need she felt pulsated throughout her entire being.

"No begging," he promised, his own voice husky with longing.

The next moment, Adam covered her mouth with his own, kissing her deeply. In less than a heartbeat, he became lost within her.

Sealed by that physical act alone, they were instantly one. Nothing mattered right now to Adam but this overwhelming, screaming need inside of him, this need that demanded satisfaction, some sort of an outlet before it completely tore him apart.

The moment he silently surrendered control, it was as if someone had suddenly fired a starter pistol in the air, signaling the beginning of this explosive interlude. Adam found himself hardly able to remember how he got from one stage to another. Couldn't actually recall how his clothes had disappeared from his body. One second, he was dressed, the next, he wasn't. Had he done it, or had she? He was unclear as to the steps. Similarly, he wasn't even sure if his hands had urgently tugged her dress from her while she had been similarly engaged with his clothes, or if they simply divested themselves of their own clothes.

He was only aware of movement and shedding.

Through it all, his mouth remained urgently sealed to hers as if his very life depended on it.

In a way, it did.

And just like that, she was nude. Her flesh was tender and pliant beneath his hands. He felt as if he was on fire just touching her, sliding his palms along her soft, soft breasts, caressing her supple curves and re-committing them to memory.

This was only the second time he'd made love with her, and yet every touch, every pass, teased forth a memory from within him. Her body was oh-so-familiar to him even though, as he trailed his hands along her curves, he felt on the brink of an exciting new adventure.

Over and over again his mouth slanted over hers, kissing the sensitive area along her throat, seeking out the hollow of her neck, the dip in her now-flat belly. Her moan of pleasure in response to his questing tongue set him off the way Adam thought nothing ever could, making his head spin.

She had never told Adam that he was her first lover. It wasn't the kind of thing a woman broadcasted, even though, in her case, she had never met anyone she'd wanted in her bed. In her heart, however, Eve was certain that someone with Adam's experience would know. She, on the other hand, had nothing to compare except perhaps the first time that he'd been with her. What she vividly recalled was that she'd been utterly, hopelessly lost in ecstasy.

This time around, the ecstasy had doubled itself so that she could hardly contain the wild feelings rushing through her. It was as close to an out-of-body experience as she would ever hope to have.

She didn't want it to end.

Something told her this would only be a onetime thing. Last time, there'd been no encores because she'd discovered his secret life. This time around, she had a feeling that the cause for the lack of encores would be his.

But if it came to that, she wanted this isolated moment in time to last as long as possible.

Eve bit down on her lower lip as the first climax suddenly exploded over her, a depth charge coming from oblivion and targeting her. There'd been almost no warning. One moment, there was deliciously mounting pleasure, the next moment, fireworks.

Bucking, raising her hips to absorb every ray of heat, every movement of his mouth over her inner core, she cried out his name and something more. With lightning flashing through her brain, Eve couldn't even say for certain what it was that she had cried out.

But Adam could.

He'd heard it even though he told himself he'd imagined it.

At moments like this, with control wrenched away from him, it was easy to hear things that weren't said, see things that weren't there.

With his last scrap of strength, he forced himself to deny what part of him had thought he'd heard, burying the words "I love you," even though, with all his heart, he wished he could acknowledge them, press them to his chest and echo them in kind.

Instead, he drew himself up along her body, igniting them both as flesh rubbed against flesh. And just like that, he was hovering over her, looking down into her eyes, his gut tightening. Feeling things he couldn't acknowledge, wanting to say things he couldn't say.

It was just the moment that caused him to get carried away, nothing more, Adam silently swore to himself.

Even so, he gathered her into his arms, holding himself back as much as he could while positioning his hips over hers.

And then he was inside again, entering as gently as he could, ever alert for any sign that he was hurting her. That she had, at the last moment, changed her mind.

There was no sign.

Her arms tightened around his neck and she held on as hard as she could, mimicking the rhythm of his hips, determined to feel the peak of the crescendo at the same moment as he did. And then, it seized her, sending a rainbow of stars shooting all through her. She held on as hard as she could, praying that the moment would never end.

Mourning because she knew it had to.

Chapter 12

At first, Eve couldn't register the sound on the outer perimeter of her consciousness. Still in the throes of the final stages of euphoria, it took her several seconds to identify the insistent, soft buzzing.

A cell phone, set on vibrate.

Since hers played the first few bars of "When the Saints Go Marching In," a song she vividly remembered from her childhood, Eve knew the buzzing cell phone had to belong to Adam.

The last vapors of her euphoric state evaporated. The outside world invaded this piece of paradise they'd managed to construct. It was to be expected.

But on Thanksgiving?

Because she'd unwittingly stumbled across Adam's double life eight months ago, unbidden suspicions instantly crowded her brain. She tried to fight her doubts. Harboring suspicions would taint this perfect moment for her.

They already did.

The cell phone stopped and then started ringing again. And again. Whoever was on the other end obviously didn't want to go to voice mail. Eve suppressed a sigh.

"Your phone's buzzing," she finally said.

He was aware of that. He'd secretly been hoping that his caller would go away. But no such luck.

It was either his handler, or the reason he was being handled.

The phone vibrated again.

"Shouldn't you answer it?" Eve asked, wondering why he wasn't. Fearing that she knew.

Adam turned to look at her. All he wanted to do at this moment was make love with her again.

"I don't want to," he told her truthfully.

Was that because he couldn't take the call with her so close, or because Adam was having the same thoughts about the moment as she was? That it was too perfect to spoil.

Too late.

Shifting, she moved away from him and began patting the articles of clothing entangled and scattered all over the floor, searching for the telltale lump that was his phone. Adam instantly came to life and started looking for the offending cell phone himself. He needed to get to it before she did.

But Eve found his cell phone first. Pulling it out of the pocket of his jeans, she glanced at the LCD screen as she held the phone up to him. "You'd better answer it. They don't sound like they're going to go away."

He glanced down at the display. It said "Private." That would be his handler.

Flipping the phone open, Adam murmured, "Hello?" as his mind scrambled, searching for a way to get rid of the man without arousing Eve's suspicions.

"Where the hell were you? I called your damn phone four separate times."

"Three," Adam corrected, keeping his voice even. "And it's Thanksgiving."

"Yeah, I know. My wife's not happy about me ducking out on her and her family. The whole bunch should be locked up in an insane asylum," he grumbled, allowing himself a personal moment.

It wasn't like Hugh to complain about his life. His handler was careful to keep a definite line drawn between his work and his private world. Adam couldn't help wondering if something within the mission was going south. "What's so important it can't wait until tomorrow?"

Hugh's tone was clip. "Intel has it that the incoming shipment's been moved up. Might not be accurate, but get ready to roll in the next couple of days or so anyway. Might even be tonight," he amended. "Whoever that college punk's main man is, he keeps everyone on their toes."

Adam focused on the only thing he considered crucial. "Tonight?" He saw Eve looking at him, the curiosity in her eyes growing.

"Maybe," Hugh responded. "I just wanted you to be on standby."

"Right," Adam muttered.

The connection on the other end of the line went dead.

Glancing toward Eve, Adam continued talking as if his caller was still there. "Well, you handle it. I've got faith in you. Call the police and give them whatever information you can pull from the surveillance tapes. Okay, fine. If they want to talk to me, I can come down to the store to answer questions. But try to handle it yourself first. Yeah, Happy Thanksgiving to you, too," he added for good measure. "Goodbye."

"Police?" Eve echoed once he shut the cell phone. "What was all that about?"

Adam tossed the phone back down in the general vicinity of his jeans. He sighed and shook his head, as if the idea of vandalism was beyond him. "That was the new clerk I hired last week. He said the security company called him because someone tripped the alarm, breaking into the bookstore tonight. Can you believe it? On Thanksgiving. Whoever it was that broke in probably figured nobody would be around."

She pulled her dress up to her chest, partially covering herself. It seemed strange somehow to be carrying on a conversation naked like this, with the heat of passion drifting into the horizon.

"This security system you have, it's hooked up to a surveillance camera, right?" she asked.

He found her sliver of modesty really arousing.

"Absolutely," he told her. "I've got a lot of valuable books in that shop. And some of them are rare, one-of-a-kind editions. Doesn't make any sense not to have an interactive security system."

She thought of the pure joy she'd seen on her father's face when she'd given him that Mark Twain first edition for his birthday. "I'm sorry," she said with feeling. "What did they take?"

She was being so sympathetic, he felt guilty about lying to her. "Bill has to go over the inventory to see what's missing."

"But he's sure someone broke in…?"

Adam nodded. "He said the security company said that the alarm was tripped."

"Could just be a faulty system," she suggested hopefully. "Maybe nothing was taken."

"That's always a possibility," he agreed. He'd forgotten how optimistic she could be. It was one of the things about her that reached out to him.

She shook her head, crossing her arms before her tightly. "Books should be sacred."

"Nothing is sacred," Adam responded, looking at her intently. *Except, maybe for you.*

"Do you think you should go, make a report?" she suggested, mentally crossing her fingers that he wouldn't feel the need to do so.

"No, Bill can handle it. He spent the holiday with friends and was on his way home when the security company called him—"

"Why him and not you?" she asked.

"Because I knew I wouldn't want to be interrupted," he told her, his eyes caressing her. "Bill has no family here so he can handle it for the time being, unless the police need to talk to me," he said.

Banishing Hugh's call from his mind, as well as the fact that he'd been forced to lie to her again, Adam gave in to his urges. He gathered Eve into his arms. The heat of her body stirred him just as much now as it had before they'd come together tonight.

He swept the hair away from her face. "Now, where were we?"

He watched the smile bloom on her face. "In ecstasy as I remember," she teased.

"Ecstasy, right. Sounds familiar," he agreed, bringing his mouth down to hers.

There were no more calls that night. He'd made sure that he'd shut off his cell phone, just this once.

Adam frowned. He could feel the tension building in his body.

Every hour that passed without a call from the cocky Sederholm was another hour in which to wonder if something within the operation had gone desperately awry. Or if whoever currently headed up this deadly daisy chain was on to him and had decided to pull up stakes, cutting his losses before the trap snapped around him.

There was no way of telling. Hugh's informants on the street, as well as the one that he himself had cultivated, said there were no rumors about a possible shift in power or even that a shipment was being moved.

It was as if no one knew anything, a highly unlikely scenario.

Adam grew progressively antsy, but at least he had a story in place if he had to suddenly leave Eve's house.

Unless, of course, the play went down in the wee hours of the night, he thought darkly, nodding his head at his last customer of the day as he rang up a rather worn copy of *The Catcher in the Rye*.

Walking the man to the door, Adam flipped over the closed sign and secured the locks.

Ten minutes later, he was on the road, his thoughts reverting back to the precarious situation he was in. Again.

Although the narcissistic college kid had a flare for the dramatic, Adam was fairly certain that he didn't have to worry about a middle-of-the-night call from the supplier. He knew for a fact that Sederholm preferred conducting his business in the light of day. Despite his bravado and incredibly poor imitation of Al Pacino, the brash student felt safer when he didn't have to remain alert, worrying about who or what was hiding in the shadows.

Practically on automatic pilot, Adam blinked and realized he needed to turn off on a street where a strip mall was still in its infancy. He'd decided to pay Eve a surprise visit. This was where Eve and Vera had moved their practice in order to accommodate the needs of their growing clientele. The new animal hospital had space for new X-ray machines.

This was the best part of his day, Adam thought. The part where he got to see Eve and the baby. Where he got to pretend that he was actually just a regular person with a regular life.

For how much longer?

He shut away the annoying voice in his head.

Because of what he did, there was no point in his thinking too far ahead. All he had was right now and he intended to make the most of it, the most of every moment he had with his family.

His family. It had a nice ring. Even if it was a false one.

As he pulled into the parking lot situated before the Laguna Animal Hospital, Adam didn't see her car. Eve usually parked off to the side, leaving the area right before the hospital entrance clear for her four-legged patients and their owners. Right now, the parking lot was fairly empty. Where was Eve's car?

Something was wrong. He could feel it.

Susannah was seated behind the front desk, focused on several beige folders spread out before her. She was working on their billing statements. The brunette looked up the moment she heard the door open. Recognizing him, the perfunctory smile she flashed at the owners of their patients faded. In its place was a look of grave concern.

He was right. Something was wrong. Ever mindful of his surroundings and the dangerous tightrope he walked, Adam swept his eyes over the immediate area. But nothing seemed out of place.

"Hello, Mr. Smythe."

There was a note of hesitation in her voice. Was the animal technician debating telling him something? Again Adam glanced around, searching for some telltale sign that would give him a clue. Had one of Sederholm's lowlifes come here to threaten Eve?

He dispensed with the niceties. "Where's Dr. Walters, Susannah?" he asked the technician.

Susannah seemed genuinely distressed as she began her narrative. "Dr. Walters had to rush to the hospital."

His brain instantly spun scenarios. He forced himself to bank them down. Eve was a veterinarian. Susannah could be referring to the emergency animal trauma center located in Bedford.

"Why did she have to rush off, Susannah?" he asked, striving for patience.

"It's the baby," the receptionist blurted out.

Okay, now he could panic. "What about the baby?"

One word came tumbling out after another. "Brooklyn started coughing and sneezing and it looked like she was really having trouble breathing. Dr. Walters called Brooklyn's pediatrician—"

"Name, I need a name," he said, interrupting her when he couldn't recall the physician's name.

All he could remember was that it was a woman and that she was associated with the same hospital, Blair Memorial, that the ambulance had taken her to right after Eve had given birth to their daughter.

Susannah stopped dead for a moment, apparently drawing a blank.

"It's Dr. Collins," Vera told him, walking into the reception area from the rear of the clinic. Eve's associate heard Adam's voice and came out to fill him in. "Dr. Sarah Collins," she specified. "Dr. Collins told Eve to meet her with the baby in Blair Memorial's E.R." Approaching the desk, the short, ordinarily perky blonde pulled out a pad and a pen from her lab coat pocket. "I can give you the address—"

"No need," he thanked her, hurrying out again. "I've already got it."

"I offered to drive her," Vera called out after him, following him to the door. "But she wanted someone to stay to take care of the dogs scheduled for appointments."

That sounded like Eve all right. Even in the middle of a possible crisis, her mind was on her responsibilities. Hell of a woman, he thought.

"Don't worry," Vera yelled after him, holding the door open so he could hear her. "Brooklyn's going to be just fine."

"Thanks," was all he managed to shout back.

The next moment, he was in his car, slamming the door. His heart raced as he gunned the engine. He'd been in life-and-death situations where a single word could blow his cover and hadn't felt half as apprehensive as he did right at this moment.

Being a father changed you. He'd never fully appreciated that until this very minute.

Traffic was heavy this time of day. Not wanting to get hemmed in by gridlock, he avoided the freeway altogether and took side streets instead. With one eye on his rearview mirror, ever on the lookout for police cars that might further impede his progress, Adam drove to the hospital as if his engine was on fire and he needed to reach his destination before it exploded.

For the first time since his sister had overdosed, he prayed.

The nurse at the information desk looked as if she was ready to summon one of the security guards. With effort, Adam lowered his voice and reined in both his impatience and his fear. "Look, my little girl was brought in a little while ago. She's only six weeks old. Dr. Sarah Collins is her doctor—"

At the mention of the doctor's name, the nurse seemed mollified. "Why didn't you say so?" Typing something into the computer database, she skimmed her finger along the resulting list that appeared on the monitor. "What's your daughter's name?"

"Brooklyn. Brooklyn Walters." He was going to get that changed as soon as he could, he thought. He wanted there to be no doubt that she was his.

"They admitted her. Second floor. Room 213." She raised her eyes to his face. "The elevators are—"

But he was already running not toward the elevators, but to the stairwell. He could make faster time on his own instead of waiting for the elevator.

Brooklyn had been admitted. This was worse than he thought.

Adam stopped short in the doorway of 213. There were five cribs inside the room. Four of them were empty. The one in the middle was not. Encased in a see-through plastic tent, the sight of which made his blood run cold, Adam saw his daughter.

She looked tiny. Tinier somehow than she had when she was born. And he had never felt so utterly helpless in his life.

It took him a second to take the rest of the room in and realize that Eve was sitting in the chair beside the crib. Keeping vigil.

Crossing the threshold, he came up behind her. With his hands on either side of her shoulders, he bent over and kissed the top of her head.

Eve never took her eyes off the face of the sleeping infant in the oxygen tent. Reaching up for the hand on her right shoulder, she laced her fingers through his, silently taking comfort from the contact.

She'd sensed Adam's presence the moment he'd entered the room. All afternoon, when she wasn't praying for the baby's recovery, she'd been praying that he would come. All her attempts to reach him on his cell had ended with irritating messages conveyed to her by a metallic voice. Signals were not going through.

Eve liked to think of herself as a strong person. She believed that she was able to handle anything that came her way. She had so far. But the mere possibility of something happening to her daughter had completely undone her.

There was a lump in her throat and she had trouble talking through it, even after clearing her throat twice. "Dr. Collins says she's going to be all right," she whispered. Her voice cracked as she felt tears choking her.

"I know. I ran into her in the hall." He'd rushed to the baby's room when he all but ran right into the woman. She'd given him a brief update, starting with the prognosis and working her way backward. He came around to stand beside Eve, next to the crib. "Why didn't you call me? I would have dropped everything."

"I did. But I couldn't get through and I didn't want to leave her to go looking for a pay phone." She pressed her lips together, gazing at Brooklyn. The baby had been so uncomfortable earlier. "She looks so little and helpless in there."

Adam shook his head. "She might be little, but she's not helpless. She's like her mother, a fighter," he told her. In his heart, he held on to that. On to the good news that Dr. Collins had given him. That Brooklyn was responding to the medication. Right now, he was concerned about Eve. "Have you had anything to eat?"

"I don't know," she answered truthfully. Turning from the crib, she looked up at him. "I don't think so. It all happened so suddenly. First a sniffle, then a tiny cough—it almost sounded cute." She should have been paying closer attention, she silently upbraided herself. "And then she was having trouble breathing." Eve paused to take a deep breath, trying to still her rapid pulse. "I was never so scared in my life."

"But she's okay," he reminded Eve, his voice, low, soothing. "Dr. Collins said Brooklyn was just staying here overnight to make sure everything was all right. Lots of kids get the croup."

She didn't care about lots of kids, all she cared about was *this* kid. "But she's not even two months old."

"All her vitals are fine." Taking her hand, he raised Eve to her feet. "She's going to be fine. And look at the bright side."

"Bright side?" Eve echoed, puzzled.

He brushed her hair out of her eyes and smiled at her. "Yes. You can hold this over her head when she acts out."

With a laugh that was half a cry, Eve turned to him and buried her head in his chest, grateful beyond words that he was here with her.

And then all the self-control she'd employed, holding tightly on to her panic, her fears, dissolved. Her fingers wrapped in his shirt, Eve felt the dam break inside of her. There was no holding back the tears.

Chapter 13

"You're sure about this?" Josiah inquired, his tone giving no clue that the information surprised him.

The deep, slightly raspy voice on the other end of the landline answered, "Absolutely."

Just for a moment, Josiah closed his eyes, absorbing what he'd just been told. Who would have thought? And then he took a breath and said, "Thanks, Harry. I owe you one."

The man known as "Harry" to only an assorted few chuckled. "You owe me five, Turner, but who's counting?"

"You, obviously. And you still have trouble with your sums." Moving forward on the finely creased brown leather chair that had memorized his imprint from years of use, Josiah prepared to hang up. "See you on Saturday as usual?"

"Wouldn't miss it."

The receiver made contact with its cradle. Sitting back again, Josiah stared off into space, reviewing what he had just learned.

The truth was a lot better than he'd thought. It removed the need of having to do away with Eve's Adam. He hadn't been in a position to have to rely on that set of skills in a while. Admittedly, he'd gotten a little rusty although he knew that ultimately it was like riding a bike. You never really forget. Still, his eyesight wasn't what it used to be. The task would have fallen to Lucas.

Josiah allowed himself a hint of a smile. His lips were not given to curving and the action was somewhat unfamiliar to them. Anyone passing by would have thought he was grimacing.

"Bad news?" Lucas asked, walking into the study less than a heartbeat after the phone conversation was terminated.

Josiah raised his eyes to look at Lucas's face. The grimace widened.

Away from prying eyes, the rapport between the two men was a great deal less formal than when they were out in public. But even so, it was a given for Lucas that Josiah was and always would be his superior, his mentor, the way it had once been when they had worked at the Bureau together. Furthermore, Lucas never lost sight of the fact that it had been Josiah who had saved his life in the field.

Unable to give a hundred percent to the job, Lucas had handed in his resignation rather than be relegated to a desk job. His life seemed to have lost its purpose.

When Josiah retired from the Bureau several months

later, he made it a point to look Lucas up and promptly hired the still young man to be his "man Friday," a position which entailed doing everything and anything that needed doing. If that included occasionally falling back on past talents and conducting a little investigating, so be it.

However, this time around, because it was Eve, Josiah had decided to undertake the investigation himself. He wound up pleasantly surprised for his trouble.

Josiah paused for a long moment before answering. "Strange news."

They had been together a long time. Lucas knew enough to wait for the older man to elaborate. Prodding Josiah usually had the opposite desired effect. The former senior special agent had the ability to imitate the tight jaws of a clam when he wanted to.

Josiah decided to share his intel with Lucas, a man who he had allowed, over the years, to get closer to him than anyone else, even his daughter. And, during that time, he had come to regard Lucas as the son he had never had, although he never said as much out loud. Words to that effect were not necessary. Besides, he had a feeling that Lucas knew anyway.

"Do you remember how upset Eve was when she first came back to Laguna?"

Lucas nodded. "She tried to hide it, but yes, I remember."

"It had to do with that bookstore owner."

"Brooklyn's father," Lucas said to clarify things.

Josiah inclined his head in agreement. "Yes. She had just begun to come around, to be her old self, and then her father died. That sent her into a tailspin. I thought she was just having trouble coping with her grief…" His voice trailed off for a moment as he relived the episode in his mind. "When she began to show, I realized she was trying to come to terms with something more than just grief." He looked directly into Lucas's eyes. "I sensed that she needed to talk to someone."

Lucas merely nodded, not saying a word. They both knew that in his day, Josiah was known to be at the top of his game when it came to getting confessions out of people. He never had to resort to torture or the threat of using it. There was just something about the way he looked at a person, about the way he made them feel— as if whatever was said behind closed doors would be understood and kept confidential even though no promises were made.

"She told me that she'd left Santa Barbara abruptly when she discovered that the man she was in love with turned out to be a drug dealer." Josiah took a breath, as if he was attempting to keep his anger under control. Lucas couldn't remember a time when he had seen the older man lose his temper, but wrath, when it came, would enter his eyes and was a terrible thing to behold. "I wasn't exactly happy to see him turn up here. I don't make it a habit of butting into other people's lives—"

"No, sir, you don't," Lucas agreed, silently congratulating himself for not giving in to a sudden, nearly overwhelming desire to laugh. The older man might have felt that he didn't interfere and although not intrusive in an obvious way, Josiah took it upon himself to handle things offstage as it were.

"Eve told me that Adam had changed. That he had come here, not looking for her, but wanting to make a fresh start. I found that highly suspicious," he went on, "for him to just 'pick' the same area that she had come to, but I didn't say anything to her. However, I could tell that Eve was concerned that his promise to her was written on the wind."

They'd been together, operatives and civilians, for close to two decades. In that time, Lucas had made a study of his former mentor and he could tell now that Josiah wanted some indication that he was interested in this unfolding tale.

Taking his cue, Lucas dutifully asked, "And was it valid?"

At this point, Josiah surprised him with a sound that passed for a laugh. "You have no idea."

Perhaps not an exact idea, Lucas thought, but from the gleam that had entered the older man's eye, he had a general notion where this story was ultimately heading.

"Adam Smythe isn't a bookstore owner, is he?"

Josiah stroked his chin and the neatly trimmed Van Dyke he sported. "No, he most certainly is not."

Lucas ventured a step further. "And he's not a drug dealer, either, is he?"

Josiah shook his head. "You do take some of the fun out of this, Lucas."

Lucas inclined his head in a silent tribute. "I was trained by a master."

Josiah's lips twitched just a little, a testament to his amusement.

"All right, *Grasshopper,*" he said, invoking the nickname of a character in a classic series that had once been a cult favorite, "you tell me. Just what is Eve's Adam?"

It wasn't hard to connect the dots once certain assumptions were made. "My guess is that he's some kind of law enforcement operative." Lucas paused, thinking. "Since drugs are involved, best bet is that he's with the DEA."

Admiration flared in Josiah's intense gray eyes. "The Bureau lost a valuable man when you decided to leave them."

Lucas shrugged away the compliment. "Since I couldn't give a hundred and ten percent anymore, it just seemed like the logical thing to do. How about you?" he asked. "What are you going to do with this information?" He had to admit that his curiosity had been aroused. "Are you going to keep it to yourself, or tell her?"

Ordinarily, other people's secrets were their own. But this wasn't exactly an ordinary set of circumstances. They involved someone he cared about. Someone he had been watching over since her unexpected return. His path was clear.

"The poor girl is worried that her baby's father might get sucked back into 'the life,'" he reminded Lucas. "The very least I can do is give Eve some peace of mind."

Lucas knew better than to even vaguely suggest that Josiah hold off in case something the DEA agent was involved in was going down. As a civilian, Josiah's allegiance was still to his country in general, but the circle of people who meant something to him was very small and he put them first whenever he could.

This was one of those times.

* * *

What a difference an hour made.

An hour ago, Eve thought ruefully, she'd been watching the clock, eager to close the clinic's doors and get home so that she could have a romantic evening with Adam.

She had everything planned: the menu, the music, even some of the conversation. And she had made it a point to stop by the mall during her lunch hour and had picked up possibly the hottest, sexiest lingerie she had ever seen.

But all her plans had come crashing down about her head when she'd stopped to leave Brooklyn with Josiah, who, along with Lucas, had agreed to babysit her daughter for the night. He'd told her more than once that he would be happy to do it. She knew he loved nothing more than playing the doting grandfather, but since his son-in-law had taken a post in England and taken the family with him, Josiah very rarely got the chance. He didn't talk about it, but she knew he missed his daughter and granddaughter a great deal.

"I'm not a sentimental man, Eve, but there are times that I do miss interacting with a child," was the way he'd put it. "Anytime you need an evening to yourself, I would be happy to look after Brooklyn."

So, when she'd had this idea of an evening of sizzling romance in the middle of what was judged by many to be the most hectic season of the year, his offer seemed perfect.

How was she to know that everything would come apart so quickly?

After patiently listening to her review Brooklyn's

routine, he'd taken the baby from her and then said, "Eve, I think you need to know something."

She had no idea why she'd felt an unsettling tightening within her stomach at his words. Still, despite the premonition, she definitely hadn't been prepared for what came next.

"What is it?" she'd asked him, her thoughts still racing around, checking off things she had listed only in her head.

Brooklyn began to fuss. He patted the baby on the back, rocking slightly as he stood before Eve. Brooklyn's fussing ceased almost instantly.

"I looked into a few things and I can assure you that you can stop worrying that Adam is going to revert back to drug dealing," he told her.

"Oh?" Her heart lodged itself in her throat. Adrenaline, masquerading as fear, filled her veins. "How can you make that kind of a claim? What have you heard?" she asked, curbing the urge at the last minute to ask, "What have you done?" instead.

To get into his narrative, Josiah backed up a little. "He was never a drug dealer to begin with," he told her, stunning her. "And his last name isn't Smythe. It's Serrano." He saw the uncertainty in her eyes and repeated the full name. "Adam Serrano."

Her head began to hurt. Where had he gathered all this information? He was a retired businessman. How did a retired businessman get this kind of information?

"How did you…?"

Josiah lifted his slight shoulders in a vague movement, then let them drop again. "I have friends who have friends."

Eve ran her fingertips over her forehead. The headache dancing just above her eyes was now imitating the sound of angry war drums. The throbbing made it difficult for her to absorb what Josiah was telling her.

With effort, she asked, "And what did these friends tell you?"

"That your Adam Smythe—Adam Serrano—is a DEA agent. It's not my practice to meddle," he added as a coda, "and I wouldn't have told you, except that I know how worried you've been that something might come up that would make Adam return to the unsavory life of a dealer. Now you know that he won't." He shifted Brooklyn slightly, moving her to his other shoulder. "You mean a great deal to me, Eve, and like it or not, with your father gone I feel a certain responsibility for your well-being. I'm sorry if I overstepped my place, but I just wanted to be sure that you weren't getting involved with someone who could really hurt you."

But I am. I did.

Eve could feel her heart breaking in half even as she struggled to smile at the older man. He meant well, but she would have really rather not have found this out now. Maybe later, definitely before, but not now when she had just managed to surmount her trust issues and gotten to a place where she felt she might just be able to move forward.

Still, none of this was Josiah's fault. "Thank you. I appreciate you looking out for me."

Gazing into her troubled eyes, Josiah couldn't help wondering if perhaps, despite her thanks, he had overstepped his ground and triggered something he should have left dormant. He wasn't sorry he'd looked into the matter, but he now regretted telling her he had.

With that in mind, he tried to do a little damage control. "The life of a law enforcement agent, especially when undercover, is not—"

She didn't want him to continue, or to make any excuses for Adam whatever-his-name-was. The information that Josiah had already given her made her feel numb all over.

"I understand."

Nothing had changed—and everything had changed. All she wanted to do was run, to bury herself somewhere. But there wasn't just her to consider anymore. She was a mother. She had responsibilities. Brooklyn came first, above everything else.

Eve pressed her lips together. "Look, if now isn't a good time—" She began to reach for the baby.

Josiah continued to hold the sleeping child against him. "Now is an excellent time," he told her. "Don't worry. I'm really quite good at this. I'll look after Brooklyn as if she were my own granddaughter."

There was no way she wanted to be alone with Adam now, much less spend a romantic evening with him. Betrayal wasn't an aphrodisiac.

"But—"

Josiah shook his head. "Not another word. You deserve a little time to yourself," he insisted. "Brooklyn will be here any time you want to come by to pick her up."

And with that, the former Special Agent closed the door.

Eve heard Josiah talking to the baby as if she were another adult. At any other time, it would have made her smile. But right now, she felt as if her very insides had been gutted.

With her heart feeling like a lead brick inside her chest, Eve turned away from house and went down the driveway to her car.

To drive to a place that no longer felt like home.

Adam had had an uneasy feeling weaving through him all day, and it was just getting bigger by the hour.

It had begun with a phone call. Danny Sederholm had seemed uncharacteristically jumpy when he called to talk to him. The usual irritating, cocky bravado the student displayed was absent. Sederholm had accidentally slipped and mentioned the head of the organization's name, Cesar Montoya, when he'd blurted out that the man was seeking another connection. It wasn't difficult for Adam to put two and two together and realize that the student was now viewing him as a threat.

It hadn't been easy, but he finally managed to convince Sederholm that he wasn't out to usurp him. That he was happy with the way things were and all he wanted was to be connected to a steady supply of cocaine, heroin and meth so that he could get back to his dealers.

Sederholm had sounded somewhat reassured when he hung up, but Adam knew that the college student could be easily swayed. If the next person Sederholm spoke to had a different spin on how things were going, the kid would buy into that. And then consequently, he might find himself in a heap of trouble.

This was getting old, Adam thought. He'd been pushing his luck for too long. It was definitely time to change the focus of his work. He needed a position within the department that didn't make him constantly feel as if he needed a shower.

Funny how things changed, he mused, getting into his car. His current life seemed to suit him, especially when he only had to think about himself. But it wasn't just him anymore and he didn't want it to be. He'd come to realize that he really wanted to be part of this new family unit. Wanted to come home to Eve and the baby not just for a little while, but on a regular, ongoing, permanent basis.

Eve.

Not for the first time today, he wondered what was up. She'd made a point of calling him this morning just before noon and saying that she didn't want him swinging by the clinic this afternoon. Instead, she wanted him to come to her house a little later than usual. She'd ended by saying that she had a surprise for him.

Just thinking about the conversation made him smile.

At the same time, his conscience nagged at him, the way it did more and more frequently these days. This charade couldn't go on. He needed to tell her exactly who he was. He knew it was against all company policy, but keeping her in the dark indefinitely wasn't right.

If he hoped to have a chance with her, he needed to let her know what he really did for a living. Not the undercover details, but everything that could be safely released without jeopardizing anyone else's life. He'd already made up his mind about coming clean.

His job was important, but if she wanted him to get out of law enforcement altogether he would do it. For her. He was no longer defined by his work. Something a great deal larger came into play now.

And once he made these changes, once he either left the department or at least took on another position, then maybe she would consider marrying him. Because his life, he'd come to realize, was incomplete without her and the baby.

He hadn't realized that he was just existing, not living, until he had something to compare it to. Eve made him feel alive in all the important ways that counted.

Whistling, he pulled up into her driveway. The garage was open and he saw her car parked inside. For the time being, he banked down all his other thoughts, along with that uneasy, nagging feeling at the back of his neck that told him something was wrong. He focused instead on the evening ahead.

An evening he was looking forward to spending with Eve and the baby.

Adam rang the doorbell and waited for a moment. When there was no answer, he rang again. He was about to knock when the door finally opened.

His eyes met hers and the greeting on his lips faded. The uneasy feeling that something was wrong was back. In spades.

Chapter 14

His survival instincts instantly kicked in. Especially when she didn't step back, didn't open the door any farther to let him in.

"What's wrong?" he asked tentatively.

Everything! her brain screamed.

When he stepped forward, she mechanically took a step back, thereby admitting him into the house when she hadn't really wanted to. Where did she begin? Eve silently demanded. She was so upset, so angry, that fragments of sentences crowded her mind.

One thought stood out.

Her eyes narrowed into angry, blazing slits. "You lied to me."

The accusation drove a chill down his spine. He scrambled to make sense of it. Was she talking about the past or something current? Had she found out about his dealing with Sederholm and taken it at face value, thinking he had reverted back to the life of a drug dealer?

Adam schooled himself to remain calm. Maybe this all had some sort of logical explanation he hadn't thought of yet.

"About?" he asked cautiously.

"About?" she echoed incredulously, stunned and furious at the same time. "Just exactly how many things do I have to choose from?"

So many you wouldn't believe it.

Out loud, he tried to select his words calmly, to keep from inciting her further. "I only meant that maybe there's been some mistake and that you—"

She jumped on the word. "Mistake? I'll say there's been a mistake."

Eve felt angry tears gathering in her eyes and she fisted her hands at her sides, willing them away. She wasn't about to cry in front of him. She absolutely refused to let him see how hurt she was.

"And I made it when I thought that you and I could actually put everything behind us and build something together. Have some kind of trust together. Shows what an idiot I am." Her eyes were all but shooting sparks. "Or maybe it shows how desperate I am to make our relationship work. And you, obviously, don't feel the same way." She waved her hand at the door he'd just closed behind him. "Please leave."

For a moment, he was absolutely speechless. Where had all this fury come from? "What?"

Eve ground out the words. "I said leave."

At a loss, he grasped at the first thing that came to his mind. "Is this some kind of postpartum depression you're going through?"

He couldn't have picked anything worse to say if he tried. It was akin to waving a huge red flag in front of her.

"Oh, just because I'm a woman, right away my feelings have to be pinned on a hormonal imbalance? Well, my hormones are fine, thank you very much. They're not the ones that betrayed me." Since he wouldn't do the right thing and go, she marched over to the front door and pulled it opened, repeating her terse instruction. "Please go. Now."

Instead of leaving, Adam jerked the door out of her hand and slammed it shut. "I'm not going anywhere until you tell me what the hell you're talking about." He chose his words deliberately. "If I'm being executed, I wanted to know what you think it is I've done."

Incensed, Eve glared at him. How could he pretend to be puzzled? Had everything with him been an act? The lovemaking, the endearing words, *everything,* just an act? *This is what he does for a living. He fools people. And you're the biggest fool of all.*

"You don't know?" The question dripped with a sarcasm she didn't know she was capable of.

He made it a point not to lose his temper because that caused him to lose his focus, but it was a definite struggle to hold on to right now.

"No," he said evenly, "I don't know. If I knew, I wouldn't be asking you what the hell you're talking about, I'd be explaining to you just why you're wrong," he told her, praying that this was just some kind of mix-up.

"The only wrong thing I did was to fall in love with you."

He stared at her, stunned. "Wait, hold it. You're in love with me?"

She hadn't meant for that to come out. Not like this, not now. "Don't let it go to your head." She waved an impatient hand at the statement. "It doesn't change anything. I can't trust you—"

"Yes, you can," he told her with feeling. She could trust him to love her, to protect her, to be there for her forever.

But she shook her head. Because she couldn't trust him, his words to the contrary were meaningless to her. "And you don't trust me."

He was still shadowboxing in the dark. She could be referring to so many issues, things he wasn't at liberty to talk to her about yet. But soon. Until then, she was going to have to stay in limbo—about everything. "It's not a matter of trust, Eve." She had to understand that, even if he couldn't allow her into his world completely.

"Then what is it a matter of?" she demanded. "If you trusted me, you would have been straight with me from the very beginning," she insisted.

He had to know that she wouldn't have told anyone. That she would have taken his secret to the grave because she knew it could mean his life. Instead, he chose to keep her in the dark, to make her think the worst of him. He'd robbed her of the joy of sharing the stages of pregnancy with him, of life, of their combined love, growing within her.

"Do you have any idea how hard it is to know that?" she cried. "That I don't mean enough to you for you to be straight with me? To have you let me into your life and let me know what's really going on?"

He still didn't know if she thought he'd gone back to drug dealing or if this was about something else. Had Sederholm somehow gotten to her? Told her something? No, that wouldn't have been his way. The scum would have taken her hostage, not talked with her.

He didn't want her thinking of him as a pusher, but what choice did he have? This was almost over and once it was, he was free to really plead his case. If she'd listen to him.

"I told you, it's not a matter of trust. There're other things at stake. Other people at stake." Oh, the hell with it. He couldn't bear the torment in her eyes. He took hold of her shoulders and cried, "I'm not a drug dealer, Eve."

She pulled free and her anger was as fierce as ever. "I know that."

He stared at her, completely stunned. "You know that?"

"Yes," she fairly shouted. "And not because you told me, although I really, really found it hard to believe that you'd turned over a new leaf—"

He needed to have something answered. There could be really bad repercussions to this. "Then what is this about?"

"What's this about?" she echoed incredulously. He had a hell of a nerve, pretending to be in the dark. "I'll tell you what this is all about. It's about you cutting me out of your life, out of everything that's going on. It's about you not telling me that you're a government agent," she shouted at him.

He stared at her in silence for a very long moment, replaying her words in his head. "You know?"

"Yes, I know," she spat back.

"How did you find out?"

Eve lifted her chin stubbornly. So now he had questions and she had the answers. She was tempted to taunt him and ask how it felt. But she wasn't certain if Josiah would have wanted his part in this revealed, and right now, she was feeling a great deal more loyal to the older man than she was to Adam.

"It doesn't matter how I found out. The important thing is that I did—and you weren't the one to tell me."

If she knew that he wasn't a drug dealer, why was she still shouting at him? It didn't make sense. "You're angry because I'm a government agent?"

Eve was stunned by his question. Did this man have cotton for brains? "I'm angry because you didn't *tell* me you were a government agent. You let me think you were a drug dealer."

"I couldn't compromise the operation."

She was far from placated by his answer. "But you could compromise me, what I thought of you? Do you know how many nights I spent agonizing over this? Over the fact that the father of my baby was a drug dealer? Doesn't it bother you that you could have righted everything by telling me what you were?"

Yes, it bothered him. But his hands were tied. If she knew and one of the people he was dealing with found out, a lot of lives could be lost. He couldn't take that chance.

"It wasn't my call."

He made it sound like some kind of a sporting event, not her life he was playing with. "Sorry, I didn't know the game plan ahead of time."

This wasn't getting them anywhere. He pushed past the blame portion and worked with what was. "Okay, so you know. Why are you so angry at me? I'm one of the good guys."

He might be that to others, but not to her. Not after what he'd done—or hadn't done. "No," she said very deliberately, "you are a liar. Can't you see, it doesn't matter if you're a good guy or a reformed bad guy, a lie is a lie. That's an absolute," she insisted. "And you told not one lie but two, maybe three. For all I know there are even more."

"I didn't—" Adam started to protest, but she held her hand up to stop the flow of words.

"How do I know that?" she demanded. "How do I *know* that you're not some triple agent? A bad guy pretending to be a good guy pretending to be a bad guy?"

She'd lost him for a moment. He tried to work his way backward. "Hold it—"

"No," she declared, "I won't hold it and I won't hold you. Now please, just leave," she implored, not knowing how much longer she could hold it together.

He wanted to give her some space, but he had a feeling if he walked out that door, it would be all over between them. "No, I won't leave until you tell me that we can work this out."

She shook her head, her hair bobbing about her face. "If I said that, then I would be lying just like you and I don't lie. Maybe that's stupid of me," she sniffled, "but I don't. Because I knew that a lie, *any* lie, compromises a relationship and casts doubts on it. You lied to me and now I don't know when to believe you or *if* to believe you. Fool me once, shame on you. Fool me twice, shame on me," she said, reiterating the familiar old adage. "I'm taking that to heart."

It couldn't end this way, not when he'd finally opened up his heart to someone. "Eve, please—"

But she wasn't about to be talked out of it. "I need time to think, to sort things through. I can't do it with you around."

He pressed his lips together. "Would it help if I told you I loved you?"

She didn't believe him. She wanted to, but she couldn't. "It would—if I felt I could believe you. But you could just be saying that because it's expedient right now."

He opened his mouth to argue with her, to profess his feelings more strongly, but just then, his cell phone rang. One glance at the illuminated screen told him he was getting a text message from Sederholm.

Adam bit off a curse when he saw that the deal was going down now.

She could see the struggle that was going on within him in his eyes. She made it easy for him—and for herself.

"You'd better take that," she told Adam. "It's obviously going to be more important than me."

He wanted to shout at her that nothing was more important to him than her, but he knew that the effort would be useless. He couldn't get through to her, not tonight, not given the way she felt. He'd already seen that the more he pushed, the more she resisted. As much as he didn't want to, he knew his only recourse was to pull back and let her calm down.

And then maybe, once this major drug drop came to

pass, he could devote all his attention to sorting things out *for* her.

"I'm going," he agreed. "But I'll be back." And that was a promise she could take to the bank, whether she believed him or not.

"Only if I want you to be," she informed him just before she slammed the door, cutting him off from her.

She leaned her head against the door, feeling drained. Feeling awful. God, what an idiot she'd been. Adam had to have thought of her as the most gullible person who had ever walked the earth.

Her heart ached even as she cursed him for complicating her life like this. She remained like that for a long moment, too numb to move, too unhappy to try.

Finally forcing herself to move, Eve looked at her watch. It was still early. Early enough to go pick up Brooklyn and bring her home. The thought bolstered her somewhat. She needed something to divert her, to keep her from dwelling on this overwhelming, terrible pain she felt.

Dialing Josiah's number on her cell phone, she grabbed her car keys and her purse.

He answered on the second ring. "Turner here."

"Hi, Josiah. It's Eve," she told him, heading for the front door. "There's been a change in plans. I'm coming over to pick up Brooklyn."

"Is something wrong, Eve?"

She might have known that Josiah would pick up on that. Before she could answer, the doorbell rang.

Damn it, why couldn't Adam just go away and leave her be? She didn't want to see him again, not tonight. Not for a long time.

"No, nothing's wrong," she bit off a little waspishly as she yanked open the door. Her attention switched to Adam. "Look, I said I just— Oh!"

"Eve, are you all right?" Josiah demanded. But there was no answer.

The phone had gone dead.

This didn't feel right.

The text message he'd received from Sederholm had summoned him to this location. The buy was supposed to go down within this warehouse he was standing in front of and there were no lights, no signs of life anywhere.

And, more telling, no sign of Sederholm's flashy silver Lexus convertible, the $68,000 gift, Sederholm had haughtily informed him, from the student's clueless parents for his twenty-first birthday last year.

It was a setup. It had to be.

But even as he drew out his weapon, slowly circling the perimeter of the abandoned warehouse that had once ironically housed a toy empire before it had gone bankrupt, Adam could see that something was off.

Gaining access through a side entrance that, by the looks of it, hadn't been used for some time, he moved about the darkened area slowly and cautiously. Every one of his senses was focused on the shadows as adrenaline went into high gear through his veins.

But there was no sound of breathing, no sound of movement anywhere within the warehouse. Not so much as a mouse or a rat.

Adam carefully made his way over every inch of the warehouse, moving from one wall to the other. Finding a light switch on the far wall, he held his breath and then threw it on. It wasn't powerful enough to illuminate the entire warehouse, but did highlight that he was alone.

Why would that cretin send him out on a wild goose chase?

And then it hit him. The scum had orchestrated exactly what he'd been afraid of. Sederholm had lured him away to get to Eve.

What other explanation was there?

He pulled out his cell phone to call her. But before he could, it rang in his hand. Fearing the worst, hoping for the best, he flipped it open and put it to his ear, still holding his weapon ready in his other hand.

"Hello?"

"Get back to her house!"

The voice barking the order had a slight accent. He'd only been in the man's company twice, but he recognized the voice immediately.

"Turner, what do you know?" Adam demanded.

But he found himself talking to no one. The line had gone dead. Adam didn't bother swallowing the curse that rose to his lips.

Shoving the cell phone back into his pocket, Adam quickly ran back to the rusted door that had been his point of entry into the warehouse.

Even as he flew to his vehicle, he couldn't contain the icy chill that zigzagged down his spine. He hadn't had a chance to ask Turner what this was all about, but even so, he knew.

Something was happening to Eve. And it was all his fault.

* * *

"Who the hell are you and what do you want?" Eve demanded with all the anger she could summon. The look in the young man's flat eyes made her blood run cold.

Sederholm shoved her back with the flat of his hand, while aiming his gun at her with his other. "I'm your boyfriend's playmate and I want to make sure that he doesn't think he can cut me out of the payoff that's coming." He looked around quickly to assure himself that it was just the two of them. "You think I don't know about him going behind my back, trying to make nice to my connection? *My* connection," he shouted, hitting his chest twice for emphasis. "And you're going to be my insurance policy."

She stalled for time. She'd been on the phone with Josiah. He must have heard her open the door to this stranger. If nothing else, he would be sending his driver out to check on her to see if everything was all right, the way he had when there'd been that minor earthquake in the spring.

All she needed was a split second to throw off this cocky-looking peacock. He was hardly more than a kid and she was certain he was a pushover. If he wasn't wielding a gun, she could have easily taken him, she thought, even if he had the advantage of height going for him. But her father had been thorough when she was about to go off to college and had insisted that she take lessons in self-defense. She just needed to separate this character from his weapon.

"Insurance policy against what?" she asked him, doing her best to sound interested as her mind raced around for a solution.

"I've been watching him. That bookstore owner seems to care a lot about you, sneaking off to see you when he should be working." He laid the cold steel gun barrel against her cheek, stroking it. "I'm going to make sure he thinks I'm going to hurt every pretty little hair on your head if he decides to get ahead of himself. Only room for one second-in-command and that's me."

The sound of a window opening in the rear of the house had Sederholm jerking her closer to him and wrapping an arm around her throat.

Chapter 15

The crazed intruder dragged her to the side, so that there was a wall at his back. His arm pressed down so hard against her clavicle, Eve thought she would choke to death. She could only think of Brooklyn.

Who was going to raise her daughter? Who was going to be there for the little girl when she was growing up? When she needed a mother?

She couldn't die. Her baby needed her.

Frantic, she thought of her dog, then remembered that the animal was sedated because she'd removed a benign tumor from her side. Why had she picked today of all days to do the procedure?

She had to *do* something! Clawing at her assailant's hand rather than his arm, Eve grabbed one of his fingers and bent it back as far as she could.

Sederholm howled in pain. "You bitch!" he screamed, then tightened his stranglehold even more.

Her head began to spin as she grew more and more light-headed. Desperate, she dug her nails into him. Cursing her, the man finally loosened his hold enough for her to gasp in air.

"Come on out, Smythe!" he called out. "I know you're here." His eyes scanned wildly about, unsure which way his target would enter. "Figured it out, did you? That I sent you on a wild goose chase so I could get to your whore. You're smarter than I thought. Too bad you're not as smart as me," he taunted. The almost maniacal smile disappeared as if it had never been there. "Get out here before I shoot her—because you know I will!"

Adam cursed silently.

He had to show himself. There was no other choice. Sederholm was insane enough to do just what he threatened: shoot Eve because he could.

Adam thought about coming out shooting, but he had no way of knowing exactly where Eve was in the room and he didn't want to risk hitting her. More than likely, the cowardly Sederholm held her in front of him like a shield.

Still armed, Adam positioned his weapon, ready to fire, as he emerged from the rear of the house. He saw Sederholm swing around, keeping Eve in front of him, the fireplace to his back.

"Let her go, Sederholm," he ordered, aiming his gun at the man's head. "She isn't part of this."

Sederholm shifted so that his head was partially blocked by Eve's. His voice dripped with cynicism and evil.

"Oh, on the contrary, Smythe. You care about her. That makes her a very big part of this—maybe the most important part of all."

Adam looked into Eve's eyes for a split second. Damn it, he should have never shown up on her doorstep. He should have ignored that e-mail that appeared on his computer and just concentrated on his job.

"I'm sorry," he told her.

It was too late for that. And she didn't blame him, anyway. But she needed assurance. "Just promise me you'll take care of Brooklyn."

"Brooklyn?" Sederholm interjected.

"My daughter," she responded when he jerked her hard, demanding an answer.

"Oh, right. The kid. How touching," he mocked. "What makes you think Adam here's going to be around to take care of anything?" He laid the muzzle of his gun against her temple and gazed at the man he believed was trying to take his place in the hierarchy. "Drop your gun, Smythe. Drop it or she's dead." He raised his eyebrows. "My finger feels a spasm coming on."

Terror filled her. Adam was her only chance of surviving this. "Don't do it, Adam," she pleaded. "He'll kill us both."

"Maybe," Sederholm commented. "Then again, maybe not. All depends on how I feel." His eyes challenged Adam. "I might let the pretty lady live. But not you, though. How's that for honesty?" he asked with a chilling grin. "Now put the damn gun down," he demanded, "or I swear she's dead."

Adam believed him. Very slowly, he bent his knees, placing his gun down in front of him.

"Good boy," Sederholm mocked. "Now kick it over here."

"No, don't do it, Adam," Eve cried. "Please—"

"How do you put up with this?" Sederholm asked, nodding at his hostage, his tone light as if they were two friends kicking back and shooting the breeze. Because he wanted to shut her up, Sederholm moved his arm from around her neck and quickly covered her mouth with his hand. "Now, where were we? Oh, right, I was going to shoot y—"

A shriek interrupted his sentence. Eve had bitten down on the fleshy part of his hand. Sederholm reacted automatically and pushed her from him. "You bitch!" he screamed, aiming at her.

The second Eve distracted Sederholm, Adam dived for his weapon. On the ground, his gun in his hand, Adam swiveled around, about to fire up at the drug dealer when a shot rang out through the living-room window.

Sederholm, his eyes opened wide in shock, sank down to his knees. Blood oozed from the hole between his eyes as he fell facedown on the floor.

Scrambling to his feet, adrenaline pumping, Adam whirled around toward the shattered window, ready to fire. He hadn't had time to call for any backup. This had to be Montoya, or one of the drug lord's underlings, cleaning up what had obviously become a liability for the cartel.

Out of the frying pan, into the fire. Adam backed up, using his body to shield Eve.

"You all right?" Adam tossed the question at her over his shoulder.

She struggled to keep from shaking. "Yes. But who just—?"

There was some kind of movement just beyond the window. "I think we're about to find out. Stay behind me," Adam ordered.

"Hey, don't shoot," someone called through the broken glass. "I'm not as fast as I used to be."

Eve's mouth dropped open. She recognized the voice even before the man came in. "Lucas?"

The rest of the glass from the shattered window rained into the room as it was summarily swept away. One hand raised in token surrender, Lucas came in through the window. He held a high-powered rifle in his other hand.

"That would be me," he said amiably. "Sorry about your window." He nodded toward the shattered glass on the floor. "But I didn't have time to pick my shot. I had to take what I could get."

Eve stared at the rifle. Josiah's driver seemed so comfortable with it. And there was no arguing that he was a dead shot. Wasn't anyone what they seemed?

She looked at Adam. "Is he with you?"

Adam slowly shook his head. "Not that I know of," he qualified. And then he grinned with relief. "But he can join my team anytime he wants."

Lucas laughed. "Thanks for the compliment, but I'm retired." As he spoke, he began disassembling his rifle.

This wasn't real, Eve couldn't help thinking as she watched Lucas reduce his weapon to a sum of its parts, placing each down on her coffee table. "You're not just a chauffeur, are you?"

Lucas raised his eyes to her face. "No, ma'am," he

said mildly, his fingers never missing a beat. "I'm also a cook, a social secretary whenever Mr. Turner needs one, and—"

"A sniper," Adam concluded, no question in his voice.

"No," Lucas replied easily, placing the last piece of his weaponry on the table. "I'm not a sniper. I *was* a sniper once upon a time," he admitted.

It was getting increasingly difficult to regulate her breathing. Any second now, she would need a paper bag to keep from hyperventilating.

"Does Josiah know?" Eve asked the tall, athletic man. But even as she asked, she had a feeling that she knew the answer.

Lucas's smile transformed his tanned, serious face into one belonging to a young man who enjoyed his life. "He knows."

"He sent you, didn't he?" Adam asked. It was time to get a hold of his handler. The situation could still be salvaged if they were fast enough. Digging into his pocket, he took out his phone and flipped it open.

Lucas nodded. "Mr. Turner would have come himself," he told Eve, "but his vision isn't what it used to be—and someone had to stay with the baby. I'll be right back," he promised.

Opening the front door, he stepped out for a moment. The next moment, Lucas was back, carrying what appeared to be a leather case. Laying it on the coffee table next to the rifle parts, he quickly packed the separate pieces of his weapon into it.

"If you won't be needing anything else," Lucas said, addressing his words to both of them, "I'll be getting back to the house. Mr. Turner will be anxious to debrief me."

"No, we're fine," Adam assured the older man with feeling. "Thanks to you."

Lucas smiled his thanks for the compliment and silently left.

Shaken, Eve sank down on the closest available flat surface, in this case, the coffee table. Rather than complete his call, Adam looked at her with concern. He put his hand on her shoulder. "Are you sure you're all right?"

"Peachy," she replied mechanically, staring at the inert form on her floor. "I've got a dead man in my living room, my oldest client has a driver who carries around a rifle that breaks up into tiny pieces, and my baby's father shoots people for a living." She took a deep breath and then let it out again. Nothing got better. "I've fallen down the rabbit hole and I can't get out."

Hugh could wait a few minutes. Adam closed his phone and shoved it back into his pocket. Sitting down beside Eve, he put his arm around her shoulders. She'd been through a lot tonight and he had no idea how to make it up to her.

"I'm sorry you got tangled up in this. I never wanted to get to this point, never wanted to get involved with you," he told her honestly, "because I was afraid this could happen."

She glanced up sharply, her mind still swimming. "You *knew* Lucas was going to shoot that awful man through my window?"

"No, but I was afraid that Sederholm might think of me as a threat instead of a connection to more markets and want to find some kind of leverage to use against me." He was sorrier than he could ever express. "And you were that leverage."

"Just shows-to-go-ya," she quipped, "that you can't map out everything." Eve paused a second. "Now what?"

That part was rather clear to him. "Now I call my handler and tell him what went down and then we see what we can do to salvage the sting."

Sederholm had dropped the head man's name without realizing it. It wouldn't take much for their reformed computer hacker to find where the man was staying. Once they had that information, he'd go to Montoya and make a pitch, saying he had eliminated the middle man, in this case Sederholm, and wanted to do business with the head of the cartel directly. If Montoya bought the story, the end result could still be the same.

Eve listened quietly to Adam's answer. She hadn't been talking about the operation when she'd asked. "Now what?" referred to the future of their relationship. But obviously, she and Brooklyn were far down on his list of priorities.

Eve couldn't help wondering if she'd been part of his cover. Pride kept her from asking.

"Well, good luck with that," she said as brightly as she could, standing up on very shaky legs. Her eyes were drawn to the body of the man who had come close to ter-minating her life. "Do you do clean up?" she asked Adam.

Adam took his cell phone out again. "Just getting to that."

She nodded. "Good."

Placing the call, Adam didn't notice that she clenched her fists to her sides. Eve did her best not to unleash any of the emotions running rampant through her. Because if they came out, she had no idea if she could ever bank them down again.

Because she didn't want to return to an empty house with the baby in the middle of the night, Eve waited until morning before she drove to Josiah's house to pick up her daughter. Once her arms were safely around the baby, she couldn't keep the question back any longer.

"Who are you, Josiah?"

The older man regarded her with as much of a smile as she had ever seen on his lips. "I'm your friend, Eve."

She wasn't about to engage in some sort of verbal dance, she was still much too drained from last night. "Besides that."

He considered a moment before replying, "A retired gentleman."

Not good enough. "Who was once a navy SEAL?" she demanded. "A commando?" she supplied when he made no answer. "What?"

Josiah was silent, as if debating what, if anything, to say and if so, how much. Finally, he said, "I spent time in Special Ops and then came to work for the Bureau in a rather, shall we say, unique capacity."

It had the ring of truth about it, even if a little bizarre. "Did Lucas work in the same 'unique' capacity?"

By the oddly amused expression on Josiah's face, she knew she was asking too many questions. But she needed to know. "If you're asking if that's where I met him, the answer's yes."

"Are you still part of that…'unique' capacity?" she asked.

Josiah began to laugh. "Oh, my, no. But I do believe

that one's skills should be exercised every so often, just to keep them primed, you know." Rising, he touched her elbow, urging her to the guest bedroom where Brooklyn was sleeping. "Now take your lovely daughter and go home, Eve," he coaxed. "Lucas will follow you to make sure you get there."

"Lucas doesn't have to follow me, Josiah. I can get there on my own," she assured him. And then she paused. "Thank you for sending Lucas to my rescue."

The small shoulders lifted in a careless shrug as he walked her to the front door. "I thought your young man might need help."

So that's how Adam had managed to appear just then. Josiah had sent him, as well. "You called Adam to tell him what was going on?"

He looked at her as if to ask why she would even question such a thing. "It was only right."

Incredible. She tilted her head and kissed the older man's cheek. "Thank you."

Josiah lightly brushed the tips of his fingers along the area where she had kissed him. "My pleasure entirely, my dear," he told her with as much feeling as she'd ever heard him display.

It was over.

After months of waiting, months of preparing, months of constantly looking over his shoulder and, near the end, almost losing Eve, it was finally over.

And this time, at least, Adam thought, the good guys won.

Even so, it felt almost anticlimactic.

He supposed that was because for him, it had all

come to a head the other night, when that worthless waste of human skin had almost killed Eve. Just remembering made his stomach feel as if it was in the middle of a deadly typhoon.

Damn, but he'd earned his paycheck tonight, delivering the head man, not to mention a hell of a lot of kilos of heroin, to his boss. A lot of spoiled rich kids would have to rough it for a while, doing without their customary high.

Ordinarily, that would make *him* feel high. But he'd moved beyond that, beyond the rush a good bust brought with it. Now, in order to get that effect, he needed to have Eve beside him. Eve, making love with him. Eve, just being.

He needed to make that happen. He'd left the meeting early, letting the others celebrate. He had somewhere else to be.

As he took a sharp right, he automatically swung his hand out to keep the pizza box on the passenger seat from tumbling upside down onto the floor of the car. He didn't even remember most of the trip. He was fixated on the end goal. He hadn't spoken to her since he'd helped one of the lab boys clear out Sederholm's body. That was two days ago.

Two days felt like an eternity.

By the time he arrived at Eve's house, his heart was pounding a hell of a lot harder than it had when the final bust went down this afternoon.

Because this meant more to him.

"Here goes nothing," he murmured under his breath as he pulled up to her driveway and got out. Or rather, *everything,* he amended.

Taking the pizza box out of the car, he carried it to the front door. When he rang the doorbell, he called out, "Pizza delivery."

He was about to ring it again when the door opened.

Eve, barefoot and wearing jeans and a T-shirt, stood in the doorway, the door slightly ajar. "I didn't order any—" When she saw who it was, her mouth dropped opened. "Oh."

"No, you didn't order any," he agreed, striving to get back some of the initial charm he was supposed to have had. "But I thought you might want to celebrate."

She slanted a look at him. "Just what is it that I'm celebrating?"

"Well, the almost perfect drug bust for one," he told her. He knew it sounded like a boast, but he deserved to give himself a little praise. "As of this afternoon, there's going to be a lot less heroin on the street, at least for the time being."

"You said 'for one,'" she reminded him. "What's 'for two?'"

He studied her for a long moment. For two cents, he'd sweep her into his arms and just head for the hills. But he knew she'd never be happy with that. She thrived in crowds, around people. And he loved anything that made Eve Eve.

"Two is a little trickier," he admitted.

Now he had her curious. "What is it?" she wanted to know.

He put his hand up, as if to say all in good time. "Before I answer that, I need to spread these out."

Eve watched as he laid out what looked like old report cards on the kitchen table. Her eyes narrowed as she looked at the one closest to her. "Are those report cards?"

"Yes. Mine," he added before she could ask.

Just to verify the unusual claim, Eve picked one up and glanced over it. It was his all right. And he was a fairly decent student, she noted. She put the card back on the counter. "Why are you showing me your old report cards?"

"So you can see that I mean it when I tell you that for you, I intend my life to be an open book. I'll show you anything you want to look at," he promised. "No more secrets, Eve. Not from you. I want you to know everything there is to know about me."

This all sounded well and good, but she wasn't going to allow herself to get carried away or let her imagination run wild. She wanted everything spelled out.

"Because?" she prodded.

"Because," he began evenly, "then you can't use the excuse that I'm keeping things from you."

He certainly didn't believe in shooting straight from the shoulder. "And why would I want an excuse?"

"To use in case you want to turn me down," he told her, hating the very thought.

She almost felt like throwing up her hands. Almost. "You know, maybe it's your secret agent mentality that makes you think this convoluted way, but I've always found that the simplest path between two points is a straight line. Draw me a straight line, Adam," she implored. "What are you trying to say?"

"Actually," he corrected, "I'm trying to *ask* something."

She dug deep for patience. "Okay, what are you trying to ask? Spit it out, Adam," she ordered briskly.

So he did. "Will you marry me?"

It took her a second to come to. A second more to breathe evenly. "That depends."

He didn't understand. "On what?"

"On who's asking me," she told him, then specified her problem. "Is it Adam Smythe or Adam Serrano who wants to marry me?"

"It's just me," he told her softly, taking her hand and placing it against his heart. "Adam. Just Adam. And just so you know," he interjected before she could answer, "no matter what your answer is, I plan to love you for the rest of my life."

She could feel her heart melting in her chest.

"Well, Just Adam," she began, smiling at him, "I can't see how I can resist a proposal like that."

He laughed and hugged her close. "I was hoping you'd see it that way. Any chance that I could have a do-over on that romantic evening you were planning for us the other night?"

"You mean the night your little playdate pal tried to kill me?"

He had the good grace to wince. "That's the one."

Eve wrapped her arms around his neck and raised her face up to his. Her eyes were smiling. "Every chance in the world."

"That's what I wanted to hear," Adam murmured just before he sealed the deal with a long, soulful kiss that promised to go on forever.

And nearly did.

Epilogue

Laura Delaney pushed herself away from her computer for a moment. Not to get up, just to reflect.

A very self-satisfied smile curved her lips as she closed her eyes and savored the message she'd just read in her private e-mail account. The one that she still maintained for communications that involved the life she had once led, not her life now. Her contact at the CIA had just informed her that not only had Adam Serrrano shown up on Eve's doorstep to take responsibility for the child she was carrying, he'd actually helped deliver said child and then stuck around to marry Eve. The two now appeared to be the very definition of happiness.

Mission accomplished.

She'd never thought the old, familiar term would

feel so good to her. Sound so good to her. Heaven knew that she didn't regret leaving the Company. But she did miss that sense that all was right with the world that came over her when a mission resolved itself well. That feeling was there now, in spades. She'd set out to reunite Eve with her lover and she had. Moreover, it had turned out even better than she'd hoped. The magic that had brought them together in the first place hadn't faded. It had only grown stronger, despite the obstacles.

Would that ever happen to her? She'd like to think so, but she was realistic enough to know that most likely, she would never get the chance to find out. Finding the location of the father of her son had proven to be impossible up until now. There was no reason to believe that would change despite her efforts and the combined efforts of her old friends at the Company. God knew she'd tried.

Don't spoil your mood. You did good. Maybe, just maybe, if you put your mind to it, you can do good again. You seem to have a lot better luck locating unsuspecting fathers when they don't directly involve you.

Laura smiled again and opened her eyes. It was late, but she wasn't sleepy. Jeremy was tucked away in bed, sleeping like a little rock and she didn't much feel like watching TV tonight. The holiday season presented nothing but reruns on its schedule tonight.

Time to see if she could get lightning to strike twice.

Pulling up close to the computer again, she went back to the Web site she'd originally set up to network with other single mothers. She was curious to see if there was anything in her in-box.

A few strokes brought her to the right location. She

moved her cursor over the e-mail button and clicked it. The screen filled up with unread mail.

Settling in, Laura smiled to herself. Time to get busy. MysteryMom had work to do.

* * * * *

THE COWBOY'S
SECRET TWINS

BY
CARLA CASSIDY

Carla Cassidy is an award-winning author who has written more than fifty novels. Carla believes the only thing better than curling up with a good book to read is sitting down at the computer with a good story to write. She's looking forward to writing many more books and bringing hours of pleasure to readers.

Chapter 1

Melissa Monroe couldn't help but wonder if she was making a huge mistake. A fierce case of déjà vu filled her as she drove the Texas road. The lonely highway, the snow coming down from the overcast sky and the Christmas carols playing on the car radio all evoked memories of the last time Melissa had driven on this particular road.

It had been just a little over a year ago, only at that time the snow hadn't been comprised of pretty little flakes lazily drifting down, but rather a blizzard whiteout condition that had eventually forced her to pull over.

A sexy stranger in tight jeans and a cowboy hat had rescued her. He'd told her his name was James and they'd ridden out the storm together in a vacant farmhouse.

It had been a wild and crazy night and she'd acted completely out of character. The consequences of her actions that night were in two car seats in the back.

Joey and James, who were a little over four months old, had been completely unplanned and unexpected, but since the moment she'd realized she was pregnant, they had been desperately wanted and loved.

She glanced back now to check on them and smiled. Snug as bugs they were in their little blue coats and matching hats. They'd been sleeping for the better part of an hour and Melissa hoped to get where she was going before they woke up demanding another meal.

Thirty minutes ago she'd passed the place in the road where she'd had to pull over during the storm a year ago. It was just outside the small town of Rockport, Texas. She was now ten minutes from the Texas town of Dalhart and her final destination.

On that night a year ago she'd been on her way from her home in Amarillo to visit a friend in Oklahoma. Tonight she was on her way to someplace just on the other side of Dalhart.

Tightening her hands on the steering wheel, she hoped she wasn't on some kind of a wild-goose chase. Suddenly all kinds of doubts crashed through her mind. Maybe she was a fool to trust her cyber friend, a woman she'd never met in person but had bonded with over the past year in a chat room for single moms.

MysteryMom had been a source of support, information and friendship over the past year. She'd helped Melissa through the difficult pregnancy. Then once the twins were born she'd been a font of advice on everything from colic to diaper rash.

MysteryMom and Melissa's best friend, Caitlin, were the only two people on earth who knew about the circumstances of the twins' conception.

Melissa suspected that MysteryMom had given her directions to her place, that she was bringing Melissa to her home for a face-to-face meeting and to spend the holidays together.

For the past couple of weeks Melissa had been depressed. Christmas was only four days away—the twins' first Christmas—and she hadn't even had any extra cash to buy a tree or a single present.

She'd always dreamed of giving her children the kind of Christmas she'd never had, with family gathered close and laughter in the air. It wasn't all about a lack of money that had depressed her, but certainly financial worries played a role.

She'd been working at building her own interior design business when she'd found herself pregnant. The pregnancy had been difficult and the business had fallen by the wayside. Since the twins' birth Melissa had been living on her savings, which were dwindling fast.

It had been all she could handle to take care of newborns, but after the first of the year she was determined to somehow provide for them and delve back into her work.

She slowed as she reached the Dalhart city limits. According to the directions MysteryMom had sent her she was to turn off the main highway and onto a country road approximately ten miles from where she was now.

With a new burst of nervous tension kicking up inside her, she pulled into a restaurant parking lot and grabbed her cell phone from her purse and punched in Caitlin's number.

"Are you there yet?" Caitlin asked when she answered.

"According to the map I'm about fifteen minutes from the place," Melissa replied.

"How's the weather? I heard they were calling for snow."

"It's been spitting a bit, but nothing to worry me," Melissa replied.

"I don't know why you just didn't plan on coming to my place for Christmas instead of taking off on this adventure of yours."

Melissa smiled into the phone. "You're going to have so many fancy parties to attend, the last thing you need is me and the boys hanging around." Caitlin was single and gorgeous and working up the corporate ladder at blinding speed. "Besides, look what happened the last time I was on my way to visit you."

"It's not my fault you got stuck in a blizzard and then decided to kick it with some sexy stranger."

"True, it wasn't your fault. I've decided it was all Tom's fault," Melissa replied and tried to ignore the faint pang of her heart at the thought of her ex-boyfriend.

"Ah, don't even mention that snake's name," Caitlin replied. "I thought he was a creep when you first starting dating him and he definitely proved me right."

"Water under the bridge," Melissa replied. "Anyway, I just wanted to check in with you and let you know I'm almost there."

"You'll call me when you arrive? Tell me all about this MysteryMom of yours?"

"Definitely."

"And, Melissa, I hope you have an amazing Christmas. You deserve it."

Melissa put her cell phone back in her purse and pulled her car back on the road. Dusk was falling and she was eager to get to her destination before dark.

As she drove her mind filled with thoughts of Tom Watters. She'd thought they'd marry and build a family together and after two years of dating she'd begun to press him about setting a wedding date. He'd finally told her there wasn't going to be a wedding, that for the past six months he'd been involved with another woman, one who was much sexier, much more a woman than Melissa.

Once again she clenched her hands on the steering wheel as she thought of that moment. She'd immediately made plans to visit Caitlin, needing to get away from her dismal apartment and all reminders of Tom.

Reeling not only with a broken heart, but also with a damaged ego, she'd been easy pickings for the handsome stranger who had come to her aid.

Her cheeks burned hot as she remembered that night of unexpected passion. James had looked at her with such desire. He'd made her feel so sexy, so wanted. She'd never before experienced that kind of wild abandon and suspected she'd never experience it again.

She cast all these thoughts aside as she drew nearer to the road her directions told her to take. As she left the small town of Dalhart behind, she spied the highway sign where she needed to turn.

In approximately ten miles she should be at the destination that she suspected was MysteryMom's home. Excitement danced in her chest as she thought of finally coming face-to-face with the woman who had been not only a friend, but also a surrogate mom through the trials and tribulations of being a single new mother to twins.

If she didn't like the looks of the place she'd turn around and make the two-and-a-half-hour drive back home. If she got any bad vibes at all, she'd just drive away. There was no way she'd put her babies or herself at risk.

The first surprise was the enormous stone monuments that marked the entry to the address she sought. The second surprise was when she drove down the tree-lined narrow drive and got her first glimpse of the house. No, *house* was too plain a word for the mansion that rose into view.

The two-story home was as big as a hotel, with several equally impressive outbuildings. Lights spilled with a cheerful welcome from several of the windows as the evening had begun to thicken with night shadows.

"Oh, my goodness," she whispered to herself. The whole place breathed money.

As she drove up the circular driveway she saw that one of the outbuildings was a stable and she was more convinced than ever that this was MysteryMom's house. MysteryMom had mentioned that she loved working with horses.

She parked the car and glanced into the backseat where Joey was awake. Of the two boys, Joey was the most laid-back. He rarely fussed and seemed content to take life as it came at him.

On the other hand, James was a handful. Demanding and impatient, he was the first to set up a frustrated cry if he needed a diaper change or a meal or if she took away his beloved rattle. But, he also had begun to belly laugh when happy and the sound of it never failed to delight her.

She looked at Joey, who gazed at her with bright blue eyes. "Are you ready to go meet Mommy's new friend?" she asked. He waved his arms as if to show his excitement.

As she got out of the car she realized it had grown darker, as if night hadn't just stealthily approached but had rather slammed down without warning.

She opened the door to the backseat and first unbuckled Joey and pulled him up on her hip, then went to the other door and did the same with James. In the past four months she'd become quite adept at not only carrying both boys, but also her purse and a diaper bag all at the same time.

The cold air chased her to the front door, where she managed to use her toe to knock. Her heart hammered with excitement as she waited for MysteryMom to answer. When the door opened her excitement transformed to stunned surprise.

He filled the doorway with his broad shoulders and lean hips, and his blue eyes widened with the same shock that she felt. His gaze swept over the two babies in her arms and his face paled.

James.

For a moment her mind refused to accept what she saw. "Henry? Who's here?" a feminine voice called from somewhere in the house.

Two thoughts flew into Melissa's head. Apparently his name wasn't James and he must be married. Oh, God, this was all a mistake. A terrible mistake.

Before she could take a step backward, before she could even move a muscle, a ping sounded next to her and the wood of the doorjamb splintered apart.

Everything seemed to happen in slow motion. Another ping resounded and James or Henry or whatever his name was leaned forward, grabbed her and pulled her inside the house. He slammed the door behind them.

"Call the sheriff," he yelled. "Somebody is shooting at the house." He opened a drawer in the ornate sideboard in the entry, pulled out a gun, then without a backward glance at her, disappeared out the front door.

Melissa stood in the center of the entry, her heart

banging frantically. Mistake. This was all some sort of horrible mistake.

What kind of a man was her babies' father that somebody shot at the house the minute he'd opened his door? Was he a drug dealer? A criminal of some kind?

As Joey and James began to cry, Melissa fought back tears of her own.

Henry Randolf clung to the shadows of the house as he tried to discern exactly where the shooter might be. He thought the attack had come from the stand of trees directly in front of the house.

As he moved forward he tried not to think about the woman who had appeared on his doorstep. Melissa, that was her name. She'd crossed his thoughts often over the past year, but he couldn't think about her now or the two babies she held in her arms. He couldn't afford to get distracted while somebody with a gun was on his property.

One problem at a time, he told himself. The shooter first, then he'd have to figure out what to do about his unexpected visitor.

He clenched his gun tightly as he worked his way to the stand of trees, listening for a sound, seeking a shadow that would indicate where the attacker might be. As he thought of how close those bullets had come to Melissa and those babies, a slow seething rage built up inside him.

This wasn't the first time he'd been shot at in the past week. Three days ago he'd been riding his horse across the pasture and somebody had taken a potshot at him. His mount had reared and taken off for the stables as Henry had pulled his gun to defend himself from the unknown.

He was still outside checking the area when the sheriff's car pulled up. Sheriff Jimmy Harrick lumbered out of his patrol car like a sleepy bear exiting a favorite cave. He pulled his collar up against the cold night air as Henry approached him.

"I've checked the area. There's nobody around now. The shots came from that stand of trees over there but it's too dark to see if there's any shell casings or evidence."

He pointed toward the house. "Let's go inside and talk." Henry didn't wait for a reply but headed for the door. He hadn't felt the cold when he'd first burst outside, but now the damp December air seeped into his bones.

"Got company?" Jimmy asked as they passed the older model car in the driveway.

"Yeah, an old friend." Henry's stomach kicked with nerves as he thought of the woman who had stood on his doorstep carrying twins who looked remarkably like he had when he'd been a baby.

Damn, what mess had he gotten himself into? He had a feeling his life was about to get extremely complicated.

As he and the sheriff walked into the living room he saw Melissa seated next to his mother on the sofa, each of them with a baby in their arms.

Melissa's blue eyes were wide with fear. He couldn't blame her. There was nothing like a welcoming committee of bullets to put that expression in a woman's eyes.

Henry tore his gaze from Melissa and focused on the sheriff. "Something's got to be done, Jimmy. This is the second time somebody has taken potshots at me in the past week."

Jimmy shoved his meaty hands in his pockets and rocked back on his heels. "I'm not sure what to do about it, Henry. There's no question that you've made some enemies with your decision to run for mayor."

"And so it's okay for somebody to try to kill me? Because they don't like my politics?" Henry was acutely aware of Melissa listening to every word, watching him with those amazing eyes of hers.

Jimmy pulled his hands out of his pockets. "Now, you know that's not what I'm saying," he protested. "I'm going back out there with my flashlight and I'll take a look around, then I'll head back to town and start asking questions. I'll let you know if I find anything. If I don't then I'll give you a call sometime tomorrow."

"Fine," Henry said curtly. He knew nothing more could be done tonight and in any case he was having a difficult time thinking about anything but the woman who sat next to his mother.

He walked Jimmy to the door, then closed and locked it and drew a deep breath to steady himself. How had she found him? They'd only exchanged first names on that crazy night they'd shared a little over a year ago and he hadn't even given her his real first name.

And then there were those babies. Henry had decided he was never going to marry and he'd certainly never planned to be a father, but there was little question in his mind about the paternity of those twins. Now he had to figure out what he was going to do about it.

He returned to the living room, where the two women on the sofa didn't appear to have moved, although Melissa and the two little boys no longer wore their coats.

His mother had that look on her face she used to get when he was a kid and had done something he knew he shouldn't do. He definitely had some explaining to do.

She stood and walked over to him and thrust the baby she held into his arms. "I'm retiring to my room. It appears you and Melissa have a lot to talk about."

The little boy smelled of baby powder and gazed up at him with curious blue eyes. As Henry stared down at him the little boy's lips curved up in a sweet smile.

"That's Joey," Melissa said. "And I have James." She said the name with forced emphasis and he remembered that the night they'd been together he'd told her his name was James.

That night he hadn't wanted to be the wealthy Henry James Randolf III. He'd just wanted to be an ordinary cowboy named James. "My name is Henry. Henry James Randolf," he said.

As he looked at her several things struck him. She was still as pretty as he'd remembered her with her long blond hair and those big blue eyes, but she seemed tired and stressed.

Her cheeks grew pink beneath his scrutiny. "I don't quite know what to say. I didn't expect you."

He frowned and tightened his grip on Joey, who wiggled like a little worm. "What do you mean, you didn't expect me? You came here. You knocked on my door. Who else would you be expecting?" He sat in a chair across from the sofa as Joey leaned his head against his chest. To Henry's surprise his heart knocked hard.

"I thought I was coming to spend the holiday with a woman I met last year on the computer." Once again her cheeks warmed with color. "We met in a chat room for single pregnant women and she's been a wonderful source of support through my pregnancy and single parenting. She goes by the name of MysteryMom. She gave me this address, e-mailed me directions and told me to come here."

He eyed her suspiciously. The story certainly didn't have any ring of truth to it. "And how did she find me?"

Melissa raised a hand that trembled slightly to tuck a strand of shiny hair behind her ear. "I don't know. When we first got close I told her about the blizzard in Rockport and you coming to my rescue. All I knew about you was that your name was James and that you drove a black pickup with a license plate number that started with tin."

TIN-MAN, that's what his plate read. An old girl-friend who had proclaimed that he had no heart had dared him to get the personalized plate, and he never backed down from a dare.

"When I first realized I was pregnant," she contin-ued, "I went back to Rockport and asked around about you, but nobody had any clue who you might be. Somebody tried to kill you."

He blinked at the unexpected change of topic. "I think it was a warning, not a real attempt on my life. Our current mayor was diagnosed with cancer and has decided to resign. The city council has called an emergency election to be held in two months. I decided to run for the position and somebody apparently doesn't like my politics."

James began to fuss, waving his fists in the air and kicking his legs. "They're hungry," Melissa said. "If you could just show me to the kitchen, I'll fix them bottles, then we'll be on our way."

"On your way? You can't leave now," he protested. "It's dark and getting later by the minute and I don't know if the person who fired that gun earlier is really gone from the area." He stood with Joey in his arms. "You'll stay here tonight and we can discuss everything further in the morning."

She stood and gazed at him with somber eyes. "You haven't even questioned if they're yours or not."

For the first time since he'd opened his door to her, he offered her a smile. "They look just like me. They even have my cleft chin. And I know we used no protection that night."

"I'm not here to cause you any trouble," she replied.

Henry nodded, although he wasn't so sure about that. "Let's go into the kitchen and get those bottles ready," he said.

Time would tell if she had really been led to his

doorstep by some mystery cyber friend or if she was just another woman who had recognized who he was on the night of the blizzard and had found a way to cash in on the Randolf fortune.

Chapter 2

Melissa snuggled down in the bed in a guest room fit for a princess. The twins were sound asleep in an old playpen that Henry had found in the attic. It had been dusted off and the padding covered with a crisp, clean sheet. The boys were clad in their pajamas and sleeping beneath a cashmere throw that was as soft as a cloud.

She'd called Caitlin just to let her friend know that everything was all right and that it hadn't been Mystery-Mom's home she'd come to, but rather the man who was the father of her boys. She'd promised to let Caitlin know everything that happened when she returned home in the morning.

She was exhausted now, but sleep refused to come.

The night had been filled with far too many surprises. The first had certainly been the sight of Henry as he'd opened the door. The second had been the bullets that had come precariously close to both her and her babies.

Even after the trauma of the shooting had passed she hadn't been able to get a read on Henry. He'd said little as he'd helped her bottle-feed the boys. She knew he had to be as stunned to see her as she'd been to see him.

They hadn't spoken much, just attended to the boys' needs, then he'd shown her to her room for the night with the promise that they'd talk further in the morning.

She didn't know what would happen. She had no idea what to expect from him, if he intended to be part of the boys' lives or not.

She'd resigned herself at the time of their birth to the fact that Joey and James wouldn't know their real father. At least now she wouldn't have to tell them the humiliating story of how she'd gotten pregnant by a stranger in a vacant farmhouse during the middle of a snowstorm.

MysteryMom must have somehow traced him with the partial license plate letters Melissa had mentioned. She obviously had resources Melissa didn't have. If MysteryMom had hoped for some kind of happy ending for Melissa, she was functioning in the world of make-believe.

Despite the intimate night they'd shared, Melissa and Henry didn't know each other at all. He hadn't even given her his real name that night.

Certainly he was in a social position to date all kinds

of sophisticated, successful women. And the last thing Melissa was looking for was a man in her life.

Tom's betrayal still burned bright in her heart and if that wasn't enough, she had two little boys to raise. She didn't want a man. She didn't want anything from Henry, except for him to be a father for her boys.

She'd been hoping to spend Christmas someplace where the spirit of the holiday was everywhere. There was no sign of Christmas in the Randolf home and in any case she didn't belong here.

First thing in the morning she'd be on her way back home to her little apartment and maybe on the way home she'd stop at a discount store and buy one of those little metal trees in celebration of the twins' first Christmas.

She finally fell asleep and dreamed of that night with Henry in front of the fire he'd built to warm them through the snowy night. The heat of the flames had been nothing compared to the fire in his kisses, the warmth of his hands on her body.

When she woke up bright sunshine drifted through her bedroom window, not the faint light of dawn she was used to, but full sunlight that let her know it was late.

The boys!

She shot up and looked at the playpen. It was empty. She jumped out of bed and yanked on her robe. Henry had gotten her suitcase from the trunk of her car the night before despite her protests that the gunman might still be out there lying in wait for him. She'd held her breath until he was back in the house safe and sound.

Now her breath caught once again in her throat as she raced out of the bedroom and down the grand staircase to the lower level of the house.

She heard voices coming from the formal dining room and headed there, her heart beating frantically as all kinds of irrational fears whirled through her head. She flew into the room and stopped short.

The boys were in their car seats on the polished mahogany wood of the huge table. Henry's mother, Mary, stood in front of them, shaking a rattle at first one, then at the other as they bubbled with laughter.

"Melissa," Mary said with a smile that faltered as Melissa sagged against the doorjamb. "Oh, dear, we frightened you, didn't we?"

"I woke up and they were gone. I wasn't sure what to think." Melissa's heart slowed its frantic pace.

"It was Henry's idea really," Mary said. "You looked so tired last night and he thought it would be nice if you got to sleep in a bit this morning. So we sneaked into your room around dawn and grabbed these two little bundles of love and brought them down here. We gave them each a bottle and then I gave them a little sponge bath and changed their clothes. I hope you don't mind."

Melissa wanted to be angry that they'd obviously riffled through the diaper bag and taken her boys from their bed. But the look on Mary's face as she gazed at the twins made it impossible for Melissa to maintain anger. Besides, if she were perfectly honest with herself the extra couple of hours of sleep had been glorious.

"You know, I never thought I'd live to see grand-babies. Henry is quite the confirmed bachelor so I'd resigned myself to the fact that there would probably never be grandchildren." She smiled at the twins. "But these two are like gifts from heaven."

Melissa smiled. "You haven't changed one of their messy diapers yet. That might change your mind about gifts from heaven."

Mary laughed. "Oh good, you have a sense of humor. I'm so glad. And now if you'll get dressed I'll have Etta make you some breakfast. Henry and I have already eaten."

"Oh, that's not necessary," Melissa replied. "I'm not much of a breakfast person and besides, I'd like to get back on the road as soon as possible." She not only wanted to get back to Amarillo, but she was still deter-mined to stop someplace on the way home and pick up a few things to bring Christmas to her tiny apartment.

At that moment Henry appeared in the opposite doorway. He seemed bigger than life, his presence sucking some of the oxygen out of the air.

He looked like the rugged, handsome cowboy she'd met on the road that night. Clad in a pair of fitted jeans and a flannel shirt that emphasized the width of his broad shoulders, he let his gaze sweep the length of her before he smiled and said good morning. Even though he smiled, his eyes remained shuttered, enigmatic.

Melissa was suddenly aware of the fact that her robe was tatty and frayed and her hair was probably sticking out in every direction. She hadn't even washed her face before hurrying down the stairs.

"I'm just going to run upstairs and shower. I'll be right back."

"When you come back down I'd like to have a talk with you," Henry said.

She nodded and backed out of the dining room then escaped back up the stairs. There had been an edge in Henry's tone of voice when he'd said he wanted to talk to her that worried her.

This whole trip had been a nightmare. The unexpected presence of a man she'd never thought she'd see again, bullets splintering a door and now the promise of a conversation she had a feeling she didn't want to have.

He was probably going to tell her to take her babies and leave, that being a dad didn't fit into his lavish single lifestyle. And even though that was fine with her, it made her heart hurt just a little bit for her sons.

She knew what it was like to grow up without a father. She remembered the empty ache his absence had created inside her and she certainly hadn't consciously chosen that for her boys.

Minutes later, as she stood under a hot spray of water she found herself again wondering what MysteryMom had hoped to accomplish by leading her here. Of course it would be nice for the boys to have a father in their lives. She wanted that for them. But she wasn't in control of Henry's reaction to instant parenthood.

Mary had said he was a confirmed bachelor. It was definitely possible a bachelor wouldn't want to be saddled with two little boys who required a lot of time and attention.

By the time she'd finished her shower and dressed, nervous energy bounced around in her stomach. She certainly didn't know Henry well enough to second-guess what he might want to discuss with her, but it didn't take a rocket scientist to know that it had something to do with Joey and James.

Despite the night of desire they'd shared, since the moment she'd arrived at this mansion Henry frightened her more than a little bit. Oh, she wasn't physically frightened of him. What scared her most was the fear of him rejecting his sons, sons that he'd never wanted and had never asked for.

When she returned downstairs Mary had the boys on their tummies on a blanket in the living room. She smiled at Melissa. "That James, he's a feisty one, isn't he? He reminds me of Henry when he was a baby. Demanding and impatient, there's going to be no holding him back when he starts to walk."

James arched his back, raised himself up and grinned at Melissa, as if relishing the very idea of being independent and mobile. Meanwhile, Joey rolled over onto his back, perfectly content to play with his fingers.

"It must be hard, being a single parent to twins," Mary said.

"I manage okay," Melissa replied with a touch of defensiveness.

"I'm sure you do, dear. Henry is waiting for you in the study," Mary said. "It's down the hall and the first door on your right."

Melissa nodded and with one last look at her contented boys, she went down the hall to the study. The door was closed and she knocked on it with a gentle tap.

She heard him tell her to come in and she opened the door. Henry sat behind a massive mahogany desk and although he smiled at her as she stepped into the room, it did nothing to alleviate her nervousness.

The study was as beautifully appointed as the other rooms in the house. A stone fireplace took up one wall and floor-to-ceiling bookcases filled another. "Melissa, please have a seat." He gestured to the chair in front of the desk. She sank down and tried not to be intimidated by the surroundings, by him.

"Mom said you were eager to get on the road and head home, but I wanted to talk to you about the possibility of you staying through Christmas," he said.

"Oh, I'm not sure…" She paused as he held up a hand to stop whatever she was about to say.

"We're forever linked now by those boys and despite the fact that we had that night together, I don't know anything about you."

Oh, but he did, she thought. He knew she liked to be kissed just below her ear, that if he stroked her breasts she moaned deep in the back of her throat. A whisper of longing swept through her as she remembered that night and him. She forced herself to focus on what he was saying.

"We stopped having anything to celebrate at Christmastime three years ago when my father unexpectedly died of a heart attack on Christmas Day. Since then Christmas each year has slid by with little celebration in this house. But this year we have something to celebrate. The twins. I'd like to give them a terrific first Christmas, so please tell me you'll stay."

Her first instinct was relief, that he wasn't casting the boys out and that he apparently wanted to get to know them better. Still, there was one thing that made her relief short-lived. "I have to be honest. I haven't forgotten those bullets that flew when I arrived here," she said. "I don't want to put Joey and James in harm's way." She fought against a shiver as she thought of the bullets that had come far too close to them the night before.

"I feel more comfortable with you here rather than going back outside," he replied. "Somebody is being a nuisance, obviously attempting to make me rethink my position in running for mayor, but I won't let any harm come to you or the children."

She considered his words thoughtfully and believed him. There was something solid about him, a strength in his eyes that let her know he wouldn't allow danger to come to her or her babies.

He was their father and all he was asking was for her to remain a couple more days. Surely there was no harm in that, in giving him and his mother the first Christmas with the boys.

"Okay," she finally replied. "We'll stay through the holiday." She had no idea if it were the right thing to do or if it was possible she was making a terrible mistake.

A wave of satisfaction swept through Henry at her reply. From the moment she'd stepped into the study he'd smelled her, a familiar scent of fresh flowers with a hint of vanilla. It was the same fragrance she'd worn the night they'd been snowbound together and it stirred all kinds of crazy memories inside him.

As she stood and tucked a strand of hair behind her ear he remembered how soft, how silky her hair had been beneath his touch. That wasn't all he remembered. There was the taste of her mouth open to his, the spill of her warm, full breasts into his palms and the moans that had escaped her at his every touch. Desire slammed into his stomach, hot and wild and completely unexpected.

He had no idea if he trusted her, hadn't spent enough time with her to know if he even liked her, but that didn't stop him from wanting a repeat of what they'd shared on that snowy night.

"Good. We'll make it a Christmas to remember," he said and stood.

She backed toward the doorway, as if eager to escape him. "I'm going to take the boys upstairs for their morning naps. I'll see you later."

"Melissa," he said, stopping her before she could

disappear from the room. "I don't even know your last name."

She smiled, the first real smile he'd seen from her, and the gesture lit her up from the inside out. "Monroe. Melissa Monroe."

The minute Melissa left the study Henry leaned back in his chair and gazed thoughtfully out the window. From this vantage point he could see the carriage house in the distance. It was a two-bedroom self-contained cottage that was occasionally used as guest quarters.

Henry had been living there before his father's death. His heart constricted as he thought about his dad. Not a day went by that Henry didn't miss him. Big Henry, as he'd been called, had not only been father, but he'd also been friend and mentor to his only son. The two of them had worked side by side running Randolf Enterprises, which was comprised of not only the ranch but also oil wells and enormous financial holdings.

There were people in town who were threatened not only by the financial power Henry possessed, but also by his decision to run for the position of mayor and clean up the corruption he knew ran rife through the city offices of Dalhart.

He had a couple suspicions of who might have taken those shots at him, but suspicions didn't work for an arrest. He also suspected that whoever had shot at him hadn't really tried to kill him but rather was just warning him, hoping he'd decide not to run for mayor.

Those gunshots didn't scare him half as much as the

idea that Melissa might not allow him to be as big a part of the boys' lives as he wanted.

"Henry?" His mother entered the study, her features worried. "Is she going to stay?" She sat in front of him in the chair that Melissa had vacated.

"She didn't tell you?"

"I was in the kitchen speaking with Etta about dinner. Melissa took the babies and went upstairs before I got a chance to ask her."

"She's staying until after Christmas." He leaned forward. "I don't quite know what to make of her. The story she told me about some cyber friend giving her directions here sounded more than a little bit shady."

"You think she's after money?"

"It certainly looks like she could use it." He frowned as he thought of the rusted old car out front, the frayed robe that had hugged her curves that morning.

Mary leaned back in her chair and folded her hands in her lap. "You want to tell me how this happened?"

Henry grinned at her. "You need a lesson in biology?"

She scowled at him. "You know what I mean, Henry. I've never heard you mention this woman's name before and yet she shows up here with two babies who are obviously yours."

"Remember the blizzard we had at the beginning of December last year? The night I couldn't get home from Hilary's because of the whiteout conditions?"

"That was the night you broke up with that woman."

Henry nodded. "I was on my way home when the

conditions got impossible to drive in. As I pulled over to the side of the road I saw another car there and Melissa was inside. I had no idea how bad the weather was going to get and I'd just passed the old Miller place and knew it was vacant, so I got her out of her car and we holed up there for the night."

Mary raised a hand. "That's all I need to know about the particulars. Is it possible she knew who you were?"

Henry pulled a hand down his lower jaw. "I don't know. I suppose anything is possible. I've always been so careful. I've always recognized how vulnerable I was to gold diggers."

Mary arched an eyebrow upward. "Need we mention Hilary's name?"

Henry smiled as he thought of the woman he'd been dating and had broken up with the afternoon of the blizzard that had brought him and Melissa together.

"Hilary might be a gold digger, but she never kept that fact a secret," he replied. Since the day of their breakup the attractive brunette hadn't stopped waging her battle to become Mrs. Henry Randolf III. She called him or came by at least once a week in an attempt to seduce him back into her arms.

Mary straightened her back and sniffed indignantly. "That woman couldn't wait to marry you and have me shut up in a nursing home someplace. The evil witch."

And that had been the very reason Henry had broken up with Hilary. It was at the moment she mentioned that she thought it would be uncomfortable living with Mary and that Hilary had been searching for a nice nursing home for the older woman when Henry had recognized there would never be a future with her and certainly not a marriage.

"You don't have to worry about that," he said to his mother. Once again he leaned back in his chair and cast his gaze out the window.

"I never really thought about having kids," he said softly. "But now that they exist I want them here with me. I want them to grow up here on the ranch and learn the family business. I want to teach them like Dad taught me."

"Aren't you forgetting one little thing? Melissa might not want to move here. She might have a perfectly fine life, perhaps with a boyfriend or family of her own."

Henry frowned thoughtfully. "I find that hard to believe. I mean, according to her story she took off from her home to meet some cyber friend and spend Christmas with her. If Melissa has family or a boyfriend, why didn't she stay home to spend Christmas with them?"

"I'm sure I don't know. You know her better than I do. But, Henry, you have to remember that just because you want something doesn't mean you can have it. You're talking about a woman here, not a business deal."

Mary stood. "All I know is that I intend to enjoy each and every minute of having those babies in this house. And now I'm going to go make a shopping list. There's only two shopping days left before Christmas and suddenly I'm in the mood to shop."

She practically floated out of the study. Henry hadn't seen his mother this happy since his father had been alive.

Even though he'd had the entire night to process the fact that he was now a father, he still wasn't sure how this was all going to work. The first thing he would have to do was get to know Melissa, find out if she'd come here looking for easy street or if the story she'd told him was true.

But before he could do that he had some phone calls to make. He'd promised Melissa a Christmas to remember and Henry never broke a promise.

His mother was wrong about one thing—this *was* a business deal. Melissa had what Henry wanted and all Henry had to figure out was what price he'd have to pay to get it.

Chapter 3

Melissa stood at the window and watched as a car pulled up out front and Mary got into the car's passenger side. When the vehicle pulled away Melissa wondered if she should be doing the same thing—driving out the main gates and heading for home.

Behind her in the playpen the two boys had just fallen asleep. They usually napped for about an hour in the morning and the same amount of time in the afternoon.

Restless energy coursed through Melissa and she moved to the window on the opposite side of the room to gaze out at the pastures, corrals and outbuildings on the land. In the distance she could see what appeared to be a carriage house.

The dusting of snow that had fallen the evening before had melted beneath the warmth of the sunshine. It was a beautiful day, cold but clear.

A whisper of noise whirled her around and she saw Henry standing just outside the room in the hallway. He motioned to her and she left the room. "I thought maybe while the boys napped you might want to have a cup of coffee with me. I'd like to get to know you, Melissa."

Once again nervous energy fluttered in her chest. Of course he wanted to know her better. She was the mother of his children. "And I'd like to get to know you better," she agreed. "Coffee sounds wonderful."

She checked on the boys to make sure they were still asleep, then followed him down the staircase to the dining room where Etta, the Randolf cook, carried in a tray laden with two cups of coffee, cream and sugar and two small plates with slices of cinnamon coffee cake.

Henry introduced the older woman to Melissa. "Etta has been keeping the Randolf family well fed for the past twenty years."

"And it's been a pleasure," Etta replied. Then with a friendly smile at Melissa she turned and left the dining room.

Melissa pulled a coffee cup before her and wrapped her fingers around it. As Henry watched her she felt ill at ease and wasn't sure what to say, where to begin.

"This is awkward, isn't it?" he finally said.

She flashed him a grateful smile. At least he felt it, too. "Terribly awkward," she agreed. "I know you have no reason to believe me, but it's important to me that you know that I don't just fall into bed with strangers I meet."

She couldn't hold his gaze and instead looked down at her coffee as she continued. "That morning the man I'd been dating for two years, the man I thought I was going to marry, let me know that he had found a new girlfriend, somebody sexier than me." She felt her cheeks warm with her confession. "That night I just… It all went more than a little crazy."

He laughed, a low chuckle that was both pleasant and surprising. She looked up at him sharply, wondering if he were laughing at her.

"It seems fate had a hand in our meeting that night. I was coming home after ending a relationship with a woman I'd been dating for over a year. Maybe we were both a little reckless that night."

"But that's not who I am," she replied. "I'm usually not reckless."

He took a sip of his coffee, eyeing her over the rim of his cup. "And yet you took off with an address to an unknown place given to you by a woman you've never met before."

"A calculated risk," she replied. "If I didn't like the looks of the place when I arrived, I wasn't going to stop." She tugged on a strand of her hair in frustration. "Okay, it wasn't the brightest thing in the world to do," she conceded.

She wasn't about to tell him that it was an aching loneliness that had driven her to meet MysteryMom.

Although she loved her boys more than anything else on the face of the earth, she'd been hungry for adult conversation. The idea of spending the holiday alone had depressed her.

She reached for one of the plates and a fork. Whenever she was nervous she wanted to eat and it was impossible to ignore the heavenly scent of the cinnamon that wafted from the coffee cake.

"Okay, let's start with the basics," he said. "Henry James Randolf, thirty-five years old, rancher and oilman. I'm a Taurus. I like my steak rare and sunrise rides on my horse. I've been told that I'm stubborn but I don't necessarily see that as a fault. I'm not a big drinker but I do like a glass of scotch or brandy in the evenings. Now, your turn."

"Melissa Sue Monroe, thirty years old. I'm a Libra and I like my steak well-done. Before I got pregnant I was working to build my own interior design business. I've never been on a horse and my drink of choice is an occasional glass of wine. Oh, and I've been told I have a bit of a stubborn streak, too."

He smiled, although she noticed that the gesture didn't quite warm the blue of his eyes. "What about family?" he asked.

She shook her head and paused to take a bite of the cake. "I don't have any. My father left when I was five, told my mother he wasn't cut out for family life. I never saw him again. My mother passed away two years ago and since then it's just been me…and of course, the boys."

"You have friends who give you emotional support?"

"My best friend lives in Oklahoma, so I don't see her very often. As far as other friends, to be honest the birth of the twins has pretty much put an end to any social life for me."

"How's your interior design business?"

She considered lying. She thought about telling him that she was wildly successful, but he was obviously an intelligent man. He only had to take a glance at her car and note the worn condition of her clothing to know that the money wasn't rolling into her household.

"Nonexistent," she finally said. "The pregnancy was difficult and for the last three months of it, I couldn't work. Since then it's been just as difficult. The boys have required all my time and energy." She raised her chin. "But after the holidays I'm going to try to get back to work."

She took a sip of her coffee and wished he didn't smell exactly like she remembered from that snowy night, a scent of clean male and wintry air and a faint whisper of spicy cologne. It was a fragrance that stirred her with memories of warm hands and hot kisses.

"How have you been supporting yourself?" he asked.

"I had a small inheritance from my mother." She shifted positions beneath the intensity of his stare and took another bite of her coffee cake.

"You have a boyfriend? Somebody significant in your life?"

A small laugh burst from her. "Definitely not. The only males in my life wear diapers and drool."

This time the smile that curved his lips warmed the blue of his eyes. "At least they're cute when they drool." His smile faded. "I'm sorry I wasn't there to help through the pregnancy. I'm sorry you had to go through it all alone and I promise you won't be doing it all alone now."

She wasn't sure why his words, rather than comforting her, filled her with a new burst of apprehension. Maybe if she really knew him, knew what kind of a man he was, she wouldn't feel so worried about what he might have in mind for her and the boys.

"Having grown up without a father figure in my life, I understand how important the role of father is and will be to my boys. I want you to know that I'm open to a discussion about visitation for you," she said.

"There will be time to discuss the particulars of that over the next couple of days," he replied. He took a sip of his coffee and leaned back in his chair. "So, are you originally from Amarillo?"

She nodded. "Born and raised there." This was the kind of talk they might have had if they'd been on a date, the kind they should have had that night instead of falling on each other like two sex-starved teenagers.

"Do you have somebody special in your life? A woman you're seeing? I don't want my presence here to make any problems for you," she said.

"You don't have to worry. There's nobody special. I don't intend for there ever to be anyone special." There was a firm finality in his voice.

She took another sip of her coffee. God, the man was

so good-looking she couldn't imagine the women in the area leaving him alone. "Your mother mentioned that you were a confirmed bachelor."

"I am. The only reason I might have entertained the idea of marriage would have been to have a son to pass the ranch to when I died. You've managed to give me two without the nuisance of a marriage."

Nuisance of marriage? Funny how different they were, Melissa thought. She'd wanted to be married for a very long time, had always thought that by the time she turned thirty she'd be part of a family like she'd never had growing up.

She still hoped for that someday. The only difference her dream had from reality was that in reality her boys would have their real daddy and then maybe eventually they'd have a loving, caring stepfather.

But at the moment, any kind of relationship with a man seemed impossible. She was just too tired to even think about romance. She'd been tired for months, not that she minded. The twins were more than worth any exhaustion they caused.

"You look tired, Melissa," he said as if he'd read her thoughts. "I hope you'll take your time here and allow my mother and me to help so that you can get some extra rest. It can't be easy dealing with twins all by yourself."

"I'm fine," she assured him. "It's gotten easier since they sleep through the night most of the time now."

"Still, I hope you'll let us take some of the burden for the next couple of days."

"They aren't a burden. They're my joy," she exclaimed a bit more vehemently than the situation warranted.

He leaned forward and reached out and brushed the corner of her mouth. "You had a little cinnamon," he said as he pulled his hand back.

She grabbed a napkin and wiped her mouth and tried to ignore the electric jolt his touch had shot through her body. *He just swiped your mouth,* she told herself. A simple, casual touch and yet she felt it from head to toe.

A loud knock sounded on the front door and he pushed back from the table. "You might want to come with me to answer it," he said. "I think it's for you."

"For me? Who would be here for me?" She got up from the table and followed him to the front door.

He looked outside, then smiled and this time his smile warmed her completely. "It's Christmas, Melissa. Christmas has officially arrived at the Randolf house."

Henry opened the door to allow in the four ranch hands who maneuvered a huge evergreen tree through the door. The boughs were tied down and Hank and Tim, the ranch hands bringing up the rear, carried between them a huge pot to stand the tree in.

"It was the biggest one old man Keller had on his lot," Charlie said as they carried the tree into the living room.

"Melissa, can you help me move the coffee table?" Henry asked.

She quickly grabbed one side and he grabbed the

other. They moved the table out of the men's way. "Just set it up in the corner," he instructed.

"That's the biggest tree I've ever seen," Melissa said, her eyes round with wonder.

Henry smiled. "I told them to get the biggest one they could find. We'll decorate it this evening after dinner."

"We could string popcorn and cranberries." She flushed and shook her head as if irritated with herself. "That was silly of me. I'm sure you have lovely expensive ornaments."

He could tell she was embarrassed and he found that oddly endearing. "Actually, I've always wanted to do a tree the old-fashioned way. I think it would be fun to string popcorn and cranberries."

The look she gave him was so sweet, so grateful, that he once again felt a stir of desire deep in the pit of his stomach. When he'd brushed the trace of cinnamon from her lip moments earlier, he'd wanted to kiss it off.

He focused on watching his men wrestle the tree into the stand. Something about Melissa touched him, a vulnerability, a wistfulness in her eyes that he hadn't seen in a woman's eyes for a very long time.

He still didn't trust her. The only woman Henry really trusted was his mother, who had no ulterior motive for loving him. Any other woman he'd ever allowed close had ultimately shown herself to be more interested in the Randolf fortune than in whatever Henry could offer her as a man.

He didn't know if perhaps Melissa was just smarter

than them all and had managed to trap him like none
of the other women had managed to do.

Once the men had the tree up and the ropes off, Henry
introduced Melissa to them. "These are some of the best
ranch hands in the state of Texas," he said. "That's Hank
and Tim, Ben and Mike and Jacob and that rascal with
the black hat is Charlie, my right-hand man."

Melissa's eyes had glazed over and he smiled at her.
"Don't worry, there won't be a test later," he said.

She laughed and the sound of her musical laughter
shot a rivulet of warmth through him. "Good, because
you lost me at Hank." She smiled at all the men. "But
it's nice to meet you all."

"I'll be right back," Henry said to her as the men
began to head for the front door.

In the entry he touched Charlie's shoulder and
motioned for Charlie to stay behind while the rest of
them got back to their work.

"You heard about the shots fired last night?" he asked.

Charlie nodded. "Jimmy talked to a couple of us
late yesterday evening."

"I want all of you armed while on the property until
we know what's going on," Henry said. "And I'd like
to work a couple of you in shifts so that somebody is
always working the house. Talk to the men and see
what kind of schedule you can arrange."

Charlie's eyes narrowed. "You looking for more
trouble?"

Henry released a small sigh of frustration. "To be

honest, I'm not sure what I'm looking for, but twice now somebody has taken potshots at me and I don't like the idea of anyone on my property attacking me or mine."

"We'll work out a schedule and I'll get it to you this afternoon," Charlie replied.

"Thanks, Charlie. I really appreciate it," Henry replied.

"It's no problem. We can't let the boss get hurt." With these words he stepped out the door.

Henry watched him catch up to the other men. Charlie was a good worker, always pitching in for even the dirtiest jobs. When Henry had broken up with Hilary he'd worried that he was going to lose Charlie. Hilary was Charlie's sister and Henry had feared that Charlie might feel compelled to stop working for him because of sibling loyalty. But Charlie had assured him that he wasn't going anywhere and that he didn't get involved in his sister's affairs.

Henry had gotten the impression that there was no love lost between the two. In any case, he was grateful that he hadn't lost Charlie. Good workers were hard to find.

In fact, he was going to have to let Hank go. He'd noticed the tall, thin man had smelled like a brewery despite the fact it wasn't even lunchtime. Henry had already warned him twice about drinking on the job. There wouldn't be any more warnings.

He closed the front door and returned to the living room to find Melissa gone. She'd apparently gone upstairs to check on the twins. He walked over to the large floor-to-ceiling windows and gazed out to the outbuildings in the distance. The tree was only the first of the deliveries that would take place over the next two days.

The brief conversation he'd had with her over coffee had told him exactly what he needed to know. She had no family and he suspected she had few friends. That would make what he had in mind much easier. All he had to do was convince Melissa that his plan was in the best interest of them all.

He looked up as he heard the sound of her coming down the stairs, a baby on each hip. He hurried to meet her halfway and took one of the boys from her.

As he scooped the little one from her arms he tried not to notice the warmth of her body, that scent of her that half dizzied him with memories.

"Which one do I have?" he asked.

"Joey," she replied.

"How can you tell the difference?" The little boy snuggled against Henry's chest, as if aware that he was held in loving arms. Once again the heart that Henry didn't know he possessed filled with a strange wonder and a fierce sense of protectiveness.

"Once you get to know them better, it's easy to tell them apart by their personalities," she said as they hit the landing. "But the quickest way is that Joey has a tiny scar in his right eyebrow. He was reluctant to be born and the doctor had to use forceps."

Henry looked at the little boy in his arms and noticed the tiny scar at the corner of his eyebrow. Joey grinned up at him and reached for his nose. Henry laughed as he dodged the little hand.

James kicked his feet and wailed, his face turning red as Melissa wrestled with him. "He's hungry and he has no manners," she said.

"Ah, a boy after my own heart," Henry replied. "Let's go to the kitchen and get them some lunch."

The kitchen was a huge room although Henry and Mary rarely took meals there. This was Etta's space but it was also the easiest place to feed two hungry little boys.

Etta was in the process of preparing lunch, but smiled with welcome as they all entered. Henry got the car seats that were serving as high chairs and placed them in the center of the large oak table, Once the boys were settled he watched Melissa prepare two small bowls of cereal.

As she approached the table he held out his hand for one of the bowls.

"You might want to put on a hazmat suit," she warned as she gave him one of the bowls and a small baby spoon. "They not only like to eat cereal, they also like to blow it and spit it and play in it."

Feeding Joey was a pleasure like Henry had never known before. The kitchen filled with laughter as he and Melissa spooned cereal into their waiting mouths, off the front of their shirts and themselves.

"Well. this sounds like fun," Mary exclaimed as she came into the kitchen.

"Ah, the shopper is home," Henry said as he wiped off Joey's face then handed him his bottle.

"Randy is putting my purchases upstairs in my room." She smiled at Melissa. "It's been far too long since this house had such laughter in it. And the tree, it's going to be just lovely."

"Melissa thought it would be fun to string popcorn and cranberries for the tree," Henry said.

Mary clapped her hands together. "What a lovely idea. We'll have a real old-fashioned tree trimming. I'll make hot cocoa and we'll play Christmas music and have such fun."

Melissa looked from Mary to Henry. "You both are so kind," she said and once again he saw a touch of vulnerability in the depths of her eyes.

"Nonsense, you're family now," Mary replied.

But she wasn't family, Henry thought. She was still a stranger. And she would never really be family, he mentally added. Sure, he had a strong physical attraction to her and she was the mother of his boys, but she would never be anything more than that to him.

His father had spent a lot of years warning Henry about the women who would want him for his money, women like Hilary who would turn themselves into whatever he wanted or needed to access the kind of lifestyle he could provide for them. As far as his father was concerned, aside from his wife, Mary, women were cunning creatures to avoid except for the occasional physical release, and then only if protection was used.

"I was lucky, boy," his father would often say. "I was

poor as a church mouse when I met your mother. I never had to worry about if she loved me for my money or for myself. You won't have that luxury. You'll never really know if a woman loves you or your money."

He knew without a doubt that Melissa hadn't set out to seduce him that night. There was no way she could have orchestrated the blizzard and the two of them being on the road at the same time in the same place.

What he didn't know was that once fate had placed them in that position, had she recognized him and taken a calculated risk of getting pregnant? It had been a mutual seduction that night. She'd been as willing a participant as he had been.

He frowned thoughtfully as he watched her coo and sweet-talk the two little boys. But if that was the case, if she'd recognized him that night before she'd slept with him, why hadn't she contacted him the minute she realized she was pregnant? Maybe she'd been afraid he'd talk her into an abortion.

One thing was clear. Henry wanted his boys living here with him and he would achieve that goal with or without Melissa's help.

Chapter 4

The afternoon seemed to fly by. Melissa was shocked when two baby cribs were delivered and Henry had them set up in the room across from hers. And the beds weren't all. High chairs were also delivered, fancy high chairs that seated infants then changed to accommodate toddlers, along with boxes and packages in all shapes and sizes.

"This isn't necessary," she'd protested. "We're only going to be here a couple of days."

"Then things will be more comfortable for the couple of days that you're here," Henry had replied.

Dinner was a pleasant meal with the boys happily seated in their new high chairs and most of the conversation between Mary and Melissa. Henry had been quiet, watching Melissa with an enigmatic gaze that made her overly self-conscious and more than a little bit nervous.

After dinner they all gathered in the living room for the tree-trimming party. Mary supplied thick thread and needles to string the popcorn and cranberries that Etta provided, and Henry carried the two high chairs into the room and placed the boys in the seats.

"Why don't I put the lights on while you two make the garland?" Henry asked.

Mary smiled at Melissa. "He'd do anything to get out of using a needle and thread."

"Sewing is a woman's work," Henry replied.

"Stubborn and a male chauvinist, what a surprise," Melissa exclaimed.

"I'm not a male chauvinist," he protested. "I just don't like needles."

"Okay, then stubborn and a bit of a wuss," Melissa replied teasingly.

Mary laughed in delight. "Finally, a woman who can put you in your place, Henry."

Henry looked at Melissa and in the depths of his eyes she saw a flicker of heat that stirred something wild and hot inside her.

"Ouch!" she exclaimed as she pricked her finger with the needle. She instantly put her finger in her mouth and Henry's eyes flamed brighter.

"And that's why I don't like needles," he finally said and turned his attention to the string of Christmas lights.

There was definitely something between them, she thought. Something hot and hungry. She wasn't in love with him, didn't know him well enough to gauge exactly what she thought of him. But there was no denying the strong physical attraction that existed between them.

"I always wanted to do a tree like this," Mary said. "Old-fashioned and simple. Big Henry was into flash and gaudy." A soft smile curved her lips. "That man wouldn't know simple if it tapped him on the head."

"You miss him," Melissa said.

Mary leaned back against the sofa cushion, the smile still lingering on her lips. "He was stubborn as a mule, ridiculously opinionated and could make a saint weep with frustration, but yes, I miss him each and every day." She tapped her heart with a finger. "But he's still with me in here."

That's what Melissa wanted, what Mary and Big Henry had apparently shared, a love that would last through eternity. "I'm so sorry for your loss," she said and covered Mary's hand with hers.

Mary smiled and gave her hand a squeeze and then released it and began to string popcorn once again. "Thank you. I'm just sorry he's not here now to meet his grandsons. He would have been so pleased to know that there will be another generation."

"I'm going into town tomorrow and thought you might like to take the ride with me, Melissa," Henry said. "Mom can babysit the boys for an hour or so."

"I'd be happy to do that," Mary agreed.

"Oh, I don't know," Melissa said hesitantly. She'd never left the boys for a minute since their births.

"I promise I won't beat them or chain them to their beds," Mary said gently.

Melissa laughed. "That never entered my mind." She looked at Henry. "Aren't you afraid to go out? I mean it was just last night that somebody shot at you…at us."

"I won't be a prisoner in my own house," he said with a tone of steel in his voice. "Besides, I've got my men watching the grounds and we'll be safe in town. Nobody would risk trying to hurt me with so many other people around."

Melissa was torn. She was reluctant to leave the boys for any amount of time, yet there was a tiny simmer of excitement as she thought of an hour or two without them. The idea of a trip into town was appealing, but she was surprised by how cavalier he was about somebody trying to hurt him.

"I keep telling you that I don't believe my life is really in danger, that I think somebody is just trying to aggravate me, trying to manipulate me into throwing in the towel on my plans to be mayor," he said.

"Okay, I'll go with you," she finally said, unsure if it was just another reckless decision on her part.

"Good. We'll plan on going after breakfast and we'll be home before lunchtime," he replied.

"It will be fine, dear." Mary reached over and patted

Melissa's hand. "I remember the first time I left Henry with somebody. He was just about the twins' age and Big Henry had decided I needed a night out. I must have called home a dozen times to check on Henry in the two hours we were gone. Big Henry finally decided to bring me home."

Melissa smiled. "They're getting to the age where if you blink you feel like you've missed a first."

"I've already missed too many firsts," Henry said with a touch of vehemence.

He would make a good father, Melissa thought. Whenever he looked at the boys she saw a fierce love shining from his eyes. As crazy as it sounded, there was a tiny part of her that wished that same expression were in his eyes whenever he gazed at her.

She recognized the foolishness of such a wish. He was a confirmed bachelor and in any case he was the kind of man who could choose from a harem of successful, beautiful women if he ever did decide to end his bachelorhood.

She'd be a fool to entertain any kind of happily-ever-after ideas where Henry was concerned. He was right in that they were forever bound because of the boys, but the ties that bound them would be dual parenting and nothing more.

When the phone rang Henry went to answer, leaving Mary and Melissa alone. Melissa looked at the woman who had been so kind to her.

"I can't imagine what you must think of me," she said.

Mary smiled. "I certainly wouldn't want anyone to look at some of the things I've done in my life and make a judgment. I'm not about to do that to you."

"I appreciate that," Melissa replied gratefully.

As Melissa thought about all the ways coming here could have been so terrible, she was even more grateful to Mary and to Henry for their welcome, for embracing the boys and her into their home.

As Henry came back into the room James exploded in one of his rich belly laughs. Henry froze, the look on his face one of sheer wonder and delight.

"What's so funny, little man?" he asked as he leaned down and picked up the rattle James had dropped. He handed the rattle back to James, and James promptly threw it on the floor once again and looked at Henry and laughed. Henry laughed as well and picked up the rattle and once again gave it to James, who tossed it over the edge of the high chair tray yet again.

Melissa laughed. "That's his new game and he'll play as long as you will."

Henry's eyes sparkled with a new warmth she hadn't seen there before. "They're amazing, aren't they? It's obvious already that they're smart."

Melissa smiled. It was fun to see him being a proud daddy, certain that his boys were more intelligent and cuter than any other babies on the face of the earth.

The rest of the evening passed quickly. They drank hot cocoa and strung the popcorn and cranberry garlands on the tree, then added tinsel and ornaments that had been in the Randolf family for years.

Mary knew the history of each and every ornament and Melissa was entranced by the stories she told.

"I picked these up while I was out today," Mary said as she grabbed a box from the bookcase that Melissa hadn't noticed. She took the lid off the box and pulled out two ornaments and handed them to Melissa.

The ornaments were little cowboys and each sported the words *Baby's First Christmas*. For a moment as Melissa gazed at them her heart was too full to attempt speech. "I don't know what to say," she finally managed to sputter. A sudden mist fell in front of her eyes. She quickly blinked them away. "Once again, thank you for your kindness."

"Pick a good spot and hang them on the tree," Mary said. "It's the beginning of a new tradition. There will be an ornament every year for each of the boys to add to the collection. When they leave home and have their own trees, they can take them with them."

Melissa got up from the sofa and approached the tree, vividly aware of Henry's eyes on her. She'd felt him watching her all evening long, an intense, almost preda-tory gaze that had kept her in a state of anticipation.

It was still there between them, that crazy, wild attrac-tion, that white-hot desire that had exploded out of control on the night of the snowstorm. She saw it in the depths of his eyes, felt the electricity in the air whenever he was near.

She hung the ornaments and then James began to fuss.

"It's past their bedtime," she said as she unbuckled James from his high chair and pulled him up into his arms.

"I'll get this one," Henry said and picked up Joey.

"I think I'm going to call it a night as well," Melissa said to Mary. "Thank you for a wonderful evening and I'll see you in the morning."

Mary kissed each of the boys on their foreheads and smiled at Melissa. "Sleep well, Melissa."

As Melissa went up the stairs she was conscious of Henry just behind her. She could smell the scent of him, felt a stir in the pit of her stomach. It was easier to be around him with Mary in the room. Being alone with him made her think of how his lips had felt on hers, how his eyes had burned electric blue as he'd taken her that cold, wintry night.

She carried James into the bedroom across from where she'd slept the night before, where the two new cribs awaited. The boys were already dressed in their sleepers, but each needed a diaper change before going to sleep.

"You can just put him in that bed," she said. "And I'll take it from here."

"What else needs to be done?" he asked.

She smiled and unsnapped James's sleeper bottom. "Diaper duty."

"Toss me one of those diapers and I'll take care of Joey," he replied. She looked at him in surprise. "I wrestle cattle. I think I can handle wrestling a diaper on a little bottom," he said with a smile.

Within minutes the boys were changed and half-asleep. Melissa kissed their downy heads then walked to the doorway and turned out the light. A night-light glowed from a socket in the corner as she and Henry stepped back out into the hallway.

"That's it? Now they'll just go to sleep?" Henry asked.

"If we're lucky. If it's a good night," she replied.

"And if it's a bad night?"

He stood so close to her she could feel the heat from his body radiating to her. Memories of the night they'd shared shot through her mind. She remembered the feel of his hand around hers as they'd raced through the blinding snow to the abandoned farmhouse, his gentleness as he helped her pull off her wet shoes and socks.

He'd rubbed her feet between his hands, then had gotten a roaring fire started using a stack of wood that had been left by the fireplace.

As crazy as it sounded, that night in the arms of a stranger she'd felt more loved, more cared for than she'd ever felt in her life. It was a pathetic statement on how lonely her life had been up until now. She suddenly realized that even with Tom she had felt lonely.

She also realized he was looking at her expectantly, that he'd asked her a question she hadn't yet answered.

"If it's a bad night then I usually walk them or rock them until they finally go to sleep," she said. "Hopefully they won't have a bad night while we're here so they won't wake up you or your mother."

"You don't have to worry about them waking up Mom. Her rooms are on the other side of the house. And

I don't mind if they wake me up. I'd be happy to walk or rock a baby back to sleep."

She was quickly developing a crush on her babies' daddy and she found it appalling. "Then I guess I'll just say good-night," she said as she backed away from him.

"Good night, Melissa," he replied then turned his attention back to the bedroom where the boys slept.

It wasn't until Melissa was in her nightgown and had slid beneath the blankets on the bed that the first stir of uneasiness filtered through her.

The new cribs, the high chairs, even the ornaments on the tree suddenly took on an ominous meaning. She'd worried that Henry wouldn't want to be a part of Joey and James's lives but now her worry was exactly the opposite.

What if those things hadn't been bought to make her visit more pleasant? What if they'd been bought as the beginning to creating a permanent place here for the boys?

Henry certainly had the money and the power to make a play for custody of the boys and Melissa was in no financial position to be able to fight him.

Don't jump to conclusions, she told herself, but she couldn't stop the burning fear that somehow, someway, Henry intended to take her babies away from her.

Chapter 5

"Are we ready to take off?" Henry asked Melissa the next morning when they'd all finished breakfast. She looked so pretty in a bright pink sweater and worn jeans that hugged her hips, but she'd been unusually quiet since she'd gotten up that morning.

She glanced at the boys still seated in their high chairs. "Go on, Melissa. I can take it from here," Mary assured her. "Go enjoy a little shopping or whatever. It's a beautiful day and we won't see many more of them."

"I just need to get my coat," Melissa said.

As she ran up the stairs, Henry walked to the entry hall and retrieved his gun and shoulder holster from the drawer. He quickly put them on and then pulled on his winter coat.

He didn't want the presence of the gun to frighten Melissa, but he also didn't intend to go out the door without it. Although he anticipated no trouble, he intended to be prepared if trouble found him.

As she came back down the stairs he felt a tiny fluttering heat in the pit of his stomach. He was looking forward to spending some time with her, without the boys, without his mother as a buffer between them.

She intrigued him. He couldn't get a handle on her. He didn't know if she was really what she seemed—a nice woman who had acted uncharacteristically the night she'd been with him, a loving mother who had come here to find a friend, or a schemer who was like so many of the other women who had drifted through Henry's life.

"Ready," she said as she reached the landing.

He'd already had Charlie bring his truck to the driveway and as he stepped out the door he was on alert. As Charlie got out of the driver seat, Henry helped Melissa into the passenger side.

Once she was in he met Charlie at the driver door. "Thanks, Charlie," he said.

"No problem. You watch your back in town."

Henry nodded. "I'm sure we'll be fine. You keep an eye on things here while I'm gone. Oh, and Charlie, tell Hank I'm giving him three weeks' severance pay, but he's fired. I warned him about his drinking, but he didn't take my warning to heart."

Charlie's expression didn't change. "I'll tell him, boss."

Within minutes Henry was in the truck and they were pulling out of the ranch entrance and onto the main highway that led into Dalhart.

He cast her a sideways glance. "You've been rather quiet this morning."

She looked out the side window, making it impossible for him to see her face. "I was up most of the night. The boys were restless and fussy." She paused a moment and then continued, "You know it's not all fun and games, dealing with the boys. You've seen them on their best behavior, but they can be so difficult. They cry and fuss and keep you up all night. They spit out their food and make a big mess."

He frowned, wondering where she was going, what had brought on this little diatribe. "I'm aware that parenting isn't all fun and games," he replied.

She turned to look at him. "How could you possibly be aware of that? You've only been around them for a day and a half." Her eyes were wide and her lower lip trembled slightly.

"Only a fool thinks it's easy to raise kids, and I'm not a fool," he replied.

Once again she cast her gaze out the side window. She appeared at ease, but he could feel the tension wafting from her. Something had put a burr on her butt and he couldn't imagine what had caused it. Maybe she was just one of those moody women who got mad at the world without any provocation. Maybe this was a negative character trait that he would have seen if they'd dated for any length of time.

He figured eventually he'd know what had set her off. "Are you warm enough?" he asked as he turned the heater fan up a notch.

"I'm fine," she replied. She turned her head and he felt her steady gaze on him.

They rode in silence for only a few moments, then she sighed, an audible release that sounded weary. "You're obviously a man who is accustomed to getting what you want in life."

"I do all right," he replied cautiously. They had entered the town and he pulled into a parking space in front of Nathan's General Store. He unbuckled his seat belt and turned to look at his passenger. "Melissa, something is obviously bothering you. You want to tell me what's going on?"

Her eyes were filled with anxiety as she studied him. She raised a hand that trembled slightly to shove a strand of her long, pale hair behind her ear. "You scare me, Henry. Your power and your money scares me."

He looked at her in surprise. "It's been my experience that most women find my power and my money exciting—even intoxicating."

"Then I'm not most women," she replied. "Maybe those women had nothing to lose, but I do." Her voice thickened. "I need to know if you intend to take the boys away from me."

"What makes you think I'd do that?" he countered.

"Because you can," she replied and her eyes flashed with a touch of anger. "Because it's obvious you've already taken them into your life. You've bought cribs and high chairs and heaven knows what else and don't tell me you bought those things in order to make my visit with you more pleasant."

"I have no intention of taking the boys away from you," he said.

For a long moment their gazes remained locked. He saw the internal battle going on in her eyes, knew she was trying to decide if she could trust him or not.

"Melissa, I'm not going to lie to you. I want those boys living at the ranch. I want them to grow up here. I don't want to just be a weekend dad. I want to teach them to love the land, to be a part of Randolf Enterprises, which will one day be their legacy."

Her eyes narrowed with each of his words and he watched her stiffen in protest. She was a mother bear, sensing danger to her cubs and he liked that she looked as if she were about to rake his eyes out.

"I have a suggestion so that the boys will remain with you, but I also get what I want," he said.

"And what suggestion is that?" she asked dubiously.

"There's a carriage house behind the main house. It's a two-bedroom fully functional unit. I'd like you to consider moving there with the boys."

"That's a crazy idea," she said immediately. "I have a life in Amarillo."

He raised an eyebrow. "A full life? From what little you've told me, it sounds like a lonely life."

"But it's mine," she replied fervently. "It's my life, not yours."

Henry stifled a sigh of frustration. She'd said she was stubborn and at the moment that stubbornness lifted her chin and flashed in her eyes. "Look, I'd just like you to consider making the move. It would be great for the boys to have not just me, but my mother in their lives on a full-time basis. Just think about it. That's all I'm asking of you."

Once again those beautiful eyes of hers studied him thoughtfully. "And you promise that you won't try to take the boys from me. You won't use your money to try to get custody of them from me?"

"I promise," he replied.

"How do I know you aren't lying?"

He opened his truck door. "I guess you're just going to have to trust me, just like I'm trusting that the story you told me about some mystery woman bringing you to my house is true. Now, let's do a little shopping and let me show you the charms of Dalhart."

In all honesty, he hadn't really seriously considered going to court to take the boys away from her. They were babies, not some company he could buy or sell.

Besides, he knew how important a mother was to children. He had a wonderful relationship with his own mother and would never deprive his children in that way. He hoped Melissa could put away her fears at least for the duration of their outing and she appeared to as she got out of the truck and offered him a tentative smile.

"I'd like to pick up something for your mother while we're out," she said.

"You don't have to do that," he protested. He knew that money was tight for her.

"It's something I want to do," she replied, her chin once again lifted in that stubborn thrust. "She always smells like roses so I was thinking maybe some rose-scented soap or lotion."

He was surprised both by her observation about his mother and by her thoughtfulness. "Okay, I'm sure we can find something like that in one of the stores. I've got some things to pick up, too."

He gestured her toward the door of the store. Shopping at Nathan's General Store was kind of like delving into a treasure hunt.

The floor-to-ceiling shelves were stuffed full of items with no rhyme or reason for their placement there. Candles sat next to disposable diapers, jars of peanut butter next to boxes of cereal.

"Wow," Melissa exclaimed as they entered the store. "It looks like you could find whatever you need in this one store."

"If you can find what you need," Henry said dryly. "Nathan has an unusual way of arranging things."

"I can see that," she replied. "But that's just going to

make this fun." As she drifted toward a shelf, he watched her and wondered what it was that so drew him to her.

Granted, she was pretty, but it wasn't the heart-stopping beauty that could make a man yearn. She was pretty in a girl-next-door kind of way. But she wasn't a girl. She was a woman with lush curves that he remembered intimately. She also had an intriguing aura of a combination of strength and vulnerability. Certainly she had to be strong to take on the job of raising twins alone. But there were times when he saw a wistfulness in her eyes, a yearning for something that he had an idea had nothing to do with his money or his lifestyle.

A blue sweater, he thought suddenly. That's what she needed. A sweater the exact color of her eyes. He'd like to buy her several things, but he wasn't sure if his gifts would please her or make her angry.

He'd like to buy her a new robe to replace the one she'd been wearing yesterday morning. He'd like to buy her a new car to replace the junk on wheels that she'd driven to his house. But besides her strength and stubbornness he sensed more than a little bit of pride.

He liked that about her and yet knew it was that very trait that might make it difficult for him to get what he wanted.

Although he wouldn't mind another night of pleasure with her, he certainly didn't want to marry her. He didn't even want a romantic relationship with her. All he had to figure out was a way to convince her that it was in everyone's best interest for her to move into the carriage house. That's what he wanted more than anything and he would stop at nothing to get what he wanted.

Despite the anxiety that had weighed heavy in Melissa's heart from the moment she'd opened her eyes that morning, she was enjoying the unexpected shopping time with Henry. The talk in the truck had helped ease some of her fear. He'd promised he wouldn't try to take custody of the boys and she only hoped that she could trust that promise. She'd steadfastly refused to think about his offer of the carriage house. She might think about it later, but she didn't want her ambivalence to ruin a perfectly good day out.

They'd wandered in and out of stores and she'd been successful in buying rose-scented lotion and body soap for Mary.

Dalhart was a charming little city that Henry explained got an influx of tourists each summer.

In August there was a three-day celebration that included the largest free barbecue in the United States, a rodeo and three nights of live music and fun.

"See that building over there?" He pointed to a four-story brick structure on the corner. "That's the Randolf Hotel. I bought it six months ago and it is currently undergoing massive renovations. I'm going to need an interior designer when the renovations are done. I'd hire you if you were living here."

"Sounds suspiciously like a bribe," she replied lightly.

He grinned. "Maybe a little one. But I have to hire somebody and it might as well be you."

"You don't even know if I'm good at it," she exclaimed.

"I have a feeling you're good at whatever you put your mind to," he replied.

As they continued to walk the sidewalks Henry pointed out other places of interest and eventually led her to a café where he insisted they go inside and have a cup of coffee before heading back to the ranch.

She agreed. Although she was eager to get back to the kids, she was also reluctant for this time with Henry to end. He'd been charming, making her laugh with a surprising sense of humor and making her feel as if she were the most important person on the face of the earth.

He'd introduced her to people that greeted them and she'd seen the respect, the genuine admiration Henry's friends and neighbors had for him.

In the café they were led to a table in the back where they sat and ordered coffee. "I thought you said you had things to buy," she said once the waitress had poured their coffee and departed from the table.

"I got them," he replied.

"But you don't have any packages." She reached for the sugar to add to her coffee.

"I always have my purchases delivered to the house."

"I guess that's one of the perks about being you," she said dryly.

He grinned and the charm in that gesture kicked her in the heart. "I'm not going to lie. There are definitely perks to being wealthy. For instance, I never go to bed at night and worry about how I'm going to pay the rent. You'd have that same luxury if you'd move into the carriage house."

"That's not true. I would never expect to live someplace free of charge. I pay my way, Henry." She wrapped her hands around her coffee mug. It was one thing to be independent, but it was another to make the boys suffer from her independence.

"There are two things I'd ask of you," she said after a moment of hesitation.

"What's that?"

She realized this close that his eyes were really more gray than blue. Almost silver, they were the kind of eyes a woman could fall into, eyes a woman could lose herself in.

"I haven't been able to afford to get them health insurance," she said. "Maybe it would be nice if you could put them on your policy."

"Done," he answered without hesitation.

"The other thing is that maybe you could help me with a college fund for them. I didn't have the opportunity to go to college, but I'd like my sons to."

"You didn't have to ask for that. I'd want to make sure they go to college," he replied. "Why didn't you go?"

"There were several reasons. Financially it was impossible, but even with a full scholarship I couldn't have gone." She paused to take a sip of her coffee and then continued. "When I was a junior in high school my mother developed health complications due to diabetes. She lost most of her eyesight and they had to take one of her legs. There was no way I could leave her to go to college. She had nobody but me to take care of her."

"Quite a sacrifice on your part," he observed.

Melissa smiled. "I never considered it a sacrifice. I considered it a privilege to take care of the woman who had always taken care of me."

"One of the reasons I broke up with the woman I'd been dating for a while was because she thought it was time to put my mother into a nursing home."

Melissa looked at him in stunned surprise. "What was she thinking? Your mother certainly doesn't belong in a nursing home."

"My sentiments, exactly," he replied. "And you don't even need me to tell you what Mom thought of the idea. Needless to say Mom wasn't upset when I broke it off with Hilary. Now, tell me how you got involved with interior decorating."

As Melissa told him about working in a furniture store and finding her calling in arranging rooms and décor, she once again remembered the thrill of his mouth on hers, the way his arms had felt holding her tight.

"Shouldn't we be getting home?" she asked when she'd finished telling him about her struggling business. "It's been a couple of hours and I don't want to take advantage of your mother."

"We'll head back," he agreed. "But I can promise you

my mother wouldn't feel taken advantage of if we were gone all day. She's absolutely crazy over those boys."

Melissa smiled. "I can't tell you how wonderful it is that the boys not only have a father like you, but also a grandmother like Mary. I'm well aware of the fact that James the cowboy could have been a man who wanted nothing to do with them."

He looked at her sheepishly. "I want you to know that night was the first and only time I've lied about my name." He motioned for the waitress to bring their tab. "To be honest, that night I just wanted to be James the cowboy, not Henry Randolf III."

The café had grown busy with the approach of the noon hour and Melissa was aware of several people looking at her with curiosity as she and Henry left their table and headed for the door.

They were just about to reach the door when a tall, willowy brunette walked in. "Henry!" she cried in obvious delight, then her gaze swept to Melissa and her smile faltered slightly.

"Hilary, this is Melissa Monroe, a friend visiting from Amarillo. Melissa, this is Hilary Grant," Henry said.

"Nice to meet you," Hilary said to Melissa, then turned her attention back to Henry. "I was going to stop by your place this evening. I made a batch of that fudge you love and was going to bring it to you."

"That's not necessary," Henry protested.

"Well, of course it isn't necessary, but it's something I want to do. Will you be home this evening?"

"We'll be home, but it's Christmas Eve. It's really not a good time," he replied.

Her lush red lips pursed with a hint of irritation. "Then I'll give the fudge to Charlie to give to you tomorrow," she said. "I made it especially for you, Henry."

He smiled at the beautiful Hilary. "That was very nice, Hilary, and now we'd better get out of here. We're blocking the entrance."

"Nice to meet you, Hilary," Melissa said.

She nodded and returned Melissa's smile but there was nothing warm or inviting in the dark centers of her eyes. She swept past them toward a table where another woman sat as Melissa and Henry stepped out into the cold late morning air.

"Hilary knows Charlie?" Melissa asked.

"They're brother and sister," Henry replied.

She glanced up at him. "That must have been a bit awkward when you broke up with her."

"Actually, it was fine. Charlie doesn't seem to get involved with his sister's life. I get the feeling that they aren't real close."

They had gone only a few steps down the sidewalk when they came face-to-face with a short, squat man. Melissa felt Henry's instant tension. "Tom," he said and gave the man a curt nod.

"Henry. Heard you had some excitement out at your place the other night."

"And you wouldn't know anything about that,"

Henry replied. His eyes were cool, steely in a way Melissa hadn't seen before.

"Just what I hear through the grapevine. Sounds like there are some folks who aren't too happy about your decision to run for mayor."

"Just a handful, mostly the people who have something to lose if I get into office. You wouldn't be one of those people, would you, Tom?"

"Taking potshots at a man with a rifle isn't my style. You'll see me coming if I come after you." Tom gave Melissa a curt nod, then stepped around them and walked by.

"Who was that?" Melissa asked as they arrived at Henry's truck.

"Tom Burke, city manager and the man who definitely doesn't want me to become mayor." Henry opened her car door and she slid in and watched as he walked around the front of his truck to get into the driver side.

She could tell he was irritated. A muscle ticked in his strong jaw and his shoulders looked more rigid than usual.

"You don't like Tom Burke?" she asked as he got into the car.

"I think he's a criminal masquerading as an upstanding citizen," Henry replied as he started the truck. "He knows that if I get into office I'm going to do everything in my power to see that he loses his job."

"So, you think he's behind the attacks on you?"

He backed out of the parking space before replying. When he was on the road that led back to the ranch he visibly relaxed. "Yeah, Tom Burke is definitely at the top of my list of suspects. He knows I believe that he's been taking kickbacks from inferior contractors doing work for the city and he knows that if I succeed in being elected, his days are numbered."

"Have you told the sheriff this?"

He nodded, his dark hair gleaming in the sunshine that danced into the truck window. "Jimmy knows. Unfortunately Tom isn't the only councilman who I think is on the take. The corruption in this town runs deep and I'm determined to do some housecleaning."

"And what do the townspeople think?"

"I think they're behind me, but nobody has been brave enough to speak up. I'm hoping they'll speak by voting for me."

Melissa admired what he wanted to do. Like an old Wild West hero he was riding into town filled with outlaws with the intention of cleaning it up.

"She's very beautiful," she said.

He didn't pretend not to know who she was talking about. "She's okay."

She'd been more than okay, Melissa thought. Hilary Grant was stunning. Tall and slender, with lush long dark hair and exotic olive eyes, she'd looked like a model in her long, fashionable coat and boots.

"What does she do?" she asked curiously.

"She's a beautician and she does some local modeling gigs. She and Charlie had a pretty rough life and mostly Hilary is looking for somebody to change all that rather than figuring out how she can change it herself."

"She's in love with you, you know," she said.

"She was never in love with me," he scoffed. "She was always in love with my money."

"Were you in love with her?" Melissa was surprised to realize that his answer mattered. It mattered much more than it should to her.

"No, but there was a weak moment when I considered marrying her."

"You'd marry somebody you weren't in love with?" Melissa asked with surprise.

"I considered it a business deal," he replied with an easiness that astounded her. "Hilary would have made a good wife when it came to giving parties and acting as hostess for social affairs. In return she would have been able to live the lifestyle she desperately wants."

"And you'd do that? You'd marry as a business arrangement instead of for love?" Melissa asked.

"As far as I'm concerned love is overrated." He cast her a wry look. "I suppose you're one of those hopeless romantics?"

"Absolutely," she exclaimed. "I'll only marry for love. I want to marry somebody who loves me mindlessly, desperately, and I want to love him the same way. I want somebody to laugh with, to love, somebody to grow old with and love through eternity. And I won't settle for less."

As if to punctuate her sentence there was a loud pop. The truck careened wildly to the right side of the highway as Henry muttered a curse.

Melissa saw the deep ditch in front of them and knew they were going to hit it—hard. She squeezed her eyes closed and screamed as she felt the truck go airborne.

Chapter 6

Henry fought the steering wheel hard, trying to keep the truck on the road, but he lost the battle as the vehicle flew far right, hit the lip of the ditch and flew with all four tires off the ground. It came down with a crunch and a hiss, jarring the teeth in his head as it finally came to rest.

His heart raced and he quickly looked at Melissa. "Are you all right?"

She opened her eyes and gave a slow nod, but her face was chalky pale. "I'm okay." She drew in a deep breath and her hand shook as she shoved her hair away from her face. "I hope you have a spare," she said.

He pulled his gun from his holster with one hand and

reached for his cell phone with the other. Melissa's eyes widened at the sight of his weapon. But he didn't have time to deal with her fear.

He handed her the cell phone. "Call Jimmy." He rattled off Jimmy's cell phone number. "Tell him we're three miles from my place on the highway and somebody just shot out my tire."

As she made the phone call, Henry kept his gaze on the wooded area on the right side of the highway. He was ninety-nine percent certain that a mere second before the tire had blown he'd heard the unmistakable faint crack of a rifle.

"Jimmy said he's on his way," she said, her voice higher than normal in tone.

He felt her fear radiating across the seat, but he didn't look at her. Instead he kept focused on the area where he thought danger might come. He didn't know now if the attack was over or if the blown tire was just the beginning. Was somebody approaching the truck now, knowing it was disabled and that he and Melissa were sitting ducks?

Minutes ticked by—tense minutes of silence. He was grateful that Melissa understood his need for focus, for complete concentration, and didn't attempt to engage him in any way.

His heart continued to bang unusually fast, but as the fear began to recede, anger took its place. Who was behind these attacks? Dammit, there had to be something he and Jimmy could do to figure out who was responsible and get them behind bars.

Henry didn't relax until he saw Jimmy's patrol car pull up on the side of the road. Henry lowered his gun and opened his window as Jimmy got out of his car, gun drawn and headed across the ditch toward them.

"You're becoming a full-time job, Henry," Jimmy said as he reached the driver side of the truck. "You both okay?" He bent down to look at Melissa. "Ma'am?"

"I'm fine," she replied, her voice a little stronger than it had been moments before.

"You sure the tire was shot out?"

"I heard a crack right before the tire blew. I think it was a rifle shot."

Jimmy scanned the area. "You have any idea where the shot came from?"

"Somewhere in those trees, about a quarter of a mile back," Henry replied. "I'm sure whoever it was is gone now. If the intention was to do more harm, then he would have come after us while we were sitting here waiting for you."

"Any ideas on who might have taken the shot?" Jimmy asked.

"The usual suspects," Henry replied dryly. "Oh, and I have a new one to add. I fired Hank Carroll this morning before we left for town. You might want to check him out. Can you get somebody out here to take us home?"

Jimmy nodded. "I'll radio for Gordon to come out and give you a ride. Meanwhile I'll check out the woods and see if I find anything. You armed?"

Henry showed his gun. "Nobody is going to sneak

up on us. You see what you can find and we'll wait here for Gordon."

Jimmy nodded, hitched up his pants, then turned to walk back to his patrol car.

Henry shot Melissa a quick glance, pleased to see some of the color had returned to her cheeks. "I don't think we're in any danger," he said softly. "And I appreciate the fact that you haven't fallen into hysterics."

She offered him a faint smile, although her lips trembled slightly. "I'm really not the hysterical kind of woman. You fired Hank?"

He nodded and returned his gaze to the outside. "I'd warned him twice about drinking on the job, but he was half-lit when he carried in the tree yesterday."

"I noticed," she replied. "Would he do something like this?"

Henry frowned thoughtfully. "To tell the truth, I don't know. He hasn't been working for me very long. I hope this doesn't change your mind about living in the carriage house."

"I haven't made up my mind about living in the carriage house," she replied. "And I'd say now is definitely not a good time to ask me how I feel about living here."

At that moment a deputy car pulled up and Gordon Hunter got out. Jimmy returned as Henry and Melissa were getting into the backseat of Gordon's car.

"I couldn't find anything. I don't suppose you'd do me a favor and stay inside that secure castle of yours until I can figure out who's after you? I mean, tomorrow is Christmas, surely you don't have to be out anywhere."

"I won't be out and about for the next couple of days, but, Jimmy, I'm not going to become a prisoner in my own home," Henry replied.

Jimmy frowned. "I know, Henry. I'm doing the best I can but these drive-by shootings, so to speak, aren't giving me much to work with."

Henry clapped his hand on Jimmy's shoulder. He knew Jimmy was as frustrated as he was by these sneak attacks. He also knew Jimmy was a good man who took his job seriously.

"I'll arrange for Willie at the garage to pick up your car," Jimmy said. "And I'll be in touch in the next day or two. In the meantime, try to have a merry Christmas."

Henry nodded and got into the back of Gordon's car next to Melissa. "Okay?" he asked her.

"Never a dull moment with you, is there?" she said.

There was still a tiny flicker of fear still in the depths of her eyes and he reached over and took one of her hands in his. She immediately curled her cold fingers with his as if she'd desperately needed the contact with him.

He was surprised by the sudden surge of protectiveness that filled him holding her small, slender hand in his. He wanted to keep her from harm. Surely it was only because she was the mother of his children and nothing more.

Still, he was equally surprised to realize that he had no desire to release her hand until Gordon deposited them at the front door of his house.

Melissa grabbed her shopping bags and Henry ushered her into the house, where Mary met them at the door. "What happened?" she asked, worry thick in her voice.

"Nothing serious, just a blowout," Henry said quickly before Melissa could reply. "The spare was flat and Gordon just happened to be driving by so we hitched a ride home with him."

The last thing he wanted to do was worry his mother, but he wasn't sure if Melissa would play along with his story.

She did, not countering his story to his mother. "How were the boys?" Melissa asked. "Did they behave for you?"

Mary's face lit up. "They were absolute angels," Mary said as Henry flashed Melissa a grateful smile.

As Melissa and his mother disappeared into the house Henry headed for his office. He needed to call the garage about his truck and he needed to talk to Charlie to see how things had gone with Hank.

The main thing he needed was some distance from Melissa. Even with the concern that somebody had shot out his tire, he couldn't stop thinking about how nice her hand had felt in his, how the scent of her had dizzied his senses all morning long.

He wanted her. He wanted her naked in his arms, gasping beneath him as she'd been on the night they'd shared. But she'd made it clear what she was looking for—that happily-ever-after and love forevermore nonsense. That definitely wasn't what he'd be offering to her.

Would she be interested in a night of passion with him with no strings attached, no promise of love or commitment? It was possible.

He knew she wasn't immune to the sparks that snapped in the air between them. He'd seen an awareness in her eyes when he got too close to her, noticed the way her gaze lingered on him when she thought he wasn't looking.

He sank down at his desk and realized it was much easier to speculate on how to get Melissa into bed than trying to figure out who in the hell was trying to kill him.

"You're perfectly safe here," Henry said later that evening to Melissa. "The house has a state-of-the-art security system. Nobody can get in here without me knowing about it."

Melissa nodded and took a sip of her wine. Mary had just gone to bed, the boys were also down for the night, and Henry and Melissa were sitting in the living room with the glow of the Christmas tree lights the only illumination in the room.

There was no question that the safety of her sons had been on her mind all afternoon and evening. How could she even consider moving here knowing that somebody wanted to do harm to Henry? Knowing that it was possible she or her boys could be casualties in whatever war was being waged?

"I can't seriously consider moving here until the

issue is resolved, not that I'm seriously considering it anyway," she said, giving voice to her thoughts.

"But I want you to consider it seriously," Henry said. He paused to take a sip of his scotch. "The special election is in February. Certainly by then I'm confident that Jimmy will be able to figure out who is hassling me. It would probably take you that long to make the move anyway."

"Hassling you?" She raised one of her eyebrows at him. "Honestly, that's a pretty weak description for what's happened just since I've been here. That tire blowout could have killed us both. The truck could have rolled and we wouldn't be sitting here right now."

"I swear I won't do anything to put you or the boys in danger," he replied.

She shrugged. "It doesn't matter now. I plan on going home tomorrow afternoon."

"But it will be Christmas Day," he protested. "You can't leave tomorrow. You'll break Mom's heart."

She smiled at him. "Ah, first you try to bribe me with a job offer and now you're using your mother to manipulate me. You should be ashamed of yourself."

He laughed and that familiar warmth shot through her at the pleasant sound. "I refuse to feel guilty if it forces you to stay a little longer. Besides, Etta will be making a traditional Christmas feast for lunch tomorrow and what difference does another day or two make?"

"You just want more time to try to talk me into moving here," she said.

He nodded, his eyes teasing her. "There is that," he agreed.

"Okay, I won't leave tomorrow. But the next morning we've got to get back home."

He finished his scotch and set the glass down on the coffee table. "And what then?" The teasing light in his eyes vanished. "When will I see the boys again?"

Melissa realized that her life was about to get more complicated. She'd been thrilled that Henry wanted to be a part of the boys' lives, but now she was faced with the logistics of how they would make it all work.

"I guess I can commit to twice a month driving here for a weekend visit," she said. "I know it isn't ideal, that you'd like to see the twins every day," she added as she saw the dismay on his face. "But, Henry, you have to work with me here."

"I know." He leaned back against the sofa and frowned thoughtfully. "I never knew how kids would make me feel, how much they'd make me want to be there for them, to protect them and teach them. I never dreamed that thoughts of them would be so all-consuming."

She smiled, finding him even more attractive than ever with love for his children—for her children—shining from his eyes. "Welcome to parenthood."

He shook his head and smiled. "I never knew it would be like this." His features were soft in the glow from the Christmas lights and Melissa found herself wishing for things that could never be.

She wished she and Henry were married and

tonight after checking on their children they'd get into bed together and make love all night long. She wished they'd share breakfast the next morning and talk about their shared dreams, laugh over secret jokes and know that they would face each other over their first cup of coffee every morning for the rest of their lives.

Foolish wishes, she knew. Wishes brought on by the glow of the Christmas tree and the warmth of family that permeated this house. She was slowly being seduced by Henry and his mother and she knew she'd be a fool to hope for anything except weekend visits for the boys and nothing more.

Still, she'd allowed him to talk her into staying another day because she'd been reluctant to leave this house of warmth, reluctant to leave him.

"Are there twins in your family?" he asked, pulling her from her wayward thoughts.

"Not that I know of. What about yours?"

"I think there were twins on my father's side of the family," he replied.

The doorbell rang and Henry checked his watch with a frown. "Who could that be?" Melissa watched as he rose from the sofa with a masculine grace.

When he disappeared from her sight, she leaned back in her chair and released a sigh. She'd enjoyed the day with him far too much.

His ideas about marriage had shocked her. Was he so afraid a woman would take his money? Did he not believe that he was worth anything simply as a man? What good was it to have money if all it made you do was worry about who might take it away from you?

She wondered what had made Henry so cynical about love. Had some woman hurt him in the past? Certainly Tom had hurt her, but even the pain of his rejection hadn't made her belief in true love waver.

When he returned he carried his car keys with him. "That was Willie from the garage. He delivered my truck." He pocketed the keys and sat back down on the sofa.

"Henry, do you have a computer?" she asked. She knew he had never really embraced her story about MysteryMom and more than anything she wanted him to believe that she had no interest in any of his money for herself.

"Sure, in my study. Why?"

"I was wondering if maybe you could let me use it to see if I can connect with MysteryMom. This is the time of the evening when I normally could find her in the chat room. It's important to me that you believe what it was that brought me here to you."

"You haven't given me a reason not to believe you."

She heard the faint edge of doubt in his voice and the *yet* that had remained unspoken. What he meant was that she hadn't given him a reason not to believe her *yet*.

"Maybe not, but for my own peace of mind I'd like to show you."

Once again he got up from the sofa. She finished her wine and then followed him down the hallway to the study. The room had seemed enormous the first time she'd been in here, but as he gestured her into the chair behind the desk and he stood immediately behind her, the room seemed to shrink.

They waited for the computer to boot up, and she was intensely aware of his scent, that provocative scent of clean male and spicy cologne. She could feel his warm breath on the nape of her neck and she fought a shiver of pleasure and hoped he didn't notice that she was suddenly breathless.

"There you go," he said. "You're Internet connected and can go wherever you want to go."

She placed her hand on the mouse and began to maneuver her way to the chat room where night after night for months she had talked to MysteryMom and other single mothers and mothers-to-be. But when she tried to find the room where she had spent so much of her time, bared so much of her soul, it was gone.

"I don't understand," she muttered softly as she clicked and whirled the mouse in an effort to locate the chat room. "It's not here." She felt a sick frustration welling up inside her.

"Melissa, it's Christmas Eve, that's probably why nobody is there." He placed his hand on her shoulder.

"No, you don't understand. The room always had a virtual sign welcoming single mothers and it's gone. The room itself isn't there anymore."

She looked up at him, surprised to feel thick emotion rising up inside her. She'd wanted to prove to him that it had been MysteryMom who had brought her here and not his money or the lure of a life on easy street.

"Do you have an e-mail address for this Mystery-Mom?"

She shook her head negatively. "We always just talked in the room. If we wanted to talk privately we instant messaged each other. I only got one e-mail from her and that was the directions here, but when I tried to answer her back my reply bounced back to me." She covered his hand with one of hers. "You have to believe me, Henry. It's so important to me."

He gazed at her for a long moment. It was a piercing gaze, as if he were looking into her very soul. "I believe you, Melissa. You don't have to prove anything to me."

He pulled his hand from her shoulder and turned off the computer. "Come on, it's getting late and Santa will come early in the morning."

She was ready to get out of the study, ready to get away from him. His scent, the gentle touch of his hand and the way he'd gazed at her had all combined to make her feel more than a little weak in the knees.

They left the study and as they walked back through the living room Henry turned out the Christmas tree lights, then turned on a switch that illuminated the stairs. They climbed up the stairs side by side and again Melissa was struck with a wistfulness that things were different between her and Henry. Everything would have been much less complicated if they'd dated for a long time, fallen in love and then she'd gotten pregnant.

And if wishes were horses, I'd have a whole herd, she thought. When they reached the top of the stairs she went into the boys' room and Henry followed right behind her.

She went to Joey's crib first and her heart expanded in her chest as she saw him sleeping peacefully. He had a little smile on his lips, as if his dreams were happy.

She then checked on James, unsurprised to see that he'd managed to wiggle himself sideways in the crib and had worked the blanket off him. She didn't attempt to move him from his position, but covered him again with the blanket, then backed away from the crib and into the hallway.

"James is a restless sleeper. He's more easily awakened than Joey and never keeps his blankets on," she said softly as she moved across the hall to her bedroom doorway. "I guess then I'll just say good-night."

"Melissa, I enjoyed spending the morning with you." He took a step toward her and stood so close she could feel the radiating warmth of his body.

"I had a nice time with you, too," she replied as her heart drummed a little faster.

There was a heat in his eyes that excited her and when he reached up to smooth a strand of her hair back from her face his simple touch electrified her.

"I thought about you often after that night," he said, his voice a husky whisper that stirred a simmering fire inside her. "I wondered if you'd gotten where you were going okay, if somehow, someway, our paths would ever cross again. I can't believe how little we shared and yet how much we shared."

"It was a crazy night," she replied half-breathlessly.

"I'm feeling a little crazy right now." He didn't give her time to think, time to process what he'd just said. He pulled her into his arms and his lips claimed hers.

It never occurred to her to step back from him, to deny him and herself the pleasure of kissing him. Just as she remembered, his lips were a combination of tenderness and command, of controlled hunger.

She opened her mouth to allow him to deepen the kiss. His body was rock-hard against hers as his hands slid down her back and pulled her closer to him.

Their tongues swirled and danced and Melissa felt herself falling into a sensual haze of instant desire. No man had ever been able to stir her like Henry. No man had ever made her feel as alive as she felt in his arms, with his mouth on hers.

He released her suddenly and stepped back, his eyes hooded and dark. Melissa fought for composure when all she really wanted was to grab him by the arm and pull him into the bedroom with her. Then she was struck by a thought that dashed all desire away.

"You've tried bribery and manipulation to get me to agree to move here. Is seduction your next weapon to use?" she asked.

A slow grin curved the edges of his mouth upward. "I promise you I will never seduce you in order to get you to move into the carriage house. The only reason I would seduce you is strictly for my own personal pleasure and nothing more."

He reached out and touched her lower lip with his index finger. "And I do intend to seduce you, Melissa. But, for tonight, sleep well and I'll see you in the morning."

Chapter 7

Henry awakened the next morning with a sense of excitement he hadn't felt since he'd been a very young boy. The air smelled of Christmas, of baking cinnamon rolls and fresh evergreen boughs and the cranberry-scented candles his mother loved to burn.

For a moment he remained in bed, thinking about the day ahead and the night before. Kissing Melissa had been an early Christmas present to himself. He'd wanted to kiss her all day.

As he watched her wander through the stores, her lips pursed thoughtfully as she considered her purchases, all he could think about was capturing that lush mouth with his own. Even in those moments immediately after the blowout he'd wanted to cover her trembling mouth with his and kiss her until the fear in her eyes transformed to something else.

Kissing her had been just like he remembered. Her lips had been soft and hot and welcoming and he hadn't wanted to stop. He'd wanted to take her by the hand and lead her to his bed.

Afterward he'd told her good-night and he'd gone back downstairs and spent the next several hours wrapping presents and placing everything he'd bought and the items that had been delivered over the past twenty-four hours under the tree.

By the time he'd finished it looked like toy land had come to the Randolf home. As pleased as he was about what he'd bought the twins, he couldn't wait for Melissa to open her presents from him.

It had been a long time since Henry had been excited about giving to somebody else. Sure, he was a generous contributor to a variety of charities, but buying for Melissa had given him a special kind of pleasure.

He pulled himself from bed and after a shower left the master suite. It was just after six when he passed Melissa's door and glanced inside to see her still in bed.

She was nothing more than a short, lean lump beneath the blankets, her hair the only thing visible. He wanted to crawl beneath the blankets with her, pull her into his arms and make love to her as the sun crested the horizon. That would definitely make it a Christmas to remember.

Instead he backed away from the doorway and checked on the boys, who were still sleeping soundly. He drew in a deep breath of their baby scent and felt a piercing ache at the thought of having to tell them goodbye even for a brief time.

He continued down the stairs. The tree was lit up, candles burned on the mantel and two stockings were hung, each with one of the boy's names in big glittery letters. His mother had been busy already.

He found her in the dining room, sipping a cup of coffee. She stood as he entered and gave him a kiss on the cheek. "Merry Christmas, Henry," she said, her eyes twinkling as brightly as the lights on the tree.

He hugged her and returned the greeting. "You're up early," he said as he poured himself a cup of coffee from the silver coffeepot in the center of the table.

"I couldn't stay in bed another minute. I can't wait for Melissa to see everything we've bought for the boys. I can't wait to see them in the little outfits I bought for them." She smiled and shook her head. "Christmases are going to be wonderful from now on."

"When Melissa and I sit down to discuss the visitation, I'll insist that the twins are here at Christmastime," he replied, although the words certainly brought him no comfort.

He wanted the boys here all the time. He wanted to see their first steps, he wanted to hear the first time they said da-da. He didn't want to wait days or weeks at a time between visits.

"You haven't managed to talk her into moving here? Staying in the carriage house?" Mary asked.

"Not yet. But I still have until tomorrow to make my case," he replied.

"She's leaving tomorrow?" Mary's dismay showed on her features.

"That's what she says."

"It would be nice if we could talk her into staying until after New Year's Eve."

Henry grinned knowingly at his mother. "Then we could try to convince her to stay until after Valentine's Day, or maybe Easter."

Mary laughed and nodded. "I don't have a problem with that." Her smile grew thoughtful. "It's not just the boys. I like Melissa. She's the kind of girl I once dreamed that you'd marry and build a family with."

Henry scowled. "You know that's not happening so don't even start." Most of the time Mary seemed to respect his decision to remain single, but occasionally she launched a sneak attack in an attempt to get him to change his mind.

"If not Melissa, then surely you can find some nice woman to fall in love with," she continued as if he hadn't spoken. "I hate the idea of you growing old alone. I want you to have what your father and I shared."

He paused to take a sip of his coffee. "I have sons who will keep me company as I grow old and that's all I need."

"I'm just saying it would be nice if they all could be here full-time."

Henry leaned back in his chair. "I have a feeling she isn't going to make a decision about moving here until I can assure her that it's safe. The greeting committee of bullets flying has to play a role in her not even considering it right now."

"Jimmy still doesn't have any idea who is responsible?" she asked with concern.

Henry shook his head. "He's coming over tomorrow and we're going to sit down and discuss the whole thing."

At that moment Melissa appeared in the doorway, a twin on each hip. Both Mary and Henry jumped up to take the boys from her.

"Merry Christmas," she said, her eyes sparkling brightly. She looked beautiful in a cheerful red sweater and jeans. Her cheeks were flushed with color and her hair was shiny and smooth to her shoulders.

"And the same to you," Mary said as she took Joey from Melissa's arm.

Henry took James, who offered him a half-cranky smile, then fussed and kicked his feet. "They're hungry," Melissa said. "I'll just go make them some cereal and I'll be right back."

Henry watched her disappear while he put James into his high chair. The fussing stopped, as if James knew he was about to get what he wanted. Within seconds Mary had both boys giggling as she made funny faces and silly noises. The sound of their laughter welled up inside Henry, filling him with such love it brought unexpected tears to his eyes.

Sons.

His sons.

He still couldn't quite wrap his mind around it and he was thankful for the blizzard that had brought him and Melissa together for that single night that had resulted in Joey and James.

There was no way he wanted a long-distance relationship with them. What if Melissa tired of the drive back and forth from Amarillo to here? What if eventually she fell in love and married a man who resented sharing the boys?

Fear clutched his heart at the very thought. He had to convince Melissa to move into the carriage house. It was the only way Henry could get what he wanted—a full-time position in his sons' lives.

He smiled as she came back into the room carrying two cereal bowls. "You sit back and enjoy your coffee. Mom and I will do the honors," he said as he took the bowls from her. "Did you sleep well?"

"Like a log," she replied. She poured herself a cup of coffee and sat in the chair next to Henry. Instantly he could smell the scent of her, clean and floral and intoxicating.

"Etta should have breakfast ready in about fifteen minutes," Mary said as she spooned cereal into Joey's mouth. "And after that we'll go in and see what Santa left for us."

"Santa has already given me more than enough," Melissa said. Her eyes were filled with warmth as she looked first at Mary, then at him. "The welcome you've both given me is more than I ever expected to find this Christmas."

"Maybe later today you would let Henry show you the carriage house," Mary said, surprising Henry with her forwardness. "Just have a peek at it before you definitely make up your mind one way or the other."

"I guess I could do that," Melissa agreed slowly, but she lifted her chin in the gesture Henry had come to know as stubborn pride.

At that moment Etta entered the dining room carrying a tray of fist-size biscuits, a bowl of gravy and a platter of scrambled eggs.

Breakfast was pleasant with he and his mother telling tales of Christmases past and Melissa sharing some of her fond childhood memories of the holiday when her mother had been alive. Henry found his gaze drawn to her again and again. She looked so soft, so inviting and it was more than memories of the sex they'd shared that attracted him to her.

He loved the sound of her laughter. He liked the habit she had of shifting that shiny strand of hair behind her ears when she was thinking or when she was nervous.

He felt a little like he had in seventh grade when he'd had a crush on a girl named Angela. She'd been blond-haired and blue-eyed like Melissa and it had taken him months to work up his nerve to ask her to a school dance. The experience had been his first taste of how materialistic women, even very young women, could be.

He shoved the ancient painful memory away as he

focused on the conversation and the musical ring of Melissa's laughter.

When they were all finished eating they adjourned into the living room, where the first thing his mother insisted they do was dress the boys in the little Santa suits she'd bought for them.

As the women dressed the little ones, Henry moved the high chairs into the room, as excited as a kid to distribute the presents to everyone. When the boys were in their little Santa suits, Mary took dozens of pictures and Henry knew she'd be sporting those photos all around town, bragging about her grandbabies.

Henry donned a Santa hat that James found incredibly funny. As the little boy laughed that rich burst of joy, Henry knew this was definitely going to be a Christmas to remember.

Melissa sat on the sofa next to Mary as Henry began to unveil the bigger presents hidden under sheets. Rocking horses and walkers and stuffed animals as big as Henry himself were just the beginning. There were boxes of clothes and diapers and educational toys. Of course, the boys liked the shiny wrapping paper best of all.

Mary opened her gift of the lotion and soap from Melissa and exclaimed that it was the brand and scent that she loved.

Melissa was already feeling overwhelmed when Henry gave her a present. "You shouldn't have," she said to him.

He smiled. "Open it, Melissa. I picked it out just for you. It's the exact color of your eyes."

Melissa couldn't help the way her heart fluttered at his words. She carefully removed the wrapping paper and opened the box to display the most beautiful blue sweater she'd ever seen in her life. It was soft as a whisper and she was touched by his thoughtfulness.

"Oh, Henry. It's beautiful." She felt the ridiculous burn of tears at her eyes.

"That's not all." He handed her a larger package. "I hope you won't be offended by the more personal nature of this gift, but I couldn't resist it."

She frowned at him, wondering just how personal the gift might be, aware that his mother was seated right next to her. It was a robe, a beautiful long burgundy robe with a satin collar and belt. He must have noticed the worn condition of her robe.

One of the things she was grateful for was that although he had been extravagant with the things he'd bought for the boys, the things he'd bought for her had been ordinary presents, as if he'd known she'd be displeased if he went overboard for her.

"I have something for you, Henry." Melissa got up from the sofa and grabbed the small present she'd slipped under the tree when she'd come downstairs that morning. He looked at her in surprise, took the gift and sat in one of the chairs to open it.

"There's not much I can buy for a man who appears to have everything," Melissa said. "But I know it's something you don't have, something I think you'll want to have."

He looked at her curiously, then ripped the paper off to expose two small frames. Inside the frames were the newborn pictures of the boys and two cigars with bands that exclaimed, "It's a Boy."

His eyes filled with emotion as he gazed at the gifts, then back at her. "It's the most perfect present you could have given me." He stood and kissed her on the cheek. "Thank you."

Her skin burned with the press of his lips and once again she felt overwhelmed by the warmth, by the feel of family and by the gifts he and Mary had bought for her sons.

By ten o'clock most of the mess from the morning had been cleaned up and the doorbell rang to announce a guest. Henry went to answer as Melissa finished placing the last of the wrapping paper into a large garbage bag.

She tensed as she heard the familiar female voice. Hilary. The sharp pang of jealousy that roared through Melissa stunned her. She shouldn't feel jealous of any woman Henry might have in his life. She had no right to feel that kind of emotion.

As Hilary walked into the living room she stopped short at the sight of the twins in their chairs. She looked at the boys, then at Henry, and her pretty features tightened with stunned surprise.

"Hello, Hilary," Melissa said. The woman was exceptionally beautiful and sophisticated in a gold sweater and tight black slacks. Her dark hair was pulled up and gold earrings danced at her dainty ears. She carried in her hands a platter that Melissa assumed was the famous fudge she'd promised Henry the day before.

"Merry Christmas, Mary and Melinda," Hilary replied.

"Melissa. My name is Melissa."

"Of course," Hilary said, then turned her attention to Henry. "Could I speak to you privately for a moment?"

"Okay. Let's go into my study." Henry gestured her down the hallway.

"I can't imagine what he ever saw in that woman," Mary said the minute they had disappeared.

"She's very beautiful," Melissa said as she put the last of the wrapping paper into the trash.

"Maybe on the outside, but it's inner beauty that really matters. Now, if you'll excuse me, I'm going to go help Etta with the lunch preparations."

"And I'm going to put the boys down for their nap," Melissa replied.

Minutes later Melissa stood in the doorway of the room she now thought of as the nursery. Joey had fallen asleep almost immediately and James was almost there, fussing a bit as he fought sleep.

As he finally gave up the battle, Melissa turned from the door and gasped in surprise at the sight of Hilary in front of her.

"He won't marry you, you know," she said softly.

"I don't expect him to marry me," Melissa replied.

Hilary smiled. "He's not going to marry me, either. I'd hoped that eventually I could wear him down, but Henry has no interest in being married. You seem like a nice woman and it would be a shame for you to get hurt."

"I appreciate your concern, but trust me, Henry has made it clear to me a hundred different ways that he's not the marrying kind. Besides, what makes you think I would want to marry him?"

Hilary looked at her and released a dry laugh. "You're kidding, right? I mean, he's good-looking and nice and wealthy. Why wouldn't you want to marry him?"

Melissa couldn't believe she was having this conversation with a woman who had been Henry's lover. "My life is in Amarillo. I'll be going home tomorrow to my life."

"Well, in any case I just came up here to tell you that it was nice to meet you and I hope you have a safe trip home." With a curt nod, Hilary turned around and walked down the stairs.

Melissa drew a deep breath and went into her bedroom. While the morning had been one of the happiest she could ever remember, she felt a sudden burn of tears in her eyes.

There was no way she'd ever to be able to provide for the twins like Henry could. Would she be denying her sons by choosing not to move here? She didn't want to do the wrong thing, but she didn't know what was the right thing. Maybe she should just take a look at the carriage house and keep an open mind.

Still, she couldn't ignore the fact that somebody was trying to hurt Henry and it was possible she and the boys might become accidental victims.

"Melissa?"

She whirled around to see Henry standing in the doorway. "Everything all right?" he asked.

"Everything is fine," she replied.

"I know Hilary came up here. She didn't say anything to upset you, did she?" He gazed at her worriedly.

Melissa smiled. "Not at all. She simply told me that it was nice to meet me and she hoped I had a safe trip home."

He seemed relieved. "Hilary tends to have a bit of a sharp tongue."

"Don't worry, Henry. I'm a big girl and I can take care of myself."

He nodded. "I was wondering if while the twins are napping if now would be a good time to take you to see the carriage house." He smiled, that slow sexy grin that heated every ounce of blood in her body. "I was also wondering when I was going to get to see that blue sweater on you."

"Why don't you give me five minutes and I'll meet you downstairs and we can take a look."

"Great. I'll meet you downstairs."

The minute he left the room she closed the door and pulled the sweater out of the box. It fit perfectly and was exactly the color of her eyes. The fact that he'd even thought about her eyes made her heart flutter just a little bit.

It was only as she was walking down the stairs that she realized the terrible truth—she was more than a little bit in love with Henry Randolf III.

Chapter 8

The morning had gone far better than Henry had hoped. The living room had been filled with laughter, warmth and a feeling of family that had been missing from the house since his father's death.

Melissa had teased him as if they'd known each other forever, and in many ways that's the way he was beginning to feel about her. She was comfortable, and yet made him simmer with expectancy. He couldn't remember a woman who had done both for him.

He pulled on his holster and his gun and then covered it with his winter coat. Despite the fact that it was a holiday and the season of peace and joy, Henry couldn't let down his guard. He was eager to have a sit-down meeting with Jimmy the next day to see if the lawman had come up with any evidence as to who might be after him. They needed to come up with a plan to force the person out into the open.

He turned as Melissa came down the stairs, clad in the blue sweater and the jeans that did amazing things for her legs and curvy butt. Something about her stole his breath away.

Lust, he told himself. That was it. Lust and nothing more. If he slept with her again he was certain these crazy feelings would go away.

Her plans were to leave in the morning and short of locking her up in a tower, there was no way he could stop her. He pulled her coat from the closet and held it out to her. "Ready?"

She nodded. "Ready."

"I've got to say, you look sexy as hell in that sweater."

"I'll bet you say that to all the girls," she replied lightly but her cheeks flushed as she pulled on her coat.

They stepped out the door, and Henry threw an arm around her shoulder. He told himself it was because he wanted to protect her if somebody came at them, but the truth was he'd been dying to touch her all day.

She didn't pull away but instead snuggled into him as the cold wind whipped her hair against his face. They walked briskly, not speaking. Henry kept his gaze bouncing left and right, relaxing as he saw Charlie and several of his men in the distance.

When they reached the carriage house he unlocked

the door and ushered her into the foyer. "You might want to keep your coat on. We just have the minimal heat running in here right now."

She nodded, stepped into the living room and caught her breath. "Oh, my gosh. This is four times the size of my apartment."

It was an open floor plan, the living room flowing into the kitchen. The living-room flooring was a soft beige carpeting and the kitchen had an attractive tile in Southwest colors. The furnishings were simple but tasteful and the kitchen was fully equipped with every pot and pan that a chef might need.

"If you wanted to bring in your own furniture we could store all of this," he said, unable to read the expression on her face. "Let me show you the bedrooms." He led her down a short hallway to the first bedroom. It was definitely large enough to accommodate two cribs and later two twin beds for the boys. From the window the stables and corral were in view, perfect for two little cowboys.

From there he led her into the master bedroom, which was huge, with an adjoining bathroom complete with a Jacuzzi tub. For a moment his head filled with a vision of how she'd look in that tub with her shiny hair piled up on her head and her body surrounded by scented bubbles. He tried desperately to shove the provocative vision out of his mind.

She wandered around the room and when she finally turned to look at him, tears glimmered in her eyes. Instead of looking pleased, she looked achingly miserable.

"What's wrong?" he asked.

The tears spilled from her eyes onto her cheeks. "I don't know what to do. I'm so confused. I'm so overwhelmed by everything."

Henry realized at that moment he didn't like to see her cry. He walked over to her and captured her pretty face between his palms. The look in her eyes was slightly wild, as if she wanted to escape him and the entire situation.

"Melissa, don't cry," he said gently. "Tell me what's wrong."

She jerked away from him and took several steps backward. "You don't understand. This place is so wonderful and all the things you bought for the boys were unbelievable. I know they could have a wonderful life here, but they could have a wonderful life with me in Amarillo, too."

She raised her chin and swiped angrily at her tears. "Lots of children just see their father on the weekends and they survive just fine. People get divorced or never marry and visitation is worked out okay."

He stared at her for a long moment. "But that's not what I want," he said. He shoved his hands into his coat pockets and leaned against the wall. "I don't want to be a weekend dad. What can I do to make this work for you? Of course I'd take care of all your moving expenses and if you have a lease that needs to be broken, I'll take care of that, too. If you're worried about work, I'm sure I can find you some clients for your interior decorating and there's always the hotel that you could be contracted to do. I can take care of all your needs, Melissa. We can make this work."

As he'd spoken, her tears had dried and she gazed at him with an inscrutable expression. When he finished she shook her head and offered him a small, somehow sad smile.

"Henry, there are some things your money just can't buy. You can't buy me. I don't care about money or things. My mother and I didn't have money, but we were happy." She paused and frowned.

"So, this is a no?" he asked flatly.

"It's an I don't know," she replied with obvious frustration. "I've known you and your mother for a couple of days. I refuse to make a life-altering decision that quickly. What I suggest is that I go home tomorrow and think things through without your influence. I want to do what's best for everybody, Henry, and that includes what's best for me."

Although he was disappointed with her decision, he couldn't help but admire her strength in not succumbing to an easier life than the one he thought she was currently living.

"You know I won't stop trying to change your mind," he said lightly, hoping to dispel some of the tension that sparked in the air between them.

She offered him a smile. "Why am I not surprised by that?" She walked out of the bedroom and he followed just behind her.

"I told you I was stubborn," he said.

"Just be aware that you might have met your match," she replied.

As they stepped out of the carriage house he noticed that the sun had disappeared beneath a thick layer of clouds and the air felt colder than it had before.

What he needed was a good old-fashioned blizzard that would make Melissa stay long enough for him to get her to agree what he wanted.

But Henry knew there were two things he couldn't control. The weather was the first and apparently Melissa was the second.

It began to snow at nine o'clock that evening. Melissa stood at her bedroom window and stared out in dismay. If this kept up there was no way she could leave after breakfast in the morning like she'd planned.

She checked on the boys, who were sleeping soundly, then went back down the stairs where she knew Henry was probably having a glass of scotch. Funny, after such a brief time she'd begun to know his habits. He usually sat in the living room to unwind after his mother excused herself for bed.

Sure enough, he was seated in his chair, a glass of scotch at his side as he stared at the lights still twinkling on the Christmas tree. He smiled when she appeared in the doorway. "How about a glass of wine?"

"That sounds nice," she agreed and sat on the sofa while he went to the bar and poured her drink.

It was odd, anytime she was near him a sizzle of anticipation raced through her and yet she was also comfortable with him. He was an easy man to be around, easy to talk to and share things with.

As he handed her the glass of wine, she again wondered if somehow somebody had hurt him in the past. Had somebody made him believe that he had nothing to offer a woman except for his bank account and a lavish lifestyle? His money seemed to be the only bargaining chip he knew how to use to get the things he wanted in life.

"Looks like your plans to take off tomorrow morning might have to be postponed," he said as he returned to his chair.

"Don't look so smug about it," she replied teasingly. "Actually, I'm hoping it stops soon and the roads will be all right for travel by morning."

"And I'm hoping it snows until March and you're forced to stay here and I'll have all that time to convince you to move into the carriage house."

She laughed. "You're positively relentless." She took a sip of her wine and eyed him curiously. "Tell me why you're such a cynic when it comes to love. Haven't you ever been in love before?"

"The last time I was in love I was in seventh grade. Her name was Angela and I was absolutely crazy about her." He took a drink of his scotch and then continued. "It took me months to get up the nerve to ask her to a school dance that was coming up."

Melissa sensed a sad tale ahead and there was nothing worse than young love scorned. "Did she go to the dance with you?"

He smiled, and she saw a hint of sadness, a whisper of loneliness in the depths of his eyes. "She did. She told me she knew I was rich and if I'd buy her a gold bracelet she'd go with me."

"So you bought her the bracelet?" A tiny pang pieced Melissa's heart, a pain for the boy he'd been who had learned early that his worth was in his wallet.

He nodded. "Bought her the bracelet, took her to the dance and thought it was the beginning of a wonderful love match. Then when I took her home that night she told me that she'd only gone out with me for the bracelet and that I shouldn't bother her anymore." He smiled again and this time it was the smile of the cynic he'd become. "That was my first and only experience with love."

"That's horrible," she exclaimed.

He shrugged. "It was a long time ago. Tell me about the man you were dating before we met that night. Were you in love with him?"

"I believed I was at the time." She thought of Tom, who she'd once thought she would marry. There had been a time when any thought of him brought pain, but all she felt now was relief that she hadn't married a man who had cheated on her, a man who hadn't valued her.

"I loved what I thought we had. I loved the idea of getting married and building a family. I loved the idea of waking up with the same man I went to bed with day after day, year after year. We'd dated for over two years and it had become comfortable. I just assumed we'd take the next step and get married but now I'm glad we didn't. He didn't love me the way I wanted to be loved."

"Mindlessly, desperately," Henry said.

"Exactly," she replied, surprised that he'd remembered she'd said that before.

They fell silent, but it was a comfortable quiet. Melissa sipped her wine and found her gaze going again and again to him.

He was such an attractive man with sharp, bold features and that sexy cleft in his chin. But it wasn't his physical qualities that drew her. She loved the teasing light that so often lit his eyes. She loved the respect and caring he showed to his mother. He was a good man and he would make a wonderful role model for her children.

"I think I'll call it a night," she finally said. "I'm still hoping to be able to get home in the morning." She stood and finished the last of her wine, then headed for the kitchen to place her glass in the sink.

"I think I'll call it a night, too," he said and followed behind her into the kitchen. "Jimmy is coming over tomorrow and we're going to sit down and discuss what's been going on and what we're going to do about it." He placed his glass in the sink next to hers.

"What can you do about it? You don't know who is after you." She looked at him worriedly. "Even if the person is just trying to scare you, there's nothing that says he won't make a mistake and actually manage to shoot you." She was shocked by the fear that rocketed through her, fear for him.

"Yeah, that thought has entered my mind, too," he said dryly. "I'm sure Jimmy and I can put our heads together and come up with a plan to figure out who is responsible and get them behind bars. Don't you worry about it. I'll get it all taken care of."

"I can't help but worry about it," she replied. "You're now a part of my life." Emotion began to well up inside her. "I mean, I don't want my boys to grow up without their father," she said hurriedly.

As they left the kitchen and headed for the stairs, Melissa tried to get her emotions under control. It was true, she didn't want anything to happen to him for the twins' sake. But it was also true that as a woman she'd be devastated if anything happened to him.

He turned off the Christmas tree lights then together they climbed the stairs. As always, the first thing Melissa did when she reached the top of the stairs was go into the boys' bedroom to make sure they were still peacefully sleeping.

Henry followed her in and a soft smile played on his face as he looked first at Joey and then at James. That smile, filled with such love, with such tenderness, created a warmth inside her.

She would never have to worry about her sons being loved. If anything ever happened to her, Henry would make sure they not only had what they needed to survive, but he'd make sure their world had the love he refused to believe in for himself.

"Melissa." He grabbed her hand as they left the room.

She knew immediately what he wanted, what she wanted from him. For months after that night of the blizzard she'd thought about the pleasure she'd found in his arms.

She wanted it again. She wanted him again and she could tell by the heat in his eyes that he wanted the same.

She stepped closer to him and raised her face to him and he took the unspoken invitation by crashing his mouth down on hers.

His mouth was hot hunger against hers and she felt as if she'd been waiting for this since the moment he'd first opened the door to her.

Allowing him to deepen the kiss, she leaned into him, wanting him to have no question in his mind that she wanted him.

His tongue danced with hers as his hands slid down her back and pulled her hips into his. His arousal was evident and fed the flames of desire inside her.

The kiss seemed to last forever before he finally dropped his hands from around her and stepped back. "You look beautiful in that blue sweater, but I remember how beautiful you looked naked. I want you, Melissa. This has nothing to do with anything but you and me."

"I want you, too," she said, her voice a husky whisper.

"You know I'm not making any promises. I need you

to understand that there's no future with me. I'm not the man to give you your happily ever after."

"As far as I'm concerned, tonight you're a handsome cowboy keeping me warm on a wintery night and nothing more," she replied. His eyes flamed as he pulled her into the bedroom and back into his arms.

Chapter 9

This time his kiss left her breathless and aching. When he pulled her sweater over her head she was more than ready for him. There was no embarrassment as she stood before him in her wispy bra. The light from her bathroom spilled into the bedroom and she could see the flames that lit his eyes while he gazed at her.

Every bone in her body weakened and she reached out to unfasten the buttons on his shirt. The heat from his body radiated to her, urging her to unbutton his shirt and sweep it off his broad shoulders.

He was beautiful, with his chiseled chest and flat abdomen. He pulled her back into his arms and as he kissed her he reached around her to unfasten her bra.

He tugged the straps off her shoulders and when it fell away he embraced her again and she delighted in the feel of his bare skin against hers.

"I've wanted this since the moment you arrived," he said, his breath hot against her throat.

"I've wanted it, too," she confessed.

Within minutes they were both naked and beneath the blankets in bed. Even though she'd only made love with him once, his skin felt just the way she remembered, warm and firm as he pulled her against him. The familiar scent of him filled her head and she knew any other man who ever wore that particular brand of cologne would always evoke memories of Henry.

As his kisses made her mindless, his hands cupped her breasts and a low moan escaped her lips. He pulled his mouth from hers and looked down at her. "You are so beautiful," he whispered.

She felt beautiful beneath his gaze. That was part of Henry's gift. He'd made her feel beautiful and desirous that night of the blizzard, and he made her feel that way now.

He lowered his mouth to capture the erect tip of one of her breasts and she tangled her fingers in his rich, dark hair. Sweet sensations sizzled through her.

He teased her nipple, swirling his tongue and using his teeth to lightly nip. Melissa closed her eyes as all concerns about the future melted away beneath the heat of his caresses. She couldn't think about anything but him and the magic of his touch.

She ran her hands down the length of his broad back, loving the play of muscle beneath her fingertips. She felt safe with him, not just physically protected, but emotionally as well. She felt as if she could say anything to him, tell him her deepest, darkest secrets and he'd keep those secrets safe.

The love she'd tried not to feel for him welled up inside her, a love she knew would never be reciprocated. But at the moment that didn't matter. She had this night with him and she knew it had to be enough for her. She wouldn't allow this to happen again but she intended to enjoy every moment of it.

"This is much nicer than a hardwood floor beneath the scratchy blanket from my truck," he said, his voice thick with desire.

"I have very fond memories of that scratchy blanket and the hardwood floor." She could speak no more as his mouth once again claimed hers.

Every inch of her skin was electrified, for each and every place he touched, he kissed, sizzled in response.

His heartbeat was strong and quick against hers, the heart that didn't believe in love, the one that refused to believe that anyone could love him for himself.

She slid her lips down his neck, wanting him to feel loved, to feel as desired as he made her feel. Her mouth moved down his chest and she licked first one of his nipples, then the other.

He gasped, a quick intake of breath that made her even bolder. He rolled over on his back as she moved down the length of his body, kissing and nipping and teasing his fevered skin with her lips.

Tangling his hands in her hair, his entire body tensed as she kissed his inner thigh. He was fully erect and although this was something she'd rarely done for Tom, she wanted the utter intimacy with Henry.

As she took him into her mouth she let out a low groan and every muscle in his body tensed. "Melissa," he moaned as his hands tightened in her hair.

She loved the strained sound of her name on his lips, loved the pleasure she knew she was giving to him. But it didn't take long for him to push her away and roll to his side.

"Now, it's my turn," he said, his eyes gleaming with promise. He ran his hand down her body and rubbed against her. "I want you gasping for air and crying out my name."

As he moved his fingers against the very center of her, a rising tide of pleasure began to build inside her. She arched her hips up to meet his touch, needing release, wanting the wave to consume her.

And then it did, crashing through her as she cried his name over and over again. She shuddered with the force of it and tears filled her eyes. But he wasn't finished yet. He rolled over and grabbed a condom from the nightstand and while she was still weak and gasping, he moved between her legs and entered her.

For a moment neither of them moved. The pleasure

of him filling her up was so intense she feared if she moved she'd lose it again.

He froze, his arms holding him up from her chest. From the light shining in from her bathroom she could see his features. His eyes were closed, his neck muscles corded as if he were under enormous strain.

He opened his eyes and looked down at her, then slowly slid his hips back and thrust forward. That single slow movement broke everything loose between them.

Fast and furious, he stroked into her and she encouraged him by clutching his buttocks and pulling him into her.

Lost. She was lost in him and once again she felt the wild tide rushing in. As it washed over her she felt him tense and moan against her, knowing it had claimed him, too.

He collapsed on her and she wrapped her arms around his back, wishing she could hold him there forever. But all too quickly he got up and padded into the adjoining bathroom.

Melissa turned her head to one side and fought a sudden rush of tears. Of all the foolish, reckless things she'd ever done in her life, this was probably the worst. She'd chosen to make love to a man who apparently wasn't capable of loving her back.

MysteryMom couldn't have known that she was sending Melissa into a new heartbreak. The woman had probably simply wanted to unite a man with his sons, ease the burden of single parenting for Melissa.

She'd accomplished that. Melissa would no longer be alone in the task of raising her sons. She knew in her heart, in her soul, that Henry would always be a support and help in the parenting process.

But MysteryMom couldn't have known that Melissa would fall mindlessly, desperately in love with Henry. She couldn't have known that Melissa would repeat the same mistake that she'd made on that snowy night over a year ago. At least he'd used a condom and there wouldn't be another accidental pregnancy.

As he came out of the bathroom she assumed he'd leave to go to his bedroom, but instead he surprised her by sliding back beneath the sheets and taking her in his arms. He kissed her on the temple, a sweet, soft kiss that touched her more than anything that had occurred between them.

"Definitely better in a bed," he said. He lay on his back and pulled her into his side. His hand stroked her hair as she placed her head on his chest. "I really hate to see you take off tomorrow."

"It's time, Henry. It's been a wonderful holiday but now it's over and I have to get back to my real life." It was more important than ever that she leave here as soon as possible. Her heart had gotten involved in a way that already would ache when she left. More time here would only make the ache sharper when she did go home.

She raised her head to look at him. "You know I'll do whatever I can to make it easy on you to see the boys."

"I know that." He raised his hand and trailed a finger

down the side of her cheek, across her lower lip. "I can't think of a better woman to be the mother of my boys."

The tears that had hovered just under the surface sprang to her eyes at his words. "You're just saying that now because you have me naked in bed with you," she replied with a choked little laugh.

"You know that's not true," he chided. "You have the values I want the boys to have. I know you'll teach them to have integrity, to have strong but gentle hearts."

She ran her hand across his chest and placed it on his heart. Her last thought before she fell asleep was that the one thing she would teach her boys was to believe in the power and wonder of love, something apparently nobody had ever taught Henry.

Henry stood at the window in his study and watched the snow swirling in the air. It had snowed about two inches overnight, effectively postponing Melissa's plans to leave first thing that morning.

He was now waiting for Jimmy to arrive. Jimmy had called earlier to tell Henry that the snow wouldn't keep him from his appointment.

Staring at the carriage house in the distance, Henry thought of the night before. Making love to Melissa had been amazing and he'd been in no hurry to leave her bed.

Henry couldn't remember the last time he'd slept with a woman in his arms. He'd never stayed the night with Hilary, had always preferred the comfort of being alone in his own bed. But sleeping with Melissa had been not just comfortable, but comforting in a way he'd never imagined. It had been nice to feel the warmth of her next to him as he'd drifted off to sleep. And it had been equally as nice to wake up with her curled in his arms.

Surely these crazy feelings he was developing for her were nothing more than gratitude. After all, she'd given him the greatest gift a man could get—children.

He wasn't going to mention the carriage house solution to her again. He recognized that over the past two days he'd become a bore and bordered on becoming a bully in trying to get her to do what he wanted.

Whatever she decided, they'd make it work because it had to work. Even though they weren't married, he knew they'd do whatever was in the best interest of the twins.

At the moment Melissa and his mother and the twins were all in the kitchen. It was Etta's day off and they were in the process of making dinner.

As he'd walked to his study he'd heard the sound of laughter and merriment coming from the kitchen. The house would feel empty once Melissa and the boys were gone.

Actually, the house had felt empty for a long time. And if he thought about it long enough he'd admit that his life had been fairly empty for a very long time. He frowned, irritated with the direction his thoughts were taking. Maybe it was a good thing Melissa was leaving soon. She was messing with his mind in a way that was distinctly uncomfortable.

He turned away from the window as a knock fell on

his door. The door opened and Jimmy poked his head in. "Your mom told me to come on in," he said.

Henry motioned him inside. "How are the roads?" he asked as he gestured his friend into the chair in front of the desk.

"A little nasty but not too bad. The road crews are out working so if we don't get any more accumulation we should have everything under control." He eased into the chair. "You got any of that good scotch hidden away in here?"

Henry walked to the minibar in the corner and poured himself and Jimmy a drink, then handed Jimmy his and sat at the desk with his own.

Jimmy took a deep swallow and sighed. "I don't know if Willie told you or not, but he found the bullet that shot out your tire still in the rubber that was left on the truck. It was a .22 caliber. I know it wasn't Hank. At the time your truck was fired on, Hank was down at Lazy Ed's, completely sauced."

Lazy Ed's was a popular tavern for the ranch hands in the area. "I'm not surprised. His drinking is what caused him to get fired in the first place," Henry said.

"Before we get into all this, I want to know about those twin boys that your mother introduced me to in the kitchen. They sure do have the Randolf chin. You been holding out on me about your love life?"

Henry smiled and knew in an instant he wasn't about to tell Jimmy the truth about how the twins were conceived. Although Henry certainly wasn't a prude, he didn't want to give anyone in town a reason to think less of Melissa.

"Melissa is a friend from Amarillo. She's a terrific woman and we've been close for some time. When she got pregnant we agreed that we'd share the parenting of the boys and remain friends."

"I never even knew you wanted kids," Jimmy said.

Henry smiled. "I didn't know I wanted them until they were here. I got to tell you, Jimmy. They change your life. They make you want to be a better man. That's why it's so important we get this mess cleaned up, these attacks that are happening on me. I can't have them around if it's not safe."

Henry leaned back in his chair. "You know who is at the top of my suspect list."

Jimmy nodded. "Tom Burke. You scare him, Henry."

"He should be scared," Henry said with a scowl. "You and I both know he's a criminal."

Jimmy nodded. "I've been in contact with the FBI and I'm hoping they're going to look into his actions as city manager. The problem is we both know he's a likely suspect. What we don't have is any proof."

"Did you question him about his whereabouts at the time my tire was shot out?"

Jimmy nodded. "According to his wife, he was at home with her."

Once again Henry frowned. "You know damn good and well she'd lie for him."

Jimmy nodded. "I've put a couple of my men on

Tom. Full-time surveillance as long as I have the manpower. If he tries anything we'll be on top of him. It's the best I can do, Henry."

Henry nodded. He knew Jimmy was as frustrated as he was by what had been happening. He took a drink of his scotch.

"If this had all started the night that Melissa showed up here with those babies, I would ask you if you thought Hilary might be playing a woman scorned," Jimmy said.

Henry laughed at the very idea of Hilary hiding out in the woods with a gun. "No way. I'll grant you she wasn't too happy to discover I had two babies, but Hilary knew the score where I was concerned. Besides, she'd never risk breaking a nail to do anything like this."

"And the first attack happened to you before Melissa arrived on the scene," Jimmy said.

Henry nodded. "I'm telling you it's Tom Burke or it's somebody he's hired. He's the only person who has a hell of a lot to lose if I become mayor."

Jimmy tilted his glass up for another drink of the scotch. "I just wanted to come out here and tell you that I'm doing the best I can."

"What about a ballistics test on the bullet Willie dug out of my tire?" Henry asked.

"Unfortunately the bullet hit your rim and was pretty mangled. Besides, in order to do a ballistics test you have to have a weapon to compare it to and Tom Burke insists he doesn't have a rifle."

Henry snorted in disbelief. "I don't know a man in this entire county who doesn't own a rifle. This is Texas, for God's sake."

"You're preaching to the choir, Henry."

For the next thirty minutes the men spoke about other potential suspects. There were only two that Henry could think of, both council members and friends of Tom Burke.

"You definitely have the support of the people," Jimmy said. "People like you, they admire your integrity and they trust you. If you can stay alive until February there is no doubt in my mind that you'll be voted in as mayor."

"That's nice to hear," Henry replied.

Jimmy glanced toward the window. "I've got to head back into town." He stood.

"I appreciate you coming out on such a crummy day." Henry stood as well.

"I swear I'm going to get to the bottom of this, Henry," Jimmy said as they left the study.

"I just hope you do before this mysterious shooter gets lucky," Henry said dryly.

The two men walked to the front door, where they said their goodbyes. The snow had begun to fall again and as Henry closed the door he realized that he was more worried now about whoever was trying to hurt him than he'd been before Melissa had arrived in the house.

Before, he'd just been irritated by the whole thing. But now all he could think about was if anything happened to him the boys wouldn't have their father. He had every reason in the world to want to stay alive…for them and for Melissa.

The laughter coming from the kitchen pulled him away from the front door and to the source of the sound. Once there he found his mother and Melissa finishing up dinner preparations.

As he walked into the room, the twins flashed him smiles that as always filled him with warmth. "Something smells wonderful," he said.

"Melissa can cook," Mary exclaimed.

"It's just spaghetti with meat sauce," Melissa replied as she took a pot of boiling pasta off the stove top.

Henry took a seat at the table and watched as she dumped the spaghetti noodles into an awaiting colander. "You don't understand. Mom would think you were amazing if you could just boil an egg. She's the worst cook in the entire state of Texas."

Melissa shot a quick glance to Mary. "Don't worry," Mary said with a laugh. "He's quite right. It's one of the reasons Big Henry hired Etta. He knew if we tried to live on my cooking we'd all starve. Henry, why don't you set the table and I'll get the salad."

As always, dinner was a pleasant time. They chatted about favorite foods and Mary regaled Melissa with some of her war stories at the stove. The boys kept up their end of the conversation by babbling and cooing.

At one point James blew a raspberry. He looked startled and as they all laughed, he grinned and blew another one.

Henry smiled at Melissa. "You might have gotten his very first smile, but at least I didn't miss out on his very first raspberry."

After they'd finished eating Mary took the boys into the living room while Henry and Melissa cleaned up. "Dinner was terrific," he said as he stacked the dishes she rinsed into the dishwasher. "Do you like to cook?"

She nodded. "I do, but most of the time it seems like a lot of trouble to cook for one. When my mother was alive I did a lot of cooking, but not so much since she passed."

"You miss her."

She smiled with a touch of sadness. "Every day. Unfortunately diabetes is a ruthless disease and I think she was tired of fighting. It's some comfort to know she's not in pain anymore."

"I miss my father, too. He and I weren't just father and son, we were friends." Henry smiled at thoughts of his dad. "He was bigger than life, one of those colorful characters that people didn't forget after meeting him."

Melissa handed him the last plate. "And he taught you everything you need to know about being a wonderful father."

Henry smiled. "Yeah, I hadn't thought about it before, but he was a wonderful role model." He took the towel she offered him and dried his hands.

"It worried me that I was all alone," she said, her expression somber. "I worried about what would happen to the boys if I got hit by a car or had a sudden heart attack. Now I don't have to worry anymore. I know if anything happens to me you'll love them and take care of them."

"Nothing is going to happen to you," he assured her. "You and I are going to parent those boys until they're hulking adults and we're old and gray."

She smiled. "I like that plan, and speaking of the boys, I think it's probably time for a diaper change."

The rest of the evening passed and by nine o'clock it was time to put the boys down for the night. Mary said her good-night and retired to her wing of the house while Melissa carried Joey and Henry carried James up the stairs to their room.

Once the boys were settled into their beds, Melissa motioned Henry into her room. "Do you think I'm going to be able to head home tomorrow?" she asked.

Henry walked over to her window and peered outside. A light snow was still falling. He turned to look at her. "Why don't you make a decision in the morning? It's snowing now but maybe it will stop before too long. I can call Jimmy in the morning and ask him about the condition of the roads."

What he really wanted to do was have a repeat of the night before. But something in the way she stood with her arms crossed in front of her chest made him think she wouldn't be open to the idea.

"You want to go back down and have a glass of wine or something?" he asked.

She shook her head. "No, I think I'll just call it a night

now. I really am hoping that we'll be able to travel in the morning. Besides, it's been a long day and I'm exhausted."

He realized she was already distancing herself, preparing for the goodbye. He was surprised at the edge of sadness that took hold of him. It wasn't like it was going to be goodbye forever, he told himself. Most likely one way or another he'd be seeing her every weekend. If she didn't want to drive here, then he'd drive to Amarillo. But somehow he knew that once she left here things would never be the same between them again.

"Then I guess I'll just say good night," he said. He couldn't help himself. He stepped closer to her with the intention to deliver a kiss to her forehead, but instead found his mouth claiming hers.

The minute their lips connected the window where Henry had stood moments before shattered. As Henry saw the device that lay on the floor in the bedroom fear screamed inside him.

He shoved Melissa toward the door and they fell into the hallway as the bomb went off.

Chapter 10

One moment Henry had been kissing her and the next Melissa found herself on the hallway floor with Henry on top of her. The back of her head had connected hard with the floor in the fall and she was dazed and confused.

The loud explosion still rang in Melissa's ears, making her momentarily deaf. As Henry got off her, her hearing began to return. Above the din of the house alarm ringing she could hear the cries of her babies and her heart slammed into her chest with enough force to steal what little breath she had left.

"Check on the boys," Henry yelled as he pulled her up off the floor. He raced back into the bedroom and tore down the curtains that had caught on fire. As he stamped out the flames, she ran across the hall to the boys' room. They were safe, but scared by the noise.

She took them into her arms, and her heart beat so fast it felt as if it were trying to burst out of her chest. She stood in the center of the room, afraid to move, unsure what might happen next. She tried to calm the boys but with the alarm ringing discordantly it was impossible. Tears raced down Melissa's cheeks as she tried to still her own fear.

Somebody had thrown a bomb of some kind into the window of the bedroom where she'd slept, at the window where Henry had been standing only moments earlier. Her head couldn't wrap around it.

The blast could have killed him. It could have killed her. Had Henry not reacted as quickly as he had, they both could have been seriously hurt or worse.

She hugged the boys even closer to her chest and breathed a sigh of relief as the alarm suddenly stopped ringing. Now what? Had the danger passed? Was there more to come? Too afraid to move, she remained in the center of the room.

A moment later both Henry and Mary rushed into the room.

"You okay?" Henry asked her, his features taut with tension.

"We're fine," she said and felt a new press of tears as Mary put an arm around her shoulder.

"Jimmy is on his way," Henry said as he took Joey from her arms. "Let's go downstairs to wait for him."

By the time they got down the stairs several of Henry's ranch hands were at the front door. Henry opened the door to allow them inside and they all gathered in the living room.

"We heard the explosion," Charlie said, his features grim. "Then we saw the fire at the window. I'm just glad to see you're all okay."

"You didn't see anyone?" Henry asked as he shifted Joey from one arm to the other.

Both Charlie and Randy shook their heads. "Didn't hear a car, didn't see a soul," Charlie said. "Dammit, it's like it's a phantom."

"It wasn't a phantom that threw a bomb through the window," Henry said, his anger rife in his voice. He handed Joey to his mother. "I want to go out and take a look around. With the snow there should be some footprints that can be tracked."

Charlie frowned. "Unfortunately, Randy and I might have messed up any prints," he admitted. "When we heard the blast we both ran to that side of the house. I didn't even think about footprints."

"There still might be some prints that don't belong to the two of you," Henry said.

"Please, Henry, wait for Jimmy before you go out," Melissa said. She had no idea what other danger might await him if he ventured outside and she couldn't stand the thought of anything happening to him.

"Yes, Henry," Mary spoke up, her voice filled with

a mother's worry. "Please wait for Jimmy. I don't want you out there."

Melissa could tell by Henry's expression that he was chomping at the bit, needing to do something, anything that might find the guilty party.

"If you want, Randy and I can go back out and take another look around," Charlie offered.

"Trust me, if there's anyone around I'd be happy to tie him up and beat his ass until Jimmy shows up," Randy exclaimed.

Henry clapped him on the back. "I appreciate the sentiment, Randy, but the last thing I want is for anyone to get hurt. Why don't we all sit tight until Jimmy gets here?"

Charlie and Randy sat on the two chairs while Melissa and Mary sat on the sofa with the twins. Henry paced the room, looking like he wanted nothing more than to punch something or someone.

There was no question that somehow, someway, Melissa had to leave here as soon as possible. She couldn't place her children at risk. The idea that the pipe bomb could have easily been thrown through the window of the bedroom where the twins slept filled her with a kind of terror she'd never felt before.

"Randy, what I'd like you to do is see if you can find a piece of plywood in the shed to put over the broken window after Jimmy takes a look around." Henry turned to look at Melissa and his eyes were dark as midnight. "Melissa, I want you to pack a bag for you and the boys."

She looked at him in surprise. "But where are we

going?" She knew the roads were snow-packed and her tires weren't in the best shape. There was no way she'd take off at this time of night for home.

"I'm going to have Charlie check you in to a motel until the roads are safe enough for you to travel home." Henry looked at his mother. "You might want to pack a bag, too."

"Nonsense," Mary scoffed. "I agree with you that Melissa should take the twins and go but nobody is chasing me out of my home."

Henry nodded, as if unsurprised by his mother's decision to stay put. He returned his attention to Melissa. "The latest weather report I heard said that the snow is going to stick around for at least another twenty-four to forty-eight hours, so pack enough things to last you and the boys for a couple of days."

"But what about you?" Melissa asked. She wanted him to come with them, to leave this place of danger and hide out with her someplace where she knew he'd be safe.

"I'll be fine as long as I know you and the twins are safe." He took James from her arms. "Come on, I'll go up and help you get your things together."

"I'm going to head out to the shed," Randy said. "It's been long enough now I imagine whoever threw that bomb is long gone."

"And I'll wait here with Mrs. Randolf," Charlie added.

Henry said nothing as they climbed the stairs back to the room where the blast had occurred. The scent of smoke and gasoline lingered in the air.

"It must have been loaded with fuel," he said as he

surveyed the damage. "At least it wasn't filled with any kind of shrapnel."

Melissa shuddered at the thought. She pulled her suitcase from the closet and quickly packed what little she'd brought with her. They then moved into the boys' room, where she packed their clothes and diapers.

"I'll have Charlie get you settled in at one of the motels and I'll call you first thing in the morning," he said. She turned to face him and saw the worry in his eyes, a worry coupled with rage.

He stepped up to her and placed his palm against her cheek. She turned her face into the warmth of his hand. "He could have hurt you tonight. He could have hurt you and the boys."

"But that didn't happen," she said softly.

"Not this time, but I can't take another chance. I thought you were safe here, but I now realize I can't guarantee your safety. You'll be safe in a motel until the roads are clean enough for you to go home."

"Henry?" Jimmy's voice drifted up the stairs.

Henry dropped his hand from her face and stepped back from her. "Come on up, Jimmy."

Melissa and Henry met the lawman in the hallway. "You can have a look around. I'm sending Melissa with Charlie to a motel for the rest of the night. I'll be back up here as soon as I get those arrangements made."

Henry didn't say a word as they went back down-stairs. Once there, as Melissa and Mary began to put the coats on the boys, he disappeared into his study.

Minutes later he came out. "I've got you set up in a room at Ed's Motel. It's clean and comfortable and the owner is a friend of mine. The room is registered in the name of Hank James. Nobody will know you're there and the key will be waiting for you in the office."

A muscle knotted in his jaw. "Charlie will get you there safe and sound and I'll call you in the morning." He shoved a wad of cash into her hand. "There's a diner right next door to the motel. They'll deliver whatever you need to your motel-room door."

It was crazy, but as Melissa pulled on her coat and Charlie grabbed her bags, she had a sudden terrible fear for Henry.

"Please, stay safe," she said as she held the twins in her arms.

He kissed Joey and James on the forehead and then gently shoved a strand of her hair behind her ear. "Get out of here and let me do what I need to do."

It took only minutes for her and the boys to be loaded into Charlie's four-wheel-drive vehicle. While they pulled away from the house Melissa looked back to see Henry silhouetted in the front door.

Once again she was struck with the strong, inexplicable fear—the fear that she was never going to see him again.

"Henry, where are you going?" Jimmy asked as Henry pulled on his winter coat. They had just spent the last hour picking through the rubble in the bedroom.

Jimmy had collected the pieces of the device to use as evidence and now Randy was hanging the plywood over the broken window.

Charlie had returned to the ranch after dropping Melissa and the children at Ed's Motel. At least Henry had the comfort of knowing she and the babies would be safe there until she could leave town.

With each moment that had ticked by a rage had grown in Henry, a seething sick rage that begged to be released. And he knew exactly where to vent it.

"I'm going to Burke's house." Henry buttoned his coat but didn't reach for his gun in the drawer. He knew if he had it on him he might use it and as much as he wanted to hurt the man he believed was responsible for the pipe bomb, he didn't want to kill him. He was a father now, a man who had too much too lose by letting his rage get the best of him.

"Dammit, Henry, you can't go off half-cocked," Jimmy exclaimed in frustration.

"Trust me, I'm not half-cocked, I'm fully loaded," Henry replied dryly.

"Just stay put," Jimmy said. "I'll go talk to Burke."

"Then I'm coming with you." Henry didn't give Jimmy another opportunity to talk him out of it, but instead slammed out the door and walked into the snowy night.

Minutes later he and Jimmy were in Jimmy's patrol car navigating the slick roads as they headed into town. All Henry could think about was how devastating the results might have been had that bomb been thrown into the boys' room. The thought of such a tragedy stoked the flames of his rage even hotter.

"He could have killed my kids, Jimmy. He could have killed Melissa," Henry said, breaking the silence in the car.

"I know," Jimmy said. He grunted as the back of the car threatened to fishtail out. He steered into the slide and straightened the car. "We'll check out Tom's alibi for the time that the bomb was thrown through the window."

"It's possible he didn't personally throw it, but instead hired somebody." Henry frowned. "I've got to put an end to this." He stared out into the dark night. "Maybe I should withdraw from the election."

Jimmy shot him a stunned look. "You'd do that?"

"If I just had myself to worry about then I'd never quit. But it's not just me anymore, Jimmy. I've got kids and Melissa and they are going to need me."

"So they win and the corruption in Dalhart continues." Jimmy released an audible sigh. "Just give me a few more days before you make a decision. You're running on pure emotion right now. Give yourself time to calm down and let me sort this out."

Henry didn't reply. He knew Jimmy was right. He was definitely running on emotion, but as he thought of Melissa and Joey and James, he couldn't help but be filled with emotion.

He'd wanted to be a hero to the town, to clean up the mess that had been allowed to go on for far too long.

But he now wondered if the stakes were too high. He'd rather be a father than a hero.

He sat up straighter in the seat as they approached town. The only other vehicles they'd passed were snow trucks laying down salt and pushing snow.

Tom Burke lived well above his means and salary in a five-bedroom luxury home on a three-acre lot. The first thing Henry noticed was that Tom's car was parked in the driveway. Not only was the car relatively clean of snow, but tire tracks showed that it had recently been driven.

The rage that had slowly begun to wane during the drive now roared back to life inside Henry. He was out of the car before it had come to a complete halt.

"Henry, dammit, wait for me," Jimmy cried as he parked the car and got out.

Henry didn't wait. He headed for the front door with a single-mindedness and once he got there he banged on the door with his fist.

By the time the door was opened by Tom, Jimmy had reached the porch. Henry didn't say a word, but rather grabbed the short man by the front of his pristine white shirt and dragged him out the door.

"Hey, get your hands off me," Tom yelled and jerked out of Henry's grasp. "What the hell is wrong with you, man?"

"Have you been out to my place tonight, Tom? I see your car has been driven. Did you come to pay me a little visit?" Henry glared at him and became aware of Deputy Gordon Hunter joining them on the porch.

"I don't know what you're talking about," Tom exclaimed, his beefy face red. "I haven't been anywhere near your place tonight."

"Then you hired somebody to throw that pipe bomb through my window." Henry took a menacing step toward him. "I had babies in the house, you bastard."

Tom looked from Henry to Jimmy. "A pipe bomb? I don't know a damn thing about a pipe bomb."

"Then where did you go tonight?" Henry demanded. "Your car has been driven recently. Where did you go?"

"To the damned grocery store," Tom exclaimed in frustration. "We're supposed to get more snow. I needed to get a gallon of milk. Is that a crime now?"

"It's true," Gordon said. "I've been watching him, tailing him all evening. The only place he went is to the grocery store."

Henry stared at Gordon, then back at Tom. "I'm warning you right now, Tom. If anything happens to anyone I care about, I'll be back here to see you and I'll beat your ass to a pulp."

Tom looked at Jimmy in outrage. "Did you hear that? He threatened me with bodily harm."

Jimmy shook his head. "Nah, he didn't threaten you. He promised you." Jimmy clapped his hand on Henry's back. "Come on, Henry, nothing more can be done here for now."

Henry shot Tom another killer glare, then stalked back to Jimmy's car and got into the passenger seat. As

Jimmy and Gordon spoke to Tom for another few minutes, Henry steamed.

How were they ever going to get to the bottom of this? Whoever was responsible was smart enough to leave no clues behind, to do the kind of sneak attacks that made it impossible to investigate.

One thing was clear. He couldn't allow Melissa and the boys back into his home until the situation was resolved and that angered him more than anything.

It was a tension-filled ride back home. Jimmy talked the whole way, detailing his plan to investigate what had happened.

"We might be able to find fingerprints on the pieces of the bomb that survived the blast. There might be specific traceable material that was used. Don't you worry, Henry. I'm going to get to the bottom of this."

As he babbled on, Henry stared out the window, his mind drifting to Melissa and the boys. What were they doing at this moment? He glanced at his watch and realized his sons would be sound asleep and tonight he wouldn't be able to stand in the doorway and smell their scent, watch their little faces as they dreamed. Tonight he and Melissa wouldn't be able to sit together in the living room, enjoying quiet conversation after his mother had gone to bed.

The fact that some nut had taken these particular pleasures away from him reignited the fire of his anger. But by the time they finally reached the house the anger had burned itself out and he was simply exhausted.

Randy and Charlie sat with his mother in the living room and he quickly told them what had happened with Tom, then Charlie and Randy left.

"Are you all right?" his mother asked as he walked to the bar and poured himself a healthy dose of scotch.

"No. I'm angry and frustrated and I'm wondering if I shouldn't just pull out of the election." He sat on the sofa next to her.

"Is that what you want to do?"

"I don't want anything to happen to Melissa and the boys."

Mary smiled at him. "That didn't answer my question. Besides, as soon as the roads clear Melissa and the boys will return to Amarillo. You still have to live here with any decision you make."

Henry released a sigh and dropped his head back against the cushion. "I've never really been scared in my life, but the thought of how close danger came to Melissa and the boys put a fear in my heart I never want to feel again."

"Parenthood brings with it a multitude of fears." Mary patted his hand. "The first time those boys get on a bicycle your heart is going to race with fear. The day you put them on a bus to go to school you're going to be filled with a terror as you think of all the things that can go wrong. But you'll also know a joy greater than anything you've ever experienced with them."

Henry nodded.

"And then there's Melissa," Mary said softly. "You light up in her presence, Henry."

"She's the mother of my children," he replied.

"I think she could be more than that to you if you'd just open up that heart of yours," Mary said.

"I don't want her to be any more than that," he replied with forced lightness.

Mary sighed. "Your father was a wonderful man, Henry, but he was obsessed about some woman stealing your money. I worry that instead of making you careful, which was his intention, he made you incapable of allowing anyone close to you."

He was in no mood for one of his mother's attempts to get him to change his mind about love and marriage. He tipped his glass up and drained his drink, welcoming the hot burn down his throat. "Mom, it's been a long day and I'm exhausted. I have a lot of things to think about and I don't want to have a conversation about my decision to stay single."

"You're right. I'm sorry." She got up from the sofa. "I'm going to bed. I'll see you in the morning and hopefully by then Jimmy will have this all figured out and we can get back to a normal life."

"Good night, Mom." He watched her disappear up the stairs, then once again leaned his head back and released a long sigh.

He hoped Jimmy had some answers in the morning, but he didn't expect him to have any. He looked over at the phone. What he'd like to do is call Melissa, just hear her voice before he called it a night. But it was late and he didn't want to wake the boys. Besides, he'd told her he'd call her first thing in the morning.

He got up from the sofa and walked to the window. It was snowing again. Yesterday he'd hoped for snow so that he could keep Melissa and the boys here longer. Now he prayed for it to end so she could take the boys back to Amarillo where they would be safe from the madness that had become his life.

Chapter 11

It was the longest night of Melissa's life. The motel room was typical of motel rooms all around the country, equipped with a king-size bed, a television in a cabinet and a desk. It was spotlessly clean and once she'd placed the desk chair and a barricade of pillows along one side of the bed, the boys fell asleep almost immediately.

Unfortunately sleep remained elusive for her. She took a fast shower and changed into her nightgown, then got into bed and tried not to relive the events of the night.

What was happening at the house? Were Henry and Mary all right? If anything happened who would come to tell Melissa that something had gone wrong? Surely somebody would keep her informed.

She tossed and turned with worry and fear and it was during those long hours of sleeplessness that she realized the depth of her love for Henry James Randolf III. And in that realization she knew she would never be able to give him what he wanted.

The idea of making her home in the carriage house, so close, yet not a part of his life, was physically painful to consider. She could easily imagine the kind of routine they'd fall into over time.

The twins would spend a lot of their time in the big house with Henry and Mary and occasionally the desire Henry and Melissa felt for each other would rear up and explode and they'd make love. There would be no commitment, no love, just an arrangement. She couldn't do it. She couldn't sacrifice her own dreams of a marriage and love forever just so that Henry could get what he wanted—full-time access to the boys and an occasional release of sexual tension with her.

As soon as possible she was heading home and she and Henry would work out a viable visitation plan, one that didn't involve her living in his backyard.

She finally fell asleep around dawn and awakened around eight with a sliver of sunshine drifting in around the edges of the curtains. The boys were still asleep. The disruption from the night before had apparently exhausted them.

She got out of bed and pulled on the luxurious burgundy robe Henry had bought her and moved to the window to peer outside. Although it had snowed another inch or so overnight, the sun was a welcome sight. Surely by late evening or first thing in the morning the roads would be cleared enough that she and the babies could go home.

She needed the reality of her little apartment, away from Henry, where she could think clearly. Being with Henry definitely muddied her mind.

The ring of the telephone on the desk pulled her from the window. She grabbed up the receiver and said a soft hello.

"You okay?" Henry's deep voice filled her ear.

"I am now that I know you're okay," she replied. "I couldn't sleep last night. I've been worried about you."

"I almost called you last night to tell you that everything was fine, but I was afraid I'd wake the boys. I've got a glass company coming out first thing this morning to replace the broken window in the bedroom. Jimmy and his men went over it with a fine-tooth comb looking for anything that might be evidentiary. How are the boys?"

She glanced over to the bed. "Still sleeping. What happened after I left last night?" She listened as he told her about going to Tom Burke's home and confronting the man he thought responsible.

"You didn't really expect him to confess, did you?" she asked when he was finished.

"No, but it would have been nice if we could have settled all this last night. I'm hoping Jimmy will be able to get something from the pieces of the device he collected last night, something that will be enough evidence for an arrest."

"You know I can't come back to the house," she said, her heart heavy as the words left her mouth.

"I don't want you and the boys back here," he replied. "Not until this is all resolved. Last night was too close for comfort and I'd never forgive myself if anything happened to you or Joey or James."

Melissa squeezed the receiver closer to her ear as she heard the passion in his voice. He cared about her. She knew he did, but it wasn't enough for him to invite her fully into his life.

"You have everything you need there? The roads are still pretty bad but you should be able to get home sometime tomorrow."

"That's what I thought when I looked outside the window a minute ago, and yes, I have everything I need—we need."

"I'll have Charlie or one of the other men deliver your car later today or first thing in the morning. I don't want to be seen there with you." He paused a moment. "So I won't be able to tell you or the boys a personal goodbye."

She could hear the regret, a true longing in his voice, but she was almost glad that there wouldn't be a personal goodbye. There were going to be enough goodbyes in their future and she had a feeling she'd find each and every one of them difficult. "You'll let me know if anything changes?"

"Of course," he replied. "I'll call you later this evening in any case. And, Melissa, I'm so sorry about all this."

"You don't have to apologize. Just take care of yourself, Henry. My boys need their daddy."

"And I need them," he replied softly, then with a murmured goodbye he hung up. By that time the boys were awakening and she changed diapers and fixed them each a bottle of formula.

While they ate their breakfast she made a pot of coffee in the coffeemaker provided, then studied the menu she found on the desk from the diner next door.

She was starving and she knew part of it was probably stress-related. She picked up the phone and called in an order for an omelet and toast. While she waited for the food to be delivered she got dressed for the day.

The boys had just finished their bottles when her food was delivered. She sat at the desk to eat and kept one eye on the twins, who entertained themselves by playing with their fingers and toes and gurgling to each other as if sharing a secret language.

The omelet was excellent and after she'd cleaned up the mess she stretched out on the bed and played with her sons.

Maybe it had just been the spirit of Christmas that had her feeling so strongly about Henry. The days she had spent in his home had been like a fantasy of everything she'd ever wanted in her life. She didn't care about the lavish gifts or the fancy mansion; she didn't care about personal cooks and sterling silverware. She didn't need any of that.

It had been the warmth of family that had seduced her, the caring both Mary and Henry had offered to her and her children. It had been the shared laughter and the comfortable small talk.

Henry was going to make a tremendous father, but he'd warned her all along that he wasn't interested in becoming a husband. Still, somehow he'd made her want to be his wife.

Instead of thinking of what would never be, she tried to focus on what she intended to do when she got home. She was more determined than ever to jump back into her decorating business. She'd contact old clients, solicit for new ones and hopefully the business would grow.

Somehow she and Henry would work out a solution to the visitation issue, one that would allow each of them the independence to continue their own lives. Eventually perhaps she would find a man who would love her like she wanted to be loved, a man who would bind his life with hers. Although at the moment the idea of any man other than Henry filled her with repugnance.

What she'd once felt for Tom was a pale imitation of her feelings for Henry. She realized now that she hadn't loved Tom. She'd never loved like she loved Henry.

The day passed achingly slow. When the boys fell asleep for their naps, she turned on the television and watched two soap operas that she'd never seen before.

Around four o'clock she placed another order at the diner, deciding that an early meal and early bedtime would be the best thing.

The sun had continued to shine throughout the day and she'd heard the rumble of street plows working, letting her know that she should be able to leave first thing in the morning.

By five-thirty she'd eaten her dinner, fed the boys and the sun had gone down. She was considering changing back into her nightgown when a knock fell on her door.

With the chain on the door she cracked it open a mere inch to see who was on the other side. "Charlie," she said and quickly unfastened the chain to open the door. "Henry said you might come by to bring my car."

"Actually, Henry sent me here to take you and the boys back to the house," Charlie replied as he stepped inside the room.

"What?" She looked at him in surprise. "Has something happened?"

Charlie nodded. "Tom Burke has been arrested and the danger is over. Henry wants you all back at the ranch."

"When did all this happen?" she asked, a wave of happiness sweeping through her.

"Just a little while ago. I don't have any real details. Henry just told me to come here and collect you and the boys and bring you home."

Melissa looked around the room. "It's going to take a few minutes for me to pack everything up again."

Charlie smiled. "Take your time. I just know Henry doesn't want you here another night since it's safe now for you to be back at the house."

Melissa was thrilled by the news that Tom had been arrested and Henry was no longer in danger. Charlie entertained the twins with silly faces while Melissa scurried around and quickly packed her things.

She was going to have to say goodbye in person. The thought broke her heart just a little bit. It would have been easier to take off in the morning without any long goodbyes to Henry. But she knew Henry probably wanted to spend time with the twins one last time before she left for home the next day.

Tonight she would have to tell him about her decision not to move into the carriage house. It would be difficult but she was firm in her decision and he was just going to have to accept it.

Finally she had her things ready to go. While Charlie carried her suitcase back to his SUV, she got the boys into their coats. "You're going to see Daddy again," she said, buttoning Joey's coat.

"I'll carry this little guy," Charlie said as he came back into the room and picked up James. "I've still got the car seats so everyone will ride safely."

Within minutes they were all packed in the car and Charlie started the engine. "Do I need to check out or anything?" she asked.

"Nah, Henry will take care of it." He put the vehicle in Reverse and backed out of the parking space.

"So you don't know what kind of charges have been pressed again Tom?" she asked.

"No, but I'm assuming it's attempted murder or something serious like that," Charlie replied.

"I'm so happy that it's finally been resolved, that Henry is safe and can get on with his life." She stared out the window and frowned. "Shouldn't we be going the opposite direction?"

"No, I'm going exactly where I need to go." Charlie turned and smiled at her, but in the depths of his eyes she saw something cold, something calculating and the first whisper of fear edged through her.

Her throat went dry. "Do you have an errand to run before you take us home?"

"Yeah, an errand that's going to change my life." He reached into his coat pocket and pulled out a gun. "And I suggest you sit back and enjoy the ride."

Melissa stared at him with a rising sense of horror. Charlie? Why was Charlie holding a gun on her and where was he taking her?

Fear screamed inside her head, a fear for herself, but more important, a fear for the two babies who were in the backseat.

It had been a busy day but no matter what Henry did his thoughts were on Melissa and the boys. It ached in him that he wouldn't be able to give the boys a final kiss on their sweet cheeks before sending them back home, that he wouldn't be able to fill his lungs with the sweet baby scent of them.

He would have liked the opportunity to tell Melissa goodbye in person, too. One last look at that shine in her eyes, one more of her lovely smiles to end the holidays would have been nice.

But he reminded himself that this wasn't a permanent goodbye. Whether they liked it or not they were in each other's lives for at least the next eighteen years.

Etta hadn't made it in because of the snow so at dinnertime he and his mother had a quiet meal of ham and cheese sandwiches. In fact, throughout the day the house had been far too quiet.

He hadn't realized how much Melissa and the boys had filled it up and brightened every dark corner. He told himself this was just temporary, that eventually they'd be back and the house would come alive once again.

It was almost six o'clock when he sat down in his study and picked up the phone to call her. The phone rang at the motel room once…twice…three times. Henry frowned as it rang a fourth and fifth time.

He finally hung up but stared at the phone with confusion. Surely she wouldn't have taken the boys out anywhere. She didn't have a car and it was frigid outside. *Maybe she's in the shower,* he thought.

Picking up a pen, he tapped the end of it on his desk as a vision of Melissa in the shower filled his head. He could easily imagine her slender body beneath a steaming spray of water, visualize the slide of the soap across her full breasts.

He threw the pen down, irritated with these kinds of thoughts. He'd believed that if he made love to her one more time she'd be out of his system. He thought that the crazy physical attraction he felt for her would wane, but instead of diminishing, it seemed to have grown stronger.

He picked up the phone and tried her number again. It rang and rang and still there was no answer. How long did a woman spend in the shower?

He got up from the desk and paced the room, a thrum of anxiety inside his chest. Moving to the window, he stared out in the direction of the carriage house. He still hoped to talk her into moving in there. It would make everything so much less complicated.

They were going to work well together as a team in raising the boys. He was incredibly lucky that a woman like Melissa was the mother of his children.

He returned to the desk and tried to call her once again. When there was still no answer, the anxiety that had whispered through him screamed with alarm. Racing out of the study, he headed for the coat closet in the foyer and yanked out his coat. He grabbed his gun from the drawer and stuck it in his pocket.

"Henry? Where are you going?" Mary appeared in the foyer.

"I can't get hold of Melissa on the phone. Nobody answers and I've got a bad feeling."

Mary's hand flew up to her heart. "Maybe she was

in the bathroom, or stepped outside for a moment. Maybe she went to the office for something?"

"Maybe," he replied grimly. "But I won't be satisfied until I go there and check it out."

"Should I call Jimmy?" she asked worriedly.

"No, I'll call him if I need him. It's possible there's a perfectly logical explanation for her not answering the phone." He leaned over and kissed his mother on the cheek. "Don't worry."

"You'll call me?"

"The minute I get there and know that everything is all right." He didn't wait for her reply, but instead braced himself and hurried out into the cold evening air.

Minutes later as he pointed his truck toward town, he thought of all the logical explanations for the unanswered calls. Maybe she'd gone to get ice. Maybe one of the boys had been crying and she hadn't heard the ring of the phone.

There could be a dozen innocent reasons, but the possibility of those wasn't what made his heart bang in his chest. And his heart was banging fast and furious. He felt as if a wild beast had been let loose in his chest.

Fear. Rich and raw, it clawed at his guts, made him sick with worry. He'd never felt like this before. He'd never known this kind of fear.

The going was slow as the roads were slick and nasty. His hands clenched the steering wheel tightly as he prayed that nothing was wrong, that nothing bad had happened.

A lump lodged in the back of his throat. Had one of

the boys gotten ill and Melissa had somehow taken them to a doctor? Surely if that had happened, she would have called him.

By the time he reached the city limits he was almost nauseous with worry. Ed's Motel was on the south side of town along the main highway. It was a typical one-story building with connecting rooms that faced the parking lot. The office was in the center, but Henry went past it. He knew Melissa was in Room 112 and it was in front of that unit that he pulled up and parked.

He cut the engine and jumped out, his heart banging faster than he could ever remember it beating before. "Melissa?" He banged on the door. "Melissa, it's Henry. Open the door."

Nothing. No answer, no door opening. Absolutely nothing. He hammered on the door with his fist, then tried the door. It opened into a dark room.

He flipped on the light. The bedspread was wrinkled with pillows lined up against one side, but there was no suitcase, no babies and no Melissa anywhere in the room.

Maybe he got the room number wrong, he thought, but even as he grabbed onto that idea, he smelled the faint familiar scent of Melissa lingering in the air. She'd been here. Oh, God, so, where was she now?

He wouldn't have thought his heart could beat any faster, but it did, thundering in his chest with painful intensity.

He left the room and ran across the parking lot to the diner. Maybe she'd decided to take the boys there for dinner. Although he couldn't imagine her packing them up and carrying them across the way when the diner would deliver whatever she needed, he clung to the hope that this was the explanation for her absence.

Although on a normal evening at this time the diner would be packed, the weather conditions had the place nearly deserted. Henry took two steps inside the door and instantly knew she wasn't there.

His heart crashed to the floor. He stepped back outside and pulled his cell phone from his pocket. His fingers trembled as he punched in Jimmy's phone number.

"Jimmy, it's me," he said when the sheriff answered. "I need you to meet me at Ed's Motel. Something has happened to Melissa and the boys."

With Jimmy's assurance that he'd be right over, Henry walked back to the motel and into the office. Maybe he'd gotten the room number wrong. Maybe he'd only imagined the scent of Melissa in the room.

The owner, Ed Warren, was at the front desk and greeted Henry with a friendly smile.

"Henry, didn't expect to see you tonight," he said.

"Ed, that room I rented from you by phone. What room number was it?"

"112," Ed replied without hesitation. "I know because it's the only room I've rented in the past couple of days. This damned weather has practically closed me down. Why? Is there a problem?"

"Have you noticed anybody around the room? Have you seen a car or anything parked in front of it?"

"No, to be honest I haven't moved from behind this desk all day. I know a pretty lady came in for the key last night and that's all."

"The pretty lady isn't there now and she had a couple of babies with her. You haven't seen them this evening?"

Ed shook his head. "Sorry, Henry. I can't help you."

Henry reeled back out the door, almost blinded by the sickness that welled up inside him. Where were his babies? And where was Melissa?

Chapter 12

Melissa had never known such terror. There was no escape. She couldn't open the car door and jump out, not leaving Joey and James still in the car with Charlie. She was trapped and she had no idea why this was happening, what Charlie had planned for them.

As they left the city limits and began to travel on dark, lonely country roads, the terror clawed up the back of her throat and twisted her insides.

Joey and James had fallen asleep, unaware of the drama taking place. "Where are you taking us?" she finally asked, her voice reed thin.

"Don't you worry about it," Charlie replied. "If you

do what I tell you to do then there's no reason anybody has to get hurt and you and your kids will be fine."

"What do you want, Charlie? Why are you doing this?" She needed to make sense of it. "Is this because of your sister? Because Henry didn't want to marry her?"

Charlie laughed, the sound not pleasant. "I don't give a damn about Hilary. That stupid bitch dated Henry for over a year and couldn't close the deal. If she'd gotten Henry to marry her then I would have been on easy street. As Henry's brother-in-law I wouldn't have been shoveling horse crap anymore. I could have worked a respectable job with all the perks. Now I have to take matters into my own hands."

Henry had believed that somebody on the town council was responsible for the attacks on him. But he'd been wrong. "You were trying to kill Henry?" she asked.

Charlie glanced at her and laughed once again. "Trust me, if I'd wanted Henry dead, he'd be dead. I just wanted to disrupt his perfect little life, make him go to bed at night a little nervous."

"But why? What's he ever done to you?"

"I hate him!" Charlie exclaimed with vehemence. "I should be living his life. I should have his money. All he did to earn it was be born. I've been working my ass off for all my life. I came from nothing, but those babies in the backseat are my ticket to something."

It all crystallized in Melissa's mind. Kidnapped. Charlie was kidnapping her and the boys and was going to demand a ransom.

Henry had spent his entire life worrying that some woman might try to take his money from him and now because of her and the boys his fear was coming true, except it wasn't a woman about to take him, but a madman.

What if he didn't pay? Even as the possibility entered her mind she dismissed it. She'd only spent a couple of days with Henry, but she knew the man he was, she knew what was in his heart. He'd turn his bank account inside out to assure the safety of his children.

But what if something went terribly wrong? What if Charlie snapped or things didn't go as he planned? There was no question that to Charlie she and the boys were expendable. Nobody knew where they were, nobody would suspect Charlie of wanting to hurt Henry or having anything to do with her disappearance.

They were in mortal danger and at the moment she saw no way out of it. Maybe when they arrived to wherever he was taking them she'd be able to do something—anything—to get away. She grabbed on to that hope, that somehow, someway, she'd be able to figure out a plan.

She glanced at her wristwatch. It was just after six. Henry had said he'd call her sometime this evening. Had he tried to call? Did he even know they were missing yet?

It seemed like they drove forever before Charlie finally pulled to a stop. In the glare of the headlights stood a small shanty. It was dark and isolated, surrounded by trees laden with snow. There wasn't a light from a neighbor or a sign of civilization anywhere.

A shudder worked through Melissa, a shiver that had nothing to do with the cold as Charlie opened his car door. "Get the kids and don't try anything stupid. You're worth nothing to him or to me and I won't hesitate to kill you if you give me any trouble."

She believed him. The coldness in his eyes, the hardness in his voice let her know he meant what he said. Charlie knew Henry would pay whatever the demand to get his children back, but she was definitely expendable. Henry didn't love her.

She was grateful that the boys didn't awaken as she unfastened them and pulled them from the car seats. She held them tight as Charlie motioned her into the shanty with the barrel of his gun. Once inside he turned on a light that illuminated the dismal interior.

There was a sink, a small refrigerator, a two-burner hot plate, a microwave and a small table along one wall. On the other side of the small room was a single-size cot and a door she assumed led to a bathroom. A small electric heater blew warm air, but not enough to heat the entire room.

"Put the kids on the bed," he commanded.

On trembling legs she moved to the cot and gently placed the sleeping twins in the center of the small area. Tears blurred her vision as she straightened up and turned to face her captor.

"Unfortunately this is going to be your home away

from home for the next day or two," he said. "Sit down." He pointed to one of the chairs at the table.

With one backward glance at the sleeping twins Melissa did as he asked. "You threw that bomb through the window, didn't you?" she asked and was appalled by the quiver in her voice.

Charlie opened the cabinet beneath the sink and pulled out a heavy chain. The sight of it shot a new wave of fear through her. "Yeah, it's amazing how easy it is to build a little pipe bomb. I shot out the tire on Henry's car, too. My original plan was to waylay you as you left town, but Henry's decision to move you into the motel made it all so easy."

He straightened and locked one end of the chain on a metal hook that had been driven into the wall and then approached her with the other end.

"Please, you don't have to do this," she said, the tears not only blurring her vision but running hot down her cheeks. "I can talk to Henry. I'm sure he'll give you whatever you want. Just please, let me and my babies go."

"Shut up," he said. He bent down and grabbed her ankle. She instinctively kicked at him, the survival instinct roaring to life.

He stepped back from her, the gun pointed at her head. "Don't make this difficult. I told you that if you cooperate, you won't get hurt. But I won't hesitate to put a bullet through your head if you give me any trouble. You understand?"

She drew a deep breath, gulped back a sob and

nodded. She didn't want to give him a reason to kill her. She had to stay alive. She had to figure out a way out of this and save her boys.

"Now, I'm going to put this chain on your ankle. There's enough length for you to move around the room, take care of the kids and use the bathroom. There's some grub in the refrigerator and you should be fine until I get back here."

He fastened the chain around her ankle and she shuddered at the cold bite of steel against her skin. "I'll bring in your things so you should have everything you need."

With that he disappeared out the door. Instantly Melissa grabbed the chain in her hands and began to attempt to pull it out of the wall. She yanked and pulled, but there was no give at all.

She quickly dropped the chain as Charlie came back in carrying her suitcase and the diaper bag. The one thing he didn't have was her purse with her cell phone inside.

"Don't look so worried. You should only be here a couple of days, however long it takes him to get the cash for me. I'm not even going to make a ransom demand until tomorrow. I'll give him a night to worry. It will put him in a better mood to deal with me and my demands."

"Please, Charlie," she said one last time. "If you let us go now I won't tell anyone what you did."

"If and when you get a chance to tell anyone I'll be

long gone. I'll be a rich man on some tropical beach living under a new name."

"Henry will never stop looking for you," she insisted. "He'll hunt you down wherever you go. You'll live your life looking over your shoulder."

He smiled, obviously not concerned by her words. "But what a great life it's going to be. I'll be back later." He dropped the suitcase and diaper bag to the floor, then left the shanty. She heard him lock the door from the outside and then she was alone with just her sleeping babies to keep her company.

"Henry, there's no sign of a struggle or forced entry," Jimmy said. He'd arrived at the motel room with two of his deputies. "There's nothing to indicate that anything bad happened her. Maybe she just went home."

"Without her car?" The urgent burn in Henry's gut had only intensified over the past half an hour.

"Maybe she had somebody pick her up," Ben Whitfield, one of the deputies, said.

Henry shook his head. "She wouldn't have done that. She wouldn't have left without telling me goodbye."

"Maybe the scene at your house last night scared her more than she let on. Maybe she was afraid to tell you she was going home because she was afraid you'd try to change her mind," Jimmy said.

A new sick feeling swept through Henry. Had he been pushing her so hard the past couple of days that she might have taken off without telling him? Afraid that he'd push her to do something she didn't want to do? Even though their time together had been relatively brief, he believed he knew the kind of woman Melissa was and he was convinced that wasn't the case.

"I'm telling you, Jimmy, something's happened. We've got to find her." He looked at the sheriff. "She's in trouble. I know it. I feel it."

"Ben, you and Jake hit the streets, see if you can find anyone who might have seen something," Jimmy said.

"What about Tom Burke?" Henry asked.

"I already checked with Gordon. Tom is home with his family and can't have had anything to do with Melissa or your boys."

Henry grabbed Jimmy by the shoulder. "We have to do something, man. We have to find them." The emotions that filled Henry left him weak, a combination of the worst fear he'd ever known in his life.

"We'll find them, Henry. Why don't you go home and wait. Maybe she'll call."

"I can't go home. I need to do something," he said in frustration.

"Henry, take a deep breath. We don't even know that something bad has happened," Jimmy repeated.

But Henry knew. He felt it in his gut. There was no way that Melissa would have left town without speaking to him, no way she would have left her car at his house and taken off with somebody.

Something was wrong.

Something was horribly wrong.

"I'm going to drive around and see if anyone has seen her," Henry said. He couldn't go home and tell his mother that Melissa and the boys were missing.

Telling Jimmy he'd be in touch, Henry got into his truck and started to drive down the street, looking for anyone who might have seen Melissa and the boys. For the next hour he stopped at each and every business that was open and questioned anyone he found in the place.

Where could they be? What had happened in that motel room? Jimmy was right, there had been no sign of a struggle. Whoever she left with, she'd apparently gone willingly.

Surely if she'd planned on having somebody pick her up and take her back to Amarillo she would have said something to him when they'd spoken earlier on the phone. She would have made arrangements to get her car.

It was almost nine when he finally headed back to the ranch. He didn't know what else to do, where else to look. He only knew the terror that filled his heart.

The drive back to his place was the longest he'd ever made. Tears burned behind his eyes but he refused to let them fall. Tears implied sadness, grief and he absolutely refused to grieve for Melissa and the boys. He needed to stay strong.

His mother met him at the door. "What's going on?"

"They're gone." The words fell from his lips and suddenly the tears that he'd fought so hard to control spilled from him.

"Melissa and the boys aren't at the motel. We can't find them, Mom. We don't know where they are."

Mary reached for him and wrapped her arms around him, attempting to comfort him like she had when he'd been a little boy and had skinned his knee. But he wasn't a little boy and this was far worse than a bruised knee.

He stuffed back his tears and straightened. "I don't know what to do. I don't know what's happened. I've never felt so helpless in my life."

He allowed his mother to lead him into the living room, where they both sagged down to the sofa. "Jimmy and a couple of his men are out looking. I drove up and down the streets and asked everyone I saw, but nobody had seen them."

"Maybe she called a friend," Mary said, but Henry could tell by her tone that she didn't believe her own words.

"You and I both know she wouldn't have left town without telling us goodbye. That's not who Melissa is." He leaned his head back and closed his eyes and prayed that somehow this nightmare would end.

Both he and Mary jumped as the doorbell rang. Henry shot up off the sofa and raced to the door. He opened it to see Charlie.

"I just heard," Charlie said. "Is there anything I can do to help?"

Henry motioned him inside the foyer. "Last night when you dropped Melissa off at the motel did you see anybody around?"

Charlie frowned. "Not that I noticed. I made sure we weren't followed when we left here. I can't be a hundred percent certain that nobody saw her when I let her and the boys out of the car. God, man. What can I do?"

Henry raked a hand through his hair. "I don't think there's anything anyone can do at the moment. Jimmy and his men are out searching in town and I don't know what else to do."

"I'm heading home. You'll call me if I can do anything?"

"Thanks, Charlie. I will." Henry watched as the man left the house and walked to his vehicle in the driveway.

The night was dark and cold and Melissa was out there with his babies. "Maybe we scared her away," his mother spoke from behind him.

He turned to look at her.

"Maybe we came on too strong. We bought so many things, made it look as if we were making a home here for the twins." Mary wrung her hands together. "Maybe she's afraid you'll take those babies from her and so she ran away."

"No, she wouldn't do that." He knew in his heart, in the depths of his very soul, that she wouldn't just disappear. He turned back to the door and stared outside. "I think somebody has them. I think somebody took them from the motel room."

"But why?" Mary cried.

Once again he turned to face her. "Maybe as a final attempt to make me pull out of the election. I don't know. We won't know for sure until whoever has them contacts us."

"Surely whoever has them wouldn't hurt them." Mary's voice trembled with her fear.

He didn't attempt to give her false pacification. "I don't know, Mom."

"So, what do we do now?" she asked.

Henry's stomach clenched. "We wait."

Melissa wasted no time the minute Charlie left the shanty. First she worked to try to get the chain off her ankle. He'd secured it with a padlock and she was hoping maybe she could use something to pick it open. But a search of the two drawers in the kitchen area yielded nothing more than two spoons. Even the handle of the spoon was no good in trying to pick the lock.

The boys remained sleeping soundly. She was grateful for their silence. She needed to think. Even if she did manage to get herself free from the chain, then what? She had no idea where they were, no idea how far she'd have to walk with the twins in her arms to get help.

But she figured her odds were better braving the elements than staying here until Charlie returned. Henry had said that his breakup with Hilary hadn't seemed to matter to Charlie. Apparently, it had.

Charlie had seen Hilary and Henry's marriage as a ticket for him off the ranch. When that had fallen apart, she'd made the mistake of coming here and giving

Charlie a new bargaining chip. She glanced at the twins. No, two bargaining chips, she thought.

What scared her more than anything was that she didn't think Charlie intended to let her live. The twins couldn't identify their kidnappers, but she could. If she died then Charlie would be safe. He'd never have to look over his shoulder to see if somebody was after him.

For the next hour she pulled on the place where the chain was connected to the wall, hoping to break it loose. She finally sat on the floor, exhausted by her efforts and overwhelmed with defeat.

Silently she began to weep. She would never see her babies grow up. She'd never see their first step or hear them say Mommy. She wouldn't be there to put them on the bus for their first day of school, to straighten a tie when they went to their first school dance.

Pain flooded her as she stuffed a hand against her mouth to keep the sobs from ripping out of her. She wept until there were no more tears to weep and then she prayed. She prayed that no matter what happened to her, the boys would be safe. She prayed that they would live a long and happy life with Henry and Mary.

Thoughts of Henry brought more tears. She'd never see him again. She'd never see that slow slide of a sexy grin across his lips, the simmering sparkle of pleasure in his eyes.

Surely by now he knew they were missing. She looked at her watch. Almost ten. He would have called the room and gotten worried when she hadn't answered.

He was probably looking for her now. Unfortunately there was no way he'd ever suspect his right-hand man on the ranch, the worker he depended on. The last person he'd suspect would be Charlie.

She pulled herself up and looked in the cabinets, seeking something that could be used as a weapon. He might intend to kill her, but she'd like to be able to hurt him before he did. She'd like to be able to mark him in a way that might bring up some questions.

Her fingernails were kept too short to do damage to his face. But surely she could use something in the cabinets.

She searched every nook and cranny on the room and found nothing. The cabinets held only a handful of canned goods, some soup and pork and beans and corn. The refrigerator had a gallon of milk, a loaf of bread, a package of bologna and a small jar of mayo. The freezer contained five frozen dinners.

She had a feeling the food had been brought in specifically for her and there was just enough for a couple of days. This hadn't been a spur-of-the-moment decision on Charlie's part. He'd planned this and that depressed her even more.

Finally, she sat next to the bed where the twins slept and laid her head back. She could smell her babies, the sweet scent of innocence and love.

She closed her eyes with the weary knowledge that at least she knew they'd be loved by Henry for the rest of their lives, even if she wasn't around to share it.

Chapter 13

"Henry, Hilary is on the phone," Mary said.

Henry frowned. "I don't have time to talk to her now. Tell her I'll call her back later." He returned his attention to Jimmy, who sat on the chair opposite the sofa where Henry was seated.

"We're treating the motel room as a crime scene," Jimmy said. "Even though we don't know if a crime has occurred. I've got a couple of my boys lifting prints to see what we find."

"It's a motel room. You're probably going to find the prints of people who stayed there ten years ago," Henry said with a weary sigh.

"Ed's place is pretty clean. It's possible we'll lift fresh prints."

"And then what? Unless you have a matching set on file the prints won't tell us anything."

"Henry, we're doing the best we can," Jimmy replied patiently.

"I know, I know. You tell Tom Burke that if he had anything to do with this, then he wins. If he'll let them go unharmed, I'll leave him alone. I'll pull out of the race for mayor and he can continue his business practices as he sees fit."

"Henry, I don't think it's Tom," Jimmy said. "Or anyone he's hired. I've known Tom for most of my life. Sure, he's a scoundrel, he's a white-color criminal but this isn't something he's capable of."

"Would you stake Melissa's life on that? Stake the lives of my boys on it?" Henry replied.

"Of course not. I'm just telling you what my gut is telling me and that's that Tom isn't responsible."

"Then who is?" Henry asked as a hollowness threatened to swallow him whole. "Jesus, Jimmy, who is responsible? Who could hate me this much?"

Jimmy swiped his broad hand down the length of his face. "I don't know. It might not be about hate. It might be about greed. If this is some kind of kidnapping then I'm guessing that you'll hear from the kidnapper."

Henry looked at his watch. It was after ten. "We don't even know how long they've been missing. I spoke to her this morning but didn't speak to her after that."

"I checked with the diner. Dinner was delivered to the room at around four-thirty so we know she and the boys were there then," Jimmy said.

"I've made coffee," Mary said as she stepped into the living room.

Jimmy stood. "Come on, Henry, let's go have some coffee. It looks like it's going to be a long night."

The last thing Henry wanted was to sit around and drink coffee while Melissa and his boys were out there somewhere. He wanted to beat on every door in the town of Dalhart until he found the place where Melissa and the twins were being held.

But he followed Jimmy into the kitchen, where the two men sat at the table while his mother poured them each a cup of the fresh brew.

"Shouldn't we call the FBI or something?" Mary asked. She looked as if she'd aged ten years in the past couple of hours.

Jimmy shook his head. "They won't be interested until I have evidence that a crime has occurred. She's only been missing for five or six hours and we don't know if she made the decision to go missing of her own free will."

Henry frowned and wrapped his hands around his coffee cup, seeking the warmth to banish the icy chill that had taken possession of his body the moment he'd entered the empty motel room.

"If this is a kidnapping for ransom I wish to hell somebody would call me," Henry said.

They all froze as Jimmy's cell phone rang. Henry's stomach clenched as Jimmy answered. He listened for a moment. "Just keep me posted," he finally said then hung up. "That was Jake. He and Ben have questioned everyone in the block surrounding the motel and nobody has seen Melissa."

"Why doesn't he call?" Henry cried. "If somebody has them why in the hell haven't they called to tell me what he wants?"

The frustration, the fear and the rage that had been building throughout the night exploded and Henry slammed his hands down on the table. "If anybody hurts them I'll kill them. I swear, Jimmy. I'll kill the bastard responsible for this."

At that moment the doorbell rang. Henry leaped up from the table and hurried to the door, his heart thundering in the hope that it would be Melissa.

It wasn't. It was Hilary.

"Henry, I heard about Melissa and the babies missing. I need to talk to you." There was a trembling urgency in her voice.

"Hilary, this really isn't a good time," he said, unable to stop the crashing waves of pain that coursed through him.

She reached out and placed her hand on his shoulder. "Please, Henry, I think maybe I know who is responsible."

He stared at her, wondering if this was some crazy ploy to get close to him. "What are you talking about?"

He was aware of Jimmy and his mother stepping into the foyer.

"Charlie was real upset when we broke up. He thought if you and I got married then you'd get him a job that paid well, a job in a fancy office somewhere. A couple of days ago he told me he had plans to get enough money to blow this town and live the easy life. When I pressed him for details he refused to say anything more."

The words exploded out of her in a rush, along with a torrent of tears. "I might be a lot of things, Henry, but I saw the way you looked at Melissa, I saw the look in your eyes when you saw those babies and I can't condone this. I think Charlie has done something terrible and I just had to tell you."

Henry stared at her in confusion. Charlie? Henry's mind buzzed. Charlie knew where she was staying. Melissa would have trusted Charlie. She would have gone with him without questions. Still, he was reluctant to believe it. "But he was here just a little while ago. He offered his help."

"I'm just telling you what I think, Henry, and I think he has Melissa and the boys," Hilary said.

Henry pulled his cell phone from his pocket and punched in Charlie's phone number. His heart crawled into his throat as he heard it ring and ring. "There's no answer," he said as he clicked off.

"I know where Charlie lives," Jimmy said with a frown. "There's no way he could have Melissa and the twins stashed in that tiny little apartment of his. Somebody would hear the boys crying or would have seen him bring them all inside."

Henry was processing everything in the span of seconds. Charlie could have easily taken the shot at him when he'd been out riding in the pasture. Charlie would have known that Henry and Melissa had gone to town and would have known about when they would be returning home. Charlie, who then tramped through the snow to obscure his own footprints, could have easily tossed the pipe bomb through the window.

Charlie. He still had trouble wrapping his mind around it. Charlie had been his right-hand man, his go-to guy for everything around the ranch.

"Charlie has a little shack, a place he goes hunting. Maybe he has them there," Hilary said.

"Why? I trusted him. I've always treated him fairly," Henry said.

"I think he hates you, Henry. He envies you your money, your life and I think he knew how much you cared about Melissa and the boys, cared enough to pay whatever ransom he might come up with."

The slow simmering rage that had been building in Henry throughout the night once again rose to the surface. "Where's the shack?" he asked.

Hilary wiped her tears with the back of her hand. "I hope I'm not sending you on a wild-goose chase. I don't want anything to happen to Melissa or those precious babies."

"Where's the shack, Hilary?" he demanded. He suddenly felt like too much time had been wasted.

As Hilary gave them directions to the shack, Henry was already pulling on his coat. He grabbed his gun and looked at Jimmy expectantly.

"Let's go," Jimmy said with a nod. He looked at Hilary. "If Charlie contacts you, don't tell him you spoke to us. Don't say anything to warn him or I'll see you behind bars for obstruction of justice."

"Please be careful. I honestly don't know what he's capable of," she said.

As Henry stepped out into the cold dark night he had a last glance of Hilary reaching for his mother's hand. He hoped to hell she was telling the truth and he prayed that they wouldn't be too late.

Melissa was cold. She didn't know if it was because the little heater simply couldn't warm the interior of the cabin or if it was fear that had her freezing.

Waiting. Wondering what happened next, that was what had her blood icy in her veins.

She certainly couldn't sleep, although she was grateful that the boys slumbered soundly. Seeking internal warmth, she finally opened a can of tomato soup and emptied it into a pan, then set it on the hot plate to warm.

As she waited for it to heat she wondered if Charlie had contacted Henry, if he'd already demanded a king's ransom for the return of the boys. He'd said he'd wait until morning, but maybe he'd gotten impatient. She just wanted this over.

She winced as she stood to stir the soup. She'd worked so long at trying to get the chain off her ankle she'd made it bleed.

Maybe she should be sleeping. Maybe Charlie didn't intend to return tonight and she should be getting what little rest she could. But even as she thought that, she knew there was no way she could sleep. She wanted to hold her boys. She wanted to squeeze them to her heart. She wanted to hear James's belly laugh one last time, see Joey's sweet smile. She stirred the soup as tears began to course down her cheeks once again.

Henry, her heart cried. She would never see him again. The only thing she could hope was that he would tell the boys about her, about how much she'd loved them, about what a good mom she'd wanted to be.

She froze as she heard the sound of a vehicle approach. Headlight beams flashed into the window. Sheer terror leaped into her throat. Had the deal gone down? Had Charlie come back to kill her?

The footsteps on the porch sounded loud, like gunshots, and when the door opened Charlie came inside. "Hi, honey, I'm home." He snickered, as if finding the joke amusing.

Melissa turned away from the hot plate. "Have you contacted Henry?"

"Not yet. I told you I was going to give him a little time to worry. I just figured I needed to stop back here and check on my investment." He leaned against the door and looked down at her ankle. "Looks like you worked hard to get out of that. Short of chewing off your foot, you aren't going anywhere."

Melissa had never hated anyone as much as she hated him. She'd never believed herself capable of killing anyone, but she'd kill for her children and if she got the chance, she'd kill Charlie without a blink of her eyes.

He kicked out a chair and sat at the small table and she backed up against the cabinet. "You're going to kill me, aren't you?" She didn't wait for him to answer. "I won't tell that it was you. I'll say that I don't know who took us, that he wore a mask and I didn't recognize him."

She hated that she was begging for her life, but she wanted to live. She had all the reasons in the world to want to stay alive.

"Lady, I wouldn't trust you as far as I could throw you," he replied.

With those words Melissa knew that he had no intention of letting her live and a new wave of grief crashed through her.

She turned back to the soup at the same time the front door crashed in. She whirled back around and everything seemed to go in slow motion.

Henry stood at the door, bigger than life, his eyes wild and dangerous. At the same time Charlie jumped up and drew his gun and lifted it to point at him.

In an instant Melissa knew Henry was about to die. Without thinking, she picked up the pan of hot soup and threw it at Charlie. As it splashed across the back of his head, he yelled and his gun dropped to the floor. The twins began to cry as Henry let loose a thunderous roar and tackled Charlie to the floor.

Melissa kicked Charlie's gun under the bed, then ran to the twins as Henry and Charlie wrestled with each other. Her heart pounded as she pulled the screaming boys into her arms and watched the life-and-death battle between the man she loved and the man who would kill her.

A sob escaped her when Henry pressed his gun barrel into Charlie's temple, halting the fight. At that moment Jimmy burst into the room.

"I got it, Henry. Drop your gun," he said.

Henry didn't move. His handsome features were twisted into a mask of rage. His entire body trembled and it was obvious how badly he wanted to put a bullet through Charlie's head.

"Henry, don't do it," Jimmy said and touched Henry's shoulder. "Come on, man. Let him go. I'll take it from here."

Henry squeezed his eyes closed, the internal battle he was waging bringing a new fear to Melissa. She knew if he shot Charlie his life would never be the same. It might feel good at the moment but eventually it would destroy him.

"Henry." She spoke his name softly. He opened his eyes and met her gaze. In the depths of his eyes she saw the torture he'd suffered over the past couple of hours.

"Let Jimmy take him away. Please, I need your help with the boys."

With a strangled sob, he lowered his gun and rolled off Charlie. Jimmy immediately handcuffed Charlie and hauled him to his feet.

Henry rushed over to her and knelt in front of her. He cupped her face between his palms, his gaze intense. "Did he hurt you? Oh, God, did he hurt you or the boys?"

"No, I'm okay. We're all okay." The boys had begun to calm.

He glanced down at the chain around her ankle and as he tensed as if to spring up again, she grabbed his arm. "It's okay."

Henry turned to look at Charlie and Jimmy. "Search him, Jimmy. I need a key to get this chain off her."

A moment later he unlocked the chain and removed it from her ankle. As he gently rubbed her skin, she remembered how he'd rubbed her cold feet on the night that they had been snowbound together.

Then she was in his arms, weeping in the aftermath, and he held her tight, as if afraid to ever let her go again. Eventually he did let her go. Gordon arrived along with several other deputies who would process what was now part of a crime scene.

Jimmy left to take Charlie to jail and Melissa and Henry and the boys got into Gordon's patrol car so he could take them home.

The car seats were shifted from Charlie's vehicle to the back of Gordon's car and once the boys were settled in they immediately fell back asleep. Melissa sat between them, happy yet exhausted by the turmoil and the lateness of the hour.

As they drove home Henry told Melissa about Hilary telling them that she thought Charlie might be involved. When they got back to the house Mary and Hilary stepped out on the porch to greet them.

Henry carried the twins and when Melissa reached the porch Mary pulled her into a bone-crunching hug. "Thank God," she said. "Thank God you're all okay."

As Mary released her, Melissa grabbed Hilary's hands. "Thank you," she said to the beautiful woman. "You saved my life."

Tears shone in Hilary's eyes. "I'm so sorry. I can't believe he did this. I always knew Charlie had a mean streak, but I never knew he was capable of something like this." She pulled her hands from Melissa's. "I'm going home now. I'm sure you all need some time alone."

An hour later the twins were asleep in their beds upstairs and Jimmy arrived to take a statement from Melissa.

It was near dawn when Jimmy left and Mary led Melissa to one of the spare bedrooms. As they passed the boys' room she saw Henry sitting in a chair just inside the door, as if guarding the king's treasure. Daddy on duty, she thought, and knew he'd probably be in that chair until dawn.

Minutes later as she lay in bed, even though she was exhausted she couldn't shut off her mind. Not only did her brain whirl with all the events and emotions of the night, but thoughts of Henry also filled her head and her heart.

She needed to get home. She couldn't stay here any longer. She'd allowed him into her heart in a way no other man had ever been. Each and every moment she spent with him only deepened her love for him.

It was time to go.

Chapter 14

Henry felt sick.

She was leaving. They were leaving. Even though he'd known this time would come, he wasn't ready to tell them goodbye, even if it was just a temporary goodbye.

It was midafternoon and the sun shone through the window as she finished the last of her packing. "I hate to see you go," he said.

"I know, but it's not like this is a final goodbye." She shut her suitcase and smiled at him, but her smile looked forced. The sunshine found her hair and sparkled in it and a press of emotion rose up in Henry's chest. He swallowed against it, unsure why this was so difficult.

She pulled her suitcase off the bed and set it on the

floor. "I need some time at home, Henry." Her eyes weren't as bright as they usually were. "I need some time to process everything that's happened."

He nodded. "I know. At least we know now that there's no more danger here. The next time you come back things will be completely different. You'll have no reason to be afraid."

She gazed at him with an enigmatic expression on her face. "I'm just glad it's all over for you...for us."

"I'm sorry, Melissa. I'm so sorry that you and the boys were put in any danger."

She held up a hand to stop him. "Don't apologize. It wasn't your fault. You couldn't have known about Charlie. You have nothing to be sorry for." She glanced at her watch. "And now, I really need to get on the road."

He nodded and reluctantly picked up her suitcase. Together they went down the stairs, where Mary and the twins were in the living room.

"You'll come back, won't you?" Mary asked worriedly.

"Of course," Melissa replied. "And anytime you want you're welcome to come to Amarillo for a visit."

Mary smiled. "I might just surprise you."

"I'd love a visit from you," Melissa replied. She leaned down and picked up James from the blanket on the floor where they had been lying.

"I'll get Joey," Mary said. As she picked up the smiling little boy tears filled her eyes. She looked at Melissa and gave her a teary smile. "I don't know what's worse, saying goodbye to these precious boys or saying goodbye to you."

"I packed up some of the Christmas presents in the trunk," Henry said as they all left the house and walked to Melissa's car, and Mary put Joey in his car seat. "If you need or want anything else, just give me a call."

"We'll be fine," Melissa said, then leaned into the backseat to buckle James into his seat. When she straightened, her gaze held Henry's for a long moment.

In the blue depths of her eyes Henry saw words unspoken and a shine of emotion that momentarily stole his breath away. It was there only a moment, then gone.

"Thank you. Thank you both for your generosity," she said. Once again her gaze met Henry's and he thought she was going to say something more, but instead she slid into the driver's seat and waved goodbye.

As he watched her car disappear down the driveway, he was struck with the fiercest wave of loneliness he'd ever felt.

"You're a fool, Henry James Randolf," his mother exclaimed and started back into the house.

"What are you talking about? I didn't do anything," he said.

"That's right. And that's why you're a fool." She went into the front door and slammed it behind her.

Henry swiped a hand through his hair and sighed. Women. He'd never understand them. His mother was probably upset with him because he hadn't managed to talk Melissa into moving into the carriage house. But after the trauma she'd suffered the night before, he hadn't wanted to pressure her anymore about it.

There might be a time in the future to bring up the subject again. In the meantime he had some things to take care of that would hopefully take his mind off the empty ache inside his chest.

For the next three days Henry stayed as busy as he could. Everyone in town was stunned to hear what Charlie had done and Henry was shocked and warmed by the amount of support he received from friends and neighbors.

He also made a difficult apology to Tom Burke, who surprised him by saying he was resigning his position as city manager and he and his wife were moving to Florida.

It was each evening after his mother had gone to bed and he sat in his chair with a glass of scotch when thoughts of Melissa and the boys filled his head.

It was amazing how much they had imbued the house with warmth, with joy. He missed seeing her smile and hearing that musical laugh of hers as she teased him. He missed talking to her, just sharing moments of time that could never be recaptured again.

She was a wonderful woman and someday she'd make some man a wonderful wife. He couldn't help it that he wasn't the man to fill that role in her life.

He would be the best father that he could be, but that's all he had to offer her. He hadn't pretended to be anything else but what he was—a confirmed bachelor.

* * *

The time with Henry at his house had taken on the quality of a wonderful dream as Melissa threw herself back into her real life. The boys settled back into their normal routine as if they'd never been away from home and Melissa tried to do the same.

It was Thursday morning when she sat at her computer in her living room working to build a brand-new slick Web page to advertise her business.

The twins were on the living-room floor, babbling happily to her and to each other. At least they didn't appear any worse for the drama that had taken place in that little shanty. Even Melissa was surprised by how easily she'd managed to put it all behind her. She had a life to build and couldn't dwell on that night with Charlie and how close she'd come to losing everything.

She tried not to think too much about Henry. She was in his life by accident and she couldn't forget that. It hurt to think of him, to love him and know that she would always be the mother of his children but never the woman of his heart.

For the past four nights she'd spent hours on the Internet trying to reconnect with MysteryMom but she hadn't been able to find the woman in any of the chat rooms she'd visited or anywhere else. It was as if she'd been a figment of Melissa's imagination.

Melissa would have liked to tell her that she'd successfully united Joey and James with their daddy and in that respect the story had a happy ending.

And someday maybe Melissa would find her happy ending with a man who would love her, a man who wouldn't be able to wait to marry her. At the moment the idea of romance with anyone left a bad taste in her mouth. It would take her a while to heal, to get over the heartbreak of loving Henry.

At least he hadn't spoken again about her moving into the carriage house. If he brought it up again she was afraid she would confess that the reason she didn't want to live there was because she was in love with him. She didn't want to burden him with her love. The last thing she wanted to do was complicate their relationship.

It was important for the boys' sake that Henry and Melissa's relationship remain calm and pleasant, not filled with stress or tension.

She stopped working on the Web page at six and fed the boys a bottle, then snuggled with them on the sofa. This was the time of the evening when loneliness struck her the hardest.

As the twins got sleepy and fell silent, the quiet of the apartment pressed in on her. She couldn't help but remember those nights with Henry when they'd sat and talked and just shared little pieces of each other.

She had to make sure in the future she maintained an emotional distance from him. She was going to have to see him on a regular basis but somehow, someway, she had to uninvolve her heart where he was concerned.

When the boys had fallen asleep she carried them one at a time to the cribs in their small bedroom then returned to the living room. She sat back down at the computer, but her thoughts were still consumed by Henry. He'd called every day since she'd been home, short chats about the twins that had only made it more difficult for her to gain the emotional distance she needed from him.

He'd wanted her to drive back to Dalhart this weekend, but she'd told him that she wasn't ready to make the drive again. He'd been disappointed but seemed to understand and they'd made plans for him to come to her apartment the following weekend.

There was a motel nearby and he could stay there and when she went back to Dalhart she would stay at a motel and he could visit the twins there. It was important that she set boundaries when it came to the visitation. He was her weakness and it would be far too easy for her to fall into his bed if he wanted her every time they were together for visitation.

Even now as she thought about being with him, kissing him and making love with him, she was filled with a longing that knew no bounds.

She was just about to stop working on the Web page and turn on the television when a knock fell on her door. She opened the door and her breath caught in her throat.

Henry. He stood before her as if conjured up by her thought, by her deep longing for him. "Surprise," he said with a smile that looked distinctly uncomfortable.

"Henry... What are you doing here?" She opened the door to allow him inside and as he swept by her she caught the sweet familiar scent that belonged to him alone. She closed the door and turned to face him.

He looked wonderful in a pair of worn jeans and a flannel plaid shirt and his winter coat. He looked just like the sexy, handsome cowboy who had rescued her on that snowy night over a year ago.

"I couldn't wait until next weekend or the weekend after that," he said.

She frowned. "But you've come so late. The boys are already asleep for the night. You should have called and let me know you were coming."

He shrugged out of his coat and laid it across the back of the sofa. "I would have called, but I didn't know I was coming until I was in the car and on my way." He stared at her for a long moment, his gaze inscrutable. "We need to talk."

He seemed nervous and ill at ease and suddenly she was afraid. Had he come to tell her that he'd changed his mind, that he'd decided he was going to fight her for custody of the twins? Had being away from them made him decide he'd do anything to keep them with him?

"Talk about what?" She sank down on the sofa, afraid that her trembling legs wouldn't hold her up any longer. She motioned him into the chair opposite the sofa but he remained standing with his back against the door, as if he might escape at any moment.

"I want to talk to you about the carriage house," he said.

"Henry, I…"

He held up a hand to stop her from saying anything

more. "Please, just listen to me for a minute. I've never offered something to somebody and then taken it back, but that's what I'm doing now. I don't want you to live in the carriage house."

Even though she hadn't intended to move in there, his words shot a sliver of pain through her. He didn't want her there. He didn't want her that close to him.

She nodded and told herself it was for the best. It hadn't been something she wanted to do anyway. "Okay," she replied.

"No, it's not okay. Nothing has been okay since you and the boys left." He shoved off from the door and walked the width of the room to stand in front of her. He stared at her, his expression impossible to read.

He finally drew a deep breath. "I thought I had my life all figured out, then you arrived with the boys and everything got all screwed up."

"I'm sorry. It was never my intention to mess up your life," she replied. Could this get more horrible? She fought back the sting of tears, refusing to allow him to see the depth of emotion inside her where he was concerned.

With one smooth movement he sat next to her. "My mother told me that my father might have done me a disservice in pounding into my head that all any woman would ever want from me was my money. Certainly my relationship with Hilary proved him right."

"But he was wrong, Henry," Melissa exclaimed fervently. "You're a wonderful man and you'd be a wonderful man with or without your money."

He smiled then, that slow sexy grin that would always have the capacity to warm her. "Last night I was sitting in the living room alone and thinking about the boys and what the future might hold. When I thought about them mounting a horse for the very first time, you were there in my vision. When I visualized putting them on the bus for their first day of school, in my vision you were standing beside me and holding my hand. Each and every fantasy of the future I imagined had you in it."

He frowned and his gaze never left hers. "And it wasn't just the boys' future that I fantasized about. I thought about your laughter and the way your eyes light up when you're happy. I thought about sleeping next to you, making love to you and I realized there was no way I wanted you living a separate life in the carriage house. I don't want you dating. I don't want you to be alone."

She didn't say a word. She was afraid she was misinterpreting what he was telling her. She remained frozen, her gaze locked with his.

"I realize now why it's been so easy for me to be a confirmed bachelor," he continued. "It's because I'd never met a woman I wanted to share my life with, a woman I loved mindlessly, desperately, until I met you."

Melissa's heart soared. "I wasn't going to move into the carriage house because I'm in love with you and I couldn't live there and see you every day and not be a real part of your life."

Her words seemed to break something loose in Henry. His eyes flared bright and he reached out and placed his palm against her cheek. "God, I was hoping you'd say something like that."

"I love you, Henry, but are you sure your feelings for me aren't because of the boys?"

"Melissa, I love you as the mother of my children, but my love doesn't begin and end there. I love you because you're strong and beautiful. I love you because you make me feel like I've never felt before in my life. I want to spend my life with you. Marry me, Melissa. Marry me and move into my house. Let us be a real family together."

His mouth took hers in a kiss that tasted of desire, but more it tasted of the future, of promises made and kept and the family she'd always wanted.

"You haven't answered me," he said when he finally pulled his mouth from hers. "Will you marry me? Will you share the rest of your life with me?"

"Yes," she replied breathlessly. "Yes! Yes!"

He pulled her into his arms and she leaned her head against his chest, listening to the strong beat of his heart.

"I wonder if MysteryMom has any idea what she's managed to accomplish?" she said.

"I have a feeling she knows," he replied. "I'll give you the world, Melissa. Whatever you want, whatever you need to be happy."

"I don't need or want anything but you and the boys," she replied.

"There is one thing you can eventually give me, if you're willing."

She rose up and looked at him. "What on earth could I possibly give you that you don't already have?"

He smiled, his eyes lit with love. "Twin daughters."

Melissa's heart swelled inside her. She was filled with such love, such joy, that she couldn't find her voice. She could only nod as he once again claimed her mouth with his.

She would forever be grateful for the blizzard that had brought them together on that night so long ago and to a woman named MysteryMom who had led her to happiness that she knew was going to last a lifetime.

Epilogue

She sat in front of her computer and stared at the e-mail she'd just written, but hesitated in hitting the button that would send the message on its way.

MysteryMom picked up the cup of coffee sitting next to her at the desk and took a sip, her mind whirling with the words she'd just typed.

It was amazing what kind of information could be gained when money was no object and you had contacts everywhere in the world. For the past year she'd used those contacts and her money for a mission—the mission of uniting people for the sake of their children.

It had begun when she'd started dropping in on various chat rooms and began to hear stories about women who didn't know where the father of their children were or how to get in touch with them to let them know they were fathers.

The stories had torn at her heart until finally she'd decided to try to do something—use her resources to bring some sort of reunion to the men and women who had parented children.

So far she'd been successful with several couples, but this one worried her. She reread the e-mail she'd composed and thought of the man and woman involved.

A terrible fate had pulled Emily Grainger and Jagger Holtz apart after a single night together. The result of that night had been a daughter named Michelle.

MysteryMom now had the pieces of the puzzle that could potentially bring together Emily and Jagger. She knew the information contained in the e-mail could save a man's life, but might also bring extreme danger to both him and Emily.

He's already in danger, she thought to herself. And if the e-mail wasn't sent then in all probability he would die.

She owed it to Jagger Holtz to send the e-mail and she prayed that when she did Emily Grainger would survive whatever consequences might come.

Drawing in a deep breath, the woman who called herself MysteryMom hit the send button.

* * * * *

THE SOLDIER'S
SECRET DAUGHTER

BY
CINDY DEES

Cindy Dees started flying airplanes while sitting in her dad's lap at the age of three and got a pilot's license before she got a driver's license. At age fifteen, she dropped out of high school and left the horse farm in Michigan, where she grew up, to attend the University of Michigan.

After earning a degree in Russian and East European Studies, she joined the US Air Force and became the youngest female pilot in the history of the Air Force. She flew supersonic jets, VIP airlift, and the C-5 Galaxy, the world's largest airplane. She also worked part-time gathering intelligence. During her military career, she traveled to forty countries on five continents, was detained by the KGB and East German secret police, got shot at, flew in the first Gulf War, met her husband and amassed a lifetime's worth of war stories.

Her hobbies include professional Middle Eastern dancing, Japanese gardening and medieval re-enacting. She started writing on a one dollar bet with her mother and was thrilled to win that bet with the publication of her first book in 2001. She loves to hear from readers and can be contacted at www.cindydees.com.

My warmest thanks to Carla Cassidy and Marie Ferrarella for their inspiration and support with this series. You two wear some pretty classy coattails— thanks for letting me hitch a ride on them!

Chapter 1

Jagger Holtz crouched in the dark as the helicopter overhead peeled away, ostensibly to continue tracking traffic jams on the highways below. They'd hovered over the AbaCo building a total of twenty-eight seconds. Just long enough to drop him on a zip line to the roof of the twenty-story-tall glass-and-steel tower. And hopefully not long enough to trigger the intense security of AbaCo Inc., one of the largest—and most shadowy—shipping firms in the world.

Bent over at the waist, he ran for cover, ducking behind a giant air-conditioning vent and taking a quick time check. He'd give AbaCo's goons three minutes to respond. Then, barring any company on the roof, he'd move on to phase two: infiltrating the building proper. He didn't expect to find his missing colleagues tonight—Hanson and MacGillicutty were fellow government agents sent into AbaCo undercover months ago. And both of them had disappeared. No messages. No distress signals. No evidence of foul play. They were just…gone. When his superiors had approached him, he'd leaped at the chance to do this risky mission.

It was starting to look as though his rooftop landing had gone unnoticed. He tied off a rope to a sturdy steel grille and checked his rappelling harness one more time. Down the side of the building, in through an office window and then they'd see if the password they'd bought from the snitch worked.

Without warning, all hell broke loose. The heavy steel doors on each of the four stairwells leading to the roof burst open with a deafening crash. Armed men rushed out, sweeping the roof with automatic weapons. They sprinted forward, quartering the roof with brutal efficiency.

Holy crap. Commandos for a helicopter overhead for twenty-eight seconds?

He slammed to the ground just as a high-intensity flashlight beam passed over his position, barely missing lighting him up like a Christmas tree. He was trapped. He gripped the metal grille in front of his face in frustration as they closed in on him. Warm, moist air blew at him like an incongruous sea breeze on this frigid Denver night.

Air. An air vent. It might be a dead end, but it was better than lying here and getting captured or killed in the next few seconds. He grabbed his pocketknife and used the blade to unscrew the nearest fastener holding the vent shut. He lobbed the thumb-sized screw as hard as he could across the roof. It clattered loudly, and shouting and a scramble of men reacted instantly.

The second screw popped loose. It went flying in another direction.

C'mon, c'mon. The last screw finally popped free. He grabbed the bottom of the grille and yanked. Someone was shouting irritably at the guards in German to quit running around like chickens, to form up and to search the roof methodically. Not good. AbaCo's serious security team was up here if they were speaking German.

Working fast, he slapped the clip from the rope he'd already tied off onto his climbing harness and rolled over the edge. He fell into space, fetching up hard as the rope caught. He bit back a gasp of pain as his groin took a hit from the harness that all but permanently unmanned him. Oww. So much for the glory of being a special agent.

The vent was about six by six feet square. Twisting until his feet braced against the side, he walked backward down the galvanized aluminum wall, doing his damnedest to be as silent as possible. The echo of any noise in here would be magnified a dozen times.

How far down the black shaft he descended, blind and lost, he had no idea. He counted steps and tried to estimate how far he'd gone. But it was hard to focus with periodic bursts of air from below knocking him off the wall and sending him spinning wildly in space, hanging on for dear life at the end of his single, skinny rope.

Hopefully, the AbaCo powers that be would declare the whole thing a false alarm and satisfy themselves with complaining to the radio station about its helicopter parking in their airspace. Otherwise, guards were probably waiting for him at the other end of this shaft, licking their chops at the prospect of nabbing themselves a third hapless federal agent. The idea of failing galled him, not only because he never failed, but also because it would mean Hanson and MacGillicutty were no closer to being found, their families no closer to any answers. Both of them had wives. Kids. Christmas last week had been hard on them all.

He guessed he was about halfway to the ground floor when the main shaft narrowed enough that he was forced to stop using his feet. He lowered himself hand over hand down the rope until his arms went so numb he could no longer feel them. His watch said the descent took twenty-four minutes. It felt like twenty-four hours.

Plenty of time to ponder the symbolism of his descent. Into darkness and silence and utter isolation. The hell he so richly deserved. He pushed away the encroaching panic. He could *not* afford to lose it now. He was a long way from out of this mess.

The air rushing up at him began to smell of car exhaust. The underground parking garage, maybe? Hmm. It had possibilities. Light began to glow faintly from below. Between his feet, he made out what looked like a metal grille. It was a miniature version of the big one on the roof.

The screws holding it in place were unfortunately on the other side, out of reach. He paused, listening carefully for any sound of humans nearby. Nothing. He damn well didn't intend to climb all the way back up that rope, some twenty stories. He slammed both feet into the metal panel, jumping on it with his full body weight. The slats bent slightly. He jumped again. And again. After a few more tries, a tiny gap showed at the edge of the grille as the metal began to buckle. He kicked again.

Crud. It sounded like Godzilla tearing a car apart with his teeth. Metal screeched, protesting harshly. This had to be drawing the entire cavalry to the garage. His only hope was to break through fast and get away from here before they arrived.

The grille's fasteners gave way all at once. He tumbled to the floor below, landing hard on the concrete. He grunted and rolled fast toward the nearest large object, a sedan parked on the slanting ramp, pulling his sidearm as he went. He scrambled under the car, then paused, scanning the area carefully for any feet. The goons weren't here yet.

He froze as a car drove past his position, winding its way out of sight into the bowels of the parking garage. Hurrying, he unzipped his backpack and pulled out a dark gray tweed suit coat before he stuffed the pack behind a concrete pillar. He donned the jacket over his black turtleneck and black slacks. A quick tug into place, and he was instantly transformed from commando to party crasher.

Now to find a patsy. A single female to walk him past the inevitable security. He glanced around at the cars. Mostly modest domestic cars and the occasional junker. Perfect. The worker bees' parking level.

The party was scheduled to start at eight o'clock. His watch said it was 8:05 p.m. The guests should be arriving in quantity right about now. He stood in a shadow near the elevator and settled in to wait. He pulled out a pack of cigarettes in case he needed a quick excuse to be loitering here. He didn't smoke, but the many other handy uses of cigarettes—including convenient cover story—made them a staple in his arsenal of secret-agent equipment.

In a few minutes, he spotted a vaguely human shape coming down the ramp toward him. Pink parka. Scarf wrapped around the face. Mittens. Ski hat under the parka hood. Fleece-lined suede boots. The apparition looked like a four-year-old kid bundled up by Mom to go out in the first big snow of the year to play. But more importantly, the apparition was alone.

Bingo. He had target acquisition. Or at least a way into the party.

Emily Grainger looked up, alarmed, as a tall man stepped out of the shadows next to the elevator. He stopped beside her, staring at the elevator door for a moment before surprising her by speaking. Men didn't usually speak to her. "Cold night, eh?"

She had to turn her whole upper body to see him out of her deep hood, and she did so awkwardly. She caught her first good look at him and started. Men like him definitely didn't speak to her. "Oh!" she exclaimed softly. "Uh, yes. I guess it is. Cold, that is."

She looked away, embarrassed at the way she was staring. He wasn't so much handsome as he was intense. His cheeks were deeply carved, his skin tanned as though he spent most of his time outdoors. His eyes were pale blue, nearly color-less, and as intense as the rest of him. His mouth was a little bit too wide, his nose a little too big. But still, it was a face a person would struggle to look away from. The man looking out through those intelligent, all-too-observant eyes was captivating.

He looked ready to explode into motion at the slightest provocation, just like…just like James Bond. He gave off that same restless, devil-may-care charm guaranteed to sweep a girl right off her feet. And he'd just said hello to her! Well, then.

She stared straight ahead at the stainless-steel elevator door. It threw back at her a blurry reflection of a pink whale.

Her entire life, she'd dreamed of meeting a man like this. Of becoming a different kind of woman—adventurous, bold and sexy—the kind of woman a man like this would fall for. And here he was. Her dream man in the flesh. She wasn't fool enough to believe a man like this would come along twice in her lifetime. This was it. Now or never.

"I don't think we've met before," he murmured. "What de-partment do you work in?"

"Uh, I'm in accounting," she managed to mumble in spite of her sudden inability to draw a complete breath. The elevator dinged and the steel panel started to slide open.

"Accounting. That's interesting."

Liar. Accounting wasn't interesting at all. It was boring. Safe and predictable and orderly. She couldn't count how often she wanted to jump up from her desk in her neat, bland little cubicle and scream. What she wouldn't give to be a sexy international spy like James Bond courteously holding the elevator door open for her now.

Her imagination took off. He had no idea who she was. She could be that other woman with him tonight. Flirtatious. Aggressive. The kind of woman who went after men like him and seduced them with a snap of her fingers. She envisioned ritzy casinos, champagne flutes and diamonds. Lots of flashy diamonds.

"What's your name?" James Bond murmured.

"Uh, Emily. Emily Grainger." Lord. Even her name sounded boring and safe. And it was too late to lie and call herself something exotic and alluring.

He smiled at her.

Stunned, she turned to face the elevator's front and about fell over her own feet. Ho. Lee. Cow. He had the greatest smile she'd *ever* seen. It was intimate and sexy and dangerous—all the things she imagined Bond's smile would be and more. It drew her in. Made her part of his secret double life. Promised things that no nice girl dared to think of.

"I'm Jagger," he murmured. "Jagger Holtz."

The name startled her. He didn't look like one of the Germans of the heavy contingent of them within AbaCo. And yet she probably shouldn't have been surprised. He had that same leashed energy, the same self-contained confidence that all the German security types within the firm had. But the way he'd pronounced it had been strange. Her understanding of the German language was that *J*s were pronounced like Americans pronounced a *Y.* So shouldn't his name have been Yagger? Why would he Americanize the name when none of the other Germans in the company bothered to do so?

She turned her whole upper body to look at him again. "What nationality is that name?"

He grinned self-deprecatingly, a lopsided, boyish thing that charmed the socks right off her. "I'd like to say it's a German name, but the truth is my mother was a Rolling Stones groupie. I think I'm actually named after Mick Jagger."

Her laughter startled her. A girl wasn't supposed to laugh at James Bond, was she?

The door opened, and she jumped when he reached out to steady her elbow. "Watch your step," he murmured.

Electricity shot down, or rather up, her arm, skittered across the back of her neck and exploded low in her belly. Whoa. Did James Bond have this effect on all the girls? No wonder he landed whoever he set his cap for! One touch from him and the women were putty in his hands!

Breathe, Emily. Breathe. Or more accurately, stop hyperventilating, Emily.

How she made it out of the elevator without falling over her feet, she had no idea. Her lower body had come completely unhinged from her central nervous system thanks to that devastating touch on her elbow. Not to mention that clutzy was her middle name. Particularly when she was flustered. And Jagger Holtz definitely flustered her.

"Maybe you'd better just take my arm," he said.

Good call. Give James credit for knowing a damsel in distress when he saw one. Or maybe he just knew he had that effect on all women.

She'd have been embarrassed, except he offered her his forearm with such obvious pleasure at the prospect of her touching him that she was more stunned than anything else. Was he blind? Or so hopelessly nearsighted he didn't realize how plain she was? How…completely average?

Of course, he hadn't actually seen much of her, truth be told. She was wrapped up like a mummy and only her eyes and the tip of her nose were visible. She sighed. He'd figure out soon enough that she was a mousy little thing and not even close to flashy enough to be seen with him. He was the sort of man who would look at home with a supermodel on his arm. The fantasy had been fun while it lasted, at any rate.

They stepped into the lobby of the AbaCo building. The soaring atrium, nearly eight stories tall, was decorated from top to bottom with metallic silver Christmas decorations. Personally, she didn't like them. They seemed too cold and impersonal. Hard, even. But then, that wasn't a bad approximation of the personality of her employer, she supposed.

The shipping firm was intensely German, although it had offices in a dozen major cities around the world. But AbaCo took its Teutonic persona very seriously. There were rules for everything, the rules got followed and the cargo got where it was going on time. Or else heads rolled.

"Can I hang up your coat for you?" Jagger asked pleasantly.

She looked up from bending over awkwardly as she tried to pry off one of her boots. She'd brought a pair of shoes to change into for the party, in her bulky purse. "Uh. Wow. That's really polite of you. I guess so."

She postponed her boots and straightened. He was behind her immediately, slipping her parka off her shoulders as gracefully as if it were a mink coat.

"Nice dress," he murmured on cue.

Man. He didn't miss a trick. He'd clearly aced Date Etiquette 101. Whoa. Back up. Date? They'd met in the parking garage and ridden up in the elevator together. She'd indulged in a momentary fantasy, and that was about as close to a date as they were ever going to get. He was already striding away from her, in fact.

Although in defense of her fantasy, he was carrying her coat to the cloakroom for her. Presumably, he would return with a ticket for her to pick it up later. So he would have to speak with her at least one more time tonight. One more moment to indulge in the idea of a "them." Her and James Bond. She smiled blissfully. In her world, these little fantasies were about as close as she ever got to the real thing, so why not enjoy them?

If only she had the guts to turn her daydreams into reality.

One thing AbaCo did very well was throw a party. Caterers had set up a buffet line at the far end of the atrium, and she knew from previous New Year's Eve parties that the food would be delicious. A band was playing background music at the moment but would shift into dance music as midnight approached. And then there was the open bar, of course. Bartenders ranged behind it, ready and waiting to serve nearly a thousand employees and their guests at this, the North American headquarters for the company.

Jagger was back almost before she'd had time to slip into the daring pair of red stilettos she'd given herself for Christmas. She would never dream of wearing them to work, but she hadn't been able to resist them when she'd seen them. They reminded her of Dorothy's shoes from *The Wizard of Oz,* but naughtier, with their open toes and sling backs. She was suddenly fiercely glad she'd splurged on them as Jagger strode back toward her. Her hands went to her hair nervously, smoothing the static electricity from her hat out of its silky brunette length.

His mouth quirked into a smile as if he enjoyed her sudden self-consciousness. Laughter jumped into her eyes in response. After all, it really was a very good joke to think that he might actually find her attractive.

His gaze rather improbably slid lower as he moved toward her. Right. As if there was anything to look at in her drab body. She supposed she was reasonably proportioned, but she was no supermodel. She actually had breasts and hips, and her legs, although shapely, weren't a mile long. She barely topped five foot four.

Even more improbably, a slow grin spread across Jagger's face as he took in the view, from her slinky red dress all the way down to her sexy shoes and back up again. *Oh. My. Goodness.*

He must be drunk. He was acting as though he actually found her attractive.

He held both hands out to her as he reached her, taking her hands in his. "You look fabulous," he declared. A security guard had drifted over toward them and Jagger turned to the guy. "Have you ever seen Emily look so fantastic?"

The guard, Horace Lighterman, grinned and nodded at her. "You do look great tonight, Miss Grainger."

Okay, so the male half of the human race had all gone mad. But she was willing to roll with that. Especially if by some strange miracle the madness included her suddenly being perceived as cute. Or even hot.

In keeping with the party spirit of the evening, she replied playfully, "Thanks, Horace. You're looking pretty spiffy yourself. I love the hat." The guy had on a pointed cardboard affair that looked utterly ridiculous with his police-style uniform. The silliness of the combination somehow poked fun at AbaCo, and she found that immensely appealing. Her employer could stand to be ridiculed now and then. Any other day of the year, Horace wouldn't have dared to wear that hat, and she wouldn't have dared to find it funny. But New Year's Eve was about letting loose. About taking chances. About new starts.

Someone called for Horace from the security desk just inside the lobby and he turned away from them.

"Come on," Jagger announced. "Let's go have fun."

Let's? As in him and her? As in wow. There must be definite magic in the air tonight. Either that or a hallucinogen in the water supply.

They'd barely stepped into the atrium proper when there was a ruckus behind her. Several plainclothed AbaCo security guards clustered at the front door, looking like angry wasps. One of them was holding what looked like a black backpack.

"Dance with me," Jagger announced, more of a command than a question.

His arms went around her and he swept her into a waltz, spinning her effortlessly across the dance floor. Most of the couples dancing were older, executive types. She recognized several vice presidents and their wives, and frankly, she felt a little funny out here with them. But Jagger was such a spectacular partner that she rapidly lost all self-consciousness. He guided her exactly where she needed to be, kept her precisely on the beat and whisked her around the room like Cinderella. Who knew waltzing could be so much fun?

She wasn't sure what made her dizzy. It could have been the swooping, turning flight he took her on around the dance floor, or maybe it was the way he smiled down at her—as if she were the only person in the entire world and the two of them were alone at their own private ball. Either way, it was pretty sensational.

The dance ended, and he walked her off the floor, steering her toward the bar and a cool drink as if he could read her mind. She sipped at the gin and tonic he brought her. She never drank under normal circumstances. But in the past ten minutes, she'd already established that tonight was anything *but* normal.

"How come I haven't seen you around here before?" she asked curiously. Which was to say, how on earth had she missed spotting or at least hearing about a hunk like him if they worked in the same building?

He laughed easily. "I was just thinking the very same thing about you."

"Ah, well. I work in my little cubicle most of the time. They hardly let me come up for air, let alone poke my nose outside of the Special Cargo Department."

His gaze flickered, but his smile never faltered. He murmured, "Let's not talk about work tonight, shall we? Tell me more about you."

She rolled her eyes. "I guarantee you, I have led the most boring life in the history of mankind."

"A woman who wears shoes like those? I find that very hard to believe."

She laughed. "Busted. I never wear shoes like this. They were an impulse buy. Pure foolishness."

"I like the impulse."

His eyes sparkled with laughter, but his voice slid across her skin like forbidden sex. It sent a shudder through her that bordered on orgasmic. This wasn't happening to her! She looked up at him, perplexed.

"What?" he asked, immediately serious.

"Are you for real?"

One eyebrow lifted and the devil-may-care grin was back. "Does it matter? Or shall we both just lose ourselves in the moment and see where it leads us?"

A very James Bond-like response. No wonder the Bond girls never held out for a long-term commitment from him. He was so attractive they were willing to settle for a night or two with him rather than never be with him at all. Of course, the possibility of something more than a one-night stand wasn't off the table between her and Jagger yet, either. Heck, she was thrilled that the prospect of a one-night stand was even on the table!

Which was to say, the world had definitely gone mad this New Year's Eve.

She sipped her drink and smiled back at him coyly. "The night *is* young, isn't it? Let's see where it goes, indeed."

Chapter 2

Jagger was staggered by Emily Grainger. Not in his wildest dreams would he have guessed that a parka could unwrap to reveal this jewel. She was perfect. And scary as hell. He didn't go for real women, the hearth-and-home kind a guy could envision having his babies and keeping a home with. Oh, no. She was not his type at all.

So why, then, was he so attracted to her he could hardly keep his hands off her?

Not good. Not good at all.

The first thing he noticed about her was her flawless, translucent skin. Contrasted against her lush brunette hair, the combination was beyond striking. Her eyes were big and dark, her lips ripe for the kissing. He preferred her rosy mouth after the first gin and tonic lifted away that pale pink lipstick. She looked eminently more kissable now.

But what absolutely blew him away was the look of delighted wonder in her eyes. Her gaze was so innocent, so guileless, so…pure, he almost felt inappropriate touching her. In his world, the people were hard. Cynical. Out to stab you in the back before you stabbed them. All the playfulness, all the innocence had been burned out of men like him—of him—long ago. But she had both. In spades. And they drew him in as effortlessly as a spider coaxing a fly into its web. The world's most innocent spider.

He'd accuse her of being childlike if it weren't for the intelligence lurking just below the surface of that warm chocolate gaze. He could all but hear the wheels turning as she processed and analyzed everything and everyone around her. It was a strange dichotomy. But no doubt about it, he sensed a first-class mind at work. Thankfully, she seemed in total ignorance of men like him, however.

His mouth turned down cynically. He was a user. He took what he needed from the people around him and then threw them away like so much discarded trash. A girl like Emily certainly deserved better than that. But as sure as God made little green apples, he was going to use her anyway. It was who he was. He didn't know how to do anything else.

But a warning vibrated deep in his gut. This woman might leave an indelible mark on him. She was a permanent kind of woman who could shake the very foundation of his impermanent world.

He yanked his mind back to the job at hand. If and when the AbaCo security team finally relaxed a little, he'd sneak off and make his way up an elevator and into the offices above. He'd break into the company's computers and download everything he could find on the company's shipping operations. And hopefully, somewhere in there, they'd find a lead on his missing fellow agents. If he was really lucky, his colleagues would find something criminal with which to charge AbaCo and launch a wider investigation of the secretive company's practices.

But until that moment when he had to bail out on her, he

could make this a night to remember for Emily Grainger. It was the least he owed her for her unwitting help. Not to mention, he seemed compelled to flirt with the danger this woman represented to him. He fed her compliments, laughed with her and did his very best Prince Charming imitation for her.

As she continued to dance and talk with him, he plied her with equal parts alcohol and enticement until her eyes blazed with utter infatuation. And somewhere along the way, his plan of attack changed. Why ditch Emily after a few hours to take a one-shot stab at breaking in tonight when he could play out this thing between them and potentially turn her into a long-term infiltrator of AbaCo from the inside?

Hypocrite. He just wanted an excuse to spend more time with the girl.

No, dammit, that wasn't all this was about. It was good business to turn the girl.

Nonetheless, his gut twinged. Did he have it in him to make a pawn out of sweet, trusting Emily? Hell, a woman like her should never look twice at a man like him. He really should warn her off. But he couldn't bring himself to do it. God, he was a jerk. He didn't deserve Emily Grainger.

"Are you okay?" A soft hand rested on his chest, jolting him back to the present. Damn, she was perceptive.

He grinned bleakly at her. "Yeah, sure. I was just pondering what New Year's resolution I should make this year."

"Hmm. That's a good question." Laughter twinkled in her warm gaze. "Mine is going to be to wear more red shoes."

"Gonna take more chances, huh? Gonna try living on the edge?" he teased. The thought of her existing in a world like his was ludicrous. But he couldn't begrudge her the dream, he supposed. The reality was so much darker than a woman like her could ever imagine.

She nodded firmly. "Yup. That's me. Danger Girl."

He laughed, genuinely amused. She had no idea just how

dangerous to him she was. He commented lightly, "Well, then, my resolution is to help you make your resolution come true."

Her gaze snapped to his. Not slow on the uptake, his Emily. She hadn't for a minute missed the implications of that. He was talking about continuing to see her after tonight. He looked her in the eyes, losing himself in their sweet depths. To have a woman like this for himself, to bathe himself in all that goodness, to soak up her innocence and generosity, to be loved forever by someone like her—

He cut the fantasy off cold. Danger Girl, indeed.

"Wanna take a walk?" she murmured. "Get a little fresh air?"

He grinned. "I think that's supposed to be my line. Then comes the part where I drag you into some dark corner and try to make out with you."

She grinned back. "Who says I'm not trying to drag you into the corner to make out with you?"

He nodded his amused acquiescence. "Lead on. My body is yours to ravage."

He was shocked when she led him over to the elevators and punched the up button. She wasn't going to take him up to her office—in the Special Cargo Department, no less—was she? Surely this op wouldn't be *that* easy.

He leaned down to murmur in her ear, "Are you planning to throw me down on your desk and have your way with me?"

A fiery blush leaped to her cheeks. "Good Lord, my cubicle will never be the same now that you've planted *that* image in my mind!"

"Think how much fun work's going to be on Monday morning," he teased.

"I was thinking that we could go out to the water garden and stroll around."

Ah. The building's tenth floor was not a floor at all. Rather it was an open-air terrace sporting massive columns and housing an elaborate outdoor modern art collection interspersed with, as she'd already alluded to, a bunch of fountains. All the good stuff in the firm was above that. It was the reason he'd come in through the roof—or at least tried to until that plan went completely to hell.

The elevator opened, and she punched a security code into the number pad inside. He memorized the six-digit number as a matter of course. Emily Grainger was the brass ring and then some for getting the inside scoop on AbaCo. She so far surpassed his wildest expectations for this op that he could hardly believe his luck. And all he could do was imagine different ways to bed her. He was a cad. A sharp knife of guilt stabbed him.

While he admonished himself to get over it and concentrate on his job, she reached out shyly to loop her fingers in the crook of his elbow. He gazed down at her intently and the smile faded from her face. She stared back at him, her pupils dilating until her eyes went black as she correctly interpreted his expression.

The elevator dinged and the door slid open. She shook herself free of their mutual reverie first and stepped toward the exit. Rocked at the effect she had on him, he followed her outside. The wind was howling tonight, but glass panels mounted at intervals all around the edge of the terrace shielded the garden from the worst of it. Nonetheless, he took off his jacket and draped it over her shoulders.

He caught the surreptitious sniff she took, inhaling his scent. And something moved deep within him. Something protective. Possessive.

They'd only walked a dozen steps forward before he spotted the first surveillance camera. This place was a freaking fortress, all right. All the more reason to give up on a simple break-in tonight. Better to cultivate Emily as a long-term asset, to spy for him from the inside.

Distracted by thoughts of all those secret meetings they'd need to have with each other, he ducked his head away from the camera out of long habit, and immediately could've kicked himself for having done it. Dammit. If the camera operator was half as good as the rest of the AbaCo team, Jagger had just sent a big red flag up the pole. No innocent civilian reacted that way to a surveillance camera. But a spy most certainly would.

He sighed. Nothing to do now but brazen it out. "Are you warm enough?" He smiled down at Emily.

"It is chilly. But I enjoy the quiet."

He wrapped an arm around her shoulder, tucking her close against his side. "Better?"

"Mmm," she murmured. She sounded like a kitten after lapping up a bowl of warm milk. "Are *you* warm enough?"

He chuckled. "I love cold weather. This is bracing."

She shook her head. "Give me a tropical beach every day of the week and twice on Sunday."

"I gathered that from the way you were bundled up when you arrived."

She laughed ruefully. "My mom always told me to dress like I expect my car to break down and be stranded for hours. I confess I have been known as a compulsive safety girl before. But no more, of course. I'm Danger Girl now."

He heard the whoosh of an elevator door behind him and held himself still, not reacting. He studied a red metal abstract sculpture in front of him. "That looks like a Calder," he commented, ignoring the guards he felt approaching in the sudden twitchiness of his shoulder blades.

"I think it is. I'm not too much into modern art, I'm afraid. I like my art old—and the subject identifiable."

He laughed quietly as two pairs of footsteps became audible.

"You there!" a male voice called out sharply.

He and Emily turned as a single unit, which had the effect of making the maneuver look nice and casual. "Can we help you?" Jagger asked smoothly.

The two men halted, eyeing him suspiciously. "How did you two get up here?"

Emily laughed. "We crawled up the side of the building using our supersuction fingers and spider silk. We took the elevator, of course."

"Who's the gentleman with you, Miss Grainger?"

Emily glanced up at him in surprise. "Why, Jagger Holtz, of course."

The men frowned. "Mind if we see a little identification, sir?"

He frowned as any innocent man would at such a request, but shrugged. "Not at all." As he dug out his wallet and passed over his driver's license, he asked, "May I ask what this is all about?"

"Routine security check, sir. Would you mind coming with us?"

His frown deepened as he swore mentally. He'd had such a good thing going with Emily, and now he was going to have to run again. And this time without a rope. He let his arm drop off Emily's shoulder and he tensed to charge the two men. He'd take the smaller one on the right first and spin him into his bigger, more dangerous-looking buddy.

Emily spoke up without warning. "Actually, we would mind. Mr. Holtz and I are trying to enjoy our New Year's Eve here. There's no law against walking around the water garden."

The bigger one replied, "We've had a security breach tonight, and we're looking for a man dressed in all black and matching the general height and build of your…friend."

"I see," she replied frostily, shrugging off Jagger's coat and handing it back to him. "Now *you* can see that my friend is not wearing all black. He was merely being a gentleman and loaning me his coat."

God bless her. He couldn't have asked for a better cover story if he'd prepped her himself.

The smaller guard opened his mouth, but Jagger interrupted him, impatiently now. The average innocent guy with a few drinks in him and a hot chick beside him would be getting all kinds of irritated, so he let a hint of testosterone-induced posturing creep into the exchange. "The lady and I arrived together. You can ask Horace down at the front desk."

The smaller guard glowered but murmured into his coat collar. The reply was swift. A finger to his ear and the guard nodded reluctantly at his partner. Both looked more than a little disgruntled. "Horace remembers the two of you arriving. Sorry to bother you. Have a nice night." With that, the guards turned and left.

Emily complained, "I know this place can be a police state, but good grief."

Jagger steered her toward the elevator. "Let's go back inside. You're shivering."

"It's not the cold. It's those thugs. They give me the creeps."

"You're going to have to get used to facing down thugs if you want to live a life of adventure and mayhem, Danger Girl."

"I don't need mayhem. Just some naughty shoes and a little adventure with a hot guy now and then."

His lips curved upward. Hot, was he?

They rode the elevator down to the party in silence. In a single sweeping glance of the room, he spotted no less than twelve men with earpieces carrying themselves like more of Emily's thugs. The back of his neck started to tingle. He didn't like how they were arrayed around the room. It looked for all the world like an ambush about to be sprung. With him as the main course. Time to blow this popsicle stand.

Smiling casually for the thugs' benefit, he murmured, "Speaking of adventure, what say we relocate this party to someplace less thug-infested?"

She looked up at him in surprise. "What did you have in mind?"

"How about my place? We can take your car and that way you can leave whenever you want." In his experience, the safer a woman felt about her ability to leave a place, the more she was inclined to stay. He added, "I don't need all these security guys eyeing me like I'm some criminal for the next two hours."

She glanced around. "Good point."

"No pressure, Em. Just a bottle of champagne and a bite to eat. I don't expect any more than that."

She blinked up at him, her mouth and eyes round. Was she so innocent that it actually hadn't occurred to her that he might be propositioning her for sex when he invited her to his place?

She nodded in sudden decision. "As my first act of daring in the almost new year, I, Danger Girl, accept your invitation. Let's go."

He grinned, enormously relieved. He dared not let her leave his side until he was well clear of this place, lest the security team swoop in and grab him. He picked up both of their coats, and he made a humorous production of mummifying her in her scarf, hat, parka and mittens. It culminated with her sticking her tongue out at him and yanking her scarf up over her face. Ah, sweet Emily. She had no idea what a good act she was putting on for the cameras. He could kiss her.

Hell, he could kiss her and it wouldn't have a damned thing to do with AbaCo's uptight security team.

The two of them took the elevator down to the parking garage and walked quickly to her car. He never once glanced in the direction of the pillar where he'd stashed his gear earlier. He hadn't spotted a camera, but there undoubtedly was one down here. And just as undoubtedly, someone was watching for his reaction to the hiding place of the suspicious backpack the security team had found earlier.

"The roads aren't in great shape. Would you like me to drive?" he offered. "I have a lot of experience on ice."

"Uh, okay," she replied. He opened her door for her and then went around to the driver's side of her car. He eased the vehicle out of the parking space and started up the ramp.

"Where'd you learn to drive on ice?" she asked.

He couldn't very well tell her about his numerous illegal forays into Russia. "Alaska," he replied blandly. In point of fact, he'd done some Arctic training up there that had happened to include some offensive driving classes. Doing donuts on sheet ice was a kick for the first dozen revolutions or so. Then it just made a guy sick to his stomach.

"Cool. I've always wanted to go there," she said brightly.

"So take a vacation there this year, Danger Girl."

She looked over at him, her eyes sparkling like diamonds. "Maybe I will."

He maneuvered confidently through the traffic, wary of drunks. But it wasn't midnight yet, and the majority of partygoers wouldn't hit the highways for another couple of hours. He turned the heat up full blast, and it had the desired effect. Before long, Emily had shed most of her outer layers. The view was much better now. Despite how slender she was, she had a nicely proportioned cleavage, not huge, but full and round and tempting.

"Wow. You *are* a good driver," she commented.

"It's all about being decisive and knowing what your tires can do."

Silence fell between them and he pulled out his cell phone, dialed his hotel one-handed and asked for room service. When a female voice came on the line, he responded, "This is Mr. Holtz from room 2467. I'd like surf and turf for two in my room with all the trimmings, plus the Dom Perignon 1983. And a dark chocolate fondue for dessert. Extra strawberries, please. I'll be arriving at the hotel in a half hour. Anytime after that will be fine."

He disconnected the call. Emily was staring at him as if

he'd grown a third eye in the middle of his forehead. "What?" he asked.

"Are you sure you're not James Bond?"

Okay, then. That cut a little too close for comfort. He kept forgetting that beneath her playful innocence lay an intelligent and observant woman. He laughed lightly. "Thanks for the comparison. I'm afraid I'm just a regular guy."

Emily wondered about that, though. Jagger danced like a god, handled a car like a Formula One driver and ordered fancy midnight dinners as if they were an everyday occurrence in his world. Why wasn't she surprised when he pulled up in front of one of the ritziest hotels in Denver, flipped the car keys to a valet and casually passed her the ticket for her car?

As he escorted her through the lobby his hand came to rest in the small of her back, and he leaned in close as though he was claiming possession of her to any and all who looked. That crazy electricity thing happened again, and it was all she could do to walk across the lobby without falling on her face. Honestly. It was enough to turn a girl's head.

Enough to make her willing to bust out of her shell and try to become the kind of woman this man might want for longer than one night.

Of course, his room turned out to be a suite with a magnificent view of Denver and the black void of the mountains looming in the distance. Nothing but the best for Jagger Holtz, no, sir. So where did that leave her? Tonight's consolation prize? Except he hadn't even looked at another woman at the party. She'd barely taken her eyes off him all evening. She'd have noticed if he was checking the room for other fish.

She was Danger Girl, dammit. She was not about to let her complete lack of self-confidence overtake her now. She'd come this far…she could go the rest of the way toward making years' worth of fantasies come true.

Jagger took her ridiculous coat from her and hung it up in the front closet while she wandered over to the window to admire the view. She flung the question over her shoulder, "Why me? You could've had any woman in the place tonight."

He strolled up behind her, hands fisted in his pockets. He stopped just behind her shoulder, gazing at her reflection in the black window. "Why not you?" he countered. "You're beautiful, charming, intelligent, fun, an interesting conversationalist."

She got hung up on the very first adjective. "Beautiful? Me? I don't think so."

"Beauty's in the eye of the beholder," he murmured. "I find you positively magnificent." Tension suddenly poured from him. "Emily," he half whispered, "I can't take my eyes off you." The words sounded torn unwillingly from his gut.

"But *why?*"

It was as if she'd dug one layer too deep and hit a nerve. The deep restlessness that she sensed ingrained in him went still. His body froze for a moment. His face went blank. It was as if his entire being just...shut down.

It took him several seconds to look up at her reflection and smile crookedly at it. "Can't you just accept my...compulsion to be with you...at face value?"

He had a compulsion? To be with her? Cool. As long as it didn't turn out to be some sick obsession. Although he hadn't given her the slightest hint of any aberrant impulses.

Their dinner arrived, and he lit the tall white candles between their silver-covered plates. The candlelight twinkled off the shiny sterling flatware, lending an unbearably romantic air to the table and to the entire room. He extinguished the other lights until only the twin candles lit the room, leaving the space mysterious and sexy around them.

Jagger murmured, "Like most women, you look ravishing by candlelight."

She smiled widely. "Like most women, I know it's all about the lighting and not me."

"Untrue. Even the most perfect of lighting can only improve mediocrity so much. You're beautiful, candles or no candles."

She sighed. "You're so good for a girl's ego."

"I try," he murmured as he reached for her plate with a pair of lobster pliers.

He served her himself, pulling her lobster from the shell and even ladling dressing onto her salad for her. How was a girl supposed to resist all this pampering? By the bottom of her second glass of champagne, she was beginning to wonder why she should try. And then the fondue arrived. He fed her chocolate-dipped ladyfingers, red raspberries the size of her thumb and strawberries. Mmm, the strawberries. They were decadent.

By the bottom of the third glass of champagne, all thoughts of resisting his charms had flown right out of her head. And yet all he did after the meal was put on a smooth jazz CD and commence dancing with her. Not the big, flashy waltz of before but rather a slow and subtle swaying, just the two of them, body to body. It was…nice. Okay, maybe not nice. More like naughty. Luscious. Sexy. Fabulous.

His restraint made her feel safe. In control. And yet a little voice in the back of her head told her she was already wildly out of control. But hey. Tonight was all about taking chances.

"What kind of accounting work do you do?" he murmured as they continued to talk about anything and everything.

"I track special shipments and document the money trail from pickup to delivery."

"What kind of stuff constitutes a special shipment?"

She smiled up at him. "I don't ask, and the clients don't tell. Stuff in boxes, mostly. Commercial containers. Usually heavy and sealed airtight." She shrugged. "I figure it's illegal arms shipments."

"Seriously?" he blurted.

She laughed. "No, I'm joking of course. I have no idea what it is. I just make sure it's paid for and gets there on time."

"Do you do anything else?"

"Well, sure. Sometimes they need me to do other stuff."

"What kind of stuff?"

"You know. Exciting stuff. Like order food and toilet paper for ship crews. Or relay the fuel load a ship plans to take on when it comes into port." Her tongue wasn't cooperating quite as well as she'd like, and rather than sound tipsy, she threw the conversation back in his lap. "What do you do?"

"Stuff." He laughed down at her.

"I don't suppose I have to ask anyway. Everybody knows what James Bond does."

He laughed under his breath. "Are we talking about in the bedroom or out of it?"

She giggled up at him. The bubbles from the champagne had definitely gone to her head. "Personally, I think ol' James was a little deficient in that department."

Jagger's eyes popped wide open. "How so?"

"Well, think about it. All those women, and not a one of them ever got pregnant. And you have to admit, he isn't the kind of man who'd have a vasectomy. He's too macho to be that responsible. Which means—" she sighed for dramatic effect "—that the legendary Double-O-Seven shoots blanks. If you catch my meaning." She waggled her eyebrows exaggeratedly just to make sure.

Jagger all but doubled over in laughter, and she puffed up at the notion that he was laughing at her. "What's so funny?" she demanded.

"That an innocent kitten like you actually thinks about such things."

"I'm not innocent," she asserted indignantly. "Far from it."

He drew her closer, murmuring, "Hmm. That remains to be seen."

Not to be distracted from the subject at hand, she mused, "I suppose if a girl was looking for a sperm donor to give her a baby, James Bond wouldn't be a bad candidate—if all the equipment worked, of course. He's smart, handsome, charming, accomplished..." She batted her eyelashes up at him.

Jagger rolled his eyes. "I highly doubt James thought that far ahead. Guys like him live in the moment. They don't even think about surviving beyond the current mission."

"You say that like you know something about it."

"Not me," he replied blandly.

They danced in silence for several more minutes, and then he abruptly strode over to the television and turned it on. A timer was counting down the final seconds to the new year. She'd completely lost track of time in his arms.

Three. Two. One.

"Happy New Year," he murmured...

...and then he kissed her.

Chapter 3

Emily gasped. From the first moment their lips touched, it was *magic*. It was as if she'd been waiting for him all her life and, having now found him, had known him deep in her bones forever. He lifted his mouth away from hers and her eyes fluttered open.

He was staring down at her. In open shock, if she wasn't mistaken.

"Wow." Her heart was having no part of beating normally.

He cleared his throat. "Yeah. What you said."

She laughed in wonder. Happy New Year, indeed.

And then he all but inhaled her. Of course, she all but inhaled him back. The explosion of lust between them was instant and hotter than the sun. It sizzled across her skin, searing away everything in its path, every consideration of why not to jump into bed with him, every ounce of common sense, everything but him. Just him.

She needed him just as she needed to breathe. More.

"What have you done to me?" he muttered against her neck as he bent down to reach for the hem of her dress.

The slinky fabric slid off her body with a sexy glide of fabric on flesh. "I don't know, but you did it to me, too." She fumbled at the hem of his turtleneck, tugging it over his head to reveal a chest fully as gorgeous as hinted at under his clothing. "Do it some more," she urged.

His laugh was low and charged.

Score one for Danger Girl. Heck, score a million. Game over, Danger Girl won this round, hands down. Why, oh, why hadn't she discovered this side of herself years ago? How could she have hidden in the pink cocoon of her safe little world for so long? She'd never dreamed *this* was out there waiting for her. A man like Jagger. This wild pleasure that was a fire in her blood.

The rest of their clothes came off quickly, and the lights went off, leaving only the twin candles still guttering over the remains of their supper. An alto saxophone wailed a smoky blues tune from the stereo, and the air was redolent of chocolate, deep and dark and rich.

He carried her to the bed, laying her upon it and then standing back to look at her. Normally, she'd be absolutely mortified to be examined naked by a man she barely knew. Except this was Jagger. And Danger Girl thought it was glorious to have him look at her like this, as if she was his and he was never letting go of her. Maybe it was just the champagne. Or maybe he brought out the brazen hussy in her. But either way, she wasn't about to cower in front of this man. She wanted him. All of him. She planned to act out every naughty fantasy she'd ever had, tonight.

She held out her arms to him. "Come here, you."

He didn't wait for her to ask twice. He placed a knee on the bed beside her. Then he did a slow-motion press down to her, stopping when their mouths were a hairsbreadth apart.

"Are you sure about this?" he murmured. "No pressure. If you want to stop, just tell me."

She laughed and scowled up at him. "Don't you dare stop."

"As the lady commands." He sank the rest of the way down to her, gathering her close and rolling onto his side. They snuggled for a moment while he seemed to simply savor the feel of her against him. She appreciated the fact that he wasn't in any rush. That he could take his time and savor every bit of this experience. No green boy was Jagger Holtz, no, sir. He made her feel as though she was in good hands. Confident hands. Hands that were starting to roam up and down her spine and do the most delicious things to her entire body. Who'd have guessed so many nerves in so many places were hot-wired directly to her backbone?

She couldn't help it. She wriggled impatiently against him.

His chuckle tickled her ear, and he seemed to know the time for teasing her was over. "Show me what you want, Emily."

And then all that heat and urgency and muscle were hers. She wrapped herself around him like a freezing person embracing a roaring furnace. She kissed his chest, his neck, his jaw. And all the while, his hands roamed over her body, skimming across her skin and leaving a trail of utter destruction in their wake.

He shoved her hands up against the headboard and slid down her body as her urgency increased, driving her crazy with his mouth. He muttered, "What am I going to do with you? This is madness, but damned if I can stop it."

"More," she managed to gasp. "I want more."

She arched up into him, shuddering uncontrollably as his blazing mouth closed on her. He worked his way back up her body, incinerating everything that was left of her. Only then did he plunge into the very core of her, groaning his pleasure.

Their twin suns went supernova then, combusting so bright and hot that the explosion defied comprehension. They rode the incendiary wave, blasting outward from their cores on a solar storm that reached far out into the cosmos, finally flinging them into a void so silent and peaceful, Emily wasn't sure she was still alive.

"You've killed me," Jagger breathed.

She managed to gather enough breath to laugh. "I was thinking the very same thing."

"Well, then, I think we've established that you are no innocent, Ms. Grainger."

"Just call me Danger Girl."

"Right. And a more apt name there never was. You are more than dangerous, my dear. You're lethal."

"I hope you mean that in a good way," she chuckled.

"Indubitably."

"Thanks, Double-O-Seven."

His answering smile was serene. Contented. "You're welcome. And thank you."

He pulled her across his chest, draping her over his body until they were joined practically as one. His heart still pounded like a jackhammer beneath her ear, belying his outward calm. Had she done that to him? Cool.

She smiled in utter contentment of her own. How had she ever lived without him in her life? This was more than love at first sight. Was there such a thing as soul mates at first sight?

No doubt about it. She'd break out of whatever shell she must to keep this man. She'd move heaven and earth to be with him.

His lips moved in her hair. "You probably won't believe me, but this sort of thing doesn't happen to me often."

Her answer was prompt. "You're right. I don't believe you."

He laughed. "I'm serious."

She made a colossal effort and lifted her head enough to gaze at him. "You're telling me a man like you can't have any woman he wants anytime?"

He laughed. "I don't *want* any woman anytime. I have my

standards, you know." He pressed a finger against her mouth as if he knew she'd ask how in the world she possibly met his standards. "But you...you're incredible, Emily. I think you've ruined me for any other woman."

She laughed. "Now I know you're lying. But thanks. That's sweet of—"

His mouth swooped down on hers, and he kissed her with such passion she completely lost the rest of the thought. When she was breathless and clinging to him in panting need, he whispered, "I mean it. You...you're...magic."

She knew the feeling exactly.

He continued, murmuring contemplatively, "Would you think I was weird if I said I feel like I've been looking for you for a very long time?"

"Not if you promise not to think I'm weird for thinking the very same thing."

Their laughter mingled as they stared out into the cold night outside the windows. She couldn't imagine anything more perfect than being here with him, right now, in the relaxed afterglow of their lovemaking. She couldn't ever recall being more warm and content than she was in this exact second. The peace of it reached deep into her soul. She would never forget this moment as long as she lived. It was perfect. Exactly, totally perfect.

Would he disappear come tomorrow, like James Bond? Would he give her time to become Danger Girl in truth? She doubted most people got even one moment of happiness this pure in their lives, let alone a lifetime of it. Was she greedy to want more? Not that it mattered. She already knew she wouldn't be able stop herself from trying to hold on to him for as long as she could.

The next time they made love it was slow and lazy, filled with long kisses and intimate whispers. She savored every second of it, doing her darnedest to make a lasting memory of every millisecond. To wrap each piece of it carefully in her mind and pack it away in her heart's treasure chest. It reminded her of what a honeymoon must feel like. Or a wedding night.

The thought gave her a jolt, and Jagger whispered against her collarbone, "What?"

"Mmm, nothing. Just random delicious thoughts."

She felt his lips curve into a smile on her skin. He murmured, "You're delicious. Entirely edible."

She chuckled. "I thought we'd already established that."

"Yes, but," he disagreed, "we haven't yet established how you taste with chocolate fondue."

Her gaze snapped over to the fondue pot still warming on the table. "Oh, my."

In the wee hours of the morning, as she lay limp and utterly sated, she curled into the circle of his arms and knew, without a shadow of a doubt, this was the one place in the entire world she'd most like to be. Forever.

She was home. Danger Girl had found The One.

And with that thought in mind, she finally drifted off to sleep, dreaming of naughty red shoes and chocolate.

Jagger woke up feeling more refreshed in body, mind and soul than he had in years. And the cause of it was buried beneath a pile of blankets with little but her nose sticking out from under the covers. And what a lovely nose it was. He smiled indulgently. Emily might run cold when she was asleep, but she'd been plenty hot enough last night to burn him alive.

To hell with caution. So what if she was a forever girl and he was a one-night guy? She'd become his AbaCo informant and they'd work together for a good long time. Long enough to work this fever for her out of his blood and get back to being the one-night guy his work—his life—demanded of him.

He spied an empty champagne bottle on the coffee table. He

hoped she didn't feel the aftereffects of the bubbly too bad this morning. But just in case, he ought to order up a pot of coffee. Except he didn't have the heart to wake her just yet. It had been a very long night, and she deserved to sleep in nice and late.

Still, he could use some caffeine. He slipped out of bed quietly, pulled on jeans and a sweatshirt and grabbed his ski jacket. He'd just run down to the corner and get them some fresh lattes and muffins. He'd be back long before she stirred, let alone woke up.

The temperature had dropped below zero overnight, and this first day of the new year nipped at his cheeks and forehead with sharp teeth. The streets weren't exactly deserted this Sunday morning, but they weren't far from it. He jammed his hands in his pockets, hunched his collar up around his ears and set out for the coffee shop a block from the hotel.

He'd bet she liked her coffee turned into virtual ice cream with cream and sugar. He'd buy her one of every flavor of muffin, too—

Something stung him sharply in the neck, as painfully as a wasp. Oww!

He reached up reflexively to slap at the spot, and he lurched as someone grabbed him from behind. He reacted fast and hard, slamming his elbow into his assailant and whipping around to bring his feet to bear in the fight as his years of martial arts training kicked in. But his elbow blow was blunted by his attacker's thickly padded jacket, and whatever had been in the needle in his neck was damned fast acting. The street blurred and swam woozily before his eyes. *Crap. I'm in deep trouble here.*

Something huge and dark screeched to a halt at his side and three more men leaped out of the van to surround him. It was no contest. His legs were already collapsing out from underneath him. Frantically, he looked around for help. Even a simple witness to report his capture to the police. But the attack had been perfectly timed. Not a soul was in sight, let alone within shouting range.

His vision narrowed down to a gray tunnel and then to a single pinprick of light.

"Emily…" he gasped.

And then everything went black.

Chapter 4

Two years later

Jagger huddled in the tiny room, hugging his knees, drawing the darkness close around him like a security blanket. At least they were leaving him alone more these days. That was better than the constant interrogations and beatings of his first few months of captivity. But sometimes, in the dark of this endless night, he got so damned lonely he almost wished for the thugs to come back. Worse than decent food, worse than a real shower, worse almost than freedom, he craved human company. Someone to talk to him. Just normal, meaningless conversations about normal, meaningless things.

But he doubted his life would ever be normal again. Eventually, he'd catch some disease, or he'd become malnourished, or maybe he'd just give up on living. Then he was a goner. And not a damned soul would know or care. He figured his captors would push his entire crate overboard into the middle of the ocean and call it good. No more Jagger Holtz.

What kind of life was it to have lived where no one would give a crap if he died? There ought to be someone to care. But that would've meant having someone permanent in his life. Like Emily Grainger. A forever woman. But people in his line of work didn't do long-term relationships. At least not often, and generally not well.

If only he had someone to look forward to going home to. Maybe that would help him endure this unending nightmare.

He glanced at the hole he'd punctured in the corner of his crate when he was first thrown into this shipping container to rot. It served as his only marker of the passage of time. Darkness had fallen outside. Another day gone, which made this the seven hundred twenty-eighth day of his captivity. And that would make tomorrow…he checked the math and a bitter laugh rose up in his chest…New Year's Eve. Again.

For the thousandth time, he relived that fateful New Year's Eve two years ago. He should've seen the signs. His instincts should've warned him. But he'd been so besotted with Emily Grainger he'd never seen the trap coming. He'd let his guard down. Gotten distracted by a woman. No wonder James Bond never let himself fall for any of his many conquests. Ol' James understood the dangers of losing focus, apparently. Lucky bastard.

One thing he knew for sure. If he ever got out of here, if he ever found the people who'd put him into this hellhole, he was going to kill them all. Slowly and painfully.

Emily winced and looked back over her shoulder at yet another AbaCo facility festooned with those awful metallic Christmas decorations. They must be regulation company issue. At least this office had the advantage of being in paradise. She'd leaped at the opportunity to take this exotic position when it had come along. All part and parcel of her campaign to become Danger Girl for real. Jagger Holtz might have run out on her, but she would never forget how he'd made her feel. She'd been fully alive for the first time. She couldn't ever go back to the way she'd been before, Jagger or no Jagger.

The Hawaii AbaCo office occupied its own private island at the far western end of the chain of one hundred thirty-seven atolls, islets and islands that made up the Hawaiian archipelago. Although it was more of a refueling depot than an actual office. The Rock, as most of the employees called it, boasted a deepwater dock and underground fuel-storage and pumping facilities, plus a small collection of buildings.

Oddly, the staff numbered close to sixty, even though the lone office building here could probably only hold half that number—standing up and tightly packed. Two dozen long-shoremen refueled and resupplied the ships, and the security team accounted for another dozen of the tall, silent men on the payroll. She was told that AbaCo put divers in the water for security purposes whenever one of its container ships came into port, which supposedly accounted for most of the rest of the powerful-looking men that made up the staff.

But in the time she'd been here, the actual work getting done and the number of able-bodied men stationed here to do it didn't add up. There always seemed to be spare guys hanging around the small AbaCo building, going in and out of Kurt Schroder's office for hush-hush meetings. He was the site manager.

He'd seemed surprised when she'd shown up, letters of introduction in hand from the North American chief of security for AbaCo. But after Schroder read the letter, he merely shrugged and showed her to a desk. Her job here wasn't so different from what she'd done in Denver. It mostly entailed tracking shipments, making sure they got to where they were supposed to go on time, that the money got into the right accounts and answering a few phones.

The staff rotated in and out of this remote location. Two weeks on the Rock, two weeks off-duty on a Hawaiian island of personal choice. She'd chosen Kauai. It was everything she'd imagined Hawaii to be and more—tropical, lush and laid-back. She'd fallen in love with it from the first moment she'd set foot on it.

She'd even talked her mother into moving out here with her on this once-in-a-lifetime assignment to hold down the fort at the Kauai condo during the times Emily was posted on the Rock.

"There you are," a deep male voice grumbled from behind her.

Schroder. Dang. That guy could track her down anywhere. Here she was, parked on the far side of the island from the offices, and he still showed up unannounced to check on her. It bordered on creepy. It wasn't that he had any kind of a romantic interest in her. Two years ago she might have suspected that. But now she knew better. She'd experienced true chemistry once—and she and Kurt Schroder did not have *it*.

Of course, look where having *it* with a guy had gotten her. Maybe chemistry-challenged guys were a better bet if a girl wanted some sort of sane, stable life. Still, she didn't like how Kurt was constantly popping up unannounced when she least expected him.

"There you are, Emily. Strange place to take your lunch break."

She shrugged. "I was tired. I thought a hike might wake me up. I still have a little work to do this afternoon to wind things up before the New Year's Eve party."

She winced as she said the words. Would she never get past her memories of the fateful New Year's Eve party two years ago that had so completely changed her life—changed *her*?

Schroder seemed to accept her explanation. "Be careful out here. The rocks can be treacherous, and they get slippery when it rains." He cast a grim gaze up at a low cloud bank, which was indeed threatening to wet down the tiny island. The Kona Winds were blowing today, bringing in a heavy, muggy air mass and terminally bad hair to this corner of the world.

She sighed, pushed the frizzies out of her face and followed her boss back to the shipping office. So much for a moment of privacy. A person would think that there'd be plenty of alone time to be had on an isolated rock in the middle of the Pacific Ocean, but that person would obviously have failed to figure in the pervasive eye of AbaCo always watching over its employees.

She was due to rotate off the island the day after tomorrow, and she dared not leave much by way of unfinished work for her replacement, a taciturn ex-German Army man who was about as capable with paperwork as she was with a submachine gun. Which was to say, she couldn't tell the business end of a gun from the....whatever the nonbusiness end was called.

She filed the last stack of bills of lading and had all but finished matching the latest round of payments received with their various shipments when the bell on her computer dinged to indicate an incoming e-mail. She swung her chair around to face her screen and pulled up the message.

Zhow Min. 3-6-D-15472.

What on earth? She stared at the message for several seconds trying to make sense of it. There was no greeting, no signature block. The e-mail address from which the message originated was MysteryMom. Not exactly the sort of address one of AbaCo's shipping clients was likely to use. Was this message even meant for her? Emily glanced at her screen again and saw the message was addressed to her personally and not to the AbaCo office here on the Rock.

What did it mean?

The *Zhow Min* part was obvious. A supercontainer ship by that name was due in from China sometime after midnight

tonight. It was scheduled to be in port for twenty-four hours
to refuel and take on supplies. The crew would lay over in the
dormitory provided for that purpose until tomorrow evening.

But what were those numbers all about? She pulled up the
ship's cargo manifest on her computer and compared the
numbers to the various cargo shipments on the *Zhow Min*.
Nothing even remotely resembled the number sequence. Was
3-6 a date? She couldn't think of anything special about
March 6, and a quick search of the Internet revealed only that
it was Michaelangelo's birthday, the siege of the Alamo ended
that day and aspirin was patented on that date in history.

She frowned. Who was MysteryMom, anyway? She'd
never heard of the woman.

Bizarre.

She deleted the message, shut down her computer and
walked slowly across the island to her room in the employees' dorm to take a nap before tonight's festivities. But the
numbers continued to dance across her mind's eye, teasing
her—3-6-D-15472.

The cryptic message was still tantalizing her when she
finally escaped from the New Year's Eve party later that night,
unable to withstand the memories it evoked any longer.
Maybe a walk would help clear her mind.

Frankly, she wasn't a big puzzle kind of girl. And
whoever'd sent her that message had been a tad too cryptic
for her. If it was important, MysteryMom would just have to
suck it up and send her something that a normal human being
could comprehend. She wandered down to the island's tiny,
pristine beach, letting the quiet lapping of waves soothe her
troubled thoughts. It was hard to stay worked up for very long
in this balmy tropical clime.

"There you are."

Jeez. Did Schroder have a tracking radio glued to her back
that she didn't know about?

"Why did you leave the party?" he demanded.

As if he really cared about that. She knew darn good and well he wasn't asking because he took any kind of personal interest in her fun. He just got a kick out of controlling everyone's life around here.

She considered how to answer him. She couldn't very well complain about not being with her family when, a, everyone else out here was away from their families tonight and no one else was complaining about it, and, b, she'd volunteered for the holiday work cycle and the double overtime pay that came with it.

Reluctantly, she confessed a piece of the truth. "I'm not a big fan of tight places. And all those people crammed in that one room were a little much for me."

Schroder's gaze flickered as if he was cataloging that tidbit for future reference. Not that she could imagine where it would ever come in useful to him. He was always compiling lists of facts, neatly organized, about everything and everyone.

Schroder spoke in tones just shy of an outright order. "Come inside. The food just arrived. Bratwurst, sauerkraut, Wiener schnitzel and good German beer."

Ah. That must have been the speedboat she'd heard roar up to the pier a few minutes ago. Supplies were often brought over by boat from Lokaina, the nearest inhabited island. It lay about twenty miles away to the east and boasted not only a small permanent settlement, but even a tiny airport. It was from Lokaina Municipal Airport that workers on the Rock shuttled to and from their homes on the big islands of Hawaii, nearly a thousand miles to the east. Tonight's German feast had been flown in all the way from Honolulu.

Schroder commented as she hesitated to go back with him, "We've only got a few hours until the *Zhow Min* arrives. Not much time to celebrate."

Current estimated time of arrival on the ship was sometime

between 2:00 and 3:00 a.m. Reminded of that strange e-mail message yet again, she frowned. Schroder's brow lowered in determination as well. He must have misread her expression to mean she was planning to refuse his semiorder to go back inside. Although she'd much rather skip the heavy German food and stay out here to enjoy the waves and the isolation, Schroder wasn't the kind of man to take no for an answer. She sighed and turned to follow him back to the party.

The midnight meal, although tasty, was as heavy as she'd anticipated. She was glad to retire to the big dormitory and tumble into her bed as soon as Schroder seemed to think it was acceptable for her to go. Except sleep wouldn't come tonight. She lay there for over an hour and finally gave up on it. Those damned numbers kept floating around in her head, taunting her with some meaning hanging just beyond her grasp.

It was probably inevitable that as 2:00 a.m. approached she felt a compulsion to get up and go for a hike around the island. And, oh, maybe she'd stroll over and have a look at the *Zhow Min* when it came in and see if those damned numbers revealed their hidden meaning to her then.

She stepped out into the humid night. She topped the spine of rock marking the center of the island and was immediately assailed by bright lights coming from the massive pier below. The *Zhow Min* was gliding the last hundred yards or so to the dock. The top-heavy ship, loaded down with rectangular steel containers in huge stacks from stem to stern, was huge and ungainly and reminded Emily of a pregnant whale. The checkerboard of colored containers—each the size of a semitruck trailer—was brightly lit under giant banks of halogen lights that turned night into day all along the pier.

Emily moved off to her right, away from glare of the lights and toward the promontory that overlooked the pier from one side. The behemoth eased the final few feet into its slip in majestic slow motion and shuddered to a halt. Lines the thickness of Emily's waist thudded ashore to moor the *Zhow Min* to pilings the size of small cars.

The same layer of clouds that had provided soft gray cover all day obscured the moon now, and the sea was black beneath the featureless sky. From this angle, the *Zhow Min* was a building-sized silhouette. One moment Emily saw nothing, and the next, she was aware of several black forms—humans—looking like tiny ants next to the gigantic ship, scaling its hull on invisible lines.

Squinting, she counted three black-garbed figures. Were they doing some sort of maintenance? She didn't remember any being scheduled, and her master database tracked such things. The men didn't seem to be pausing anywhere on the hull as if to inspect or repair it. They reached the deck and huddled, then moved off in what could be described only as stealth toward the stern of the ship. She noticed that all of them wore backpacks of some kind. The humps on their backs made the men look vaguely tortoiselike as they crept off into the shadows.

What in the world were they up to?

Then the trio did something even more strange. They commenced climbing one of the mountains of containers. The third clump back from the prow of the ship. They climbed to the fourth layer of containers, and then made their way inward six boxes, to stop at a faded green container. Bemused, she moved farther out the cliff to get a better view. The men were hard to see as they clung to the container in the deep shadows. They were definitely acting as though they didn't want to be seen.

As she looked on, the container's door slid open. Her jaw dropped as the men disappeared inside, pulling the door shut behind them. This was not a port of entry! Without Customs present, no container was allowed to be unsealed like that! What could they possibly be doing?

She stepped farther forward, craning to see what the men would do next.

A big, blond man standing on the pier beneath a bank of lights pivoted suddenly, peering in all directions. *Schroder.*

It dawned on her that she was completely exposed up here on the cliffs like this. Emily dropped to the ground, flattening herself in the shadows behind an outcropping of low stones and praying he hadn't spotted her.

As she peered out from behind the scant cover of the rocks, Schroder held his position on the pier. Surely he'd have barged up here to check out the unauthorized observer if he'd spotted her. She exhaled in relief. Nonetheless, she stayed right where she was, hidden behind her shield of black volcanic pumice.

Within a minute or two, the container door opened again. The men emerged. They retraced their steps in as much stealth as before, rappelling down the stack of containers and sprinting along the rail to where they'd left their ropes hanging overboard. Something was different about them...then it hit her. All three men had lost their backpacks. They must have left them in that container.

What could those men possibly be smuggling in AbaCo containers? A drug shipment would be more bulky than that, wouldn't it? Illegal weapons would also be bulky and heavy. Jewels would be smaller than the three backpacks. Money, maybe? That might explain it. As she pondered the possibilities, the men shimmied down the hull almost too fast for her to keep sight of, slipped below the edge of the pier and disappeared from sight.

Interestingly enough, Schroder strode off the pier then and headed back toward the office. It was almost as if he'd been acting as a lookout for the men who'd broken into that container. What was up with that? It didn't take a rocket scientist to figure out that something fishy was going on around here. The question was, could she contain her natural curiosity and steer clear of trouble as any sensible person would?

She watched the *Zhow Min* for a few more minutes, hoping to catch sight of the men once more. But they were gone. Schroder didn't return, either.

Frowning, she made a mental note of exactly where on the ship the container she'd seen them enter was located. She ought to be able to find it in the ship's load plan the next morning. She could cross-reference that with the ship's manifest and see what was in that box they'd tampered with. It was the sort of thing she might do in the course of her regular job duties. If somebody noticed her poking around, they wouldn't think anything of it.

It wasn't as though she could report what she'd seen. Schroder was clearly in on whatever was going on around here, and he was the guy she'd have to report the incident to. If and when she found evidence of anything suspicious, then she'd have to figure out if Schroder's superiors were in on the racket out here. She could always call Customs—but they'd want hard evidence, too. Better to look into the matter quietly on her own and not make any waves for now.

She turned around to head back to her bed. She'd taken maybe a dozen steps when a dark shape emerged out of the rocks ahead to loom in front of her. She lurched, violently startled. "Kurt! I didn't hear you coming!"

Schroder was maybe a dozen yards away from her, striding toward her angrily, his eyebrows slammed together furiously. "What are you doing out here?" he demanded.

She blinked, alarmed. "I couldn't sleep after all that heavy food. I came out for a bit of fresh air."

He looked over toward the *Zhow Min* and back at her suspiciously. "What are you doing up on this cliff?"

She was a lousy liar, so she stuck to the truth as much as possible. Meanwhile, alarm bells clanged wildly in her head. "I stopped for a moment to enjoy the view. She sure is a big ship, isn't she?"

"How long have you been here?"

He asked that as if there was a definite right answer and a definite wrong one. More internal alarms and sirens warned her to answer evasively, "I just got here." As he continued to eye her angrily, she added, "Too bad it's not daytime. I can't see much in the dark. I'd love to watch one of the big container ships dock."

The stiff set of his shoulders eased fractionally. "A couple more are due in next week. Take a few minutes away from your desk and watch one. It's a surprisingly delicate maneuver considering how big and clumsy those ships are."

She nodded and then said lightly, "Well, I'm off to finish my hike around the island before I turn in. Wanna come along? I'll race you back to the dorm."

"Since when are you a runner?"

"New Year's resolution to get into better shape," she replied cheerfully.

He made no comment, nor did he make any move to join her as she turned to trot back toward her room and some privacy to think about what she'd witnessed and figure out what to do about it.

The next morning, she was no closer to an answer. She opened her cargo tracking database as usual and casually typed up the manifest for the *Zhow Min*. Third stack back. Sixth column in. Fourth layer high…and then it hit her, 3-6-D. If letters were used to designate the layers of containers, that was the exact location of the container she'd seen those men climb into. The cargo manifest said the container was a climate-controlled box—commonly called a reefer in the shipping business—with a self-contained ventilation and cooling system. This particular reefer was listed as carrying salmon, caviar and live lobsters to San Francisco. Nothing to inspire a middle-of-the-night break-in there.

She frowned at her screen.

"Something wrong?" Kurt asked from the doorway as he entered the building.

Man, that guy was irritating! And his timing was freakishly good—or bad, as the case might be. She reached up to hit the clear button as she answered, "Nope. Just checking on some cargo."

He wandered into his office along with a half dozen of those oddly unemployed men who were always hanging out on the Rock and closed his door. She glared at the panel. Schroder had blocked out an hour on his daily schedule for this meeting. Plenty of time for her to stroll down to the dock and have a look at that box.

She could get in trouble…but she could always say that she was checking to make sure the refrigeration was still working and that the seafood wasn't in danger of spoiling. It was a flimsy excuse. Was it enough to cover her if she got caught? Did she dare try it?

Her instincts screamed at her to go have a look at that container. The combination of that spooky team of men and the strange little e-mail yesterday was too ominous to be a coincidence. Obviously, something exceedingly sneaky was afoot. Equally obvious: if she got caught, she could be in more than trouble. But hey. She'd dedicated the past two years to becoming Danger Girl. This should be right up her alley, right?

Moving quickly before she could second-guess herself, she hunted up a clipboard while her printer spit out a quick copy of the *Zhow Min's* manifest. She grabbed it and headed out the door.

It was easier than she'd have anticipated to get onto the ship. She just strolled up the gangplank, flashed her AbaCo ID badge, mumbled something about needing to check the paperwork on a container and the Taiwanese sailor manning the hatch shrugged and let her pass.

An interior stairway to her immediate left beckoned. She climbed it until it ran out and stepped out hesitantly onto the main cargo deck. A towering jungle of containers loomed around her. She looked to be aft of the first stack of containers, which meant she should move to the rail and follow it aft past one more stack.

In a matter of minutes, she was staring up at the green container some twenty feet over her head. Now what? She glanced left and right and spied a tall metal staircase on wheels. She moved down to it and gave it an experimental nudge. It wasn't ridiculously heavy. It took her a couple of minutes, but she managed to maneuver it into place at the base of the correct pile of containers.

She climbed it quickly. And then she made the mistake of looking down through its mesh steps and had to stop to catch her breath while a minor panic attack passed. Note to self: never look down through see-through steps. She fixed her gaze on the green box above and forced herself to keep going. *Danger Girl. I'm Danger Girl.*

She arrived at the container. It looked no different than any other reefer container around it. She inspected the door. A heavy steel bar would have to lift clear of a latch, but then it looked as though it would open. She reached for the handle. Holy crow, the thing was heavy. She heaved on it with both hands, pushing with all her might. Thighs and back straining, she managed to pop the bar free with a loud clang.

She froze. Looked left and right in panic. Counted to a hundred, but nobody came along to check on her. She tugged on the door. Soundlessly, it opened a few inches. A strong odor of fish poured out on a gust of cold air. Starting to feel supremely foolish, she stepped into the dark space. She should've brought a flashlight. Too late to go back and fetch one now, though. She left the door cracked open and eased forward into the crowded space.

As advertised, boxes labeled salmon and caviar on ice were stacked on the left. The entire right side of the container was taken up with two massive steel containers. She lifted the lid of the first one and saw black water. Something alive squirmed a foot or so below the surface and she recoiled in horror before she remembered the live lobsters that were supposed to be in there.

So why had a team of men broken in here under cover of darkness and left backpacks of…something…behind? She kept an eye out for the black backpacks but saw no sign of them or their possible contents. As advertised, this crate seemed to contain nothing more menacing than a bunch of seafood.

She moved deeper into the crate, following a narrow aisle left open down the middle of the space. That seemed a little weird. The whole idea was to pack these things tight and not waste an inch of packing volume. These containers were not cheap to move around the world and nobody gratuitously wasted space in one.

She followed the passage deeper into the dark.

Abruptly, she came up short against a wall. And frowned. She'd thought she had another eight or ten feet to go before she reached the back wall of the container. Usually, her spatial orientation was more accurate than this. Something else was strange, too. The rows of stacked boxes stopped a good four feet from the wall, leaving a substantial gap back here. Now, that was plain wrong. No client in their right mind would load cargo this far short of the back of the box. She looked around for the contents of the missing backpacks, on the assumption that this was the spot the men must have left their loads.

Nada. The space was frustratingly empty, completely clear of anything at all. Just floors and walls back here.

She examined the exposed wall before her. It was finished with cheap paneling instead of the quilted insulation lining all of the other interior wall surfaces of this container. Indeed, all reefer units were heavily insulated to hold in cooled or heated air. Squinting to make out more detail on this oddly paneled wall, she was startled to spot some sort of electronic device mounted on the far right-hand side of it. It was tucked way back in the dark and she could hardly make it out.

She moved over to what turned out to be a numeric keypad of some kind. Her pulse leaped. This little gizmo was definitely *not* standard issue in a reefer.

As her eyes continued to adjust to the dark, the number pad glowed faintly before her. AbaCo used similar devices as locks on office doors and storage areas. Could this be a door panel of some kind? How could it not be? She was dead sure she hadn't reached the back of the container yet. There had to be a secret compartment behind the wall.

She stepped up to the pad. She couldn't very well start punching in random numbers.

Random numbers...

Could it be? She reached up and typed in the numbers that had ended yesterday's cryptic e-mail message—1-5-4-7-2. And stared in shock as a green light illuminated over the pad. A distinct clicking noise was audible. She looked for a handle but found none. Tentatively, she ran her fingertips over the paneled wall. And discovered a groove running the length of it next to the side wall of the container. She wedged her fingernails under it and gave a tug. A concealed door swung open before her.

She stepped through, terrified of what she might find. It was really dark in the closet-sized space. Only a tiny pinprick of light illuminated the far corner at floor level.

Something moved.

Something big.

She jolted violently and muffled a scream.

The thing moved again. She backed away in horror, banging into the door at her back and shoving it wide open in her haste to escape the monster lurking in the dark.

A shaft of dim light spilled into the space, vaguely illuminating the creature crouching in the corner.

Emily froze. And stared. A cold chill rippled through her and her jaw dropped in shock.

Chapter 5

Jagger lurched as steel rattled nearby. What was this? They'd fed him and given him several jugs of water last night. Nobody was scheduled to bother him for at least a week. He'd long ago figured out he was being held in some sort of shipping container. The faint but unmistakable roll of a ship and the smell of seawater gave it away. His guess was that he'd been on a ship for most of the past two years, held in international waters, tucked away and forgotten except for those times when someone came into his ten-by-ten-foot world and tried to beat or torture some more information out of him.

The first few weeks had been the worst. His captors had been making a concerted effort to break him then, to squeeze him for everything they could get out of him while his intelligence and information were freshest. But the interrogations and beatings had tailed off over time. He suspected his captors were just waiting now for him to crack up or kill himself, whichever came first.

Except he was just too damned stubborn to give in. He'd been played for a fool, and he had no intention of going out like that. He owed his captors. Big time. And he wasn't about to die until he gave them a dose of their own medicine right back. His need for vengeance—he'd long ago quit sugarcoating his fury with words like *justice* and *payback*—had sustained him for nearly two years. In occasional moments of stark honesty, he wondered how much longer he could hang on to it. When even his hate deserted him, he feared he would be done for.

He scrabbled to the back of his box as the distinctive beep of his cage's lock sounded on the other side of the wall. They would hit him with a Taser if he was anywhere near the door when it opened. A slash of light fell on the floor. Someone slipped through the narrow gap. Odd. They usually came in threes and fours. They'd learned the hard way not to tangle with him one-on-one. In fact, they'd only made that mistake once.

Had they made it again?

He coiled, ready to spring at his captor.

The guard moved suddenly, jumping backward sharply, banging into the door. He stared, bemused as the door swung wide open. What was up with that?

A gasp. And then a voice straight out of his most painful dreams gasped, "Jagger? Is that you?"

Bright lights exploded inside his head, ice picks of shock stabbing at his eyeballs as recognition ripped through him. *What in the hell is she doing here?*

What new game were they playing with him? To date, their efforts hadn't been this sophisticated. Had Emily been dragged here to seduce him? Were they blackmailing her, perhaps? Forcing her to tease and tantalize him into spilling his guts? If brute force wouldn't work, were they now going to resort to sex? He had to admit, it was a diabolical tactic. The sort of thing he might have thought of if he were the captor and not the captive.

Surely they knew how he felt about this woman. Was a team of men waiting in the wings to swoop in and drag them apart as soon as she extracted whatever information she'd been sent here to get? He squinted past her, but it was too dark in the area beyond to see how many men waited in the shadows for him.

"Jagger?" she repeated in horror.

He must look like death warmed over. Two years with no sunlight, malnourished, unshaven. Hell, even he could barely stand his own stink.

"Emily Grainger," he muttered. "Can't say I was expecting you to walk through that door, darlin'."

"What are you doing here?" she gasped.

He laughed, and even he could hear the manic edge to it. "That's funny, Em. What do you think I'm doing here? Enjoying the solitude and sea breezes?"

"What are you talking about?" she demanded, her voice barely a whisper. "Who did this to you?"

"Your cronies at AbaCo. Tossed me in this box two years ago and left me to rot."

"Two—what—how—" she sputtered. "I don't understand."

"Look. Whatever game your bosses are playing, you can just forget it. I'm not breaking. Get out of here and leave me alone. I'm not letting them sucker me into talking, even if they dangle you as bait. I'd rather have them just beat the tar out of me."

"Beat you?" A long pause. "Are you being held *prisoner?*" The last word was exhaled in a shock so profound it barely had sound. Was she really that naive? Was it just dawning on her what AbaCo was truly capable of? What did she think had happened to him two years ago when he just vanished off the face of the earth?

He replied sarcastically, "And I suppose you're here to pull off a miraculous rescue and raise my hopes that I'm actually gonna get out of here before your goon bosses grab me again. Is that what they told you to do?"

"Rescue?" She seemed to struggle to comprehend the word. "Jagger, I got an anonymous e-mail yesterday with nothing but the name of this ship and the location of this cargo container in the message. I came to check it out. I had no idea—" She broke off. "We have to get you out of here!"

"Riiiight," he drawled.

"I'm serious. Come on! My boss will only be in his meeting a little while longer. If anyone on this island is responsible for holding you prisoner, he's the one." When he didn't move, she added urgently, "Come. *On.*"

He couldn't help it. In spite of himself, a flicker of hope ignited in his gut. Dammit, he shouldn't play along with this new ploy of theirs. He knew better. But maybe, just maybe, there was a chance they would screw something up. That he could actually slip past his captors and win his freedom for real. It was absolutely a trap. But a trap could work two ways.

Of course, he might die in the attempt. But at this point, death held very little intimidation value for him. He almost wished for it sometimes.

He eased to his feet. Took a step forward. She backed up, shoving the door behind her open wider. The smell of fish grew even stronger than usual. He was never going to eat seafood again if he made it out of here.

Emily turned and disappeared from sight down a narrow gap between floor-to-ceiling wooden packing crates.

He took another step forward. *Out of the box.*

Mother of God, he was out of that box. Even if it was only for a few more seconds, it was worth whatever they did to him to have made it out of that crate alive. Frowning, he pushed the door closed behind him. It clicked shut and a tiny red light illuminated over the electronic lock. If he was actually expecting to make it out of here, he'd cover his tracks and make it look as if he were still safely locked up inside his tiny prison.

Frankly, he was stunned that a team of AbaCo's men wasn't

out here waiting for him, laughing their heads off at his pitiful hope that he'd actually been rescued. But the box seemed tightly packed with seafood, and if there were any hiding spots from which his captors were planning to jump out at him, he sure couldn't see them.

The flicker of hope in his gut grew a little stronger.

Cautiously, he made his way down the aisle, squinting as blinding light assaulted his eyes. His eyeballs ached almost unbearably from it. Nonetheless he was grateful for the pain because it meant he could still see normally.

Emily paused short of the door at the far end of the box.

He asked, "How do you plan to get out of here with me? Just walk out?"

She frowned. "Have you got any better ideas? You can't exactly jump overboard. It's too far to fall without killing yourself when you hit the water, and besides, someone would hear you."

He stepped into the doorway and reeled back, unprepared to be twenty feet or more above the deck with only a flimsy, metal mesh staircase between him and a nasty fall.

Emily continued, "The men who came in here last night came aboard using ropes. They climbed up the side of the ship and went back down the same way."

"You *saw* them?" He didn't associate AbaCo's people with being so careless.

"Well, I wasn't supposed to. But I couldn't sleep and I happened to be out for a walk when the *Zhow Min* docked, and I happened to be standing at the right angle to see the silhouettes of the men climbing the hull."

"Do they know you saw them?"

"I don't think so. They had a lookout posted and he didn't seem alarmed by anything. Only problem is that just as I was leaving the area, my boss found me."

"Was he suspicious?" Jagger asked quickly.

"He's always suspicious. But I think he bought my story about not being able to sleep after the big meal the company served at the party."

Party. Right. New Year's Eve. His gut twisted violently at the reminder of the import of that particular date in his life. Except, if this little escape attempt of Emily's, which supposedly had been prompted by events on this New Year's Eve, turned into real freedom for him, he might have to revise his currently low opinion of the holiday.

Speaking of escaping, he looked around quickly. "We need to get moving. If I had a rope, I could climb down the hull, too."

She started down the stairs, whispering over her shoulder, "Maybe I can find you one. Stay here while I go have a look."

Right. As if he was waiting around for the goon squad to close in on them. Not a chance. He hurried down the steps on her heels. Interestingly enough, she made no comment. She headed to her left and he spied a deck railing not far ahead of her. She leaned out over the side of the ship, looking in both directions, then hurried back to him where he lurked in the shadow of a giant pile of shipping containers.

"There's a rope hanging almost all the way down to the dock about fifty feet to your right as you reach the railing. You can't exactly stroll down the dock barefoot and looking like a mountain man, though. Somebody'd spot you for sure."

No lie. He eased forward, sticking to the shadows as much as possible, until he could lean far enough forward to peek over the railing at the pier below. It wasn't busy, but neither was it deserted.

"Do you know if the pier is hollow or maybe constructed of wood? Can I get beneath it?" he asked under his breath.

"I think so. But you'll have to be careful. AbaCo has divers in the water to make sure no one sabotages a ship while it's here."

He blinked in surprise. She probably shouldn't have told him that if she was supposed to be protecting AbaCo's security.

She continued rapidly, "This island is about one mile in diameter. On the far side of it from here is a little beach. It's surrounded by thick underbrush. If you can make it over there, you can hide in that area. Unfortunately, most of the rest of the island is bare rocks. I'll have to wait until tonight, but I ought to be able to bring you fresh clothes and supplies at the beach. And then we can figure out what we're doing from there."

"This is an island?" he asked sharply. "Where are we?"

"They call it the Rock. It's a private island at the far western end of the Hawaiian island chain."

He swore under his breath. No wonder AbaCo's guys were in no hurry to close in on him. They knew he couldn't go anywhere. "How do people get on and off the island?" he asked.

Emily answered, "Boats, mostly. Sometimes helicopters. They head over to Lokaina, which is the nearest permanently settled island, and fly from the airport there to the bigger islands. It's almost twenty miles from here."

He thought fast. "Can you get us a boat?" It was the only realistic option for him. No way could he swim twenty miles of open ocean. He wasn't that fit. Heck, Navy SEALs were hardly that fit.

But if he could snag a boat, twenty miles wasn't far at all. An hour, maybe. And an airport on Lokaina? That he could work with. If he could just make it over there, he might stand a real chance of getting free of his captors. As soon as he contacted his superiors they'd send in whatever forces it took to retrieve him.

"Can cell phones call off this island?"

She shook her head. "Only satellite phones, and they're pretty expensive. The office has sat lines that everyone's allowed to use."

Yeah, and AbaCo was sure to monitor every last one of them. Yup, he'd have to get his butt over to Lokaina before he could call in the cavalry.

Damn. This was starting to feel like a real escape. Of course, his captors were probably getting a kick out of giving him a few hours of illusory freedom like this. No doubt they planned to close in on him at this supposed rendezvous tonight and take him down then. Or at least they'd try.

But then, he wasn't entirely incapable of throwing them a few surprises of his own.

He grabbed the thick nylon line and swung his foot over the railing. "When will you come to the beach?" he asked.

"An hour after dark?" she replied questioningly.

He nodded. "Done. I'll see you there."

To say she was shell-shocked was a bit of an understatement. Emily stumbled off the *Zhow Min* in a fog, barely aware of having closed the reefer unit's outer door and pushing the stairs back to where she'd gotten them.

Jagger had been held prisoner all this time? Incredible. Worse, he believed AbaCo was behind his kidnapping. Unfortunately, in her heart of hearts, she believed that AbaCo was absolutely capable of doing such a thing. She should have left the company a long time ago. But the money and benefits were excellent, and she'd preferred to be safe and secure in that steady paycheck.

Some Danger Girl she'd turned out to be. She'd continued to work for the evil supervillains, even after she strongly suspected they were up to no good. She'd let her wallet rule her ethics.

Thank God MysteryMom had sent that e-mail to her. Even if she'd had no idea what it meant, it had made her edgy and sleepless enough to see those men climb aboard the ship last night. Without that, she'd never have found him.

Nausea rumbled through her gut at what would have happened to him had she not investigated that broken-into reefer unit. Would he have died in that box? How could he not have? It wasn't as if AbaCo could turn him loose to press charges against them and testify about his captivity.

She glanced down at her watch and gasped in dismay. Schroder's meeting was due to end in a few minutes and he was super punctual. Crud. She picked up her pace until she was all but running.

She slipped into her desk chair, hot and sticky, her hair flying every which way, about two minutes before Schroder and his cronies emerged from their meeting, laughing. She managed to compose her facial expression, but her heart still pounded in fear at the sight of him. She reached for her in-basket and knocked over a coffee mug in her haste. Blessedly, it was empty, but Shroder looked up at the thud. She smiled lamely, her face red, and with exaggerated care, righted the cup.

The afternoon seemed to last about a week, but finally, the clock said five o'clock. All her work was done, and she shut down her computer quickly. She was surprised to notice that her hands were shaking. She had to get a grip on herself if she was going to be of the slightest use to Jagger.

She made her way back to the staff dormitory where the employees all had their own small room on the island. It allowed folks to permanently store clothing and toiletries and not have to move personal possessions back and forth to the Rock when it was their turn to work. It kept hauling luggage out here down to a minimum, and she supposed that saved the company money on top of being convenient for the workers.

Her plan this evening was to break into the room next to hers, which was held by a guy currently not on the island, and borrow some clothes for Jagger. The two men were reasonably close in height and build. Her room shared a kitchenette with her coworker's and only a simple lock held the door to his room shut.

It only took about fifteen seconds and an ice pick to pop the lock into the guy's quarters. It was disconcerting to realize just how insecure she'd been all this time on the island. She stepped into the dim room and made her way to his closet.

Slacks, a golf shirt, shoes, socks and underwear went into her waterproof canvas beach bag. She glimpsed the bathroom behind a partially open door and swung in there for a razor, nail clippers and a comb. She hit the jackpot when she spied a new toothbrush still in its wrapper. She grabbed it and some dental floss while she was at it.

In her own room, she added bottled water, snacks, a small first aid kit, a pocketknife and a flashlight to her bag of goodies. Last, she picked up the coup de grace. During Schroder's afternoon coffee break, she'd managed to lift a spare set of keys to the island's small runabout boat from a drawer in his desk.

Twilight had settled over the island but it wasn't dark yet. She gulped down something tasteless out of the microwave and stared anxiously at the clock beside her bed. Her mind was blank, filled only with terror that she was going to screw this up and get Jagger hurt or worse. Danger Girl must not fail!

When she judged an hour had passed since full darkness had fallen, she put on her running shoes, picked up her bag and headed out. Here went nothing.

The beach bag converted to a mini-backpack, so she slung it over her shoulders and took off jogging down the trail that followed the coast all the way around the island. She prayed she could keep up a credible pace until she topped the ridge and disappeared from sight of the clustered buildings.

The rocks rose behind her and hid her from sight. She slowed, panting. Lord, she hated running. She walked carefully as her eyes slowly adjusted to the dim conditions. Although the trail was mostly smooth, washes of loose sand and gravel made it treacherous in spots. It descended the far side of the island's spine in a series of sharp switchbacks that wound toward the eastern shore, but as she approached the lee side of the island, it leveled out. She watched carefully for the turnoff that led to the beach where she said she'd meet Jagger.

There. In the shadow of a koa tree. The faint white stripe of a trail. She turned down it, ducking into the lush undergrowth. This little corner of the island, protected from the worst of the trade winds, was thick with native Hawaiian plant life.

The tiny beach came into view. Maybe only fifty feet long, it was tucked between a pair of giant volcanic boulders at each end. Foot-high waves lapped quietly onto the sand, funneled up the beach by the outcroppings at each end of the inlet.

There was no sign of Jagger. Had he been caught? Panic turned her knees to jelly. Now what was she supposed to do? It would take hours for any police to arrive on the Rock, assuming they would even respond to an outrageous claim of a man held hostage for two years in a cargo container. Besides, Schroder and his men could have Jagger off the island and spirited away into a new and even more obscure captivity long before the police could get here.

"Jagger?" she called out quietly. "It's me."

Nothing.

She frowned. Maybe he'd already found some other way off the island. In which case, she'd wait here for a while, figure out she'd been stood up and return to her room. And then what should she do? Let him disappear again from her life? Spend the next two years wondering if he was AbaCo's captive or worse? Knowing what she knew now, how would she survive that?

Losing him the first time had been more painful than she could've imagined. They'd formed such a close bond so quickly, had clicked so well, that when he ditched her she'd been utterly devastated. She never had actually gotten over him or moved past him. But then, how could she? She saw his face every day. Couldn't help but think of him every day. Heck, she'd transformed herself into Danger Girl to be the kind of woman he'd be attracted to. It was as if that one magical night had taken over her life, as if it had never really ended. The whole past two years had been about Jagger.

And if she had to go forward again into another endless abyss of unanswered questions, of self-doubt, of missing him, she didn't know if she could take it.

Of course, the whole blessed thing was out of her hands. He would either keep their appointment here or he wouldn't. She hated being powerless like this! *C'mon, Jagger. Show up.*

Jagger crouched in a crevice high in the rock outcropping that bounded the south end of the tiny beach. Emily was sitting in the sand, jumping a mile high at every little night sound. He hadn't spotted the trap yet, which worried him. Enough for him to continue holding his position here while he waited for AbaCo's goons to show themselves. From time to time Emily glanced at her watch, but she gave no other visible signal to anyone who might be lurking nearby, watching her.

An hour passed. She was growing more agitated and jumpy by the minute. Still no sign of the ambush, though. Was it possible that she'd been telling the truth earlier? That she wasn't in league with his captors, willingly or otherwise? He dismissed the idea as preposterous. How could she not be doing their dirty work? She was out here on this godforsaken island earning a paycheck from AbaCo, wasn't she?

Her shoulders began to droop. If he wasn't mistaken, she wiped away tears from her cheeks at one point. The stress must be getting to her. It was getting to him, too. Had he not spent the past two years sitting in a box, he'd have been squirming hard an hour ago. He had to give these AbaCo guys credit. They were patient.

His attention jerked back to Emily as she stood up with an audible sigh. His gaze narrowed as she made her way over to the outcropping practically at his feet. She put down a dark bag, wedging it into a crack at the base of the boulder and murmured, "Godspeed, wherever you are tonight, Jagger."

As she trudged up the beach with her back to him, he hopped down silently and picked up the bag. He pulled the drawstring open and peered in at the contents. Something cracked painfully in his chest and his next breath was hard to draw. He stared down at the clothing, food and toiletries, flummoxed. What was she up to?

He glanced up and she was just disappearing into the trees. Still no movement whatsoever. No sign of an ambush anywhere. He should turn around and leave. Take the peace offering without looking back and use the gear and clothing to get off this rock.

But instead, he ran lightly across the beach and darted into the woods, parallel to the path, ducking from shadow to shadow. As hard as he found it to believe, he was forced to conclude that there was no one else out here.

Still, it was sheer insanity to call out low, "Emily. Wait up." But call he did.

She whirled, peering into the trees, trying to spot him. He held his position cautiously, his eyes roving urgently, looking for other reactions to his voice. Nada.

"Go back to the beach," he murmured.

She complied instantly, all but running back toward the strip of sand. He turned slowly to follow. Either there was more to this situation than he was seeing or he was the biggest idiot in the universe to fall for the same trap, baited by the same woman, twice.

There was only one way to find out for sure. And apparently he was going to do that one thing, since his feet were already carrying him back to the beach and whatever awaited him there.

Chapter 6

Emily's heart lodged in her throat at that husky, familiar voice caressing her skin out of the darkness. Memories long repressed surged back into her consciousness. Sweat-slicked skin on skin, his hard power driving into her, her body arching up into that mind-blowing pleasure, all her fantasies and more come to life.

She stopped at the edge of the minijungle, waiting for him to join her, huffing from the quick hike. Yeah, that was the reason she was panting. The hike.

Only the waves and the wind in the palm fronds overhead broke the night's sultry silence. But then something hard slapped over her mouth and she about jumped out of her skin. Heat caressed her ear—oh, God, his mouth—and he whispered, "Don't move. Don't make a sound."

She nodded her head fractionally beneath his hard hand. The unrelenting pressure eased slowly. Had he not told her to be still she'd have turned in his arms and flung herself at him in her relief. She stood there for a long time, his presence druggingly close and emanating heat and sex, but never, not once, touching her after his hand fell away from her. It was maddening.

Finally, an eternity later, he murmured, "What's in the bag?"

Her gaze snapped over to the beach bag still sitting at the base of the boulders across the beach. He'd seen that, huh? Then why hadn't he shown himself earlier? *Ah*. It hit her. He'd been waiting to see if it was some kind of trap. She answered, "Clothes. Food. Supplies."

He nodded, almost as if she'd passed some sort of test. Then he muttered, "I need to get off this island before I'm discovered missing."

She replied lightly, "Ya think? By the way, can I move now?"

His low chuckle stirred her hair and her heart. "You know the drill, Danger Girl. Hold your hands well away from your body and no sudden moves."

He remembers Danger Girl. What other details of that one night together did he remember? Then his terse instructions registered. "Sheesh, Jagger. I'm not a criminal. I'm helping you, for crying out loud."

"It's not you I'm worried about," he responded. "I can take you. But a half dozen of your partners in crime? Not so much."

He could take her? He undoubtedly meant that as in to take her down in a fight, but the images his double entendre sent spiraling through her mind stole her breath away. Dang it, where had her knees disappeared to all of a sudden? They'd gone squishy and would hardly bear her weight.

She whispered, "There's no one else out here as far as I know."

The sound he made in response was skeptical. Appalled, she looked at the surrounding undergrowth, peering fearfully into it in search of bogeymen and bad guys. She hadn't seen anyone follow her out here, and she'd looked over her shoulder constantly on the hike across the island.

If she didn't understand that he'd been through a horrendous ordeal and wasn't yet clear from danger, she'd be hurt by his lack of faith in her. But as it was, she fully understood his caution. She only prayed he was wrong.

Her scan brought her gaze around full circle back to him. Even in the moonlight his face looked paler than it should be. So thin he was. As if all of his excess being had been pared away until only the essentials remained. His was the physique of a man who'd survived immense suffering.

"I know how we can get you off the island," she offered.

"Do tell."

"I borrowed the spare keys to a boat this afternoon."

"One of the cigarettes?" he asked hopefully.

"No such luck. It's a twenty-two-foot ski boat that the staff uses for recreation—snorkeling and diving and some water-skiing when the seas are calm. But it'll take us to Lokaina."

"And where are these keys?" he asked intently.

"In my right pants pocket."

She started to reach for them, but he lurched violently and leaped forward to stop her movement, gripping her wrist in a vise that all but crushed her bones.

"I'll get them," he bit out.

Man. Touchy, touchy. But then his big hand slid into her pocket, only a thin layer of cotton separating his fingers from her groin, and her brain froze. Or maybe *overheated* was a better description. Her body went hot and liquid and achy all of its own volition, and suddenly her spine felt completely unhinged.

"While I've got my hands on you, I may as well go ahead and search you. I'll have to do it sooner or later anyway."

She blinked at his muttered words. He didn't sound particularly thrilled at the prospect, and disappointment coursed through her. Was touching her like this doing nothing at all to him? Her pulse was far too thrilled for its own good at the prospect of having his hands roam all over her body once more. He took a step forward, looming in front of her, so close she could count his eyelashes.

And then his hands touched her ribs underneath her T-shirt. Her breathing hitched, suspended somewhere between a gasp and a groan. His palms skimmed up the sides of her breasts, across the ticklishness of her armpits, tracing her collarbones and then swooping down between her breasts. His hands spread apart then, cupping her breasts. Surely through the thin lace of her bra he could feel that she wore no surveillance wire. Of course, just as surely he could feel the way her nipples had pebbled up hard and eager in response to his touch.

Her face flamed. Not because she was embarrassed. Oh, no. It was far more humiliating than that. She was aroused. By a man who'd blatantly seduced her, and then disappeared from her life for long enough that she should've been *way* over him by now. By a man who made outrageous claims about being a prisoner in a box for the past two years and had some evidence to support him. By a man she barely knew and yet of whom her memories were mostly naked and intensely sexual.

One of his hands emerged from under her shirt to spear into the hair at the back of her neck while the other hand slid around to her back. Hard, hot fingers trailed down her spine, dipping into the crevice as the base of her spine possessively. She arched forward reflexively, away from the intimate invasion, and her hips ran squarely—and informatively—into his groin.

Well, then. He wasn't completely unaffected by this search, either. Did it mean anything at all? Or was it purely a function of him not having touched a woman in two years? Whereas she could hardly stay on her feet as lust slammed into her, he merely shot her a shark's grin that gleamed briefly in the dark. Clearly, he was enjoying torturing Danger Girl. If only she had the same power over him. Then the contest might be a little more even.

A quickly as he'd commenced the search, it was over. His

hands withdrew, leaving her shivering and bereft. His voice, as calm as a glassy sea, flowed over her. "Okay. So we've ruled out a wire. Do you have a burr or some other tracking device on you? Will you tell me the truth or do I need to strip you naked and dunk all of your clothes in the ocean?"

Hmm. He could always have left her clothes on her and told her to swim out into the water a ways. But no. Getting her naked was on his mind, instead. Maybe the contest between Danger Girl and the Super Spy wasn't quite so uneven after all.

She answered him earnestly, "I'm not wearing a radio or tracking device or anything else like that. I give you my word."

He stared at her for a long moment. "I shouldn't believe you," he mumbled under his breath. "I know better."

She frowned. What was he talking about? He'd commented earlier something to the effect of her helping AbaCo set him up. Of course, that was sheer lunacy. She would never have done such a thing, particularly not to him. Not a man she'd been wildly infatuated with and had even bedded. Heck, one with whom she was still wildly infatuated.

"Where's this boat of yours?" he asked abruptly.

"That way." She pointed off to her right. "At the employee dock. It's tied up with the two cigarette boats and some Jet Skis, but I don't have the keys to any of those."

"Is this dock guarded?"

"From who? Everyone here works for AbaCo."

"Perfect," he purred. "Let's go."

Apparently, he was expecting her to assist in the next bit of grand larceny. She frowned. "I can't go with you."

"Yeah, you can—and are," he retorted.

"But I've got responsibilities. I need this job."

"Do you need to be dead also?" he snapped.

"I'm serious, Jagger. I don't mind helping you escape, but I can't up and leave. I'm not that carefree bachelorette you met two years ago."

He snorted. "And when they discover my crate's empty, what exactly do you think they'll do?"

"I don't know."

"I'll tell you, Emily. They'll pull the surveillance tapes from the dock and spot you going aboard the ship. They'll go through the ship's security camera logs and find you going into that container and both of us coming out of it. And then they'll come after you. Not to fire you. To kill you."

She gaped at him, too horrified to say a word.

"Come on. You're leaving tonight. With me."

Stunned, she didn't argue as he dragged her forward by the hand toward the black bag of supplies and then off toward the boat dock. What he said was logical. It just refused to compute. Someone would try to kill her? Not possible. She was a regular person living a reasonably regular life—even if her job was in an exotic locale. It was still mostly pushing paper at a desk. Danger Girl was about making adventurous choices, not fighting supervillains and risking death!

Jagger dragged her along for several silent and scary minutes. Then without warning he dropped to a crouch and yanked her down beside him. "That the dock?" he breathed.

She looked ahead and saw the small pier jutting out into the ocean. "Yes. That's it."

He watched it for several nerve-racking minutes and then announced, "It looks clear. Here's what you're going to do. Walk down to the dock and untie the boat. Don't get in it and don't start the engine if there happens to be a key in the ignition. You and I are going to tow the boat clear of the dock and out into open water before we crank her up. Otherwise we risk drawing someone's attention."

"How are we going to tow it—"

He cut her off. "Just go untie the boat. And wait for me if I'm not there before you." Before she could ask any more questions, he darted off down the beach toward the boathouse and was gone. How were they going to tow a boat? Why couldn't she start the boat if there was already a key? Did he think it would blow up or something? And most important of all, how was she supposed to inform him that she wasn't this kind of Danger Girl at all? That she was actually Giant Chicken Girl when it came to doing anything that involved adrenaline or death?

If he was right, it would be more dangerous for her to stay here on the island than it would be for her to march down there and steal a boat. That one fact alone was the sole reason she stood up and forced her feet into motion.

Her skin crawled with the nakedness of standing out here on the rocks like this. She tried reminding herself that she had every right to be here and her presence shouldn't raise any but the mildest suspicions in anyone's mind if she was spotted. It didn't help. Danger Girl was officially retired. Trembling, she stumbled forward and nearly pitched face-first onto the volcanic rock. She righted herself at the last moment and stood still, panting, until she caught her breath.

Darn it, she could do this. She'd rescued Jagger and that had been way more scary than this. Besides, whether he admitted it or not, he needed her help. He was by no means operating at full strength physically, and probably not mentally or emotionally, either.

Doggedly, she pressed on. She fixed her gaze on the wooden dock and strode down to it, gazing neither left nor right as she approached it. If someone was out here watching her, so be it. There wasn't a thing she could do about it. She would just have to claim sleepwalking or a sudden urge for a moonlit cruise around the island. Neither one would fly with Schroder—he was far too clever for that—but the excuse would have to suffice. It was all she had. That and a burning need to be with the man who'd stolen her heart and never given it back.

As grim thoughts of what Schroder would do to her if he

caught her flitted through her mind, she made her way out the narrow pier to the ski boat. Two lines moored the craft. Despite her shaking hands, she managed to unleash the boat from its hitching post. Now what? Jagger had told her to stay put until he joined her. What did that mean? She risked a look back toward shore and saw no sign of his familiar silhouette approaching.

And then a voice whispered from practically under her feet, "Push the boat back. Then sit down on the dock and slide into the water."

What? She stared down in shock.

"Move."

She lurched into motion at Jagger's sharp order, doing as he said. Until her feet dangled over the water, that is. "I'll get my clothes all wet," she complained under her breath.

A snort rumbled out of the darkness. "And that's so much more important than getting shot, after all."

She sighed and eased off the pier into the Pacific Ocean. The water was nearly up to her chin here, and when a wave came in, her feet lifted briefly off the seabed.

"Grab this tow line," Jagger murmured. "I've made a loop in it. Put it under your armpits and that'll free up your arms to swim."

She did as he suggested while he rigged another line in similar fashion for himself. It was slow going pulling the boat out of the tiny marina. They reached the end of the dock and Jagger made to turn left. But then inspiration hit her.

"Go right," she urged. "There's a riptide beyond the marina, just past those rocks over there. AbaCo doesn't allow any swimming in that spot because of it."

He frowned. "That way takes us back toward the buildings."

She argued, "Once the tide catches us, it'll pull us out to sea about a hundred times faster than you and I can swim against the surf to tug this monster offshore."

He considered briefly. Then said decisively, "Okay. Let's go get your riptide."

It turned out to be surprisingly easy. One minute they were swimming laboriously, getting nowhere fast, and the next, the boat was floating out to sea so quickly it was tugging them along in its wake. Jagger had to help her make her way hand over hand up the rope toward the boat, in fact. He crawled in first and lowered a ladder over the side for her to scramble up. They drifted for a few more minutes. The riptide petered out about a half mile from shore. As the boat slowed and began to drift south, Jagger started the engine. He left the running lights and instrument lights off, however, as he turned the craft east, and the Rock retreated to a speck in the distance.

Jagger opened up the throttles, checked the dashboard-mounted compass and made a minor course correction. The craft could make a steady twenty knots, but the sea was choppy enough tonight that he backed off to more like fifteen. At this rate, it should take them a little over an hour to reach Lokaina.

He kept glancing back over his shoulder behind them. It took her several times looking back herself to realize what he was doing. He was watching for pursuit. She thought of the sleek cigarette boats back at the dock and suddenly her exhilaration at being out here with the wind in her hair and the sea spray on her skin morphed into cold, damp terror.

But as the miles passed and the sea remained a featureless black sheet behind them, she began to breathe more normally.

They'd been on the water an hour when Jagger shouted suddenly over the motor, "Are there binoculars on this tub?"

She indicated that she didn't know but would have a look. She opened up one of the storage chests under a seat in the back of the boat and fished around. Life jackets, flares and coiled ropes. She shifted over to the other storage chest. This one held a variety of small tools and gadgets…and a nice pair of Zeiss binoculars. She grabbed them and headed back to the cockpit.

"Here ya go."

"Thanks." He took them and scanned the horizon, first behind them, then in front of them. With a low exclamation of pleasure, he turned the boat to the northeast and pushed the throttles forward. She looked in that direction. She couldn't be sure, but that might be a twinkle of lights low on the horizon.

A few more minutes confirmed her suspicion. A line of lights was visible, and before long, the black hump of an island. Lokaina. They'd made it.

Relief soared through her and she grinned over at Jagger.

And then he frowned. Lifted the binoculars again and scanned carefully behind them. He swore under his breath. He pushed the throttles all the way to the forward stop and the boat leaped over the waves, jarring her in her seat.

"Take the wheel," he bit out grimly.

She slid over into his seat as he stood up and moved aside. "What's up?" she shouted.

"We're about to have company."

Chapter 7

Emily's heart dropped to her feet. She looked back over her shoulder but could see nothing through the rooster tail of spray. Not that she needed to. She knew exactly what was back there. A big, black, lethal boat bearing down upon them. Fast.

Jagger tossed her a life jacket with a terse command to put it on as he fished out what looked like a waterproof bag. He tied it around his waist with one of the ropes from the equipment chest. Quickly, he stuffed the entire knapsack she'd brought for him into the bag and sealed it shut.

He put his mouth close to her ear and shouted, "I'll get us as close to shore as I can. They're probably going to shoot at us. When I tell you to, dive overboard. Stay underwater as long as you can. When you come up, only come up enough to get some air and then go back down. When you can't hear their boat anymore, surface and swim for shore. It may take a while for them to leave the area, so be prepared to bob in the water for a while. Got it?"

She nodded, too terrified to do anything else.

He continued, "It's me they're after. Just get away from me as fast as you can and you should be safe enough."

Horror flowed through her. "I'm not leaving you!"

Jagger scowled. "You don't have to pretend to be a hero for me. I know the score. You drew me out, now they'll finish me off. No hard feelings, babe. Dying like this is a hell of a lot better than spending another day in that damned crate. I knew what I was walking into when I left that box with you."

"What are you talking about?" she demanded.

He frowned but didn't reply. She opened her mouth to insist on an explanation, but before she could say anything, a roar became audible behind them.

"Don't forget what I told you," he yelled. And then he was behind her, slipping into the driver's seat as she slid out of his way. He took over the wheel. "Get down!" he ordered. "Lie flat back there and stay out of sight until I tell you to jump."

The boat slapped down on the waves, jarring her teeth, but Jagger just continued to shove the throttle as far open as it would go. The boat swerved violently, first left, then right. And the roar from behind them was all around them now. Their small craft rocked violently, as if it had crossed another boat's wake at an oblique angle.

Jagger shouted, "Get ready, Emily! Jump over the port side on my command!" He must have realized she'd have no idea what port was, because he shouted again, "Jump over the side opposite me!"

That she understood. She pushed up to her hands and knees, but the way the boat was bouncing around, that was about all she could manage. She checked the straps on her life vest.

And then he shouted, "Go!"

She didn't stand up and jump so much as slither over the side of the boat on her belly and flop into the water. Except it felt more like crashing into concrete than hitting water.

With an oomph, the air slammed out of her lungs and frigid blackness closed in on her. The shock of it stole away what little breath she had left.

Up. Which way was up? A moment of panic clawed at her until she stopped sinking. The life vest kicked in then, pulling her up toward the surface. She kicked and pulled with her arms. Her clothes were unbelievably heavy, even with the vest's buoyancy to help. Her lungs burned and her eyes stung ferociously as salt water hit them. A faint glimmer above caught her attention, and then she broke through to the surface. Her face felt cold air upon it and she drew in a gulping, desperate breath. One more breath, and then she remembered Jagger's instructions. She pulled in a last deep breath and bobbed under the water, using her arms to push herself down against the upward push of the life jacket.

She surfaced again, this time registering the roar of boat engines nearby. She said a quick prayer that one of them wouldn't run her over.

She'd ducked and bobbed a few more times when, as she held herself underwater, a tremendous concussion of sound and pressure slammed into her just as a bright orange flash exploded overhead. The water around her glowed with it. *Ohmigosh. What was that?*

She stayed under as long as she could, but the demands of being an air-breathing creature finally won out and she headed for the surface. The sight that greeted her made her blood run cold. Their ski boat was split in two, its halves flaming while burning oil and debris littered the surface of the ocean around it. The bastards had blown up the boat!

And Jagger? What of him?

She looked around frantically for any sign of him in the water. And realized belatedly that the fires had effectively illuminated the entire area, to include her. She took a hasty breath and ducked under again. The next two times she breathed, she barely broke the surface with her mouth and nose before heading back down. Even then, she still heard the rumble of the AbaCo boat circling the wreckage. Schroder's boys were no doubt checking to make sure they'd killed Jagger.

After an eternity, she finally surfaced to the sound of silence. Cautiously, she stayed afloat, turning in a full three-hundred-sixty-degree circle. No sign of the AbaCo boat. A swell lifted her up and she gazed around once more. There. Off to her left. The lights of Lokaina. Jagger had told her to swim for it. And it wasn't as if she could float around out here indefinitely. She started paddling.

It was slow going with the bulky life jacket on, but it allowed her to flip over on her back and rest now and then. And in those moments, it was worth its weight in gold. She hoped Jagger had one. Heck, she just hoped he was alive.

How long it took her to swim to shore was anyone's guess. Two hours, maybe. Long enough that she was dog tired and never wanted to taste seawater again in her life. But finally, she stretched out on the beach, the cold sand clammy and wonderful beneath her cheek.

Her clothes were sodden and stuck to her, but as she lay there, they gradually dried out a little. Her shoes sloshed when she stumbled to the edge of the narrow strip of sand. The airport was on this side of the island. Her wallet was still in the back pocket of her sweatpants. Which meant she had a credit card. Which meant she could hire a plane and a pilot to get her the heck out of here. She suddenly felt a burning need to get home. To her family. To safety.

She stripped off most of her clothes and draped them over bushes to drip while she dried out and warmed up a bit. Then she sat down on a boulder to figure out what she was going to do next.

Shock was her main emotion. Someone had just tried to kill her. Or at least the person with her. Things like this didn't *happen* to people like her! And Jagger? What of him? Was he dead or alive? Floating around out there in the ocean too hurt to swim ashore, or maybe blown into tiny little pieces of shark bait? God, she hated not knowing.

Again.

The same questions that had been her constant companions for the past two years surged back, stronger than ever. Where was he? What had happened to him? Was he all right? Did he want to be with her?

She couldn't do this again. It would kill her this time, knowing what she did now. She stared out to sea, scanning the detritus of the explosion that washed ashore, watching for some sign of Jagger. An article of clothing or something, anything, to wash up onto the beach that let her know what had happened to him. She couldn't imagine losing him again like this, without any warning at all. One minute he was there, and the next he was gone. Damn her fickle heart. Why couldn't she just let go of him once and for all and be done with him?

Of course she knew the answer to that. They had a bond between them that could never be severed, for better or worse.

After a while, her thoughts began to stray. The AbaCo gig was pretty much a goner. It had been a good job while it lasted. Too bad she wouldn't be getting a recommendation from her boss. It would've helped her when she started job-hunting again. But hey, at least she was alive.

How long she sat there hugging her knees and shivering, partly in cold and partly in shock, she didn't know. The moon climbed high into the sky before she finally roused herself and picked up her clothes. Shimmying into soggy sweatpants was the pits, and her T-shirt stunk of seaweed. Yuck. But she couldn't exactly stroll into the airport in her underwear. She shoved her feet into her shoes and was leaning down to tie them when a voice from nearby startled her violently.

"Going somewhere?"

She lurched, laces forgotten. "Jagger!" She flung herself at him, wrapping her arms around his neck.

He grunted in pain and staggered, hanging on to her until he righted himself. And then he reached for her wrists and unwrapped them gently, setting her away from him.

"You okay?" he rasped.

"Just wet. You?"

"A little singed around the edges, but I'll live."

"What happened?" she asked urgently. "I saw the boat explode and you weren't in the water and I was so scared they'd killed you—"

He cut her off. "That was the idea. To make them believe they'd killed me."

"Oh." A pause. "So are we safe now?"

He snorted. "I doubt it. AbaCo is nothing if not thorough. Until they find my body, or at least parts of it, they'll keep hunting me. Speaking of which, I've got to get out of here." He glanced around tensely. "Thanks for your help."

He took a step away from her as if he was going to leave her there. Ha! Not bloody likely she was letting him slip away from her again.

"What are you talking about?" she asked lightly. "I'm not leaving you alone for a single minute. Every time you leave my sight, something disastrous happens to you. Only way to keep you safe is for me to keep an eagle eye on you, mister."

He stared in naked surprise for a moment, but then, inexplicably, his gaze hardened. "So. The game goes on, does it? What's the next gambit?"

Huh? Half the time she didn't have the faintest idea what he was talking about. When they got somewhere safe and quiet, she was going to do whatever it took to force him to explain himself. Clearly.

In answer to his question, she said, "I have credit cards with me. We can hire a plane and get out of here."

His right eyebrow arched. "Indeed? They're really going to great trouble to make me believe I got away. What do they want from me, anyway?"

He was doing it again. Talking in riddles. She said patiently, "The airport's on this side of the island. We're probably a five-minute walk from it."

He nodded. "Let me change into dry clothes if you don't mind."

She shrugged and he stepped off into the trees for a moment. The stuff she'd filched back at the Rock didn't fit him half-bad. Of course, he'd look suave and sophisticated wearing a burlap sack.

He led the way through a bit of underbrush, and then they emerged onto a dirt road. "Left or right?" he asked.

She considered briefly. "Left, I think. But I'm not a hundred percent sure."

"Good enough for me," he murmured.

It turned out to be more like a ten-minute walk to the airport, which wasn't bad, considering. It was a whole lot better than swimming forever. She pointed out the charter service that AbaCo used, and whose owner she knew fairly well. She told Jagger the guy might do her a favor if she asked him nicely.

Jagger led the way into the tiny office, which she was surprised was even open at this time of night. It must be pushing midnight.

Don Pinkerton, the owner of the island's lone charter aviation business, emerged from a back room when they walked in the front door of his place. A television muttered in the background. He peered at her in disbelief. She must look like a drowned rat.

"Emily Grainger? Is that you?"

"Hi, Don." She gave him her best smile. He flew most of the AbaCo employees back and forth between here and the other Hawaiian islands, and in the past two years, she'd developed a passing acquaintance with him. He'd flirted with her enough to signal that he'd be willing to turn their friendship into more, but she'd never taken him up on it. Her personal life was complicated enough without adding him to the mix.

"What brings you here at this hour...and soaked to the skin?"

She looked down at herself and laughed ruefully. "Long story. I have a huge favor to ask of you. My friend and I need to get out of here as soon as possible. When's the first flight?"

"Where y'all headed?" Don asked around the toothpick hanging precariously in the corner of his mouth. "Going home to Kauai?"

"Uh, ye—"

Jagger cut her off. "Actually, we could use a lift to the big island. I have to get stateside ASAP."

Don shrugged. "How big a hurry are you guys in?"

Emily exchanged glances with Jagger. She didn't know for sure how to answer that one. Thankfully, he caught the hint and answered smoothly, "As big a hurry as money can buy. I've been recalled to my unit and they'll reimburse me whatever it costs."

Don perked up. "You military? What service are you in?"

"Marines. I'm stationed at Quantico."

Emily stared. Seriously? How come he'd never mentioned that during their magical night together?

Don nodded. "Thought so. You have the look about you."

Jagger leaned an elbow on the counter as if to settle in for a chat. "You ex-military?"

Don replied eagerly, "I'm ex-army. Pulled a couple tours flying choppers with the Rangers in Iraq before I got shot. Bum knee now. Had to get out."

Jagger winced in sympathy. "Too bad. What're you flying now?"

"Sweet little Lear jet. I shuttle the AbaCo folks in and out mostly. Couple a' rich guys on the other side of Lokaina use me to fly to Tokyo once a month. They have a standing date with some geishas."

"Cool. Have you got extended-range fuel tanks on it to make the Japan run?"

"Yup. Just upgraded the avionics, too…"

Emily tuned out as the men talked airplanes and electronics. She recognized the male bonding ritual for what it was and let it take its course, even though her skin was crawling with dread and her gut screamed at her for them to get moving. *Now.*

Before she knew it, Don had offered to take Jagger out to the ramp to have a look at his jet. She tagged along without comment. She saw now where Jagger was taking this. Clever.

Sure enough, they spent about five minutes crawling all over the sleek plane, and Don piped up, "Hey, if we top off the tanks, I could fly you to the big island tonight. I haven't been drinking and I'm not sleepy. I'd have to charge you for a hotel room at that end, but I'm up for it. Whaddaya say?"

Jagger grinned. "Awesome. Any chance I can sit in the copilot seat for the takeoff if I promise not to touch anything?"

"Absolutely."

Emily rolled her eyes as the two men fueled the plane together and talked vintage sports cars. Gearheads, both of them. Strangely enough, she thought she registered a note of strain creeping into Jagger's voice. And he seemed to be favoring his right side a little. As though maybe he'd hurt it when the boat had exploded around him and the pain was just now starting to set in. Which made sense. Almost dying must have sent his adrenaline sky-high. It would've taken a while to wear off.

Don took about a half hour to finish refueling, file a flight plan and preflight the plane. And then they were rolling down the runway and leaping into the air as the jet engines surged behind her. It was strange being all alone in the back of the plane. She was used to being crammed in a corner with a bunch of burly AbaCo employees jammed in around her.

When the plane reached cruising altitude, Jagger crawled out of the cockpit and came back to check on her. At least that was what he said. But she noticed a line of white around his mouth and the slight hitch that had entered his breathing.

"Are you hurt?" she murmured.

"A little."

"How little?" she retorted sharply. "Lemme see. It's your side, isn't it? I noticed you pressing your elbow against it earlier." She reached for his shirt.

He protested, pushing her hands away, but she persisted. "Don't you mess with me, Super Spy. Pull your shirt up and let me have a look before I tackle you and make you do it," she threatened.

That brought a grin to his face. "You and what army, Danger Girl?"

"If AbaCo can't keep a hold of you, I doubt anyone can," she retorted.

Dang. She should've thought before she blurted that out. Her comment wiped the smile from his face and put back the heavy frown that had been momentarily missing. For a few minutes there, he'd almost looked like her old Jagger again.

Reluctantly, he lifted his shirt.

She gasped. A long, jagged piece of what looked like fiberglass was impaled in his right side. The piece came out of his back about two inches below his ribs. "Oh, my God," she cried in horror.

He looked down and grimaced. "I don't think it's as bad as it looks. I'm still breathing reasonably well."

Twin trails of blood trickled down his front and back from the two exit wounds.

"You're bleeding," she declared. "You've got to get to a hospital right away!"

Her exclamation drew Don's attention from the cockpit. He swore and unbuckled his seat belt. He joined them in the back, eyeing the injury.

Emily asked, "Uh, Don, if you're back here, who's flying the plane?"

"The autopilot." Then he turned to Jagger and said briskly, "Take off your shirt and lie down in the aisle here on your side so I can get a better look at that."

Jagger did as ordered. "You a medic?" he gritted out from between teeth that were definitely clenched now.

"Naw, but all us Rangers got decent combat first-aid training." The pilot leaned down to take a closer look at the white fragment.

It was nearly a foot long and roughly two inches wide.

Don asked lightly, "You get jumped by a canoe in a bar fight, dude?"

Jagger's pale lips turned up. "Yeah. It was a hell of fight, but you ought to see the boat. I tore it to shreds."

Don announced, "We can't move the shrapnel. Don't want you to bleed out accidentally. You're gonna want a doctor to do that in case you punctured something major. I can't believe your lung hasn't collapsed. That thing goes right across the top of your diaphragm."

She winced. She could seriously do without the medically accurate blow-by-blow.

Don moved to a narrow closet behind the cockpit and rummaged around in it. He emerged with a first-aid kit. "This ain't much, but I can at least sterilize the wounds and pack 'em. Stop the worst blood loss for now. Nearest hospital's on Ranauatu Atoll. It's about an hour's flight from here. It's more of a clinic than a hospital, but they're 'bout all that's nearby for medical care."

Jagger hissed as the pilot blotted peroxide directly onto the wounds. Then he gritted out, "No hospital for me. Sorry."

She stared at him, appalled. "Why not?" It was more an exclamation of disbelief than an actual question.

Jagger answered her nonetheless. "I don't trust AbaCo. They'll have people on the payrolls of any hospital, government offices—" His glance flickered to Don. "They probably pay Don here to keep them apprised of strangers coming and going from the area."

The pilot grinned, unabashed. "They pay stupid big amounts of money for me to do it, too. But funny, I have a hell of a hard time remembering to mention when marines pass through."

"Thanks, man," Jagger ground out.

Don sat down in an empty seat, staring down at Jagger on the floor thoughtfully. "Speaking of marines…there's a guy…'bout halfway back to the main islands…ex-marine. Owns a little island with a dirt strip on it. I think someone told me once that he was a field medic in Vietnam. He could probably handle an itty-bitty piece of shrapnel like that. Want me to radio him?"

Itty-bitty, her butt. That thing was the length of her forearm!

Jagger started to shrug, then broke off, sucking in a sharp breath. "It's worth a try."

In short order, Don had radioed the guy, explained the situation and altered their course. In about forty more minutes, he began a descent and quietly told Emily to buckle up. Jagger stayed on the floor, lying on his side. He'd gone quiet and had sucked down every painkiller in the first aid kit. Worse, he'd gone pale under the small overhead lights and his breathing had taken on a raspy quality.

The medic, a silver-haired man who introduced himself only as Lyle, met them at the plane with a golf cart. He and Don helped Jagger lie down across its backseat while Emily climbed in the front.

Don commented, "There's no air traffic coverage out here and nobody'll ever know about this little stop. So you two rest up, and when you're ready to go, you gimme a holler."

Jagger nodded. He seemed to be struggling to maintain consciousness now.

Don moved to her side and murmured, "I'm gonna fly on to Hawaii and build a cover story for you two there, but I'll need your credit card. I'll charge the room to it." He added drolly, "And I promise not to max it out, Mom."

She grinned and dug in her wallet. "Do your worst with it, Don. Max it out if you want. It's not nearly thanks enough for your help."

The ex-chopper pilot ducked his head. "Pshaw. Ain't nothing for a fellow marine. You take good care of him, ma'am."

The medic murmured, "We need to get going. This young man's trying to get shocky on me."

Don nodded and stepped back as the golf cart lurched into motion. Jagger moaned from behind her.

Emily whispered, "Hurry, Lyle. I can't lose him. Not after I just found him again."

Chapter 8

How she and Lyle horsed a now unconscious Jagger up the steps and into the ex-marine's kitchen, she had no idea. Adrenaline-induced superstrength, probably. But they managed to lay him out on his uninjured side on the kitchen table, which was covered with a clean sheet and brightly lit by several floor lamps with the shades removed. A kettle bubbled merrily on the stove, presumably for sterilizing surgical instruments. She didn't want to know.

Lyle went to work immediately, giving Jagger an injection of something and then cutting away the field dressing Don had put over the twin wounds. He told her, "Grab his shoulder and hold him down if he starts to thrash around."

She did as ordered while Lyle probed the wounds. A gush of blood made her turn her head away, her stomach roiling. Jagger groaned once but made no other protest as Lyle worked quickly. He picked up a scalpel and commenced cutting into Jagger's side. She handed the medic various implements as he asked for them. A ferrous smell of blood permeated the air.

"Dunno how this didn't catch his lung. Damned lucky," Lyle muttered to himself. Then, "Dirty as hell. Sure to get infected. Gonna need more antibiotics."

He didn't sound as though he expected a response from her, so she offered none. Besides, her teeth were clenched too tightly together to speak. And then it was done. An enormous length of bloody fiberglass lay on the table beside Jagger, the bleeders were cauterized, the wounds were stitched and bandaged and Lyle mopped sweat off his forehead.

"Thirsty?" the older man asked her casually.

She turned away from the hellish remains of the surgery. "Is he gonna be okay?"

Lyle shrugged. "He looks tough."

"That's not an answer."

"Here's the thing, Miss Grainger. The shrapnel didn't clip any major organs or blood vessels. That's the good news. The bad news is the wounds were filthy. He's bound to pick up the mother of all infections. He's lost a lot of blood, and he looks malnourished. That's the worst news of all."

"Can't you load him up on antibiotics and…and protein drinks or something?"

Lyle grinned. "In the morning I'll go to town and see if I can sweet-talk the doc there out of some Zithromax. May have to claim I've picked up the clap to get it." He grinned over at her. "I hate to wreck my sterling reputation like that, but for a fellow marine…"

Man, these marines took the whole brotherhood thing seriously! She nodded gratefully. "Is there anything we can do for him tonight?"

Lyle shrugged. "Let him sleep off the morphine I shot him up with. You look like you could use a shower and some shut-eye yourself."

Now that he mentioned it, exhaustion dragged at her eye-lids until she could hardly hold them open. She kept the shower short and cool lest she fall asleep in it. As soon as she'd pulled on the clean, oversized T-shirt Lyle had laid out for her, she stumbled into the living room in search of sleep.

She noticed vaguely that the rustic cabin looked native Hawaiian. The ceilings were high-beamed and looked covered with some sort of dried leaves that formed a thatch overhead. There was no glass in the windows, just wooden shutters that closed over the spaces. Indeed, a pleasant trade wind blew through now. Just cool enough to need the light blanket Lyle handed her with a pillow. She'd insisted on curling up in the armchair beside the couch they'd moved Jagger to.

She slept deeply, dreaming of smiling blue eyes and fires burning on water.

In what seemed like only minutes, she awoke to something kicking her foot. Sharply. She blinked her eyes open and stared, horrified.

Lyle was pointing a gun at her. He didn't look amused.

Ohmigod. She and an unconscious Jagger were alone on a rock with a madman! Or worse, had Don delivered them right into the clutches of Jagger's captors? Again? Sick terror washed through her.

"Uh, what's up, Lyle?" she mumbled.

"Care to tell me why the FBI's put out an APB on our patient?"

What? The FBI? But…but Jagger worked for the federal government. Why would they want to arrest their own man? Had he been lying to her about who he was? Had AbaCo been in the right to hold him prisoner?

Questions piled on top of questions in her fuzzy brain. Whom to trust? Whom to believe? Follow her head or her heart?

She asked carefully, "If you don't mind my asking, what are the charges against Jagger?"

Lyle shrugged. "The APB says he's a violent criminal. Attacked and killed a couple guys from some shipping company and is wanted in connection with smuggling and selling government secrets."

Okay, one thing she knew about Jagger Holtz. He would never sell out anyone he worked for. He was nothing if not loyal. Suddenly certainty flowed through her. "The charges are fake."

Lyle snorted. "Girlie, I hooked directly into the FBI Web site. There's nothing fake about the charges against the man lying on my couch."

She shook her head. "The people who tried to kill Jagger, they must've planted incriminating information against him when he escaped from them. They can't afford to have him tell the U.S. government what he knows about them, so they've trumped up these charges against him to force him not to testify against them."

"And is that how you explain the warrant for your arrest, too?"

"*My* arrest?"

Lyle nodded. "The complaint against you says you broke into this shipping company's records. Says you broke into sealed cargo containers, too, and violated international customs laws."

She sighed. "Well, those charges are true. But I did it to free Jagger. He was locked up in a cargo container on a ship for two years. I found him and let him out." As Lyle stared in shock, she added defiantly, "I'd do it again, too. Even if it means I have to go to jail."

The marine studied her closely and eventually nodded. "You're telling the truth. Maybe you two have been set up." He glanced over at Jagger's bandaged form. "And I've got to admit that boy's injuries look like the kind you get when someone is trying to kill you, not when you're trying to kill someone else."

She commenced breathing again as Lyle lowered the

weapon and eased the hammer of his pistol back into place. He said firmly, "You go on back to sleep."

As if that was going to happen anytime soon! Her heart was still stuck somewhere in the vicinity of her throat.

He continued, "I'm heading to town to get more medical supplies. I'll be back in a few hours. Keep your boy still and give him water if he wakes up and asks for it."

She listened until a motorboat retreated in the distance. Was Lyle heading to the nearest town with police in it to report them? Would he return with a squad of AbaCo men? She sighed. It wasn't as though she could do a darned thing about it now. Jagger was still unconscious on the couch. And even if he could move, where would they go? They were on an island in the middle of nowhere.

What were the two of them going to do? The U.S. government believed Jagger was a traitor, and she'd become a wanted criminal. Who would help them now? If only he'd wake up. Maybe he'd know how to proceed. But what if he didn't? What if there was no way out of this mess?

She must have fretted herself to sleep eventually because a moan ripped her from a troubled dream some time later. She jolted upright. Jagger was thrashing on the couch, swearing up a blue storm.

She leaped to his side. "Hey, cool it or else you'll rip out your stitches."

Unfocused eyes stared up at her. "I'll never talk. You understand? Never. I know you're going to do whatever you have to, and I'm going to scream and suffer and you're going to do even more to me. But at the end of the day, you're getting nothing from me. Just so we're clear on that."

He must be dreaming about his captivity.

And then she knew it because he started to scream. It wasn't a high-pitched sound of fright like a woman reacting to a mouse. This scream came from the depths of his gut, torn from his throat, raw and feral in its agony. Right then and there, her knees collapsed out from under her. She needed no further explanation of what had happened to him as AbaCo's prisoner. That one scream said it all.

She leaned forward, grabbing Jagger's shoulders as he twisted back and forth, begging him to stay still. She practically had to sit on him to slow him down, and he cursed at her all the while. And the things he ranted about in his delirium…the torture he described…the days on end alone and isolated…his longing for decent food or for just a glimpse of sunlight…

Bit by bit, he tore her heart out as she pieced together the story of his past two years in his ramblings. It was hard for her to believe that AbaCo could do that to anyone and get away with it. But it was even harder to believe he'd survived it all. His mental and physical toughness, his raw courage, his sheer, ferocious will to live boggled her mind.

She heard a motorboat returning and her pulse leaped. She clutched Jagger's hand tightly, still registering how hot and dry it was in her panic.

The kitchen door opened.

Nobody shouted for her to put her hands over her head. No gang of armed men rushed into the room.

Lyle's craggy visage poked around the door. "Any change in your fellow while I was gone?"

She all but sobbed in relief. "He thrashed around for a while and he's been talking in his sleep."

"Fever's setting in. He's going delirious on us. Lemme go get my bag of goodies."

Emily hovered, feeling in turns helpless and protective as Lyle started an IV drip on Jagger, rigging the saline bag to one of the floor lamps from the kitchen last night. Into it, the medic injected a cocktail of antibiotics and sedatives. And then he ordered her to take another shower, announcing that she still stunk like rotten seaweed.

Under other circumstances, she'd have savored the hot rainwater, sluicing the remaining salt off her skin and out of her hair. But today she raced through her shower, impatient to get back to Jagger.

He was quiet through the day and into the night. But late in the evening, his temperature started to rise once more.

"Here it comes," Lyle announced grimly. "The primary infection. We're in for a fight, girl, if we want to save your man."

She sat up with Jagger through the night, her panic rising exponentially along with his fever. Funny how just a few days ago she was so mad at him she could hardly stand to think about him. And now here she was, praying nonstop for him to pull through this crisis.

Just when she thought she had life all figured out, it went and threw a monster curveball at her. She spent hours staring at Jagger's face, rememorizing the planes and angles, sharper now, but still the old Jagger. The new lines and shadows gave him more character, an added maturity that was intensely appealing.

Lyle had told her to expect Jagger to say all sorts of crazy things and not to freak out over it. Thing was, Lyle had no idea that most of what Jagger talked about *was* real. That was a burden she got to bear alone.

Lyle took his turns looking after Jagger so she could catch a nap now and then, and he ordered her to wake him up if Jagger's temperature hit one hundred and five.

When it was just her and Jagger alone in the quietest, darkest heart of the night, her thoughts strayed to the first time she'd spent a night with him, that magical New Year's Eve two years ago. It had been about as different from this as was possible. But the sense of rightness, of peace way down deep in her soul at just being with him, remained the same. She didn't know what it was about him, but she'd never met another man like him. He was simply meant for her and she for him. There was no logic to it, no reason for it. It just was.

She'd spent the past two years fighting this thing between them, but after a single day back in his company, the old attraction was back full force. And this time they had so much more between them. Not that he was aware of it at the moment, of course. After he beat this infection she would tell him all about it. And maybe they could properly celebrate the past two New Year's Eves they'd missed.

Of course, first he had to live. His temperature climbed steadily to one hundred and four degrees and then passed up the mark. And that was when he began to talk again. At first it was just mumbled words and phrases. And then his rantings began to take shape. He muttered her name several times.

She leaned over him and whispered, "I'm here, Jagger."

"Bitch," he muttered.

She stared, shocked.

"Set me up…great actress…actually believed she gave a damn about me…alone so long in my job and then she came along…so innocent…but it was a lie…led me right to you bastards…"

She recoiled in horror. *No. It can't be. It's just the fever talking.*

"If I ever find her…"

"What, Jagger? What will you do if you find her?"

"Kill her…no…too easy. Make her suffer…Yeah, suffer…"

Oh. My. God. He couldn't possibly believe she'd set him up on that New Year's Eve two years ago! But as he continued to mutter about how she'd been in league with his kidnappers and had served him up to them on a silver platter, it was clear that was exactly what he did believe.

She spoke urgently. "Listen to me, Jagger. I didn't set you up. I swear. I had no part of AbaCo's goons kidnapping you. We met by chance and I was crazy about you."

His head turned back and forth restlessly. "No chance about it," he mumbled. "I needed into that party…I approached the girl…thought she'd be such an easy mark…I never dreamed…"

Emily sat back, frowning. Was *she* the girl he was referring to? Memory of him standing in that parking garage waiting for the elevator flashed through her head. He'd been using her? She tried again to penetrate his delirium, asking forcefully, "Jagger, what were you going to use me for?"

"Had to find our men. AbaCo snatched them…need proof to move on the company…grand jury wants some evidence before they get involved…"

AbaCo had kidnapped someone else? Were these other men riding around the world in cargo containers, lost and forgotten, too? "Who were they?" she asked.

Jagger sat bolt upright and his eyes popped open. The expression in them was wild. Unfocused. "Gotta find them!" he burst out.

"Lie back down, Jagger," she soothed. "We'll find your colleagues when you're feeling better. I promise." She'd learned the hard way over the past several hours that she wasn't anywhere near strong enough to force Jagger to do anything. With a little more cajoling from her, he finally lay back down.

She smoothed his damp hair off his brow, worried by the fine sheen of perspiration there. She stuck the electronic thermometer in his ear again. Up another tenth of a degree, 104.5. She pondered waking Lyle, but the medic had gotten practically no sleep last night and wasn't exactly a spring chicken. He'd mentioned trying to bathe Jagger to help cool him, but it was imperative that his wounds stay dry.

Inspiration struck. She headed for the kitchen and rummaged around until she found a mixing bowl. She filled it with water and ice and then snagged every dish towel she could find.

She soaked a towel in cold water and laid it across Jagger's chest. She folded another wet towel and laid it across his forehead. Another one across his hips below the bandages, several more on his legs. By the time she laid the last one across his feet, the first one on his chest was warm to the touch. She dipped it in the cold water, wrung it out and replaced it.

Jagger's body was much as she remembered, powerful and lean, brimming with vitality, even in his current state. As she worked, though, she spotted a myriad of new scars. And something hot and demanding began to build in her belly. *Rage.*

A thin scar on his neck looked like some sort of slashing wound. His captors must have toyed with slitting his throat. Several small round scars clustered on his belly looked like cigarette burns. Then she found a whole series of tiny marks on his back over both kidneys. She recalled hearing somewhere that the most painful form of torture was to stick needles in the human kidney. Apparently, the nerves from the incredibly sensitive organ were wired to the brain so a human couldn't pass out from that pain. And then she found the scars on the bottoms of his feet. Dozens of them. Scars on top of scars. The width of her finger in a crisscrossing pattern as though they'd caned his feet bloody. More than once. Many times more than once.

And that was when her rage spilled over.

She was going to kill someone for this. No, Jagger had the right of it. She was going to hurt someone very badly and *then* kill them. How could anyone visit this sort of damage on another human being? Whoever'd done this to Jagger didn't deserve to live. She'd track them down. Hunt them herself if she had to.

No wonder Jagger was so furious with her if he thought she'd had some part in doing this to him. Frankly, she was amazed that he was only enraged. How had he clung to sanity at all? New awe at his mental and physical endurance filled her.

She continued draping him in cool towels all through the

night. His temperature stabilized at 104.5, but he continued to drift in and out, sometimes still and apparently asleep, and other times mumbling and tossing. And sometime during that endless night, the worst of her rage settled into grim resolve to help Jagger find his captors and do whatever he wanted to them. But first he had to live.

A little before dawn, Lyle came into the living room to check on his patient.

"How's he doing?" Emily asked anxiously.

Lyle shrugged noncommittally. "The next twenty-four hours will tell the tale. Go get some sleep and I'll take over towel duty. Good idea, by the way."

As skeptical as she was that she'd get any sleep, she lay down in Lyle's bed—the only bed in the house—and closed her eyes. She awoke to brilliant sunlight streaming through the window into her face. Shading her eyes, she glanced over at the alarm clock and was stunned to see it read nearly noon. She jumped up and rushed out to see how Jagger was doing.

She frowned. His head was lying in the mixing bowl she'd used earlier, and the thing was half-filled with ice water. "Are you washing his hair?" she asked in surprise.

Lyle glanced up grimly. "No. I'm trying to keep his brain from frying. His temperature spiked about an hour ago, and we've got to keep his head cool or he'll get brain damage. Go get me another tray of ice, will you?"

She headed for the kitchen. Dismayed, she stared at the array of shallow bowls and plates of half-frozen water now filling the freezer along with several ice-cube trays. Lyle must think this fever wasn't going away anytime soon. She grabbed a tray of ice cubes and rushed back to Jagger's side.

She worked towel duty while Lyle dumped the ice cubes in Jagger's head bath. "How long do you think this fever will last?" she asked.

"Until it breaks or he dies."

Dread filled her, as icy as the water bathing Jagger. "When will we know which way this is gonna go?"

Lyle frowned. "I've seen a lot of wounds go septic. Guys usually last a day. Maybe two at most."

"Isn't there anything you can do?" she cried.

"I doubled up the antibiotics this morning. I'm giving him all the help I can."

"I'll call Don to come get him. Fly him out to the nearest hospital." Frantically, she fumbled for her cell phone before she remembered it had been ruined in the ocean.

Lyle shook his head. "Boy's too sick to move. The flight would kill him. Besides, there's not much more a hospital could do for him. They have fancy refrigerated blankets to help hold down fevers, but your towels will work nearly as well. They'd give him the same medications I am, and then they'd wait just like we are. If you want to do something more to help, say a prayer."

Lyle enlisted her to help to change the dressing on Jagger's wounds, and she flinched to see the angry red swelling around them. The medic commented, "I'd open those up and clean 'em again, but the kid can't afford to lose any more blood than he already has." He shook his head direly.

Emily piped up, "My blood is O positive. Anyone can take that type, can't they?"

"Yeah," Lyle answered cautiously.

"You've got needles and tubes and all that intravenous stuff, right? Take a pint of my blood and give it to Jagger. That way you can clean out his wounds."

Lyle studied her speculatively. "Any chance you've got AIDS or hepatitis?"

She shook her head in the negative. "Haven't had an injection or slept with a guy in two years and I don't do drugs."

"It might be worth a try. He's not doing so great."

"Do it," she urged. "Please. We've got to do everything we can."

"All right. Lemme go sterilize up some needles."

In a few minutes, Lyle came back with a big glass of orange juice in hand. "Drink this. I don't need you passing out on me, too. One sick patient at a time is enough for me."

She downed the juice quickly.

Lyle explained, "I'm gonna stick you and then plug you directly into his IV."

She winced at the needle stick in the bend of her elbow, but in a matter of seconds, the clear tube turned dark red as her blood began streaming into Jagger's arm. Satisfaction filled her. This felt right. Her life force flowing into him, becoming part of him. Lyle timed the transfer carefully.

"There. That's about a pint," he announced.

She actually felt bereft when he disconnected her from Jagger. But then Lyle drafted her to assist while he carefully snipped the stitches and lanced the wounds. She did her best to block out seeing what emerged from the wounds. Suffice it to say it was a good thing that Lyle opened Jagger back up again. The amount of blood was alarming, but eventually it ran a healthy red, and Lyle stitched Jagger up once more.

Maybe it was the blood she'd donated, but she felt utterly drained both physically and emotionally by the time it was over. Jagger was more pale than ever and utterly still now. She almost wished for the return of the thrashing and ranting. At least then she knew he was still alive, still fighting. But this deeply unconscious state of his was the most frightening of all.

He was the same through the evening, lying zombielike on the sofa without so much as a twitch. Lyle's expression went from grim to grave. She was losing him. Jagger was slipping away before her very eyes. She prayed and then she cried and then she prayed some more. She felt so damned helpless! Surely there was something she could do.

Around midnight, his breathing started to labor, coming in painful rasps. She called out, "Lyle, do something!"

The medic came in from the kitchen and examined Jagger yet again. Then the man said gently, "Honey, there's nothing more we can do. It's up to God and Jagger now. Either he has something to live for, some work left undone here on earth, or it's his time to go."

And that was when she knew exactly what she had to do. "Could I have a moment alone with him?"

The older man nodded and stepped outside onto the porch. The door closed behind him.

She knelt by Jagger's side and took one of his hot, limp hands in hers. She put her mouth close to his ear. "Do you need something to live for? Well, try this on for size. That night we spent together two years ago? New Year's Eve, remember? You and I have a daughter, Jagger. Her name is Michelle. She's fifteen months old and looks just like you. And she deserves to meet her daddy someday. Don't you die on her. You fight, by God. You *live*—you hear me? You owe it to her. You left us before, but now you've come back to us. Don't you dare leave us again."

Chapter 9

Jagger gradually became aware of floating within a peaceful silence. It cocooned him gently in a white, weightless mist. It was a nice change from the constant dark and he was in no rush to get back to the real world. But eventually, he couldn't resist checking in on reality and opened his eyes.

He squinted into bright sunlight. That was odd. He was awake, but he wasn't in his box. What were his captors up to now?

Someone moved nearby. He looked off to his left and saw a strange man approaching. He surged up, then collapsed back, gasping as hot knives of crumpling agony stabbed his left side.

"Easy, kid. I'm one of the good guys," the stranger soothed. "But I'm gonna be pissed if I have to stitch up your side again."

The man sounded American. All of his AbaCo captors had been distinctly German. Suspiciously, Jagger asked, "How do I know you're one of the good guys?"

The man frowned. "That's a good question. How 'bout

this?" He shoved up his sleeve to reveal a Marine Corps eagle, globe and anchor tattoo on his left biceps. "Don't know too many bad guys sporting one of these."

Jagger sagged back to the cushions in relief. *"Semper fi,"* he sighed.

"Semper fidelis, my young friend. Lemme go wake up Emily. She's gonna be over the moon that you're coming around. Girl's been sitting up with you practically around the clock."

The gray-haired man left the room before Jagger could ask any more questions. Emily was here? He'd have pegged her for the type to cut and run when the shooting started. And she'd been sitting with him around the clock? Why? How long had he been out of it, anyway? Two years ago, he'd have described the pain in his left side as excruciating. But now...now he'd classify it as annoying but tolerable. Funny how pain was all a matter of perspective.

"Jagger?" Emily rushed into the room, her hair sticking up every which way. It was actually incredibly cute. She looked like a rumpled kitten. "Are you really awake? How do you feel?" To the older man she blurted, "Has the fever truly broken?"

The marine grinned. "Yup, 102.1 and dropping."

Fever? He'd been sick, then? He felt as if he'd been run over a couple of times by a Mack truck.

She moved to his side, smiling down brilliantly at him— in relief if he wasn't mistaken. "I *knew* you'd make it."

She said that as though it had been in serious doubt. He asked, frowning, "How sick was I?"

The man answered, "'Bout as sick as I've ever seen anyone be and still live. That was a hell of an infection you got, boy. Had to lance your wounds twice. Finally had to install tubes in 'em to drain 'em."

Wounds? Plural? "What's wrong with me?" he asked in alarm.

The man said, "Name's Lyle, by the way. Marine medic,

'Nam, '66 to '72. You took a piece of fiberglass through your left side. I've got it in the kitchen if you want a souvenir. 'Bout the size of a bowie knife blade. Did about as much damage as one, too."

Jagger reached gingerly for his side and encountered heavy white gauze wrappings.

"Easy, son. Tubes are still in. Shrapnel missed your lung by a hair. Tore up your diaphragm—breathing may be a bit hard for a few weeks. Don't run any marathons for a couple months, okay?"

Jagger nodded. Now that the immediate concern for his health was past, the next pressing concern was... "Where in the hell am I?" he blurted.

Emily fielded this one. "When we realized you were hurt and you refused to go to a hospital, Don diverted his plane into this island so Lyle could look after you."

Jagger glanced over at Lyle, who added, "I own this chunk of rock. It's just a pretty little spot in the middle of nowhere."

From a box to a rock. Jagger supposed that was a step up.

Lyle continued. "Stay as long as you like. It's kinda nice having some company for a change."

Jagger nodded cautiously. Don. The name sounded familiar. But he wasn't putting a face with it. Last thing he remembered, he was driving a boat across the open ocean with no land in sight anywhere. Fuzzy recollection of an explosion throwing him high into the sky tickled at his memory, but that could be from a dozen war zones he'd fought in over the years.

Emily's palm was cool against his forehead. "He still feels warm," she said worriedly.

Lyle shrugged. "It may be another day or two before the fever's completely gone. We're still gonna have to watch for relapses for a few days."

Emily nodded and glanced down. "Are you hungry, Jagger?"

"Yeah. I guess I am."

Lyle cautioned, "Go easy on 'im. Start with something simple like chicken noodle soup. He'll need to work his way up to your world-famous enchiladas."

Emily grinned. "Aha. The truth comes out. You just want us to stay for my cooking."

"Damn straight, girl." Lyle laughed.

Jagger never dreamed that a simple bowl of soup could taste so good. Maybe it was the not eating for several days. Maybe it was two years of tough jerky and rotting fruit and tasteless oatmeal. But either way, he savored each and every drop of the rich broth. And then came orange juice. Surely it was God's own nectar. He'd never tasted anything so zesty and refreshing.

Lyle helped him to his feet a little while later and guided him to the restroom. Afterward, he noticed a door that looked as if it led outside. Jagger murmured, "Any chance I can step out for a minute? It's been a long time since I saw the sun."

Lyle threw him a knowing look. "I was one of the medics who repatriated POWs in Germany when they came out of 'Nam. If you wanna talk, I've heard it all."

Jagger nodded. He wasn't ready for an amateur shrink quite yet. He just wanted to feel sunlight on his skin before this dream faded away and was replaced by the harsh, cold reality of another crate.

An ocean breeze caressed his skin as he stepped onto a long, covered porch. Emily was already out there sprawling in a chair, eyes closed and face lifted to the sun.

"Hey," he murmured as he eased gently into the chair beside her.

Her eyes flew open. "Should you be up and about yet?"

He shrugged. "Lyle didn't stop me from coming out here."

They sat together in silence for a time. It was tranquil. The sound of the waves a hundred yards away was soothing. He'd gotten so sick of listening to water over the past two years, he was surprised to find it pleasant today.

"How much do you remember of the past few days?" she eventually asked cautiously.

"Not much. Why?"

"Just wondering."

He frowned, suspicions aroused. That was the sort of question people asked when they were hinting around about something. There was more to it than idle curiosity. What was she worried about him remembering?

She distracted him by murmuring, "You talked a fair bit in your delirium."

Delirium? Holy— "Did I say anything interesting?"

"You said quite a few interesting things. You talked about your captivity mostly." She hesitated and then added, "When I was draping you in cold towels, I saw your scars."

Ah. Mentally, he winced. He'd figured at the time he picked up most of the injuries that he'd be pretty much done with the ladies after his ordeal was over. No woman would find his freakishly scarred body attractive. His captors had marred him pretty much from head to toe.

"It's an impressive collection," she commented neutrally.

"Impressive? Is that what you'd call it?" he asked bitterly.

In a flash she was on her knees before him. He stared down at her, startled.

"Jagger, I *swear* I had absolutely nothing to do with your capture. I had no knowledge of it and I didn't set you up. I was furious, in fact. I thought you ditched me the morning after—well, you know what after."

He stared down at her skeptically. Words were cheap. Just because she said so didn't mean he ought to believe her. But there was something…hovering just beyond recollection. Something important that happened during his fever. Did it have something to do with this? The gaping hole in his memory was frustrating.

"Does Lyle have a telephone?" he asked.

She shook her head. "But he has an Internet hookup if you

want to e-mail someone. Friends or family…" She broke off leadingly as if she was fishing for information about his personal life.

"I was thinking about my superiors, actually. They must think I'm dead by now."

"Uh, there may be a problem with that."

Here it came. The smooth redirect to keep him from contacting any outsiders to let someone know he wasn't shark bait.

"It seems that AbaCo planted some false information with the FBI about you and me. Well, false in your case. The stuff on me is true. But anyway, there are federal warrants out for both our arrests."

As annoying as that was, he couldn't say he was entirely surprised. It was definitely AbaCo's style. "I still need to contact my superiors. The only way we're going to straighten this out is to talk to them."

"Jagger, I can't stand by and watch you go from one jail cell to another!" She sounded genuinely distraught at the prospect. He had to admit, he wasn't crazy about the idea, either. But at least in an American jail he'd have decent food and some rights.

"Where's the computer?" he asked determinedly.

When he made to stand up, Emily was there instantly, supporting his right elbow. Damn, he was weak. With her help, he managed to totter into the house. He sat down at the computer in the corner of the kitchen and typed out a short message from Lyle's e-mail account to his headquarters in Quantico reporting that he was alive and would return to make a full report and clear his name as soon as he was strong enough to do so. There was no immediate response. He realized belatedly that if it was late afternoon here in the Pacific, it must be the middle of the night in Virginia.

He headed for the couch, inexplicably exhausted. Or maybe not so inexplicably. He caught a glance of a substantial shard of fiberglass on the kitchen counter. It did, indeed, remind him of a cross between a wicked knife and a small machete. And that thing had punctured him through? No wonder he'd almost croaked.

He lay down, grateful to rest, and it was morning the next time he awoke, with the sun streaming in from the other side of the room. Emily dozed in a chair beside him but roused the moment he shifted his weight.

She poked a thermometer in his ear. "Ninety-nine point nine," she announced. "You're almost back to human again."

"Is that why I'm so hungry I could eat the arm of this sofa?"

She grinned. "What's your pleasure? Pancakes? Eggs and bacon?"

"Do you know how to make French toast?" he asked.

"Coming right up."

In short order, she carried in a big plate of French toast, swimming in butter and confectioners' sugar and dribbled with syrup. She'd already cut it into neat little bite-sized pieces for him. Cripes. She was treating him like a four-year-old. But when he shifted to sit up, he froze as searing pain impaled him.

Emily winced along with him. "Lyle discontinued the morphine drip last night. He was worried about you getting hooked on it. He said you'd be a little sore this morning."

Jagger snorted.

She grinned commiseratingly. "Actually, I believe his exact words were that you'd hurt like a son of a bitch today."

"He wasn't wrong," Jagger managed to grit out.

He didn't complain when she lifted a forkful of French toast to his mouth for him. But he did groan—in pleasure—when he tasted it.

"It's the vanilla," she murmured. "Makes all the difference."

He didn't care if the secret ingredient was arsenic. This stuff was to die for. He ate every bite and then slept again.

For the next three days, he followed that pattern pretty

much around the clock. Sleep. Eat. Soak up a little sun. Sleep again. And somewhere in there, he began to feel human. He was starting to gain a little weight if his face in the bathroom mirror was any indication. He didn't look quite so gaunt anymore. Emily delighted in cooking for him and spent hours in the kitchen whipping up some new delicacy each day.

He was actually starting to believe that maybe, just maybe, this wasn't some elaborate scheme by AbaCo to screw with his head.

And then Lyle hollered from the kitchen on the fourth morning, "You've got an e-mail, boy. You better come take a look at it."

He pushed up off the couch and went to the kitchen to read it over Lyle's shoulder. Emily was already there, frowning at the message.

Step outside at 10:16 a.m. Turn your face up to the sky.

"What's that about?" Lyle inquired.

"Satellite must be flying overhead then. They want to get a visual on me to see if it's really me."

"Jeez. You're telling me they can ID you from space?" the older man asked.

Jagger nodded. "Yup."

"The military's come a long way since my days in the service," Lyle grumbled.

Emily was grim. "How do we know this isn't from AbaCo? Maybe they're going to fly a helicopter over at that exact moment and shoot you."

"I thought I was supposed to be the paranoid one."

She scowled. "I lost you once before. I'm not losing you again."

Something clicked in his head. Those words. He'd heard her say something like that before. Sometime during that black hole in his memory. Bits and pieces of it were starting to come back. He remembered being chased by a black cigarette boat off the coast of Lokaina, now. He vaguely remembered the interior of a small business jet. And being unbearably thirsty.

He frowned, racking his brains for more to this new fragment of memory, but nothing came.

At 10:10 a.m. or so, he went outside. In bright daylight like this, he wasn't likely to spot the spy satellite crossing overhead. But he walked down to the dirt airstrip, which was the most open spot on the island, and looked up, certain the satellite was out there.

He stayed on the field until 10:30 a.m., and then he made his way back inside and sat down at the computer. He didn't have long to wait. The e-mail came through and he opened it immediately.

If you and your accomplice turn yourselves in immediately, the federal prosecutor will take that into account when he files his formal charges. A team is standing by at Quantico to conduct a full debrief and take your statement.

He groaned under his breath. He knew precisely what was entailed in a full debrief. Days of grueling interrogation, full-bore efforts to break down his story, sleep deprivation, emotional duress, whatever it took. But after AbaCo's efforts to extract information from him, he highly doubted Uncle Sam could throw anything at him that would freak him out. But Emily—

The thought of her undergoing the same sort of browbeating made something growl way down deep in his gut. She was too innocent, too sweet, too damned soft to be put through something like that. As the gut feeling about her bubbled up into conscious thought, he froze. Was he falling for her again?

Was home-cooking and a cool hand smoothing his brow all it took to make a complete sucker out of him?

Or was he a sucker at all? Was it possible that she was for real? Sometimes when he glanced over at her quickly, he caught pain in her big brown eyes. Pain for him. She bent over backward to make him comfortable, to anticipate his every need, to do little things constantly to show how much she cared for him. All of that went way above and beyond the call of acting concerned for him. It was hard to draw any other conclusion than the obvious one. She really did give a damn for him.

He turned his gaze back to that order, thinly veiled, for him to get his butt back to Quantico and face the charges against him. He'd bet they were interested in hearing from him, all right.

He typed back, Will return as soon as able to give complete statement and answer all questions. Am recuperating from serious injuries sustained in my escape from captors. There. Let them chew on that.

"Everything okay?" Emily murmured.

"Just ducky," he replied, grinning.

She inhaled sharply and he looked up at her quickly. Her eyes were wide, and she was staring at him like a starstruck kid meeting a movie star. He raised an inquiring eyebrow.

She answered, "That's the first time you've really looked like the old Jagger. The one I met and fell—" she broke off "—the one I met two years ago."

She met and fell for? Was that how she was going to finish that sentence? Huh. It didn't matter. He shouldn't care. He *didn't* care. That was not pleasure spreading like warm honey in his gut.

He slept through most of the afternoon, but as the sun began to set, he woke, restless. "Walk with me, Emily," he murmured.

They headed down to the beach, where Mother Nature treated them to a spectacular sunset in shades of pink, peach, crimson, lavender and violet. He sat down in the warm sand as the last vestiges of the show faded from the sky.

Emily plopped down beside him.

Perhaps it was the prospect of returning to Virginia, or maybe he was just healing enough to face it now, but tonight his thoughts turned to his captivity and the grueling torture he'd endured.

He spoke quietly, without looking at her. "My captors told me you'd betrayed me. That you'd helped them set me up and had led me to them. They showed me pictures they had of the two of us at the party and surveillance pictures of us going into the hotel."

She gasped.

"I didn't believe them at first. I'd looked into your eyes. Held you in my arms. Hell, made love to you. There was no way you faked what I felt between us. But over time…" He took a steadying breath and continued. "You've got to understand. Being under that kind of physical and emotional pressure messes with your head. You start to believe stuff. Even crazy stuff. I believed them."

She made a sound of protest, but he waved her to silence. He wanted to get this off his chest.

"Funny thing is, I think maybe that's the one thing that kept me alive. I was so damned mad at you for playing me like that. There were times when my rage, my determination to find you and get even with you was the only thing that sustained me."

He stared out at the black ocean for a moment, searching for words. "So it's a little weird for me now, after hating you so passionately for two years, to suddenly find out that the one thing I was living for was all a lie."

She opened her mouth to say something, thought better of it and closed her mouth.

"What?" he asked. "Talk to me."

She smiled a sad little smile. "I feel a little stupid and a lot guilty about how mad I was at you for sneaking out the morning after like that. I swore never to speak to you again. To cut you completely out of my life, out of my thoughts—"

her voice hitched "—out of my heart. I vowed to myself never to need you again. Never to ask anything of you."

When she didn't go on, he prompted, "And now?"

"And now it's all I can do not to fling myself at you and beg you never to leave me again. But I have no right. I did, in fact, work for the very people who did this to you. For all I know, they did use me without my knowledge to set you up. You'll never look at me and see anything other than a collaborator with your enemies."

He peered at her in the dusk, trying to make out the expression in her eyes. But she'd averted her face until all he saw was a glistening track down her cheek.

After a moment, she continued, "If there's anything I can do to help you catch the people who kidnapped you, I'll do it. No questions asked. Anything at all. Just say the word."

He turned over her words for a while. Finally he said gravely, "I do have one request of you."

"Name it."

"Kiss me."

Chapter 10

Emily inhaled sharply, stunned. "Seriously?"

He made a sound that was half laugh and half something else that sounded like pain. "For better or worse, I've been thinking about you nonstop for two years. Is it any surprise that the first woman I want to kiss now is you?"

Memory of his bitter words against her during his delirium flashed into her head. Was this some ploy to get inside her guard so he could take his long-sought revenge? Or was it the innocent request he made it sound like? Was she the paranoid one now—and did it matter?

Truth was, she'd desperately wanted to kiss him almost from the first moment she'd seen him again. Even if he was setting her up for a one-night stand with the intent to leave her high and dry for real this time, she didn't think she had it in her to say no to him. Her addiction to him ran too deep, too permanent, to deny. No matter what his motives were, she wasn't going to say no to kissing him once more.

She surrendered to her heart. "I guess it's not a surprise that you want to kiss me. I want to kiss you, too."

He smiled, but it was too dark to see if the smile reached his eyes or not. She rose to her knees and moved closer to him. And then very carefully, very slowly, she leaned forward. Their breath mingled and she paused, startled by intense recognition of the spicy scent. A cold night, a candlelit suite, an evening of magical seduction were all tied to that masculine aroma. The taste of it was potent and familiar on her tongue, more complex and delicious than any fine wine. Just like the man.

His fingertips touched her cheeks. Slid down her jaw to rest on her throat. Her whole body pulsed with awareness of him, undulating toward him, drawn like a magnet.

She tilted her head. Their lips touched.

Oh, my. His mouth was as warm and resilient and restless as she remembered. But there was more to him this time. A depth of experience. Wisdom and a measure of sadness hardearned. Less of the devil-may-care recklessness. He was more of a man and less of a playboy. And absolutely irresistible because of it. She arched into him, her arms looping around his neck as need exploded inside her.

How could she ever have convinced herself she could cut this man out of her life? He was as much a part of her as her arms or her legs. More so. He was part of her soul.

His arms swept around her and he pushed her down gently to the sand, following her eagerly, their mouths never parting. Her lips opened and his tongue was there, tasting and testing, caressing and cajoling. Not that she needed any encouragement. His desperate urgency was contagious

"Are you real," he murmured against her lips, "or is this a dream?"

She ducked her head into his shoulder and laughed under her breath. "And here I was, asking myself the exact same thing. Does it matter?"

"Nope. I'll take it either way. This is a hell of a lot better than anything else I've dreamed in the past two years. Although there was that recurring dream about eating steak in a bubble bath…"

She replied playfully, "That can be arranged."

"Have you seen Lyle's bathtub? It looks like half a whiskey barrel. To sit in that thing I'd have to stick my knees up my nose. There's hardly room for bubbles, let alone you and a steak."

"Oh-ho! So the dream involved a girl in the tub, too, did it?"

Jagger grinned. "Well, yeah. You starred in many more of my dreams than I wanted."

She winced at the reminder that for the past two years he'd thought the absolute worst of her. "And now?"

"Oh, you're still in my dreams."

She whispered, "So let's make one of them real, shall we?"

His eyes went even darker and more turbulent than they already were. He lowered his mouth to hers and kissed her with restrained violence. And which dream of his was this? One where he seduced her with cold calculation and walked away with the pieces of her heart in his pocket, or one where they made sweet, tender love until they couldn't lift a finger between them? Sadly, she didn't care which. She'd take him any way she could get him.

His mouth and hands roamed over her body, burning her until the cool night air felt wonderful against her heated skin. Her cheeks must be cherry-red, they felt so hot. Her breasts, her belly, her entire body felt flushed and hypersensitive. She was abjectly grateful when he came up for air long enough to peel her out of her clothes and strip off his as well.

She murmured, "Did you ever imagine this with me in the past two years? A moonlit beach all to ourselves on a tropical island? Just the two of us, naked and together?"

His eyes closed in pain. "I didn't want to. I hated myself for thinking about it. But…yes." The hoarse word sounded torn from his gut. "Yes. I hated you for it, but I still wanted you."

"Me, too," she whispered. "I never stopped wanting you. I dreamed about you. About…doing things with you."

"Like what?" he asked against the tender flesh at the base of her ear.

His mouth made it nearly impossible for her to concentrate on an answer. She mumbled, "You know. Things."

"Tell me."

How could she refuse him? Not after all he'd been through. Not any more than she could deny a starving man food or a parched man water. "I imagined making love with you to the rhythm of waves crashing on a beach. Under the stars. Just the two of us. Free to do anything and everything we want to."

She felt his lips curve up in a smile against the base of her throat. "Kind of like here and now?"

"Um, yes. Kind of exactly like this."

His fingers drifted down her side, along her thigh and curled around the back of her knee. "You know what they say. Sometimes dreams come true."

A low moan of need slipped out of her, and Jagger needed no further permission to proceed. He pulled her leg up over his hip, opening her to more intimate exploration. She tried to be careful of his bandages, but he was having no part of it.

At first, it was all skin and mouths and hands and frantic hurry. And then, as the reality of the moment set in for both of them—awareness…and then belief…that this wasn't a dream on the verge of slipping away at any second—they slowed down. Way down.

They lay side by side on the sand, gazing deep into each other's eyes, and ever so slowly reacquainted themselves with each other's bodies with languid hands and gentle mouths. She learned the new contours of his leaner form, while he explored the changes the past two years had wrought in her as well.

"You're curvier than I remembered," he murmured. "Less of a girl and more of a woman."

Alarm jabbed her. Not a place she wanted to go just yet. Not now. Not when the reason for her curviness had so much potential for strife. Instead, she laughed lightly. "Is that a polite way of telling me I've gotten fat?"

"Good Lord, no! It's a polite way of telling you that you've grown up. Become a beautiful woman in her prime. It suits you."

How close he was to truths left unspoken scared her to death. To distract him, she commented, "You, on the other hand, are thinner than you were. Harder. It's like all the excess has been stripped away and left just muscle and sinew and bone."

He sighed. "How true."

She laughed. "Never fear. I'll have you fattened back up in no time, Jack Spratt."

"Not if you work it all off of me making love." He kissed her then, adding, "By all means do your best to pack on the weight and take it right back off of me like this."

She shook her head in mock dismay. "I knew it. Sex and supper. That's all you want from me." The phrase "barefoot and pregnant in the kitchen" slid through her mind, but she cut the thought off in panic and prayed the same phrase hadn't occurred to him.

The humor bled out of his gaze until it was so black and so intense she could hardly bear to look at it. "Honey, sex and supper don't even scratch the surface of what I want from you tonight." His voice dropped to a husky whisper. "Tonight, I want it all."

And what about tomorrow?

He didn't bring it up, and she was vividly aware of the omission. He always had been a James Bond kind of guy. Love 'em and leave 'em. Apparently, two years in a box hadn't changed that about him. And two years hadn't changed her need for him, either. Hadn't diminished it one bit. Which meant she was left exactly where she was before, suspecting that they'd just have this short time together before he left her. Again. Could she survive that twice in one lifetime?

Truly, it was amazing that one of the scores of women left trailing in James Bond's wake never caught up with him and murdered him in bereavement or an excess of passion. Ian Fleming might have understood spies, but he sure as heck didn't understand women.

And then Jagger's hands closed on her body and all concern about anything beyond this exact moment flew away into the night.

Their lovemaking was achingly slow. Jagger seemed to want to savor every single second of it. A slight frown of concentration wrinkled his brow until she finally murmured, "You look so serious. Are you not enjoying yourself, or have you just forgotten what comes next?"

A snort of laughter escaped him. "I think I remember, thanks." He added more seriously, "I'll die remembering this moment with you."

"No talk of death tonight, okay?" she replied softly.

"You've got it. I'm alive. You're alive. Let's celebrate that."

And with that he wrapped her in his strong arms and rolled down the beach with her until the cold surf washed up on their feet. She squealed and he laughed, pulling her on top of him. Their laughter mingled as she looped her arms around his neck and gazed down at him with her heart in her eyes. The laughter drained out of his gaze until nothing was left but raw need that stole her breath away.

He whispered, "For a while there, I didn't think I was going to make it out of that box alive."

"But you did."

"It was a close thing. I was on the edge of breaking when you opened that door."

"But I did."

"I wasn't going to leave with you at first, you know. I thought it was a trick."

"I wouldn't have left you there, Jagger. I'd have found a way to get you out of that crate, even if I had to call in the National Guard."

"I doubt that rock is American soil, honey. But thanks for the thought."

She grinned down at him. "I always could have messed with a cargo manifest and gotten your reefer unit off-loaded someplace and then conveniently lost track of."

He pushed her hair back and tucked it behind her ear. "My brave little innocent. AbaCo's goons would've caught you."

"I dunno. I'm pretty familiar with their computer systems. I know my way around most of their safeguards. And after all, I am Danger Girl."

He laughed quietly; then a speculative gleam entered his eyes. After a moment, he shook his head. "Later. I don't want to talk business right now."

Everything about their lovemaking was exactly as she remembered—but better. His hardness to her softness, his relentless energy, his finesse, his uncanny ability to know exactly what felt best to her as he stroked her with hand and mouth and body to a fever pitch. Bright lights exploded behind her eyelids, electric shocks zinged across her skin and orgasm after orgasm ripped through her.

She gasped his name, clinging to him as the universe dissolved around her. Likewise, he buried his face against her neck and groaned as his body shuddered deep within hers.

Gradually, she became aware of dampness on her neck. "Jagger?" she asked.

He lifted his head to gaze down at her, and she was stunned to see tear tracks on his cheeks.

Right then, right there, her heart broke. It split wide open, its vulnerable interior exposed and raw. Then into the fissures flowed something warm and soothing, something entirely right. Love. For this man. This wonderful man who'd endured so much suffering and come out the other side of it able to give of himself, able to forgive.

She reached up and tenderly wiped away his tears.

He flashed her a crooked smile. "Guess I'm still a little messed up in the head."

"It's not messed up to shed a tear. You've been to hell and back. You're authorized to be a little emotional."

He took a deep breath. "It's real, isn't it? I'm really free, aren't I? You're not going to make a phone call and have AbaCo's thugs swoop in and haul me back to my box, are you?"

She smiled at him and reached up to smooth the frown off his brow with her fingertips. "No, I'm not. And yes, Jagger. You're really free. I never would have helped them, particularly not with harming or kidnapping you. Nobody's coming to get you."

He stared at her for a long time as the truth of her words seemed to gradually sink in. Eventually, he shrugged. "We do still have the FBI to deal with. They may not be a walk in the park to convince that we're innocent."

Well, he was innocent. She hoped that the extenuating circumstances of saving a man's life would get her cleared of the charges against her, but it wasn't a guaranteed thing. She said bravely, "Once they hear your side of the story, they'll drop the charges against you."

"From your mouth to God's ear, eh?"

She gazed at every nuance of his expression as the worry slowly gave way to more hopeful thoughts. He had every reason to be cynical, she supposed. Everyone had abandoned him, believed him dead. Nobody had fought hard enough to find out how he'd died or to verify if it was even true.

Renewed guilt poured through her. Even she'd been willing to think the worst of him. "I'm sorry I didn't come looking for you sooner, Jagger."

He smiled down at her. "Don't worry about it. I'll be eternally grateful to you for getting me out of there."

"No, really—"

He laid two fingers across her mouth. "No, really. You're forgiven. It's fine."

He was a remarkable man. She didn't know if, in the same situation, she could find such generosity of spirit in herself. How on earth had she ever caught the attention of a man like him? She had to be the luckiest woman alive. She drank in the sight of him greedily. And that was probably why she noticed the faint frown that flitted through his eyes.

"What?" she murmured.

"It just occurred to me that we didn't use any kind of protection just now. Lord knows I haven't been exposed to any diseases in the past two years, but we still should've taken precautions against a preg—"

He broke off.

Panic erupted in her gut, clawing at her ribs. She held her breath, hoping against hope that she wasn't reading the memory in his eyes correctly. But she knew she was.

"When I was sick…" he started.

Oh, God.

"You said something to me. Something about…" He frowned as if struggling to retrieve the memory.

Please, please let him fail.

Triumph flashed in his gaze. "A baby—"

A thunderous frown gathered on his brow. He lurched upright, staring down at her in mingled disbelief and fury. "*Our* baby."

Still she said nothing. He hadn't actually asked her a question, after all.

His voice was terrible in its piano-wire-tight restraint. "Is that true? Do we have a child? Or did you just say that to get me to fight to live?"

It would be so easy to take the out he'd offered her. To let the glib lie roll off her tongue. Yeah, sure. That was it. She'd lied about a kid to make him fight to live. Except she had a responsibility to her daughter. To their daughter. And at the end of the day, she had a responsibility to him, too. He had a right to know.

She sighed. Took a deep breath. Said a mental goodbye to their great connection and happily-ever-after future. And answered, "It's true. Her name is Michelle and she's fifteen months old. Lest you wonder whether or not she's yours, a, I hadn't been with anyone else in over a year, and, b, you only have to take one look at her to know. She's the spitting image of you. But if you want to do a paternity test on her, I'll consent to it."

Jagger jerked away from her, taking his warmth and safety with him. He sat in the sand with his back partially turned to her, his shoulders hunched, his usual restlessness completely absent. He stared at the ocean for a long time and then shifted his gaze to the thick dusting of stars overhead. But still he said nothing. The silence was deafening.

He'd shut her out. Drawn away from her totally. No part of him was open to her. It was as if she didn't exist, and the love they'd just made had never happened. In an instant, he was a stranger to her.

The loss was devastating. As bad as losing him before had been, this was a hundred times worse. He'd left her again, and yet he was sitting a foot away from her. She'd thought his physical disappearance made her feel abandoned. *Now* she knew the true meaning of the word.

She felt an odd and painful ache in her chest. Oh, wait. That was her heart shriveling and turning to dust. Slowly, she pulled herself upright. Hugging her knees, she cautiously glanced over at him. What was there to say?

In a small voice, she murmured, "I'd have told you right away if I had known how to get in touch with you."

"Did you continue with the pregnancy because you object to abortion?"

"Good Lord, no! I kept her because I wanted her. I wanted your—our—child. She's the greatest kid ever! Wait until you meet her—" She broke off abruptly. "If you want to meet her, of course. I don't expect you to dive into parenthood just because she exists. It's your choice…"

She trailed off as he stared at her blankly. She couldn't read anything at all in that flat gaze. Until he gave her some indication of his reaction, she didn't dare say more at all.

He stared at her for a long time. Four hundred sixty-two seconds. She counted each one. And then he said neutrally, "Of course AbaCo knows about Michelle. You're on the company's health care plan, no doubt."

"Not to mention I've taken her into the office from time to time for company parties."

"Do they know she's mine?"

"Truly, Jagger, to look at her is to know she's yours. She's a tiny, female version of you. The resemblance is startling." A cold chill was spreading through her. When she'd found out the FBI wanted her, she'd known better than to contact her mother by phone or e-mail. She'd just assumed, though, that Jagger would make it all better. But the way he was frowning right now was alarming in the extreme.

He swore violently under his breath. Then he spoke urgently, his voice hard. Tight. "We've got to call Don to come get us. We need to fly out of here as soon as possible. Tonight if he can swing it."

Horror exploded in her chest. "Are you leaving me when we get to the big island, then?"

His gaze snapped to her. "No, of course not. You're coming with me. But we've got to go get Michelle before AbaCo does. Hell, they've had nearly a week to snatch her." He pushed a distracted hand through his hair and muttered,

"Cripes. I didn't need a liability like this for them to use to get their hooks back into me."

Ohgod, ohgod, ohgod.

He swore under his breath some more as he sat up, continuing to mutter that AbaCo's goons were too smart to miss this opportunity to kidnap an exploitable asset like a child and that they no doubt had her by now.

Emily jumped to her feet in terror. "They have Michelle?" she cried frantically. "Come on! We've got to go!" She wrung her hands in impatience as Jagger continued to sit in the sand.

"Honey, a few minutes or hours now isn't going to matter. If they connected you to my escape, AbaCo's men showed up at your house within twenty-four hours. In that case, they've had the child for days, by now. If we're lucky, they haven't made the connection yet and she's still safe."

Emily frowned. "But she's not at my house. My mother took her back to the mainland for the holidays."

Interest lit Jagger's eyes. "Where is she now?"

"With my mother's family in Virginia."

"Do they have the same last name as you?"

"No. My mother remarried after my father died and took his name. His family is Andersons, not Grainger."

"Hmm. Maybe there's a chance then that AbaCo doesn't know where to find her. We need to get you to a phone so you can call your mother and warn her not to open the door for any strangers until we get there. If AbaCo gets a hold of your daughter, they'll use her to leverage the two of us into doing exactly what they want."

Relief flooded Emily that AbaCo probably didn't have Michelle yet. But then visions of Jagger's tiny prison flashed through her mind and a new wave of panic broke over her. Her baby couldn't end up like that! She just couldn't.

"Breathe, Em. We'll get to her first."

She took several deep breaths. It would be okay. Michelle

would be safe. She had to be. Any other possibility was simply unthinkable. The two of them quickly hunted down their clothes and she pulled hers back on, oblivious of the sand now grating uncomfortably against her skin.

As they walked quickly back to the cabin, her mind finally began to function again, even if all it did was jump from one disjointed thought to another. At least it did until one odd observation registered and then stuck in her craw. It grew into something uncomfortable smoldering in her gut. It wasn't anger exactly, but it was irritating, and she didn't know exactly how to react.

Jagger still hadn't said a word about how he felt about finding out that he was a father. Okay, she'd grant that it was a shock and might take some getting used to before he figured out how he felt. But so far he'd called Michelle a liability, an exploitable asset and leverage. Oh, and once he'd referred to Michelle as *her* daughter. Not his.

She tried to argue herself out of it. She'd determined a long time ago not to force parenthood on Jagger if she ever found him. She'd made the decision on her own to go through with the pregnancy and to be a single parent. She'd vowed to have no expectations of him.

But her jaw couldn't help but tighten at the way he'd labeled her precious daughter like some sort of inconvenient object to be managed.

Something else Ian Fleming had never bothered to reveal about James Bond—although in fairness to the author, she probably should have known it herself—he was lousy father material.

Chapter 11

A baby. Holy smokes.

Jagger stared out the window of the Boeing 777 at the featureless blue of the Pacific Ocean passing below. They'd land in Los Angeles in an hour, and then, assuming nothing went wrong, they'd be on their way to Virginia. And his *daughter.*

The concept still blew his mind, and he'd had nearly twelve hours to get used to it while Don flew to Lyle's island from Honolulu, took them back to Oahu and then they boarded this flight to the mainland. Most men got seven or eight months to adapt to the idea of being a father, lucky bastards. And based on the degree of shock he was currently experiencing, they needed all eight months, too.

Even in the low-quality home photos of the toddler that Emily had shown him, Michelle did look startlingly like him. There really wasn't any question that the child was his. And besides, Emily wasn't the kind of woman to lie about something like this. If she said Michelle was his daughter, then it was true.

He'd never even met the child, and already he could hardly sit still in his seat as he pondered the possibilities if AbaCo managed to get a hold of her. What was up with that? It was as if he'd gone from zero to protective Daddy in ten seconds flat.

He'd listened in a state of wonder approaching disbelief as Emily eagerly regaled him with two years' worth of accumulated stories about her pregnancy, birth and raising of Michelle to date. She sounded like a cute little kid—curious and cheerful and bright. But his? Whoa.

Maybe if he could get past his horror at the idea of AbaCo kidnapping a tiny child and taking her from her mother—and father—he'd be joyful at the news that he had a daughter. But instead, panic rose up to all but choke him every time he relaxed his mental guard for even a second. He didn't have time to celebrate the news. He had to keep Michelle safe—hell, keep her alive—first. And knowing AbaCo, that was going to take every ounce of his skill and commitment.

As for Emily, he had to give her credit. She was a great mom if her frantic need to protect her child was any indication. She hadn't slept a wink last night after his revelation that Michelle might be in danger. Thankfully, she'd dropped off in her seat beside him about an hour ago from sheer emotional exhaustion.

Which was a good thing. He wasn't sure he could take much more of the sudden tension that had sprung up between them. She'd done her best to mask it, but it was clear she was annoyed with him for not showing a little more reaction—good or bad—to parenthood.

But how could he? He had to focus all his energy on saving Michelle, to keep his mind firmly on the task at hand, which was to reach Michelle and secure the child before AbaCo found her. He'd have time to figure out how he felt about being a father later.

He closed his eyes. Tried to catch a nap before they landed.

But it was no use. He'd slept too much over the past week of recuperation, and frankly he was too wired with anxiety to sleep now. He occupied the remainder of the flight imagining possible scenarios when they landed that ranged from smooth sailing to their next flight to an armed party of AbaCo operatives jumping them in the terminal.

In his line of work, it was all about contingency planning. About having a plan B for every situation that could possibly present itself to a covert operative like him. Then it was a simple matter of him assessing the situation and activating the appropriate response plan. No sweat, right? He'd done it a hundred times before. So why was he sitting here sweating bullets?

It could only be the parenthood wild card. Being a father had done something weird to his gut. Something at a subliminal level that he had no control of. It was as if some violently protective switch had been flipped on toward this small person who looked so much like him.

Under other circumstances, normal circumstances, he'd have relished these new feelings. But at the moment, jitters all but rattled him out of his seat and his mind was a jumbled mess. How was he going to save anybody in this frame of mind? He had to get control of himself! Even resorting to meditation failed him in the end.

He couldn't imagine how Emily was holding it together at all. She had a two-year head start on him in loving Michelle. Plus, there was that whole mother-bear-protecting-threatened-cub instinct for Emily to deal with.

When the plane bumped onto the runway at LAX, he was relieved as Emily blinked awake to reveal grim determination in her gaze and no hint of panic. Thank goodness. He didn't need a hysterical mother on his hands.

They had no bags to collect and he rushed Emily through the terminal at nearly a run, keeping a sharp eye out for any pursuers. Their quick pace would force any small surveillance team to scramble and reveal themselves to a trained operative like him. Sure enough, as they approached the gate for their flight to Washington, D.C., he thought he spotted a furtive movement out of the corner of his eye. He cursed under his breath and Emily went stiff beside him.

"Keep moving," he muttered. "Don't give any indication that we've just passed our gate." Her head started to turn and he bit out, "Don't look around."

Her head snapped forward.

He murmured, "We're gonna have to lose the tail before we can board our flight. Just do what I tell you to and be prepared to move fast. Got it?"

"Yes." She sounded on the verge of throwing up.

"Be strong, Em. For Michelle. Be Danger Girl."

Her shoulders squared beside him. *Good girl. Or more accurately, brave Mom.*

He proceeded to weave through the terminal, ducking through stores, reversing course abruptly and generally being a pain in the ass to follow. A couple of times he spotted AbaCo operatives dodging out of his line of sight. It looked like a three-man team. Not nearly enough to stay on a guy like him who'd figured out that he was being tailed. At least the team wasn't trying to move in and snatch him and Emily. Not yet. Not in this public a place with the amount of security major airports boasted these days.

For her part, Emily was a trouper, never complaining as he dragged her around like a rag doll.

He carefully eyed the high-quality diving watch Lyle had given him. He'd have to time this practically down to the second.

One more loop through a crowded newsstand, and then it was time.

"C'mon," he bit out under his breath. He and Emily took off running at a dead sprint through the terminal. Agony speared through his side and he prayed he hadn't opened up the wounds. But he didn't slow down. As they neared their gate, the final boarding call for their flight was being announced for the last time. Two gates prior to theirs, he yanked Emily down beside him, ducking below the levels of the chairs in the waiting areas. Crouched uncomfortably, the two of them duckwalked the last few yards to their gate.

The gate agent looked alarmed as they knelt guiltily before her ticket reader, and Jagger shot her his most charming smile past the fire searing in his side. "This is my girlfriend. My soon-to-be ex-wife and her lawyer are here, looking for us."

Sudden understanding lit the agent's face, and she obligingly whisked them onto the jet bridge and closed the door behind them.

"Your girlfriend?" Emily complained as they rushed toward the jet.

"Well, it's true, isn't it?"

That seemed to give her pause. At least it rendered her silent until they dropped into their seats, panting, and the plane had taken off. But he had faith he hadn't heard the last of it yet.

He was right.

"Look, Jagger. I never intended for Michelle to be your responsibility. I made the decision to have her and raise her by myself. You're under no obligation to get involved in her life as a parent. I don't expect it of you. You don't have to have anything to do with either one of us if you don't want to."

Irritation stabbed him and his voice was sharp as he muttered back, "You don't have a very high opinion of me, do you?"

She scowled. "I'm just saying I don't necessarily expect you to dive in and embrace the whole daddy thing. I won't even ask for child support. I'm doing fine on my own. Well, I was until I lost my job with AbaCo." She added hastily, "Not that it's any great loss. I couldn't work for a company like that in good conscience knowing what I do now about it. Your kidnapping was the final straw."

He turned to look her full in the face. "You mean there were other straws? What all *do* you know about them?"

"Quite a bit, actually."

Under the roar of the jet engines he asked quietly, "Do you know anything about illegal shipments they're making?"

She frowned. "I know stuff like the fact that most of the senior managers in my department worked together in the Stasi."

That shot both his brows sky-high. His mind raced. The Stasi had been the notorious secret police fist of the East German socialist regime. When East Germany had dissolved, so had the Stasi, thrusting thousands of trained covert operatives and thugs onto the street without jobs and without pensions. It had been a no-brainer that they'd turn en masse to crime. Like the KGB, which had become the core of the modern Russian mob, former Stasi agents formed the core of today's German Mafia. Was the *entire* shipping company an elaborate front for a crime syndicate?

Emily was speaking again. "The thing I can't understand is why they held you prisoner for two years. Why didn't they release you or just kill you?"

He laughed without humor. "I figured that one out a long time ago. They were trying to brainwash me. To break my mind and then reprogram me into a double agent to work for them."

Alarm shot across her face. "Did they succeed?"

He snorted. "Nope." He paused and then added grimly, "And I've got you to thank for that. I was so fixated on my fury at you that all their efforts to crack me failed. I was too focused for their methods to work."

She winced. "So because you hated me, you were immune?"

He shrugged. "Yeah, pretty much."

"I wish I had known earlier. Found some way to save you."

He wasn't crazy about spending two years in a box and being beaten up and half starved. But it wasn't as though he could change that fact at this point. It was water under the bridge. And right now he needed to focus all his energy on reaching Michelle and making her safe. He also needed Emily completely focused on the job ahead.

He murmured soothingly, "What's done is done, Em."

She subsided but continued to look troubled.

Both of them slept for most of the transcontinental flight to Washington, D.C. He woke up when they began their descent. He had to assume AbaCo's thugs would have figured out by now where they'd flown off to and that a welcoming committee of some kind would be waiting to greet them. A welcoming committee he'd have to lose, and fast.

Before he and Emily could approach Michelle, he had to make absolutely sure they weren't being followed. He dared not lead AbaCo's men anywhere near the child. But by the same token, he doubted Emily would put up with much fooling around before she was reunited with her daughter. She might be acting fairly controlled, but he knew her well enough to know that she was pretty freaked out.

Once they landed he planned to make contact with his headquarters. He had no intention of turning himself in now, but he had to keep the lines of communication open, to make it clear that he was going to cooperate with the government, and start planting seeds of the idea that he and Emily might have been set up and might just have some fascinating facts of their own to reveal about their accusers.

If nothing else, Uncle Sam was gonna love picking Emily's brains for what she could reveal about AbaCo's "sensitive cargoes." The U.S. had suspected for a long time that elements within AbaCo were engaged in extensive international mob activity. But nobody had ever dreamed that the entire company might be a mob front. He feared that the missing agents who'd been sent in to infiltrate AbaCo before him had met a fate similar to or worse than his. He didn't know if he hoped they were still alive, or if, after all this time, they'd died and been put out of their misery. How long could any man stay sane living in a box?

Hopefully, with what Emily knew, maybe the U.S. government could build a case against the shipping giant that would stick. It was worth risking jail for. If they could bring down AbaCo, their daughter would be safe once and for all. And that was worth *anything*.

First he and Emily had to get Michelle safely in their custody. Then they'd deal with the charges against them and take apart AbaCo once and for all.

They hadn't had time during the frantic run through LAX to call Emily's mother to check and make sure Michelle was safe, and he could only hope the woman had gotten Emily's single urgent e-mail to lock the doors and keep Michelle inside until Emily arrived to explain everything.

Their flight landed at Dulles International Airport and he didn't lead Emily through any evasive measures after they disembarked. In fact, he went out of his way to act unconcerned, as if he believed they'd lost their tail in Los Angeles. He made no effort even to check for tails. In the first place, he'd be an idiot to assume anything other than they were being followed. And in the second place, he wouldn't be able to lose the tail anyway until he and Emily had picked up their rental car and hit the road. Besides, he *felt* the tail behind him. Hell, he almost smelled sauerkraut in the air.

He supposed it was technically possible that this was just paranoia and irrational fear for Michelle's safety kicking in. But he doubted it. Either way, it didn't make any difference in how he behaved. He stopped at a kiosk and bought an outrageously overpriced cell phone and a bunch of prepaid minutes, then calmly guided her through Dulles toward the rental car counter.

Emily incorrectly interpreted his calm to mean they were in the clear, and she relaxed accordingly. Which suited his purposes just fine. He didn't disabuse her of the notion that they were safe. She needed the break from her continuous panic of the past twenty-four hours.

He drove when they left the airport. He had a sinking feeling that his specialized offensive driving skills were going to be called upon before this day was over. He pointed the car south out of the airport, winding along back roads southward into Virginia.

"So where exactly are your mother and Michelle in Virginia?" he queried once they were well away from the airport. "Can you find it on the map the car agent gave us and show me?"

"Sure. They're in Chestnut Grove." She fumbled with the map for a minute, then pointed at a speck in the Shenandoah Valley, right in the heart of Virginia horse country.

"We'll stop at the next gas station and get a more detailed map of the state. I'll need you to find three or four different routes to reach Chestnut Grove."

She frowned. "Are you expecting trouble?"

He replied with false levity, "Better safe than sorry, Danger Girl."

Over the next half hour, he had no luck spotting the AbaCo tail. And that worried him. He went so far as to guide the car onto a highway and push the speed up to twenty miles per hour over the speed limit for a few minutes. Nobody matched their speed behind him. Swearing under his breath, he pulled over at the first rest stop they came to. The lack of a visible tail could mean only one thing.

He sent Emily inside to buy snacks for them. Once she was out of sight, he commenced examining the car in detail to check for an electronic tracking device. It was the only explanation. AbaCo's men were hanging back out of visual range and using a radio to follow them.

He wasn't at all surprised to find the small black disk magnetically attached to the top side of the muffler of their car. It was very well hidden. Professionally, in fact. But unfortunately for AbaCo, he was a pro, too.

With the transmitter in his pocket, he strolled into the rest stop to join Emily. It was an easy enough matter to find out that the college student in the line in front of them for hamburgers was headed to Richmond. When the kid laid the keys to his rental car on the counter to pay for his food, it was even easier for Jagger to read the make, model and license plate number of the kid's car off the key tag.

While Emily ducked into a restroom, Jagger strolled outside and attached the tracking device to the underside of the kid's rear bumper before the student pulled out of the truck stop.

Jagger timed their departure so they actually followed the kid for a few miles, just in case the AbaCo tails had closed in to visual range while he and Emily had been stopped. Once AbaCo saw their car moving in the same direction as the tracking beacon, the goons would back out of visual range again. And the fact that they were following the wrong car hopefully wouldn't dawn on them until the student had arrived in Richmond several hours from now—long after Jagger and Emily had disappeared into the rural back roads of the Shenandoah Valley.

Jagger drove erratically, speeding up and slowing down, slamming on the brakes and making last-second turns, and even pounded down a few dusty dirt roads. No plumes of dust kicked up behind them. Eventually, he became convinced that no one was following them, at close range or otherwise.

He held out a hand across the car to Emily. "I need the cell phone."

"The phone! I'm so used to being on the Rock and not having one I forgot we had it. Let me call my mother—"

He cut her off gently. "Me first. Please. It's important."

"Uh. Oh. Okay. Here."

He dialed with one hand and held the device up to his ear. A marine clerk answered the line.

"This is Captain Holtz. I need to speak to—"

He got no further with the clerk. The familiar voice of his boss came on the line. "Jagger. Damn I'm glad to hear your voice again. Thought we'd lost you there, for a while. Where are you?"

"Not far away, actually."

"That's excellent news. You're still planning to turn yourself in, right? Do you have the woman with you?"

He glanced over at Emily. "Yes to both."

"Come in ASAP. The sooner we get statements from you, the sooner we can sort this mess out and clear your name."

"Right. About that. I've got some good news and some bad news for you, sir. The good news is that between the two of us, Miss Grainger and I should be able to hand you enough information to bury AbaCo once and for all. The bad news is we have something else to take care of first. We can't turn ourselves in just yet."

"Jagger." The colonel's warning tone was grim. "If you run around like a fugitive, the credibility of your entire story will be called into doubt. Your only shot at clearing yourself is to get your butt in here now."

Jagger winced. "Sir, I know you're right. Nonetheless, I have to take care of this problem first. It's not negotiable. You can tell the FBI that I'll be in touch with them in a few days."

"How many days?" the colonel demanded.

"As many days as it takes, sir. We'll come in, I swear. Just not yet."

"You're putting me in an awkward situation, son."

A heavy silence fell between them. There was nothing more for Jagger to say. His daughter came first. Before his career, before his safety, before his *life*. But then inspiration struck. "Could you do me a favor, sir?"

A harrumph rumbled in his ear. "What kind of favor?"

"Broker a deal for me. If the FBI will help me take care of this personal problem of mine first, I'll turn myself in and cooperate fully with them when it's successfully resolved. I'm not exaggerating when I say we can bury AbaCo. Turns out the entire company is a front for German Mafia activity."

The colonel went dead silent. Jagger heard the guy's mental wheels turning fast. "That's pretty tempting bait. The entire company, you say? But the firm's worth billions. If we took that out, we'd financially gut the German Mafia. Crime in Europe would plummet. Countries all over the world would owe us big time…" His voice trailed off. "I could work with that."

Jagger held his breath. This might be just the break they needed. With the full resources of the FBI to help them, AbaCo wouldn't stand a chance of getting its mitts on Michelle.

"It may take me a day or two to work this deal, Jagger. You gonna be okay in the meantime?"

"Yes, sir. We'll be lying low and taking care of business."

"I'll do what I can. But if they turn down your offer, they're gonna come after you hard. They're pissed that an operative of your experience turned on them."

"I didn't turn, sir." The colonel said nothing in response, and Jagger added a little desperately, "C'mon. You know me better than that."

"Yeah. I guess I do. Either way, be quick about your business."

"I hear you loud and clear, sir. And thank you."

A snort. "Don't thank me. If you want to cover my ass and yours, turn yourself in."

Jagger disconnected the call thoughtfully. Problem was, once the colonel found out that he and Emily had a child together, all hell was going to break loose anyway. Government operatives were emphatically not supposed to become romantically involved with their informants or human assets. By using her to gain entrance to the AbaCo party, he had cast Emily in the role of an agent, albeit unwitting, of the U.S. government. Still, it was enough of a professional entanglement that she was entirely off-limits to him romantically. It was going to be just a wee bit difficult to get around the fact that they had a daughter whose age placed her conception firmly on that New Year's Eve two years ago when Jagger had used Emily on a mission.

He was screwed either way. That being the case, he might as well save Michelle and unite Emily with her daughter before he went down in flames.

Grimly, he handed the phone to Emily. "Don't give your mom any details over the phone. Just tell her to stay inside with other members of your family, don't open the door to any strangers, and for God's sake, don't let Michelle out of her sight for an instant."

Emily nodded and made the call. Even across the car, Jagger heard Mrs. Anderson's agitation at the other end of the line. Apparently, the danger of the situation had been adequately conveyed and understood. Good. The way he figured it, a grandma was a mommy once removed, which made a grandmother almost as deadly as a mother when her grandchild was threatened.

"How much longer?" Emily murmured as she put away her phone.

"An hour."

It was a tense sixty minutes. He fought his urge to stand on the accelerator and barely managed to hold the car somewhere close to the speed limit. The more time he had to process the idea of having a child, the more connected he felt to her—and he'd never even met Michelle! It bordered on bizarre.

His anxiety climbed with every mile closer they came to her. He was about to meet his daughter. A human being that he'd helped create. The enormity of it overwhelmed him.

What would Michelle think of him? Would she be scared of the grim stranger with her eyes? Would she instinctively recognize him and cut him a break? What did a person do with a fifteen-month-old, anyway? Was that too old for peekaboo? Should he have tried to find her a toy in that rest stop? What did kids that age play with, anyway?

He checked his rampant nerves sharply. She was a baby, for crying out loud. She wouldn't quiz him on his qualifications to be a parent, thank God, because he was grossly unprepared. The brain freeze induced by the mere thought of facing a diaper or a bath was proof enough of that.

"Are you okay?" Emily asked him abruptly.

He started. "Why do you ask?"

"You look about ready to throw up."

He grimaced. "Impending parenthood does that to a guy." He knew the words were a mistake the moment they left his mouth.

Emily's face went closed, and she turned to stare out the passenger window, hurt written in the lines of her neck and shoulders.

"I didn't mean it like that, Em. I'm just nervous. I want Michelle to like me." He took a deep breath and confessed, "I don't know the first thing about kids."

"Neither did I. But you'll catch on fast enough. That is, if you feel like sticking around."

He huffed. "Of course I'll be sticking around. I have every intention of stepping up to my new responsibilities."

Emily flinched again. What had he said now? He was looking forward to becoming a dad. Eager to change the subject, he said, "When we reach your uncle's house, I'll stay outside and make sure we don't have any company while you go in and get Michelle."

She started. "What? I thought we were going to stay with my aunt and uncle for a while."

He frowned. "Of course not. We've got to get away from anywhere AbaCo might look for the child."

Skepticism dripped in her voice. "So you're going to…what? Run around acting like a superspy with a toddler in tow?"

That *had* been his plan. Although when she put it like that… "Have you got a better idea?"

"Well, no. But I don't think that's much of a plan. Little kids are pretty high maintenance, and it's not like you can strap her into her car seat for hours on end, stick a bottle in her mouth and call it good."

Damn.

Emily must've read his mind because she snorted. "She's not a newborn. She sleeps about ten hours at night and takes either one long or two short naps each day. The rest of the time she's busy climbing and exploring and generally destroying everything she can lay her hands on."

Oh, Lord. The weapons and delicate electronics that were part and parcel of his job being pawed by a toddler—yikes. Time for a new plan.

He blurted, "Do you know anybody in Virginia who's an old friend? Somebody you haven't contacted in years? Like not since you worked for AbaCo?"

"No. Nobody. Just my mom's family."

"How about your mother or your aunt and uncle? Would they know someone who'd take you and Michelle in?"

"What? And bring AbaCo's thugs to their doorstep? I can't do that to a family friend, or to someone I've never met for that matter!"

As a trained operative, he didn't hesitate to use anyone and everyone around him to accomplish a mission. And frankly, now wasn't the time to stand on ethics. It was time to marshal whatever resources they could and use them, no matter what the risks to others. "Em—"

She must have heard the lecture coming in his voice because she waved it off. "I don't want to hear it. It's bad enough that Michelle and I are in potential danger. I won't do that to anyone else. Find a way to keep us safe without involving other people."

"I'm not superhuman," he snapped.

"I don't know. From what I've seen of you so far, you come pretty close. Not many people could've survived what you have. And certainly not with their minds and bodies and souls intact."

In an attempt to lighten the mood he reminded her, "Hey, you're Danger Girl, not me. I'm just some guy, remember?"

"No, you're Super Spy. You're not just some guy."

"Danger Girl and Super Spy. We make some pair, huh?"

She wasn't about to be derailed so easily, however. "You've come through stuff intact that would have killed other people. You can do this, Jagger. I know it."

He wasn't sure anything about him was intact. "Then you've got to let me do what I know how to do, the way I know how to do it. Don't fight me on this. We need to take Michelle and get her away from anyone that AbaCo might somehow connect to the two of you. They know we're in the Washington, D.C., area, and they'll scour your records for any contacts in this part of the country. Your entire family is at risk as long as we're with them. Likewise, they'll be watching every hotel, restaurant, bus station, you name it. We can't go anywhere public. We've got to go to ground."

She stared at him. Hard. He avoided meeting her gaze under the guise of watching the road.

She huffed. "Fine. We'll do it your way. But you get to tell my mother."

Chapter 12

Emily didn't wait for Jagger to get out of the car. She raced for the front door, which opened without her having to ring the bell. "Michelle!" she cried.

"Mamaaa!"

Her relief when that sturdy, beloved little body rushed into her arms spilled down Emily's cheeks unchecked in hot, wet tracks. She buried her face in her daughter's silky curls. Out of the corner of her eye, she just caught a glimpse of the shotgun her stepfather leaned inside the door before he followed his granddaughter outside. Good. They'd taken her warning seriously.

"Mama?" Michelle frowned up at her, as if unsure whether or not she should be crying, too.

"I'm crying because I'm happy, sweetheart. I missed you, munchkin. Did you miss me?"

The little girl reached up to touch Emily's damp cheeks. Then she smiled and wriggled free, eager to be on the go once more. Emily laughed. "Hold on a second, sweetie. There's someone I want you to meet."

She scooped up Michelle before she could take off like the world's cutest bullet, and turned.

Jagger was standing beside the car. His face was devoid of expression, but he stood absolutely still, his intense gaze riveted on his daughter. Something about him must have captured his daughter's attention, too, for she stuck a thumb in her mouth and stared back, her own restless nature, so much like her father's, curbed for the moment.

"This is my friend Jagger. Jagger, this is Michelle."

He moved then, easing forward cautiously. He stuck a finger out and touched one of the child's bouncy curls carefully. Michelle made a fast grab and captured his finger, promptly stuffing it into her mouth.

A look of wonder spread across Jagger's face as she gnawed enthusiastically on his fingertip.

"Teething," Emily murmured apologetically. "Sorry."

"That's entirely all right," he murmured back.

Her mother's voice startled her from the front door. She'd completely forgotten about her mom in the magic of the moment. "Who's your friend, Emily? Aren't you going to introduce us?"

"Oh. Sorry, Mom. This is Jagger Holtz. Jagger, my mother. Doris Anderson."

He nodded gravely. "It's a pleasure to meet you, ma'am."

Her mother's shrewd gaze flitted back and forth between Michelle and Jagger and comprehension dawned. Emily winced. So much for that cat. One look at Michelle and Jagger side by side, and the feline was irrevocably out of the bag as to who was Michelle's father. Thankfully, Doris merely pursed her lips and said nothing.

Emily's stepfather boomed, "Well, come on in and sit a spell."

She looked over her shoulder at Jagger. "That's Al. I told you about him. He's my mother's husband."

"Handy with a shotgun, I see," Jagger muttered.

Emily grinned. "Oh, yeah. Terrorized the few dates I managed to land in high school."

Jagger grinned. "Stupid boys. Didn't know what they were missing when they let you get away. You're worth braving howitzers over, let alone a measly shotgun."

She smiled into Michelle's hair as they went inside. She turned the toddler loose within the confines of four walls and watched until the toddler raced out of sight. She spoke briskly to her mother. "We need to pack up a few of Michelle's things. Jagger and I need to leave with her right away."

Thunder landed on her mother's brow. "I don't think it's a good idea to go haring off all over the countryside with a baby in tow, young lady—"

"Don't young lady me, Mom. Some really dangerous people are after us."

"All the more reason not to go running around."

She'd feared her mother might be obstinate about this. "Jagger knows what he's doing. He can handle the people who are chasing us. He just needs to know that Michelle is safe and that she won't be used to get to us."

"She won't be if she stays here. Al's brothers are hunters, too. They all know their way around a gun if it comes to it."

Emily sighed. "We're not talking about a handful of bubbas with shotguns here. These men are ex-Stasi agents. They're mobsters. Violent criminals."

"So call the police and let them deal with this." Ever practical, Doris was.

Emily glanced over at Jagger. "Help me out, here."

He spoke quietly. "Think of a team of Special Forces commandos storming your home and killing everyone in the place so they can grab Michelle. They'll come in all at once through the windows and doors, toting submachine guns that shoot through your walls like tissue paper. They'll attack at night using night-vision goggles and you'll be completely blind. Not that Al or his brothers will get a shot off at them anyway before the team mows them down like sheep. Their weapons will literally cut you in half with bullets."

Everyone in the room stared at Jagger, aghast.

"Who are you?" Al finally asked.

"I'm a covert operative trained in the same methods as the people who are coming after Michelle. The assault I just described is what I'd do in the same situation. These guys are professionals. They're armed to the teeth and they're ruthless. With all due respect, sir, you and your family are no match for them."

Doris spoke up tartly. "Sounds like you're no match for them by yourself, either."

He smiled ruefully at her. "I'm not. That's why Emily and I have to leave and take Michelle someplace where we can hide until the authorities catch up with these guys."

Al grunted. "So surround the house with police or FBI or whoever."

Emily winced. "Right, well, there's a problem with that. Jagger and I have had a little misunderstanding with the FBI and they've got federal warrants out for our arrest. We'll be able to clear up most of the charges as soon as we talk to them, but first we have to make sure that Michelle's safe. That's why we need to take her and leave."

Doris announced firmly, "You're not going anywhere until both of you get a decent meal into you. You look half-dead with exhaustion."

A hot meal was Doris's cure-all for everything that ailed a person. Emily sighed. She looked over at Jagger for approval. He nodded reluctantly and she turned back to her mom. "All right. We'll stay for supper. But then we'll have to go."

Rather than argue anymore with her mother, Emily headed for Michelle's room and began to pack clothes, diapers and toys for her daughter. Doris stomped up and down the hall and did a lot of mumbling under her breath but did not interfere. Emily was relieved to be left to pack in peace.

Over the course of the next hour, however, a repeat of the initial argument occurred, first between her and Al, and then between her and Jagger against everyone again. In the end, Jagger reluctantly agreed to stay at the house until he and Emily had someplace specific in mind to head for.

But over the meal, Jagger recruited Al's family to help him find someplace to go. He laid out his requirements succinctly. They needed someplace isolated to hole up with Michelle where the FBI could eventually come and interview him. That place needed to be free of any family or friends of Emily's, Doris's or Al's that AbaCo could track down. It needed to be reasonably close to Washington, D.C., and it needed to not be connected to any commercially traceable databases, like those used by hotels or stores.

Doris frowned. "In other words, you need to find the home of a complete stranger who will take you in despite the fact that you bring life-threatening risk with you."

Jagger grimaced. "Pretty much."

Emily's mother excused herself from the table. "I may know just the person, and now's the perfect time to catch her."

Emily and Jagger cleared the table and started washing and drying the dishes while her mother signed on to the computer in the dining room. Doris was online a total of maybe two minutes, and then she marched into the kitchen, smiling broadly.

"I've found a place for you three to stay. However, I'm not telling you where it is unless you agree to take me with you."

Emily groaned. Jagger cocked an eyebrow and commented wryly, "I see where you get your stubborn streak from, Em."

"Well?" Doris demanded belligerently. "You'll need a babysitter if you plan on running all over creation, and I'm not letting that baby out of my sight until I know she's safe."

Jagger shrugged. "You have a point. Emily and I may be

a bit occupied over the next several days with security arrangements and after that with debriefings."

Yeah, and going to jail if the FBI didn't buy their respective stories about AbaCo. In that event, Doris would need to be nearby to take custody of Michelle. Emily glanced over at Jagger and saw the exact same thought mirrored in his troubled gaze.

Her mother beamed. "I'm already packed." When Emily scowled, her mother continued. "I did it while you were packing Michelle's things." She added defiantly, "I won't be any trouble."

"Right, Mom. No trouble at all. Now I've got you to worry about, too."

Doris shrugged. "Take it or leave it. I go, too, or I don't give up the location to you."

Emily looked over at Jagger. He said in resignation, "All right. You go, too, Doris. Two mother bears protecting the cub has to be better than one."

Once the decision was made, they left almost immediately. There was a brief flap when Jagger refused to let Doris tell Al where they were going. But when Jagger gently suggested that if Al was captured and tortured for the information it would be best if the older man didn't, in fact, know where Jagger, Emily and Michelle were, everyone subsided in horror.

Thankfully, in anticipation of picking up Michelle and a bunch of baby gear, Jagger had rented a full-sized car. They set out into the night.

"So who are we going to visit?" Jagger asked after about a half hour of evasive driving designed to make sure they had no tail.

Doris replied, "I belong to an online chat group for single moms and the occasional grandma. One of the moms lives in this general area. When I went online and asked if she'd mind a few houseguests, she invited us right away."

Emily asked sharply, "Does she understand the risk in taking us in?"

"I made it clear there were some legal problems and that Michelle's safety was an issue. I wasn't sure how much I should explain over a computer, though."

Jagger nodded. "You did well to keep it vague. We'll fill in our hostess when we arrive and she can decide if she wants us to stay or not."

Emily murmured, "Can't we just drive to Washington, D.C., and walk into FBI headquarters tonight?"

Jagger frowned. "In the first place, I have every reason to believe AbaCo's men will be staking out the place. I doubt we'd make it anywhere near downtown D.C. before they snatched us.

"In the second place, I want to bag these bastards once and for all. The only bait we know for sure that AbaCo will bite at is me and you. As soon as you and I give our statements to a federal attorney or two, we'll have all the backup we need. Then we show ourselves to AbaCo's goons, they make a grab for us and Uncle Sam grabs the lot of them. A couple of days. Maybe a week. And then this will all be over."

It sounded so easy. If only she could believe it would work out like that.

Jagger drove grimly into the night. His plan sounded straightforward enough. Except he'd been in the field enough years to know exactly how many things could go wrong between now and happily ever after. He'd had two long years to contemplate those things. He wanted nothing more than to head for the nearest armed fortress of government agents. But he had faith that if he tried to reach any kind of government installation in this part of the country, they'd find their way blocked by a wall of AbaCo guns. He and his family just had to be patient a little while longer and let events take their course. The stakes were far too high for him to screw up the end game now.

His family...he kinda liked the sound of that.

Michelle was adorable. Of course, he hadn't had to walk the floors with her all night over colic or whatever babies got that kept them up. And she hadn't had a screaming meltdown or a stinky diaper or a food-throwing tantrum yet. He tried to imagine the little bug doing something messy and babyish but was completely unable to muster up any real dismay at the prospect. Clearly, he was already head over heels for her.

Their destination would take them back toward Washington, D.C., but was still deep in the heart of Virginia horse country. The hour-long drive passed quickly as he studied his rearview mirror and tried to form a speech that would honestly spell out the danger they posed to their hostess without scaring off the woman entirely.

All too soon, they arrived at a mailbox that bore the number they were looking for. But beyond that, he saw nothing but a dirt path winding away into a forest. Well, he'd wanted isolated. Looked as though he'd gotten it. He turned onto the driveway.

And drove. And drove. The thing wound into what must have been a mile of woods before the trees finally gave way to rolling horse pastures and four-board oak fences on either side of the drive. They topped a hill and a towering, wrought-iron security gate blocked their way. Wow. Talk about a fortress.

Jagger pulled up before the security camera and intercom box.

Doris leaned forward. "Tell her Graminator is here."

"Graminator?" he asked gravely as Emily rolled her eyes beside him.

Doris glared. She looked prepared to turn him over her knee and spank him if he said anything more. Thankfully, a pleasant female voice came out of the intercom before he could give in to the temptation.

"Come on up to the house. Drive around back, and I'll open one of the garage doors for you. Pull in there."

He thought he detected a note of businesslike competence in the woman's voice. This might just work out after all.

The big gates swung open and he guided the car through, waiting until the gates had closed behind him to continue. No sense waxing sloppy at this late date. He eased forward and the drive topped yet another hill. He whistled through his teeth. A magnificent Colonial mansion rose out of the valley before them. Trees bordered the structure on three sides, but from this angle, a long, manicured lawn stretched from their feet all the way to the front doors.

The driveway took them down the lawn, around a four-tiered fountain and past the east end of the gracious home. As promised, when he pulled around back, one of five garage doors was invitingly open. He pulled inside, and the garage door slid shut behind them. He directed Emily and her mother to stay in the car until the door was entirely shut. And even then, he murmured for them to stay put while he checked things out.

He eased out of the car, crouching beside it, weapon drawn. He made a cautious circuit around their vehicle, ending up back at the driver's-side door.

A spill of yellow light fell into the dimly lit garage and a slender figure was silhouetted in the doorway. The same calm, businesslike voice from before said easily, "I'm unarmed but feel free to verify that for yourself."

A woman stepped forward, her hands held wide away from her body, palms up, as if she'd been checked for weapons before. She approached to within a dozen feet of him and then turned her back on him, waiting expectantly.

"I'm sorry about this," he murmured. "But I can't be too careful."

The woman answered casually, "I fully understand. I'd be equally cautious were I in your position."

He duly frisked her, keeping the exercise as quick and impersonal as possible. Then he nodded over his shoulder at the car. Emily stepped out, carrying a sleeping Michelle, followed by Doris.

Their hostess smiled. "I'm Laura Delaney. Welcome to my home. I'll do everything I can to ensure your comfort and safety during your stay here."

Jagger frowned. She sounded as though she knew exactly what she was getting into, here. How was that? Who was this woman?

"I assume you scanned your car for tracking devices?" she asked him.

He nodded. "I found one and passed it off to a kid headed to Richmond for college."

"You only found the one?" the woman challenged.

He frowned. "I was in a rest stop. I couldn't exactly dismantle the car in the parking lot."

Quick alarm lit the woman's features. "Let me take the ladies inside and get them settled. Then I'll come back out and help you go over the car with a fine-tooth comb."

Jagger frowned. "You think there's a second device?"

"It's what I'd do if I were tracking someone I really didn't want to lose."

Crud. He really had gone soft in that box. Maybe he'd lost the edge. And now his entire family's lives were depending on him. A sharp jolt of alarm zinged him. Was he up to this fight, after all?

As they scoured the rental car for bugs, Jagger went over the general story of his past two years. Laura offered to look into the charges against him, and it wasn't as though he was about to say no. If his boss failed to cut a deal with the FBI, he'd need to find another way to approach the bureau to arrange their surrender.

He found the second device inside the dashboard. Thankfully, it was a passive homing device and not an active transmitter that could send detailed information to AbaCo's thugs.

Jagger took great pleasure in stomping the tracker into dust. Then he asked his hostess tersely, "Do you think we should leave your place?"

"They probably know the general area in which to search for you, but I doubt they had time to triangulate your exact location. It's late and your girls are exhausted. Let's get all of you a good night's sleep and we'll figure out what to do in the morning."

The stress of the past two days was catching up with him all of a sudden. Coffee could keep him going for only so long, and the moment she mentioned sleep, a wall of fatigue slammed into him head-on. Nonetheless, he murmured gamely, "I'll stay up and watch your place."

Laura laughed. "You'll do no such thing. You're dead on your feet. I've got the watch tonight."

"You have some experience in such things?" he asked cautiously. She sounded like some sort of soldier or covert operative. She might not want to reveal her government connections, though.

She replied with equal caution, "Yes, you could say that. Suffice it to say that you should feel free to sleep very soundly. You've got nothing to worry about."

He caught the significant undertone in her voice. Yup, she was a pro. An operative of some kind. Hallelujah. They could use a little support from the home team right about now.

As Laura led the way through an enormous kitchen, she opened a broom closet and took out a lethal-looking Dragunov sniper rig. Furthermore, she looked entirely at ease handling the weapon. Holy crap. Was she more of a pro than he'd guessed? More than a government agent? Some sort of mercenary, maybe?

"Do I want to know who you are?" Jagger asked even more cautiously.

"Let's just say you and I play for the same team. Or at least we both used to."

He nodded. Fair enough. In his line of work, that was more information than many operatives would volunteer. It—and that Dragunov—were all the identification he needed. No civilian would ever have gotten her hands on the specialized military weapon. She was an operator just like him. Or maybe not just like him, but close enough.

She showed him upstairs to a two-bedroom suite joined by a sitting room. Doris was already snoring gently in one room, and Emily was curled up, unconscious, with Michelle in the king-size bed in the other room.

"Get some sleep, Mr. Holtz. And rest assured, this estate has a few security tricks up its sleeve. No one's getting near the house tonight without me knowing about it. My son and I like our privacy."

He nodded and stretched out on the sofa in the sitting room, his pistol clutched in his hand.

Which maybe didn't turn out to be such a great idea. He awoke with a jolt to bright sunlight and someone plucking his gun from his limp grasp.

"Whoa there, kiddo," he exclaimed. "That's not a toy for you, Michelle." He managed to retrieve his gun from the toddler's chubby hands just as Emily came around the corner on the hunt for the escapee.

"There you are, munch—oh. I'm sorry. I was hoping you could get a little more sleep."

He grinned up at Emily. "Not with this little kleptomaniac on the loose."

He glanced at his watch, stunned to see that it was after 9:00 a.m. He actually felt pretty close to human.

Emily announced, "I think I smell breakfast cooking. My mom got up a while ago and said she was going to go down and whip up a little something for all of us."

The mention of food sent his stomach growling against his spine. "You go on down. I'll join you in a minute."

And that was why he was alone in the upstairs hallway when Laura announced sharply from someplace toward the front of the house, "Incoming!"

Chapter 13

Emily froze at the foot of the sweeping staircase as Jagger came barreling down from behind her, bellowing, "Get away from the windows!"

She wasn't anywhere near a window, but his shout sent her tearing toward the kitchen instinctively. He was right on her heels. Doris had already snatched up Michelle and was holding the now-crying toddler close. Jagger threw open the oven door where a batch of muffins was browning, then pulled Emily, Doris and Michelle into a giant bear hug in front of it. Heat poured out on all of them until it felt as if she were a muffin baking in the oven.

"Why are we standing in front of the oven?" Emily ventured to ask.

"We're hiding," Jagger bit out.

"Standing in plain sight?"

"We're hiding from infrared cameras."

"What?"

"Helicopter's buzzing the place," he replied tersely. "Probably scanning the house for heat signatures. The heat from the oven should obscure us from their sensors."

Comprehension lit Emily's features, followed closely by panic. "They're looking through the walls?" Her entire body vibrated in his arms as a nearly unstoppable urge to bolt tore through her.

"Just stay put, honey. All they should see in the kitchen right now is a big blob of white where the oven ought to be. Trust me," he soothed.

For Michelle's sake, she corralled her rampaging terror. But bad guys could look right into a house without so much as a by-your-leave? The thought creeped her out completely.

Their hostess, Laura, came rushing into the kitchen. She smiled approvingly when she saw them clustered in front of the oven. "Helicopter's drawing away from the house. I wasn't sure if that meant they didn't see what they were looking for or if it meant they're going to fetch their ground forces. But after your quick thinking, Jagger, I'd say we can safely assume it is the former."

"So we're safe?" Emily asked.

"For now. They may be back, but I'll make a few phone calls. The regional air traffic control facility ought to be amenable to giving us a heads-up if any more unscheduled aircraft try to buzz this place."

Emily stared. "They'll do that for people?"

Jagger chuckled. "Not for all people, honey. But for our erstwhile hostess, I should think they would."

Emily's eyebrows shot up. Wow. Who *was* Laura Delaney? Just then a beautiful little boy with dark hair and his mother's bright blue eyes fringed in magnificent black eyelashes came running into the room. "Mommy! What's wrong? Is it the bad men again?"

Laura scooped up the child, whom Emily estimated to be around five years old. "Nope. No bad men here, Adam."

Jagger piped up. "Did you know that this lady here is called Danger Girl? She's great at keeping people she likes safe. Sometimes she even rescues them, too."

The little boy stared at her, his mouth a round O.

"Jagger," Emily muttered in disgust. "Did you have to?"

Laura started. "Danger Girl? You?"

Emily rolled her eyes. "It's an old—and bad—joke between Jagger and me. If anyone around here is superhero material, it's him and not me."

"Hmm." Laura eyed the two of them speculatively, but said no more. Emily got the feeling she'd missed something in the exchange.

The disrupted preparations for breakfast resumed. A few minutes later, a middle-aged Englishwoman whom Laura introduced as her son's nanny strolled into the general chaos. She took efficient charge of both Adam and Michelle, who were fascinated by each other, and led them off to the nether regions of the mansion to play.

As Doris's world-famous omelets slid neatly onto plates and the adults sat down at the table, Laura filled them in. Emily listened eagerly.

"Jagger, last night I took the liberty of looking into the charges against you. The evidence to support a claim of treason was turned over to the U.S. government almost two years ago. The assumption within the government has been that AbaCo made you an offer you couldn't refuse and that you'd been turned."

Emily gasped. "Jagger would never betray his country! He's the most honorable and noble man I know!"

Jagger grinned. "Thanks for the vote of confidence, but we'll need more than that to convince the feds to drop the charges against me."

"What about the fact that they had you locked up in a box for two years?" she demanded indignantly.

He sighed. "I have no proof of that."

"I let you out of that box! I'll testify to what I saw."

He sighed. "That only proves I was being held in a box two weeks ago. Nothing more."

"I saw how pale and thin you were—"

Laura cleared her throat politely. "Actually, there might be some evidence to support Jagger's claim. I can't go into the details of how I know, but I believe that AbaCo has engaged in a systematic campaign of holding prisoners on ships in international waters, in the same manner they held Jagger. I believe they kidnap some of their own hostages, but they also appear to be willing to hold other peoples' hostages for a hefty fee."

Emily wasn't sure she followed, but Jagger leaned forward intently. "You mean they're throwing people in containers like mine and just sailing around in the middle of the ocean with them indefinitely?"

Emily's stomach turned over. "You mean like a floating prison ship?"

Laura nodded grimly. "As long as the ship stays in international waters, there's not much anyone can do to help these prisoners. Only when they come into ports for refueling can anyone move on rescuing them."

Emily nodded. The *Zhow Min* had been at the Rock for just such a fuel stop when she'd freed Jagger. "Do you think more than one ship is involved? Or can we just alert the authorities to search the *Zhow Min* the next time it comes into port?"

Laura frowned. "If there is more than one ship, then the authorities will have to move very carefully. A bold rescue of the hostages on one ship might get all the others on the rest of the ships killed. Nobody knows for sure. The U.S. government dares not take any forceful action until it has proof one way or the other."

Emily chewed thoughtfully for a minute. "What about the ship's cargo manifests? Do they reflect the existence of these prisoner containers?"

Laura shrugged. "We've never managed to gain access to AbaCo's record-keeping system, but I highly doubt they'd leave an easy trail for anyone to follow."

Emily had to agree. She'd worked in the special cargo department for years, and she'd never run across any indication that such activity was taking place.

"As for the FBI charges against you, Emily," Laura commented, recapturing her attention sharply, "they're based on evidence that was turned over to the U.S. Customs Service about a week ago."

Emily winced. "I'm guilty of the things they're accusing me of. It's how I found and rescued Jagger."

Laura shrugged. "I'm certain that a competent attorney will be able to get the charges against you dropped, given the extenuating circumstances of needing to save a human life."

"I didn't technically know I was saving a human life. I was given a hint to peek into a certain container, and when I did, I stumbled across Jagger."

Laura smiled serenely. "It's all about how a good attorney spins it. I think you'll be all right. As for you, Jagger, it would be helpful if we could prove that AbaCo's holding prisoners in international waters. Your claims would be that much more believable."

He sighed. "They're careful. And my departure from their floating accommodations was rather abrupt. It's not like I stuck around to gather evidence to prove that I was their prisoner for two years."

"Understood. We'll just have to catch them doing something else dastardly and take pictures next time."

Jagger snorted and Emily echoed the sentiment. She'd worked for AbaCo long enough to know just how smart and devious her ex-employer could be. The next time the company slipped up could be a long time in coming.

Laura turned to her abruptly. "Emily, have you checked to see if your AbaCo computer passwords have been revoked?"

"I'm sure they were the moment I was discovered missing."

"Too bad. It would've been exceedingly helpful in helping clear Jagger's name to have been able to get into their system."

Emily grinned. "I didn't say I couldn't get into their system. I merely said my passwords were revoked."

Laura leaned forward. "Do tell."

"I happen to know my boss's passwords and those of about half my coworkers."

Jagger and Laura exchanged pregnant glances. He muttered, "They could use the break-in to track where you live."

"And they could run into the blind firewall my server throws up against traces," Laura retorted confidently.

Jagger shrugged. "Your call. I'm all over any help you can give us, but you're in no way obligated to endanger yourself or your son."

"Actually, I am obligated. It's what I do."

"Come again?"

Emily was glad Jagger asked the question. She was definitely lost now.

"I help people. Particularly moms. Single moms. It's how I pass the time. I'd go crazy rattling around this big house by myself without having projects to work on. Apparently, you folks are my latest project."

Emily liked the sound of that. Their hostess seemed remarkably connected to influential people and seemed to have no shortage of other resources to draw on.

After breakfast, Laura and Jagger disappeared into a sumptuous library on the ground floor to map out a strategy of what they were going to do when they broke into AbaCo's computers. Once they had it all worked out, then they would call her in to sign on to the company's database.

She spent most of the morning playing with Adam and Michelle. The little boy was bright and charming, much like his mother. There was one brief scare when what turned out to be a deer tripped some sort of motion detector on the grounds of the estate. She didn't think she'd ever get used to seeing Jagger whip out a gun and race around like some sort of trained killer.

Although to hear him and Laura talking casually about defense plans for the mansion, it sounded as though that was what both of them were. A few weeks ago, that concept would have scared her silly. But now...now she was thrilled that he was every bit as violently trained as he was. It was a relief to have him on her and Michelle's side.

It was nearly lunchtime when Jagger called her into the office. "Okay, darlin'. If you can get us into the cargo database, we'll take it from there."

She sat down in front of the state-of-the-art computer system and its twin plasma screens. "Do you want into the regular cargo tracking system or the special one?"

Jagger and Laura stared at her. He spoke first. "You can still get us into the special one?"

"Sure."

A slow grin spread across his face. "By all means, then. Hack away."

She typed rapidly, bringing up the hidden sign-on screen. Dieter Uling, the guy who did her job on the Rock when she was rotated off the island, never changed his passwords, and he hadn't in the past week, either, it turned out. She signed on in his name and then stood up. "Have fun, you two."

Jagger was already seated at the desk, typing rapidly. A scrolling list of outstanding shipments rolled down the screen. "Do you know how to get this to print?"

Emily snorted. "Of course. Move over." She leaned over him, typed in a set of commands and the printer beside her began to hum.

"Is there any way to tell what's in each of these shipments?" Laura asked.

Emily shook her head regretfully. "No. The actual contents of these special containers are only kept in hard copy. The ship's captain gets a set, and the customer retains a set. We destroy all other records as soon as the cargo's delivered."

"Which, in and of itself, is pretty incriminating," Jagger murmured.

"We maintain a list of the weight of each shipment, and in some cases, we record a hazardous materials status."

"But for the most part, you could be moving absolutely anything in those boxes and nobody would know."

Emily nodded. "I can show you how AbaCo runs phantom weight and balance measurements for the ships to account for the invisible containers. Here's one, right now, in fact." She pointed at the screen and a complicated set of entries beside a cargo shipment. "This is a normal shipment, but it's been linked to a phantom container. This set of numbers is the load plan corrections for the second container."

Jagger muttered, "This is a gold mine."

Laura added, "Print all you can now. We may have to back out of the system fast once they realize we're not signed on from an AbaCo office."

Emily hit the Print All command, and she'd no sooner hit the enter key than the second computer screen lit up with all kinds of security warnings.

Laura announced, "That's our cue, folks. Shut 'er down."

Jagger hit the escape button and the screen went blank.

The computer continued to spit out paper for several minutes; however, the data had successfully been batched over to the printer's internal memory before AbaCo spotted the break-in and cut off the database.

Jagger eagerly removed a thick sheaf of papers from the printer. "Let's take a look at this stuff and see if we can spot anything to take to the feds and clear our names."

Emily said, "What can I do to help? There must be something. I want to stop these guys once and for all."

Jagger snorted. "You and me both." Then he suggested, "Perhaps you could translate some of these numbers into plain English for us."

She spent several minutes going over the entries with him and Laura, explaining what the abbreviations meant until the pair had the hang of reading the information.

Jagger reached across the table to squeeze her hand gratefully. His touch was casual, intimate. As if he was perfectly at ease with claiming her as his in front of someone else.

Her face heated up as he murmured, "I think with this information, you may have just saved our future together. It looks at a first pass through this stuff like we'll be able to nail AbaCo with it."

Emily stared. To heck with AbaCo. He was talking about "their future together"? Was Jagger seriously contemplating sticking around, then? She'd hoped…but she'd dared not believe. Her heart leaped in her chest at the thought of him in her and Michelle's life for the long term. Of holidays and birthday parties and first dates experienced as a family. But she still couldn't let herself think the word *forever.* Even Danger Girl knew better than to reach that high with her dreams.

A need to be alone, to process the idea of Jagger as a fully involved father, overcame her. She murmured an excuse and rose to leave. "If you guys need anything from me, just give a shout."

He grinned. "You've already been more help than you can imagine."

Emily wandered in several times over the next few hours

and answered various questions about notations and company procedures as Jagger and Laura sorted through the documents. She wished there were more she could do. Jagger assured her that most intelligence work was like this—a few moments of terror punctuated by hours and hours of tedium, or worse, sifting through piles of boring data.

Laura had sent the nanny out for the weekend with a flimsy excuse about the woman working far too hard. But Emily suspected it had more to do with not exposing her to possible danger. Besides, Doris was having a ball with the kids and had them well in hand.

Emily and her mother fed the kids lunch and carried plates in to Jagger and Laura a little after noon. That was when Laura suggested casually that if Emily would like to check her e-mail she should feel free to jump online. It dawned on Emily belatedly that it had been a while since she'd checked her messages. In fact, the last e-mail she'd received had been that cryptic message that led her to Jagger.

She sat down at the computer cautiously. "And you guys are sure AbaCo isn't tracking my e-mail and won't find me if I sign on?"

Jagger laughed. "Not on this system, they won't find you. It's locked up tighter than Fort Knox."

Laura added laughingly, "Actually, the system will route AbaCo to an address in a slum in Mumbai. I'd love to see their guys running around there in hundred-degree heat and humidity trying to track you down. You can't believe the stench of the place in the summer."

Grinning at the notion, Emily signed online. She deleted a pile of junk mail, and then spied an e-mail address that made her pulse pound. MysteryMom. The source of that cryptic message had sent her another post. And the time-date group on it was barely an hour old.

In trepidation, she opened the message.

Veronique. 3L6H2D.

"What's wrong, Em?" Jagger asked immediately.

"I got another message. Just like the one that led me to you."

"What does it say?"

She read the message aloud.

"What does it mean?" Jagger asked.

"The *Veronique* is one of AbaCo's ships. And I assume the numbers and letters are another set of coordinates that will lead to a specific container."

"Can you access information on the *Veronique* online?" Laura asked innocently.

Emily shrugged. "I suppose so. I'd better use someone else's security code, though. I imagine ol' Dieter's having a pretty bad day right about now."

She signed in to the general AbaCo database, this time using the code of a fellow clerk from her stint in Denver.

"The *Veronique* is due in to Norfolk tomorrow night. The container at that cargo position is another reefer unit like the one I found you in, Jagger."

"Reefer?"

"Refrigerated unit. It has a self-contained generator that holds its contents at a constant temperature."

Jagger swore under his breath. "Do you suppose they've got another poor schmuck stashed in the back of the thing?"

Emily stared at him. "You think MysteryMom has found out where they're holding another prisoner and wants us to find him or her?"

He shrugged. "It makes sense. The whole reason I was sent in to infiltrate AbaCo in the first place was that we'd lost two operatives to them in under a year. They just disappeared. No trace. Just…gone."

Emily added grimly, "And you made three. How many more since then has Uncle Sam lost?"

Jagger shrugged. "Hopefully, they quit trying with me. I'd hate to think someone came in to rescue me and got captured, too."

Into the heavy silence that followed, Laura commented quietly, "If we were able to recover another prisoner and document the conditions of his captivity, it would go a long way toward corroborating your story. This time, pictures should be taken, maybe some video shot, during the rescue."

"AbaCo's got to be edgy after my escape. I highly doubt we'd be able to stroll aboard and just turn the guy loose like Emily did with me."

Laura shrugged. "So, we'll prepare more carefully, knowing that we have to plan for opposition to our extraction. No biggie."

Emily exclaimed, "Are you two nuts? AbaCo's trying to kill us and the FBI's trying to catch us, and you want to just waltz onto a giant ship in the middle of a busy port, which by the way will be crawling with government officials, and break into a container?"

Jagger commented tightly, "AbaCo's a big company. They can't watch everywhere at once. And of course we'll set up a diversion."

"Of course," Emily repeated drily.

The strain in his voice was palpable as he ground out, "Honey, if there's even the slightest chance that some other guy is stuck in a box wasting away and not another living soul knows he's there, I *have* to do something about it."

"But you have no idea if there's even anyone in this container," she protested.

"We'll figure out a way to tell. Can you look at the corrected weight on the load plan and see if this container actually weighs what it's supposed to for a load of—" he glanced down at the papers in front of him on the desk "—live orchid plants?"

Emily frowned. "I suppose I could check it out." She moved over to the desk. "Plants are a low-density cargo, but orchids need a humidifier system in the container, which adds a couple hundred pounds of motors and water." She pulled out a pen and paper. "What does the open manifest say the weight of that reefer is?"

Jagger rattled the number off and she jotted it down.

Then she asked, "Laura, can you find a load correction to any of the containers immediately surrounding that box?"

It took a minute, but the other woman exclaimed in satisfaction, "Here it is. Negative eighty-two hundred pounds and negative rolling moment of .023 degrees."

Emily ran through the calculations. Her stomach sank at the end result. Reluctantly, she announced, "That weight reduction would account for approximately one-third of the plants in the container. Which means the odds are excellent that there's a relatively large open area in that reefer, similar in volume to the one you were held in, Jagger. Or else they're smuggling air."

Jagger's jaw rippled grimly. "I can't turn my back on this lead. I've got to rescue whoever's in that box."

Emily's gut clenched in denial. She'd just found him! She couldn't risk losing him again so soon. And not this way. Not shot up or worse by the very people who'd captured him and torn the two of them apart in the first place. Both of them had already lost far too much to AbaCo. "*Please,* Jagger, call the police."

"We need the evidence, Em. We've got to move in fast and get it before AbaCo can pay anyone off to tamper with or destroy the evidence. By the time we call the police, present our evidence, they decide to move, then they get both the local and federal warrants they'll need to search the ship, the *Veronique* will be long gone. AbaCo will send it back out into international waters where no one can touch it. If the guy in that container is lucky, all they'll do is push his box overboard. If not, they'll torture him to try to figure out who's coming after him."

"But a rescue now, especially after you escaped, will be terribly dangerous—"

He cut her off. "I'm fully aware of that. Which is why I'll be careful."

"Why *we'll* be careful," Laura amended firmly.

Panic squeezed Emily's throat until she couldn't force out the words to tell Jagger how much she feared losing him. How he couldn't do this to her and Michelle. How he had to give up this foolishness—give up his career, if need be—rather than put himself at this kind of risk. She and their daughter needed him. Instead, all that came out of her mouth was a muted sound of protest.

Laura spoke gently, "Emily, it really is a golden opportunity to clear your names and catch AbaCo red-handed all in one fell swoop."

Laura was right. Emily's rational brain could accept the truth of that, but her gut was another matter entirely. Despairing, she looked over at Jagger. He came around the table to her, lifted her to her feet and wrapped her in the comforting safety of his embrace.

He murmured, "I promise it'll be okay. I know what I'm doing, honey. It'll turn out fine."

She closed her eyes and buried her face against his chest. She wished she could be half so confident. No way could she let him walk out the door by himself, leaving her to wait and wonder. That would kill her for sure.

He went on, "But I *have* to do this. I couldn't live with myself if I didn't do it."

She loosed a shuddering sigh that was half a sob. He was right. And after all, she'd heard his delirious rantings. She knew better than anyone how much he needed to take action after two years of helplessness, to get retribution against AbaCo in some way. She was going to lose this fight. Heck, she'd already lost it.

She reached for courage she wasn't even sure she had and raised her head. She wiped the tears from her cheeks and announced as bravely as Danger Girl could, "If you're absolutely set on going through with this, then you two are going to need my help."

Jagger smiled down at her in relief and gratitude. "Thank you, Emily. I know this is hard for you. And for the record, I'm counting on your help."

She shook her head and crushed an urge to continue trying to talk him out of it. It was a waste of breath—she knew that stubborn set of the jaw all too well from Michelle. She muttered in resignation, "You know this is crazy, right?"

"Crazy's my middle name, darlin'." His cocky grin faded. "And besides, I owe AbaCo one. I'll bring down those bastards if it's the last thing I do."

Emily flinched. She had a sinking feeling it might very well be the last thing he ever did if he tangled with AbaCo.

Chapter 14

Jagger invited Emily to join him and Laura after supper for a closed-door planning session. She told them everything she could think of about AbaCo security procedures and cargo-handling routines. But when they got down to the nitty-gritty of practicing how to work together in a gunfight, she visibly panicked. Her hands began to shake and her breath trembled, and she couldn't seem to sit still in her seat.

He took pity. "The rest of this planning is just technical stuff, Em. Besides, isn't it getting close to Michelle's bed-time? I bet she'd love to have her mommy tuck her in."

Emily snorted. "I dunno. Granny's a pushover when it comes to Michelle wheedling more time to play out of her. I'm the bedtime Nazi."

Jagger grinned. It was hard to imagine sweet Emily being a Nazi about anything.

Her calm facade evaporated as she rose to her feet and excused herself. Poor kid. She was running a lot closer to the edge of falling apart than she'd been letting on. He had to give her credit, though. She was stronger than she looked. She'd been a champ so far. Just one more day and this mess would be resolved, assuming everything went well.

And if things went bad, well, then not much would matter at all.

He and Laura compared notes and figured out quickly that their respective training had come pretty much out of the same playbook. Which was a huge relief.

Laura excused herself to go tuck in Adam, and he wandered upstairs, gravitating toward the squeals of laughter emanating from Michelle and Doris's bathroom. The door was partially open and he peeked in.

His daughter was sitting up to her chin in a mountain of bubbles, and had them piled on her head and hanging from her chin in a fair toddler imitation of Santa Claus. Emily and Doris were laughing, and the scene was so endearing he felt something in his heart break at the sight.

All of it could be his. The laughter, the love, the sense of family. All he had to do was reach out and take it.

Tomorrow. He just had to get through tomorrow. And then he'd take everything they had to offer him and more. He'd reach for it all.

Michelle's hands emerged from the mounds of bubbles and slapped down on the water, sending bubbles flying every which way, and drenching Emily and Doris. Michelle squealed with renewed laughter, delighted at the liberal glops of bubbles now adorning the two women.

He didn't think he'd ever get enough of that sweet sound. His daughter's laughter was a balm to his soul. As he stood there in the shadows of the doorway and watched the hilarity, the crack in his heart split wider and wider until the whole thing burst apart in an explosion of joy.

He was *happy.*

Happier than he could ever remember being. And it was all because of the laughter of a child. His child. *Their* child. The daughter he and Emily had created and whom she had shared with him in an act of generosity that stole his breath away.

Emily plucked the toddler from the water and wrapped her in a towel that swallowed Michelle whole. He retreated while Emily dried the child and dressed her in a fuzzy pair of pink footed jammies that were too cute to be legal. No doubt about it, his daughter would have daddy wrapped around her little finger in no time flat. The truth of the matter was he was already a goner.

He lurked in the next room while Emily rocked Michelle to sleep, closing his eyes and letting the quiet lullaby she sang wash over him like a blessing. And he'd thought he loved Emily before. Seeing her like this, loving his child with the full measure of a mother's devotion, filled up spaces in this new heart of his that he'd never dreamed existed.

When Emily moved to get up a while later, he glided into the room quickly and lifted Michelle from her arms. Together, they carried their daughter to the crib Laura had thoughtfully provided and tucked their angel in snugly for the night.

Jagger looped his arm over Emily's shoulder as they turned to leave.

He stopped just inside their bedroom. "She's awesome, Em. You've done an amazing job with her."

Emily blushed a little. "I'm sure I've made my share of mistakes, but I figure if you just love them with everything you've got, the rest will take care of itself."

He'd give anything if she could love him that much. But they'd thought a lot of hurtful things about each other over the past two years. He didn't know how long it would take for her to trust him completely again. Thankfully, AbaCo's lies about her had been exposed, and he'd let go of his need to hurt her. He shuddered to think, though, of what might have happened if she had not been the one to rescue him. Would he have ever believed in her innocence otherwise? Would he have thrown away bubble baths and fuzzy jammies and soothing lullabies in the name of vengeance? He feared he would have. And the thought left him chilled to the bone.

"Hey, are you okay?" Emily asked in concern. "You look pale."

He grinned bravely. "I'm fine. It's just the lighting. Super Spies don't get pale."

Emily grinned back. "Well, Danger Girl certainly does. She gets scared to death and isn't afraid to admit it."

He swept her into his arms and grinned down at her as her eyes went limpid. "Right now, Danger Girl looks a little flushed."

She murmured up at him, "You do that to me."

"I know. And I love it. Come." He drew her toward the big bed that was invitingly turned down. "Let's see how much of you is blushing for me."

Emily laughed. "That would be all of me, you forward man."

He expected to make love to Emily, but she surprised him by pushing him down gently to the mattress and indicating that he should roll onto his stomach. She checked his wounds, which were healing nicely, and then she gave him the mother of all back rubs. He was putty in her hands. But when she rolled him over onto his back and gave his front the same loving attention, tension built in him until he couldn't stand it any longer.

He rolled over, taking her with him, and stared deep into her eyes as their bodies became one. The intimacy of the moment was almost more than he could stand. But generous Emily never flinched, never pulled back. She opened her body and heart to him and gave him every last bit of herself without reservation. It was almost as if she was offering him the very sense of family and belonging he'd craved earlier.

When the shudders of their lovemaking finally died away, she reached up, smiling lazily, to cup the back of his neck with her hand. She murmured, "I could do that for the rest of my life and never get tired of it."

"Is that an invitation to stick around awhile?" he replied.

She stared up at him intently. "Yes. It is. You know I'd love to be with you for as long as you'll have me."

For as long as he'd have her? His mind spun out the possibilities of that. "I think, honey, that could be a very long time, indeed."

She smiled, but the expression didn't penetrate the darkness in her eyes. "Then how can you stand to risk all of this—you and me, being there for Michelle, our *family?*"

With her body still warm around his, the love in her eyes reaching out to embrace him, their daughter sleeping in the next room, he could see her point. Did he really dare chance losing all of this? For a possible prisoner, a stranger he'd never met and wasn't even sure existed?

Doubt sliced into him, sharp and hot. She had a point. Maybe his days as a superspy were over. Maybe he was clinging to a part of himself that no longer existed. What if he'd lost the edge? The possible consequences of failure were too awful to contemplate. So why was he trying it?

Emily stared up at him, no doubt watching the arguments play out in his eyes. She murmured, "I knew I could make you change your mind. I just had to get you away from Laura and remind you about your family—"

Abruptly angry, he cut her off. "So this sweet seduction was just a case of bedroom politics? You were just trying to get me to change my mind?"

She frowned. "No, well, yes. Yes, I was hoping you'd change your mind. But no, it wasn't just about that. I lo—"

He rolled away from her and out of the bed, striding across the room to pick up his discarded clothes. He yanked them on angrily. "I'm not that gullible. I know what I have to do and nothing you say or do is going to change that, dammit!"

To her credit, she didn't try to argue with him.

He stormed out of the room and headed downstairs.

It took him all of about five minutes to calm down and realize he'd overreacted. She was only looking out for Michelle. She wanted her daughter to have a father. He couldn't fault the impulse. And besides, he'd give almost anything to be able to settle down and raise Michelle with her. But unfortunately, he was still Super Spy, and he still had responsibilities.

First on that list was clearing their names so she could have the peaceful life she craved with her daughter. Second, and no less important, was evening the score with AbaCo so he could live in peace with the events of the past two years. Those were more important than any fairy-tale, happily-ever-after scenario she envisioned.

He pulled out the schematics of the *Veronique* that Laura had found online and printed earlier and he pored over them, walking through the plan a dozen times in his head, trying to anticipate absolutely every possible scenario for tomorrow night's rescue. It—he—must not fail.

A long time later, he crawled into bed beside Emily and gathered her warmth against his side.

She murmured sleepily, "Did you finish planning World War Three?"

"As much as I can. Operations like this never go according to plan. A certain amount of improvisation is inevitable."

He felt Emily's wince against his shoulder. She mumbled, "That's the part that worries me. All that unpredictable stuff that can go wrong."

"Don't worry too much about it. Sometimes things break the good guy's way, too. It all evens out in the end."

"Yeah, well, I found you and freed you, and that's about as much as I'm willing to demand from fate."

He smiled into the darkness. "Sleep, honey. One more day and it'll all be over."

He thought he heard her mumble under her breath, "And then what?"

He didn't have an answer for her. Not yet. He had to focus entirely on the moment at hand and not to lose concentration by speculating about a future he couldn't guarantee that they'd have. He could only pray that the Fates had one more lucky break lined up to fall his way.

He slept deeply. So deeply that when he lurched upright, sweating and sure he was back in that damned box, he didn't know where he was right away. He threw off the covers, which felt far too much like ropes tying him down. His old scars ached and he rubbed them to convince the nerves there that they were not under attack.

The dark of the bedroom was as oppressive as the blackness of his crate and played tricks on his mind until he slipped out of bed and padded over to the door to Michelle's room. He cracked it open to admit the glow of her night-light.

He couldn't resist. He tiptoed into her room to peer down at the little girl. She slept on her stomach, sprawled in abandon, with one arm flung over a rather tattered plush bunny. Her blond curls tangled around her face, and her one visible cheek was chubby and rosy. Calmed by the sight of her, he padded back to bed and left the adjoining door open a bit.

No doubt about it. If another man was caged up in a box, missing these perfect moments with his family, Jagger had to take action. He *had* to try to save the guy.

Chapter 15

Emily crouched behind Jagger and Laura and wondered yet again how Jagger did this for a living. The sneaking around guards and over fences they'd had to do to even get to this dock had wiped her out physically and emotionally, and they hadn't even started the real mission yet.

Jagger murmured, "Is that the *Veronique?*"

She whispered back, "That's the right slip, and she's about the right size. I can't see her name from here, though."

Laura pointed to a stack of truck-sized containers not far from the pier to which the *Veronique* was tied. "I'm heading over there. I'll radio you to confirm that we've got the right ship. Then you can do your thing, Emily."

Right. Her thing. Boldly walking aboard the ship with her expired AbaCo identification and hoping against hope she didn't trigger any alarms that got her detained or worse. Jagger swore they'd rescue her if that happened, but Danger Girl was a quivering puddle of terror at the moment.

Laura darted across an open space and disappeared into the shadows beside the containers. Her radio call was all too quick in coming. "Yup, it's our ship. You're on, Emily."

Jagger stood up in front of her and she did the same. She gazed up at him in wordless fear, and without her having to ask, he wrapped her in his warm, safe arms. "It'll be all right, honey. Just stick to the plan. We'll be right behind you."

Right. Stick to the plan. She could do this. *Not.* What if it was all a giant trap?

Jagger must have sensed the direction her thoughts were taking because he murmured, "We can handle whatever happens. I know you can do this. Do it for me."

Darn it. Did he have to go and say the one thing that would prevent her from turning tail and running as fast as her feet would go? She nodded reluctantly against his chest. "Have you got the video camera?"

"Yup, everything's ready. It's time, honey."

He released her and took a step back. One gloved finger traced down her cheek and along the line of her jaw. "Be careful. If it looks like you're not going to make it, back out. Don't be a hero—we'll find another way to get aboard."

Right. No heroes here.

She took a deep breath, turned away from him and took a step. And then another. Before she knew it, her feet had carried her into the peach glow of the halogen lights bathing the pier. She walked almost halfway down the starboard side of the massive container ship and onto the aluminum gangplank leading into the bowels of the vessel.

"Can I help you?" a sailor asked in gruff surprise.

"Yes, you can. I'm with the special cargo division at AbaCo, and there's a problem with the paperwork on a shipment aboard the *Veronique*. The load plan you guys faxed to our office doesn't match the one we have on file. I'm going to have to go through the deck load container by container and figure out which setup is accurate." She rolled her eyes in disgust at the snafu.

"Oh, man, that sucks." The guy commiserated.

She fluttered her eyelashes at him, not enough to be outright flirting, but enough to capture his attention, nonetheless. Keeping eye contact with him, she pulled out her AbaCo identification badge and clipped it to her belt at her waist. Then she shifted her clipboard to partially conceal it.

"Is there any chance you could show me how to get topside? I get lost in these big ships. And—" she leaned in close to confess as the guy's pupils dilated "—I'm a little claustrophobic. Sometimes I get kinda freaked out in ships' passageways. I don't know how you do it."

On cue, the sailor puffed up. "Oh, you get used to it. You just tough it out at first, ya know."

He turned and headed down the narrow, dimly lit passage behind him. "C'mon. I'll walk you up top. Main stairwell's this way."

She refrained from glancing over her shoulder into the shadows. Somewhere very close behind her, Jagger and Laura were waiting to dart aboard the *Veronique* in the absence of the man on watch. If all went well, they'd take another stairwell and meet her on deck in a few minutes.

Her helpful sailor led her out into a towering jungle of stacked containers, looming so high overhead they cut off all but the tiniest sliver of night sky.

"Need some help?"

Emily looked around with a sigh. "Nah. I'll give a holler up to the bridge if I need any help. I've got the phone number."

"Right, then. I'd better get back to the hatch. I'll see ya when you're finished."

Emily smiled warmly. "See you in a little while."

Thankfully, he didn't stick around to flirt any longer and left her to herself. She moved farther into the containers. The one she sought would be in the aft half of the ship, near the centerline of the vessel. Jagger was concerned that it would be visible from the bridge. He and Laura had some sort of diversion planned just in case.

There it was. A rusty brown, temperature-controlled unit that wasn't the slightest bit remarkable. Was it possible that a human being was caged up in there? The container was about fifteen feet up, in the third layer of containers. This time, no rolling staircase was nearby to make access easy. She moved to the end of the row of containers and stepped close to the rail to look overboard. Oily black water swirled nearly a hundred feet below. She gulped and took a quick step back.

She leaped violently when a male voice came from the shadows directly behind her. "Hey, baby, wanna get naked with me?"

"Jagger!" she snapped under her breath. "You scared me to death."

"Work your way down this outside row of containers, and pretend to compare lading numbers to your sheets of paper. A guy on the bridge has binoculars on you."

Holy smokes. Someone was watching her? The back of her neck crawled. She hastily flipped a few pages of her fake notes and then pretended to study the packing documents pasted in a clear plastic pouch on the side of the nearest container.

Jagger murmured from the shadows again, "Laura's gonna watch the other end of the aisle while I enter the unit. Drop your clipboard and cry out like you startled yourself if you see anyone coming this way."

And then he was gone. She was alone and exposed. She moved on to the next container and repeated her paperwork charade.

She'd been at it maybe three minutes and had made her way back to near the narrow aisle between stacks of containers when she heard Jagger's voice call out low, "Em. Come here."

What on earth? That wasn't part of the plan. She strolled unconcernedly into the aisle in case the man on the bridge was still watching her. The bulk of the bridge tower disappeared from view. She sprinted to where the container door was barely cracked open.

"What's up?" she murmured as loud as she dared.

"I need your help. There's a guy in here, but he's in pretty bad shape. I'm sending him down on a rope, but he may need your help."

They'd done it! They'd found another prisoner. Now, if they could get him off the ship, they'd have all the proof they needed to sink AbaCo and clear their names!

Her pulse leaped in trepidation as the door opened wider and a shadowed form backed out of the box on his hands and knees. It turned out Jagger had rigged a loop in the rope for the prisoner to step into with his foot. Jagger lowered the man by letting the rope slide slowly down to the deck.

The man was tall with a heavy black beard, but so emaciated he looked hollow. He staggered as he stepped out of the rope and Emily wedged a shoulder under his armpit to steady him.

"Problem, Jagger," Laura called out low from somewhere out of sight nearby. "A couple of AbaCo guys are headed this way with purpose. They don't look like grunts."

"Armed?" Jagger asked quickly.

"Not visibly," was the low response. "We've got to go. Now."

Jagger slithered down the rope fast and joined Emily and the tall man. "Em, any chance you can head those AbaCo guys off while we get our friend out of sight? He's not in any condition to run. We're gonna have to hide him until the goons leave."

She blinked fast. "Uh, I'll try." Crap. She was terrible at improvising.

Laura rounded the corner and skidded to a stop in front of them. "Let's go with the zip lines over the port rail—" She broke off, staring at the prisoner. "Nick?" she whispered.

The man's head jerked up. His dull eyes grew slightly less dead. "Laura?" he croaked.

"Oh, my God," Laura cried softly. She took a step forward as if to embrace the fellow, but Jagger spoke in a sharp whisper. "Save it. We've got to go. Our friend can't handle anything strenuous like climbing ropes. We've got to hide him until we can sneak him outta here."

Laura nodded and batted at the tears streaming down her face. The man, Nick, looped his arm possessively around the woman's shoulders and the two of them shuffled slowly toward the port side of the ship.

Jagger muttered to Emily, "Keep your story simple." And then he whirled and caught up in a few strides with the couple's painfully slow progress.

Emily headed out fast to intercept the incoming AbaCo men. When she heard their footsteps about to round the corner, she stopped and commenced examining the bill of lading on the nearest container.

"Oh!" She cried out as three men came into sight and all but slammed into her. "Goodness, you startled me!"

"I'm Robert Schmeckler, ma'am. Ship's security officer. Forgive me for being blunt, but who are you? And please explain exactly what it is you're doing here."

She remembered hearing somewhere that the best defense was a good offense. A vision of Laura in tears over that starving man fresh in her mind's eye, Emily scowled and put on her best indignant tone. "I work for Hans Schroder in the Special Cargo Division. I'm *supposed* to be on vacation in Washington, D.C., right now, but he called me up from the Rock and insisted I come down here to check out an irregularity with the *Veronique's* load plan. Is one of you gentlemen responsible for it? He's going to want to speak to you tomorrow."

The three men reacted to Schroder's name and the mention of the Rock. None of them took credit, or blame as the case might be, for being in charge of the ship's load plan. Which was a relief. A true load planner would know immediately that she was blowing smoke.

She went on in tones of disgust. "Frankly, I don't know what he's talking about. Everything looks perfectly in order to me. I think the paperwork got screwed up on his end, and I'm going to tell him that as soon as I get back from my *interrupted* vacation."

"May I see your credentials?" Schmeckler asked in his deadpan German accent.

There was no help for it. She handed her ID badge over to him. He studied it closely for a minute. "This badge is expired, Miss Grainger."

She rolled her eyes. "I'm fully aware of that. I told Hans I hadn't had time to renew it before I left Hawaii, but he insisted I come down here anyway. Go ahead and throw me off the ship. It would serve him right. I swear, I'm gonna make him give me an extra week of vacation after this fiasco."

"I'll have to keep this badge."

Emily snorted. "Be my guest."

"I also have to ask you to come with me."

Ohgodohgodohgod. Michelle! If these guys arrested her, how would her daughter grow up without her?

She mumbled, "Uh, of course. Lead on." What else could she do? She couldn't possibly outrun these guys, and she'd die, literally, if she jumped overboard and splatted herself on the pier below.

The security officer turned and led the way while the other two men pointedly fell in behind her. They stepped through a hatchway and into the main superstructure of the ship. It was a short walk to a cramped office, and Schmeckler waved her to one of two chairs in front of his desk.

She jammed her hands in the pockets of her jacket and sat down where he indicated. She was *so* busted. Was she the next victim they'd throw into a container and forget? Or wouldn't she be that lucky? No way could she hold out against the kind of torture Jagger had endured. And what about Michelle? Her baby needed a mother! What on *earth* had she been thinking to go along with Jagger on this wild escapade?

She wasn't Danger Girl. She never had been. She'd always been that cautious little mouse who overdressed for bad weather in case she had car trouble. All her efforts to change—to become the kind of woman a man like Jagger Holtz might love—had been in vain. And stupid. Extremely stupid. He'd chosen the mission over her—he hadn't changed one bit. He would breeze back out of her life as quickly as he'd breezed into it.

Except in the meantime, she'd gotten into a mess way over her head, and her daughter was going to be the one to pay. This was absurd. She just wanted to go home, live a quiet life and watch her daughter grow up in peace. To heck with all this action and adventure. Jagger could have it.

"I'll need to call Schroder and verify your identity, Miss Grainger."

She nodded stiffly, and was vaguely surprised that her neck didn't shatter with the strain of that small movement. In desperation, she blurted, "It's the wee hours of the morning on the Rock. He may not answer his phone. He's prone to turning it off at some point in the night so he can get a few hours of uninterrupted sleep. But he usually comes into the office around 8:00 a.m. Hawaii time. That's just a couple of hours from now. We can wait till then to call him if we have to."

As she spoke, she groped in her right pocket for her new cell phone. She counted number pads with her fingertips and dialed Schroder's cell phone. She covered the entire phone with her palm and pressed its face tightly against her thigh, praying it would sufficiently mute the sound of her call ringing at the other end. Not to mention, she didn't want Schroder to hear any of what was going on at this end.

Schmeckler dialed his desk phone and waited impatiently. *Please, God, let my call go through first and block the line.* The security guy frowned. "I'm getting a busy signal."

She nodded knowingly. "Ah. The lines to the Rock are either all busy or down temporarily. We have to rely on satellites, and when sun spots flare up, phone service out there gets iffy. Especially the personal phone lines. If you wait a few minutes and try again, they may come back up."

Schmeckler asked one of the men hovering behind her. "Where's Zook?"

"Ashore with your conting—"

With a sudden, alarmed glance in her direction, Schmeckler made a sharp hand gesture that cut the first man off, midsyllable.

Emily frowned. Schmeckler's contingent of what? Men? What would an AbaCo security officer send a contingent of sailors ashore to do? The way the first man said it, she didn't get the impression the sailors had been sent ashore to get drunk and pick up women. And who was Zook, anyway? Assuming that was the name of an actual person?

Schmeckler looked over at her and explained from behind a falsely saccharine smile, "He's the ship's load master."

Thank God *he* was off the ship. Yet a little more time she'd bought for her partners in crime to find a way off the vessel. Meanwhile, she had to occupy Schmeckler so he wouldn't think up some creative way around Schroder's busy cell phone.

She leaned forward. "While we're waiting, if you'll pull up the ship's load plan, I'll show you the anomalies in the weight and balance that we're concerned about." She lowered her voice. "As you well know, the company occasionally carries cargo for clients that is best left…discreetly accounted for."

Schmeckler's eyebrows shot straight up. He obviously knew exactly what she was talking about, but seemed startled that she knew about it, too.

She shrugged. "I'm in charge of burying the money trail.

Of course I know where everything—" she paused before adding significantly "—and everyone is."

Schmeckler typed on his computer and then gestured her to come around his desk.

She thought fast, and only one idea came to her. It was wildly risky, but what other choice did she have? She'd do whatever it took at this point to get out of here and get back to Michelle. *And she'd never, ever, leave her daughter's side again.*

"May I?" she asked, reaching for the keyboard.

The man at her elbow nodded.

"Take, for example, the temperature-controlled unit in this position." She scrolled down to the container from which they'd just rescued Nick. "As you know, its cargo has a significantly lower weight than live plants."

The guy beside her looked thunderstruck that she was aware of that particular container. Some of the suspicion around his eyes seemed to ease as she proved that she was an extreme insider into AbaCo's extracurricular activities.

She continued pleasantly. "The weight correction for our passenger unit should have been made to this container over here." She randomly pointed at a container that was shown as loaded on the opposite side of the *Veronique*. She said a quick mental prayer that Schmeckler wasn't any great expert at load planning and continued. "But there's no notation of a load correction. That's what Hans Schroder is freaking out over. If something were to happen to this ship, the paperwork would get examined with a fine-tooth comb and then people would starting opening up containers to have a look."

She had no idea what people would open which containers, but it seemed to scare the heck out of Schmeckler.

Just then, a walkie-talkie sitting on his desk blared, and Emily jumped about a foot in the air. A voice crackled across it, "Sir, we may have an intruder on board. We just got a hit on a motion detector on deck four, and we show no personnel in that area."

Schmeckler cursed. Her German was good enough to pick out him complaining to himself about being short-handed tonight and not needing this with one of Schroder's people sitting in front of him.

Emily moved smoothly back over to the chair in front of his desk. "I'll wait here if that's something you need to go check out. Lock me in, if you want to. That way you can take your men with you."

Schmeckler frowned at her for a second, then nodded tersely. All three men stepped out, and a lock clicked shut on the other side of the door.

Now what was she supposed to do?

She thought fast. Jagger, Laura and Nick were stuck aboard the *Veronique,* too. And if she knew AbaCo procedures, a detailed security sweep of the entire ship was commencing right about now. *A diversion.* She'd bet Jagger and company needed a diversion. But what? She eyed Schmeckler's computer. She moved around the desk to check it. Ha. Not only was it powered up, but it was still signed into the ship's internal computer network. What could she do with a computer to mess up a ship?

She recalled an argument she'd overheard some months back between Schroder and another man about a hole in the company's shipboard security having to do with shipboard weight and balance systems. Schroder had wanted it fixed and the other man had said it was too obscure to worry about, since only a few senior ship's officers had access to it. And this computer was already signed in to the very system that Schroder had been upset about.

Perfect.

Now, what was it Schroder had said? The volumes of air and water in a ship's massive ballast tanks—the bladders of air or water used to balance a ship laterally and keep it from rolling over on its side—could be changed by anyone with access to the ship's onboard load planning system. He'd been concerned that someone might hit the wrong button and accidentally empty a ballast tank.

She had to hunt around a bit in the load planning system, but then she found it. An innocuous little button that said Enter Ballast Corrections. She set all of the starboard ballast tanks on the *Veronique* to fill with air and all of the port-side tanks to flood with water. She suspected some sort of warning would go off on the bridge, too, and they'd try to override the command. To that end, she quickly typed up a logic loop that would keep her manual ballast commands active in spite of any overrides attempted from the bridge. She sent the mini-program to the *Veronique's* mainframe.

When she got back a message that her program had been successfully installed, she hit the activation button to empty and fill the ballast tanks.

How long it would take for anything to happen—if anything happened at all—she had no idea. She checked her cell phone to verify that the line was still connected to Schroder's cell phone. It seemed to be. She stuffed it back in her pocket.

Diversion hopefully complete, she went to work on escaping from Schmeckler's office. She hunted around in his desk until she found a pair of scissors, and then went to work on the door's hinges. It took her several minutes and resorting to using a heavy-duty stapler as a hammer, but she finally managed to wedge the bolt out of the top hinge. She crouched and went to work on the lower hinge. The bolt burst free, and she pressed her ear to the door to listen for movement outside. Nothing.

She pried the door back enough to slip through the gap and stepped out into the hall. If she wasn't mistaken, the floor wasn't entirely level beneath her feet. She raced down the hall until she found a stairwell, and she ran down the stairs as fast as she could. A placard said she was on deck eleven. Nine decks to go to reach the one with the hatch to the pier.

By the time she got about halfway down the stairs, the tilt beneath her feet was becoming more noticeable. She heard sounds of shouting from somewhere overhead, but the voices didn't sound as though they were headed her way.

She burst out onto deck two, and straight ahead was the gangway and the shore beyond. She slowed to a fast walk and approached the sailor stationed at the door. It was the same guy as before, and he was frantic with worry.

"What 'n hell's going on?" he all but bellowed at her.

"I don't know. I was talking to Schmeckler and all hell broke loose. They said something about topside cargo shifting and overbalancing the ship. She's rolling on her side and they can't stop it. They told me to get the heck off the *Veronique* before she sinks."

The sailor exploded into a string of curses. Then he pulled himself together enough to say, "You better go now. The gangplank's getting unsafe."

She stepped up to the door and looked out. Sure enough, the metal walkway, which had been nearly level when she boarded, was now tilting down at the dock at an alarmingly steep angle.

She paused in the door to face the sailor. "You'd better get up top. They need all hands up there if they're gonna save the ship."

The sailor's eyes widened in panic and he bolted for the stairs.

She turned and started down the ramp. She ended up having to half run down the thing to keep her balance, but then she spurted out onto the pier and solid ground. She ran for shore and didn't stop until she'd cleared the main shipyard and was standing once more in the dark shadows of the visitors' parking lot beside their car.

She swore under her breath. She didn't have the car keys. And she didn't have a clue how to break into a car, let alone hot-wire one. She turned to look back at the ship. It was definitely listing to port. It was probably no more than a ten-degree angle, but in a ship the size of the *Veronique,* ten degrees made it look about ready to roll over and sink.

Sailors were running around on deck like furious fire ants, and she suspected some poor schmuck on the bridge was frantically trying to figure out why none of his commands to the ballast system were working. Personnel from the docks were starting to head toward the ship, and a number of them ran up the steep gangplank, no doubt trying to assist the disabled vessel.

Well, she'd created chaos. Now, if only Jagger, Laura and Nick could find a way off the ship in the midst of it all.

Chapter 16

Belowdecks, Jagger crouched and peeked around a corner. He'd taken point while Laura helped an exhausted Nick stumble along behind him. He was just in time to see the sailor on the watch bolt away from the main hatch into the bowels of the ship. He didn't know what the hell was going on with the *Veronique,* but it was definitely listing hard to port. Hey, he was all over any luck that came their way.

He signaled over his shoulder for the pair behind him to move out. Nick apparently knew military sign language, because he shambled forward immediately. The guy was obviously running on nothing but guts and grit, but so far, he'd clenched his jaw and managed to keep up.

Jagger approached the gangplank cautiously. Son of a gun. Not a soul was in sight. Were they actually going to be able to stroll off the ship? It seemed too easy to be true. But he was prepared to go with the easy solution right now. No telling how much longer Nick would be able to stay upright. The guy was as gray as a ghost.

Laura and Nick caught up to him and likewise gaped at the unattended hatch. "What's happening?" she whispered.

"I have no idea. But let's not stick around to find out. C'mon."

Jagger led the way, the butt of his sidearm tightly gripped in his fist inside the pocket of his jacket. This stunk of yet another AbaCo trap. But then, he'd successfully made it off the *Zhow Min* and he'd been sure that was a trap. Could lightning strike twice in one lifetime?

He headed down to the dock, looked both ways and waved Laura and Nick down. There was a tricky moment when Nick lost his balance, but Laura lunged forward and got a shoulder under the guy's armpit before he could go down.

Once they were safely on the pier, Jagger moved to Nick's other side and looped the taller man's arm over his shoulder. Between Jagger and Laura they all but carried him off the pier. And just in time, too. Behind them, a team of firefighters raced toward the *Veronique* and clambered aboard the wounded behemoth.

Jagger guided the awkward trio into the visitors' parking lot and his car. He looked around frantically. *Where is Emily?* Panic exploded behind his eyes, all but blinding him.

"Take the car and get Nick out of here, Laura. I'm going back for Em—"

An apparition rose from behind the car and he all but fainted in relief at the familiar shape of Emily coming around the rear fender. She flung herself at him with enough force to nearly knock him off his feet. She was sobbing so hard he couldn't make out a single word of whatever she cried against his chest.

"Easy, darlin'. We all made it. Let's get out of here. We'll talk later."

He opened the car door and eased her into the front passenger's seat. Nick had already half collapsed into the backseat, and Laura was climbing in beside him, cradling him close. Clearly those two had some sort of history between them. And given how badly steel-nerved Laura had fallen apart at the sight of the guy, it was an intimate emotional history.

Their departure was shockingly anticlimactic. He drove sedately out of the parking lot and pointed the car back toward the hills and valleys of the Shenandoah. The video camera was safely in his pocket, loaded with damning footage of Nick's prison and the container he'd been trapped within. Like him, Nick hadn't believed at first that rescue had arrived. He'd had to flash a few of his own scars to convince the guy that he, too, had been AbaCo's prisoner and was here to free the guy.

Jagger shuddered to remember the mental and emotional place he'd been in when Emily had done the same for him. He reached over and squeezed her hand.

"Okay, honey, it's safe to talk now. How did you get off the ship? And do you have any idea what happened to the *Veronique?*"

Emily ducked her head, abashed. "I broke into the ship's computer ballast system and filled all the starboard tanks with air and flooded all the port-side tanks. The computer indicated that the ship will only roll about eleven degrees before it stops."

Jagger gaped. And then he laughed, long and hard. He exulted. "Danger Girl rules!"

Emily's face went serious. Stubborn. "Danger Girl is dead. Your life is not for me. I can't do that again. I don't have the nerves for it, and I have a responsibility to my daughter. One parent who runs around risking life and limb for fun is enough for any child. I'm sorry, Jagger. I can't be part of your world."

He stared at her, stunned into silence. What was she saying? Was she dumping him? Was she tossing him out of her family's life? Not that he'd blame her. His world was far too dangerous for children to be around. Hell, hadn't his first thought when he found out Michelle existed been horror at what a horrendous liability she was to him?

Except those pink cheeks and bouncy golden curls and innocent laughter didn't feel like a liability. They felt like a little slice of heaven on earth. His own special angel come to save him from the dark.

"Em…" He didn't know what to say. He wanted to beg her to hang on to them, to allow him to be a part of their lives. But he didn't have any right at all to ask that of her. He clenched his jaw against the thickness in his throat and blinked hard against the burning in his eyes. Damned things had grit in them all of a sudden.

Nick passed out in the backseat. Hard to tell if he was sleeping or unconscious. Probably a little of both. Laura cradled the big man protectively in her arms and didn't look as though she planned on letting go for a very long time. Nick might actually get a happily ever after. Lucky bastard.

Emily stared out the window in pensive silence, her head turned away from Jagger. And he let her withdraw. It was possibly the hardest thing he'd ever done. But he let her go. What choice did he have? He loved her. Loved Michelle. Enough to leave them, to keep them safe from his world, to protect them from everything he did and was.

But it ripped his heart out of his chest and tore it to little shreds to do so.

They'd been driving for maybe a half hour when Emily murmured, frowning, "Schmeckler said something strange in his office…."

Jagger glanced over at her, his heart dead. "Who's Schmeckler?" he managed to choke out woodenly.

"The *Veronique's* security officer. He pulled me into his office and took away my ID badge. He was trying to call Schroder when a motion detector went off. I assume that was you guys."

Jagger nodded. "Probably. What did he say that's got you puzzled?"

"He was mad when the alarm went off. He mumbled something to himself in German about being undermanned tonight. And one of the guys with him mentioned a contingent of Schmeckler's men being ashore."

Wild alarms erupted in Jagger's gut. His every operative instinct, honed over twenty years, went onto high alert. He glanced in the rearview mirror, and Laura was staring back at him, horror written on her face.

Laura breathed, "It was too easy."

Jagger started to swear. He cursed long and hard as he stood on the accelerator and the car roared forward.

"What's wrong?" Emily cried. She might not be a trained spy, but she had good instincts, and she sensed that something was terribly wrong.

Jagger ground out, "Finding Nick's crate was too easy. The rescue went too smoothly, and we encountered practically no opposition."

"What are you saying?" she asked, with terrible certainty that she knew the answer to that vibrating in her voice.

He spelled it out. "Given that AbaCo knew they had a break-in to their special cargo database today, and they know you and I are in the local area, and they knew the *Veronique* was coming in today, does it make any sense at all that we all but strolled onto the ship, snagged Nick and strolled off again?"

Emily shook her head, her eyes the size of saucers.

"It was a diversion, Em. They drew us to the *Veronique* on purpose."

She frowned. "But they didn't catch us. Heck, they all but let me go."

"Exactly. That's because we weren't the target tonight."

"Then what was?"

"Not what," he said gently. "Who."

She stared for a moment more; then her face crumpled. "Oh, God. The children!"

Jagger closed his eyes for a moment as pain and terror slashed through him, but then focused on the road flying beneath their tires.

"What do you want to do, Jagger?" Laura asked grimly from the backseat.

He glanced over at Emily, who was a complete wreck, her fists stuffed against her mouth as if she'd scream if she moved them. "Make the call."

Laura nodded and held her cell phone to her ear. In a moment, she began to murmur unintelligibly.

Emily glanced back and forth between the two of them. "What's going on? Talk to me, Jagger!"

He sighed. "Laura's talking to the FBI. She'll ask them to send a large contingent of agents to her house. Which will protect the kids. But it will also ensure that I'm arrested."

"I'm wanted, too," she reminded him.

He nodded grimly. He knew what he had to do, but damn, it was hard. Harder even than he'd expected. He forced himself to continue speaking. "I'll drop you off outside her estate. Laura will make arrangements to reunite you with Michelle, and you two can leave the country. I've got some money squirreled away for emergencies, and you can have it. Laura will help you go someplace far, far away. Start a new life. Doris can go, too, if she wants."

"It's done," Laura announced from the backseat.

"Thanks," he replied. "I'll never be able to repay you for what you're doing for us."

Laura laughed without humor. "Are you kidding? You gave me the father of my son back."

Nick lurched beside her at that but didn't fully regain consciousness.

Emily's gaze went wild and she looked back and forth between Laura and Jagger. "No! I'm not leaving you!"

Each word was a dagger to his heart. "Honey, you have to. You said yourself that this life isn't for you. And it's not right for Michelle, either."

Emily subsided, sobbing into her sleeve. Each heave of her slender shoulders was agonizing to witness.

He reached across the car to touch her arm. "I'm so sorry, Em. So very sorry."

She shook off his hand. He let it fall.

How he stayed on the road for the next hour without wrapping the car around a tree, he had no idea. But eventually, Laura commenced calling out directions from the backseat. Apparently, there was a back entrance to the estate, and she guided him to it.

When they'd driven a ways into a stand of heavy woods and his direction sense said they were getting close to the house, he stopped the car.

"What're you doing?" Emily croaked.

"It's time, honey. You need to get out of the car, now. Laura will bring Michelle to you as soon as she can."

He climbed out of the car and went around to her side of the vehicle. He opened the door, but she merely stared up at him.

"Please, Emily. It's the only way."

"No, it's not."

His eyebrows lifted.

"I'm going with you. Don't make me choose between you and Michelle. I can't do it. You're the two halves of my heart, and I can't live without either one of you."

"But you'll be arrested, too—"

"I have faith in Laura's lawyers. They'll get me off. All I did was rescue you. And now that we've got that video, I'll be fine."

He shook his head in the negative. "I can't take that chance with you. I *have* to know the two of you will be safe—"

A faint rattling sound echoed through the trees and his head jerked up.

"Let's go, Jagger," Laura called urgently from the backseat. She'd recognized the sound, too. That was gunfire. Coming from the vicinity of the mansion. The mansion his precious daughter was currently inside.

Chapter 17

Emily's head jerked up. That sounded like...ohmigod. "Was that a gunshot?"

"Several of them," Jagger bit out as he turned and raced for the car's trunk.

Laura leaped out and joined him. The trunk slammed shut, and Emily made out the thick, tubular shapes of rifles. Several of them.

Jagger leaped into the driver's seat and rolled the car forward in the dark.

Laura shook Nick awake. "Do you think you can you shoot a rifle?"

He shrugged and answered in a rusty voice, "I'm game to try."

Laura asked, "How 'bout if I tell you your son, Adam, is inside that house down there and AbaCo's thugs are trying to break into the place to kidnap him?"

Nick sat up straighter. "Oh, yeah. I can do this."

Emily lost it, then. "AbaCo's men are breaking in?" she squeaked.

Laura grinned. "They may get into the house, but there's no way they're getting into the safe room."

"The...what?" Emily turned around to face the other woman.

"The house has a safe room. I installed an old bank vault and equipped it with self-contained power generators, air filters, even a toilet and running water. I showed it to Doris before we left and gave her the combination to the door. I told her to spend the night in there with the kids just in case."

Now, if only Doris had taken Laura's suggestion to heart and taken precautions with the children.

Jagger stopped the car just inside the woods, maybe two hundred yards behind the house. "Can you see any movement?" he muttered.

Emily scanned the area around the house frantically but saw nothing. *Please, God, let this all be a giant false alarm.*

But then a flash of light from somewhere on the other side of the house lit up the night.

Jagger said, "Laura, you and Nick go in the family room doors. Emily and I will head in through the kitchen. Assuming we meet no opposition, we'll meet at the base of the stairs. AbaCo tends to use German ordnance and the FBI should come with bigger-caliber stuff."

The pair in the backseat nodded and slid out, weapons in hand, and disappeared into the dark.

"Where's my gun?" Emily demanded.

Jagger started. "Do you know how to use one?"

"Plenty well enough for tonight's purposes. My stepdad showed me how to handle a gun, but he never did talk me into going hunting with him. But if AbaCo guys are out there, I'm all over shooting them."

Jagger grinned and passed a shotgun across to her. "C'mon, Mama Bear. Let's go protect your cub."

Grimly, she hefted the weapon and chambered a round. She stuffed the shells Jagger handed her into her pockets and then nodded her readiness. Michelle was in danger. She had to save her baby. Fear had no place in that equation and hovered only peripherally in the background of her mind.

Jagger's restraining hand on her arm was all that kept her from barging into the house, shotgun blazing. "Easy, Em. We don't know if the FBI's on scene yet. If you just charge in there, they may shoot you."

"The gunfire came from out front. I'm betting AbaCo's guys are in the house shooting out and the FBI is just arriving on scene."

"The FBI's not stupid. They will surround the house."

"But they haven't yet, or else we wouldn't have been able to run up to the back door like this."

Jagger nodded. "Good point. So let's go find those AbaCo bastards and wreck their evening."

She nodded her approval at that plan and realized her entire body was shaking. Okay, so she was actually terrified somewhere deep in her gut. But it wasn't as though she had any choice in what she was about to do. Michelle needed her. End of discussion.

Jagger whispered one last set of instructions. "Stay behind me. Your job is to make sure no one sneaks up on us from behind. I'll take care of engaging with the bad guys. Keep your head down and don't be a hero, got it?"

"Got it."

Jagger eased open the kitchen door and, crouching in the dark, made his way behind the big center island. Emily followed close behind. As they paused, silence settled around them for a moment. But then, the noises of movement came from toward the front of the house. Whoever was already in the mansion was making no attempt at stealth.

Jagger raised a hand and started to wave her forward, but

his hand froze in midair as a loud voice shouted through a megaphone from out front, "FBI! Lay down your weapons and come out with your hands clasped behind your necks."

Thank God.

Profound relief washed over Emily that help was here. But as she exhaled in gratitude, another sound caused her to stiffen once more. A voice, speaking in terse German. Giving orders.

She leaned forward and whispered frantically in Jagger's ear, "He just ordered his men to abandon the mission. They're to fall back to the kitchen and run for the woods and meet at some rendezvous point. They're coming right at us!"

Jagger nodded and settled his weapon more securely in his arms. Without him having to say anything, she did the same, fitting the butt of the shotgun firmly against her shoulder.

Running footsteps pounded down the hall. The swinging kitchen door burst open and Jagger shouted in credible German, "Freeze!"

The AbaCo men—six of them—lurched violently to a halt, their weapons trained on the kitchen island. One of them snarled, "Lay down your weapons and get out of our way or we will shoot you both."

Ohgodohgodohgod...

Michelle. She must hold her ground for her baby. For the man in front of her. For her family.

Jagger snapped back, "Not happening, you Stasi SOB. It's over. You're busted."

The German grinned. "I think not. You're not FBI. Kill them—"

His command was cut off by the sound of at least a dozen weapons clicking to the ready behind Emily. A new voice spoke calmly. "Nope, they're not FBI, but we are."

Emily all but fainted, she was so light-headed with relief.

"Everybody, lay down your weapons slowly."

Emily complied along with Jagger and the German hit

squad before them. As the Germans were straightening back up, one of them reached out fast and flipped on the kitchen lights. He dived for his weapon…

…and was dead before he hit the floor.

The other Germans froze in various bent and crouched postures in the act of reaching for their weapons.

Four FBI agents wearing black Windbreakers raced into the room, flanking the island. Another half dozen came in through the door, spreading out behind Emily and Jagger. From her prone position on the floor, they were just about the prettiest sight she'd seen since Jagger had looked up at her inside his crate.

"Glad you could make it, gentlemen," Jagger commented from beside her.

"You Jagger Holtz?" someone asked from behind them.

"That's me. Two more good guys are moving in the other end of the house—a woman and a tall, skinny guy with a beard."

"Thanks for the invite to this little party. We're looking forward to talking to you and the woman. That her with you?"

"Yup."

"Stay put on the floor while we secure these bastards. We'll get back to you in a minute."

Emily complied, watching as the FBI team handcuffed and searched the Germans. An arsenal of weapons and gear grew beside the Germans. It took several minutes, but finally the FBI men hauled the AbaCo team to its feet and marched them outside.

One of the FBI men approached Jagger and Emily. "I'm gonna have to search you both. Standard procedure after a firefight. Then you can get up."

It wasn't that bad, actually. The guy was fast and impersonal and she fixed an image of Michelle in her mind.

As soon as she was upright, she asked, "Where's my daughter?"

"We haven't found any children in the house, ma'am. But the safe room's locked down. We're guessing the kids are in there."

Just then, Laura and Nick were escorted into the kitchen. Laura asked the agent talking to them, "Could someone get some orange juice out of the refrigerator for my friend here? He's on the verge of passing out."

Nick did, indeed, look like death warmed over in the room's bright lights. Laura explained quickly that he'd also been imprisoned on an AbaCo ship, as Jagger had, and furthermore, they had video of his rescue to prove it. The FBI men looked extremely interested, and if Emily wasn't mistaken, the government agents' postures relaxed even more toward her and Jagger.

Hope turned into certainty that she and Jagger were going to be okay. They'd gotten the evidence they needed to prove their innocence. Between the four of them, Laura, Nick, Jagger and she should be able to bury AbaCo so deep it never came up for air again.

An agent poured Nick a glass of juice, which he sipped in unadulterated bliss. Jagger made a commiserating sound from beside her and muttered under his breath, "Wait till he gets his first chocolate. The guy'll think he died and went to heaven."

She murmured back, "Gee, I thought heaven was that night on Lyle's beach."

"You have no idea. Believe me. I *knew* I'd died and gone to heaven then."

Laura spoke from across the room. "Can I go open the vault now? Nick wants to meet his son, and I expect Emily and Jagger want to hug their daughter."

"Now, there's an understatement," Emily declared.

Jagger looped his arm around her shoulders and smiled down at her. "Let's go get our daughter. And remind me to thank Doris every day for the rest of her life for protecting the kids."

A team of FBI agents trailed along as the party made its

way to the front stairs. Laura opened a paneled door and a steel, bank-vault-style door loomed. Emily waited impatiently as Laura entered a lengthy code into an electronic keypad, then grabbed the heavy crossbar and gave a tug. The door cracked open.

"Doris, it's Laura and Emily and Jagger. We're out here with a bunch of FBI agents. It's okay to come out now."

A light went on just inside the vault as several FBI agents pulled the massive door all the way open. Adam ran out first, straight into his mother's arms. Nick stared in awe at his son as though he'd never get enough of the sight of the child. Laura glanced up at him worriedly, and then smiled brilliantly.

"Now that you're home, I guess my days as MysteryMom are over."

Emily gaped as Doris exclaimed, "You're Mystery Mom?"

Laura grinned and explained, "I've been searching for Nick ever since he first disappeared five years ago. To keep from going crazy while I hunted for him, I started helping other moms find fathers for their children. Their successes kept my own hope alive for one day finding Adam's father."

Emily blurted, "You sent me that e-mail about Jagger?"

"I didn't know it was Jagger, but I'd figured out that AbaCo might be keeping prisoners on ships in international waters. That one container never got off-loaded and always had a weight that didn't match up with its reported cargo."

"How did you know to send that e-mail to me, then?" Emily asked.

Doris cleared her throat. "That would be my fault. I contacted MysteryMom to ask her if she could help find Michelle's father."

Emily stared. She'd had no idea her mom had done that.

Laura continued, "I hadn't made any progress at finding Jagger, but I found out you worked at AbaCo and started poking around there. That's when I spotted the suspicious containers and started tracking them. By the way, in that printout of special cargo you ran for us yesterday, I've spotted a half dozen more suspicious containers."

One of the FBI men commented, "We'll be happy to look into those. I expect we'll be looking into a whole lot of AbaCo's activities real soon."

Jagger's arm tightened about Emily's shoulders. "So I guess I also owe my rescue to you, Laura, and to my future mother-in-law, too."

"Your future—" Emily's gaze snapped up to his. "What are you saying, Jagger?"

"I'm saying that I want to marry you. What do you say, Em?"

Joy exploded behind her eyeballs until everything was so bright she could barely look at him. The FBI men around them grinned. But then reality came crashing back in on her so hard she could hardly breathe. It felt as if an anvil had just landed on her chest.

"You know I love you, Jagger."

"I love you, too."

Whoa. She almost lost her train of thought at hearing those words from him. She wanted to beg him to say it again. To mean it enough to change for her. But then he wouldn't be the man she loved anymore.

She blurted, "But I'm not Danger Girl."

Jagger blinked down at her, clearly confused.

"Ever since that night we met, I've been trying to be the kind of woman James Bond could fall in love with. But—" she took a deep breath and forced herself onward in a rush "—it's not me. I can't live a life of danger and excitement. I'm a homebody. I like safety. Peace and quiet. I'll never be glamorous or wild or dangerous. I want to stay home and raise Michelle and live a boring, normal life. I'm just me."

Jagger listened intently to her outburst, but by the end of it, a tiny smile was starting to play at the corners of his mouth.

"What?" she demanded. Here she'd just laid out her guts for him. Explained why she couldn't marry him no matter how much she loved him, and he thought it was funny?

"Honey, I'm not James Bond. I'm not some Super Spy, either."

"Yeah, but you love this life. You love running around in the dark with guns and rescuing people. It's who you are."

"I hate to disappoint you, but my twenty-year mark in the military passed while I was cooped up in that container. I'm eligible to retire, and I have every intention of doing so as soon as I can fill out the paperwork."

"But what about tonight? Nick's rescue…" she sputtered.

"I told you I couldn't in good conscience walk away from another prisoner in a box and not try to help the guy. And yeah, I wanted to get enough evidence to sink AbaCo. But I'm done living on the wild side. Super Spy has hung up his cloak and called it quits. Within about thirty seconds of seeing you and Michelle together for the first time, I knew I wanted nothing more than to spend the rest of my nice, boring life with you two."

"Really?" she asked in a small voice. Hope hovered at the edges of her heart, but she wasn't quite ready to let it in.

"I want to watch Michelle grow up. I want to terrorize her boyfriends and give her a couple of brothers or sisters. I want to sit on my front porch in a rocking chair and watch the sun set. And I want to wake up every morning for the rest of my life and watch the sunrise in your eyes."

Tears she didn't even know were there spilled over onto her cheeks.

Jagger looked alarmed. "Hey. Are you okay, honey?"

"I'm more than okay. I'm perfect. Everything's *perfect*."

"Help me out here, Em. Does that mean you'll marry me?"

"Yes. Oh, yes!"

He wrapped his arms around both of them and squeezed until Michelle squawked, "Jaggy too tight!"

Laughing, Emily looked down at their daughter. "This is your daddy, Michelle. Can you say daddy?"

"Da-da."

Joy broke across Jagger's face that shot all the way to the bottom of her heart.

"Dadadadadadada!" Michelle squealed.

Danger Girl and the Super Spy might not live beyond this night's work, but it didn't matter. They had the strongest bond of all to protect them and keep them safe against life's struggles. A family.

Their family.

* * * * *

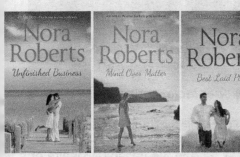
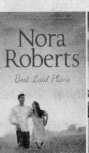
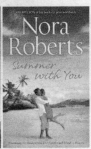

MILLS & BOON®

The Chatsfield Collection!

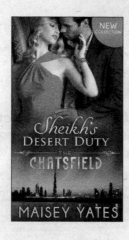

Style, spectacle, scandal...!

With the eight Chatsfield siblings happily married and settling down, it's time for a new generation of Chatsfields to shine, in this brand-new 8-book collection! The prospect of a merger with the Harrington family's boutique hotels will shape the future forever. But who will come out on top?

**Find out at
www.millsandboon.co.uk/TheChatsfield2**

MILLS & BOON®
By Request

RELIVE THE ROMANCE WITH THE BEST OF THE BEST

0415/05